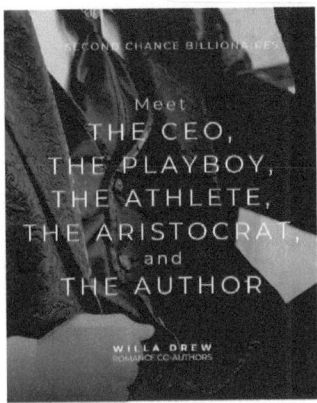

What do a grumpy CEO, a charming playboy, a retired hockey pro, a British aristocrat, and a sci-fi author have in common? A second shot at love.

They were college hockey teammates.
Now they're billionaires in the Second Chance Billionaires romance series.

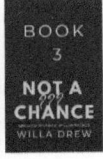

SECOND CHANCE BILLIONAIRES
BOOK 1

NOT A Fake CHANCE

by
WILLA DREW

Moving Words Publishing

Published by: Moving Words Publishing

www.movingwordspublishing.com

Cover & Interior Design: A Fabulous Production

afabulousproduction.com

Paperback: 978-1-957897-20-2

First Edition: June 2025

CONTENTS

To anyone who's ever felt like a mess of contradictions—
soft yet ambitious, scared yet sure, broken yet still trying.
This is for you.

ONE

PRESENT DAY

January

Someday, this will all be mine.

The thought lands on my head like a gilded crown—heavy, coveted, and binding. Steam from the industrial dishwasher curls into the hotel kitchen's air. No guest ever sees this part of the empire that I know like the back of my hand. My playground as a child, my training ground as a teenager, and now my battleground at thirty-five. The familiar aroma of espresso and freshly baked breakfast pastries should comfort me, but today the scents, like expectations, cling too tightly to my skin and the walls of the service hallway.

As the future CEO and heir-apparent of Haliday Hotels Group, these annual rounds I make with my mother are part ceremony, part surveillance. Our family's show of stability no matter what the numbers in the reservation system say. I'm proof to every employee, from the kitchen to the laundry room, the front desk, and the maintenance department that the prosperity of HH Group is guaranteed for years to come.

"The quarterly earnings meeting yesterday was a disaster," says the woman who's shaped everything in my life. Mom to me, and Melinda Haliday to the world, she walks ahead, her heels clicking a perfect rhythm that punctuates the hotel's backstage murmur. Even though she's the same five-foot-six as me, her presence casts a large shadow. "Going 10 percent over on your charity projects, Rose, didn't help. I told you to stop using this location for your experiments. It's our business. And your ideas"—she pauses mid-step and throws a glance at me over her shoulder—"need refinement."

Clutching the pen and notepad in my hand, I absorb the sting of her comment. Her words slice, but I've grown a callus over that spot in my heart.

"Given the social media buzz it generated, the rose wall was worth the extra cost," I say, pushing past the tight knot in my throat. "Brides will see the grand floral backdrop and think of this hotel for their wedding reception." I attempt to keep my voice steady. Weddings bring in guests, and extravagant floral arrangements are part of the cost of business in event planning.

"We need more than a few brides to keep our doors open. There are 526 rooms and 6 VIP suites in this hotel, and with the rising costs of keeping staff around, we have to improve our scheduling systems and efficiency tracking. We are bleeding money, and your side projects aren't helping."

I nod, because nodding is safer than arguing. This is how her love has always been measured—obedience in exchange for approval. The pressure she's putting me under is for my own good.

"I won't be able to protect you when I retire, you know." Mom turns and rests her palm on my forearm. "Do you really think you're ready for that?"

The ache in my throat grows as I hold in the unsaid argument. I'd grasp at any straws to prove to her I'm no longer the girl trying to learn the ropes through presentations and spreadsheets. "I'm ready, Mom."

"Before you were even born, I made a promise to your father that I would always protect you. He would have wanted nothing more than to do it himself, but . . ." Mom's thumb brushes along the row of flawless diamonds encased in platinum that encircles my wrist. The bracelet—an heirloom kept safe in our family vault until I turned sixteen—is the only tangible thing I have from my father. The platinum is cold against my skin, but her thumb is warm. It's as if she's trying to quiet the ache neither of us knows how to voice.

My mother shivers. "I might be all you've got, but everything I do is for you." She takes my hands. "Us against the world."

"You don't have to worry about me." The bitterness in my throat melts away. It's always been this way with us. She pressures me, and I shine in return. Like the diamonds on my bracelet, I improve with every challenge she throws my way.

Mom sighs, tugs at the wool of her wrinkle-free cream jacket, and leads us to the service elevator. As I push the button, the soft ding of her phone pops the tension. She checks the device, and her shoulders sag. "Shit."

"Something else wrong?"

She ignores my question and places a call. "I told you to do whatever it takes to secure the contract with TRI. I want that company," she says to whoever answers.

What TRI contract? My head snaps up as I recognize the name of the technology company I researched last year. Tailored Responsive Intelligence. A noiseless thud lands between my ribs.

On the other end of the phone, a voice mumbles information Mom clearly doesn't want to hear. Her mouth forms a thin line, and I worry about the responder's job security.

"Fine," she spits. "Find me an alternative. But it better be just as good as TRI. If I can't have the best, I want an upgrade that'll give me similar results." She ends the call.

The need to know why she's been negotiating with TRI burns in me, white and hot, the evidence heating my cheeks. I inhale and still my features. If I push too hard or if I show too much interest, she'll switch topics. Then I'll never know what's going on. "We're planning on working with TRI?"

She huffs. "We were buying TRI."

My vision blurs at the edges.

"But they won't sell." The numbers on the elevator display count down. "Their technology is exactly what we need to give us a competitive advantage in allocating maintenance, servers, and housekeeping staff. Areas where we've been in the red for over a year. I decided it was time I brought their tech in-house and cut off our competition's access to them."

She decided. Never *we*. I prepare. I perfect. I pretend. I please. She always decides. That's our choreography. I spent my life in this hotel, sacrificing weekends and summers while my peers partied and took gap years or European tours. "You didn't tell me."

Her fingers are white from squeezing her phone. "Well, it didn't go through. They declined."

"Why?"

"If I knew the reason, I'd fix it and get the deal done. Instead, I've wasted my valuable time on a contract that's dead."

"Is there no wiggle room?"

"Our lawyers threw everything at the owners." Mom's eyes flicker. It's only for a second, but I know how to read her. She's worried. "Still, Mr. Dufort and Mr. Orlov declined our offer, which was far over their asking price."

The name rings in my ears, loud and familiar.

Mr. Orlov.

Alek.

My pen falls from my fingers. I haven't heard his name in ages. Not since college. Not since . . . His absence crackles like static across my sternum. The service hallway turns warm and claustrophobic. I bend down, picking up the pen to hide my reaction. After twelve years of trying to forget him, he's still threaded through my body like wiring I can't rip out without burning the whole place down.

The elevator doors open, and Mom ushers me into the cabin. "I didn't tell you because I didn't want you to get involved with that boy again."

"Involved" is the shallowest of words to define what happened. I'd use very different terms to describe our relationship if my ability to speak hadn't vanished. The doors of the elevator close, and we ascend in silence, both of us caught between the past and what lies ahead.

Mom takes a step closer. "I only wanted to protect you."

"From what?" The question scrapes my throat. From choosing wrong? From being weak? From wanting something she can't control? From Alek?

"From getting your heart broken. I know what it feels like, and believe me, the effort is not worth the pain. All I want for you is a stable, comfortable life, where you don't have to worry about a man going after your money or abandoning you."

"Dad didn't abandon you."

"He died," she barks. "What do you call that?" She presses her lips together, eyes shining with the grief she never lets out. "At least you aren't defending your sister's father."

"Did he reach out again?"

Her chin juts up. "He wants money for a pit crew this time."

I shake my head. Unlike my father, who loved Mom and left me his inheritance, Olivia's dad only leaves invoices. Mom was seventeen when she got pregnant with me. She was eighteen when my father died a month before I was born. By twenty-five, she had turned the one hotel her grandparents left her in their will into a small LA chain. By my age, she had two kids and luxury hotels in every major city in North America. She's a force of nature, but sometimes I wish she were just my mom.

When the elevator reaches the top floor, I stride out first into the VIP suite I've been living in since my divorce two years ago.

Mom glares at my collection of half-dead houseplants on the windowsill, rescues I keep alive out of stubbornness or hope, I'm not sure which. "I'll never understand why you don't let housekeeping toss those useless plants."

"They're mine," I say.

I don't tell her they're the things I choose to save, to make whole again, to pour my love into. She throws things out when they stop blooming. I give them second chances.

Two

ALEK

September

Night shift at the Haliday Hotel isn't a bad gig. Most importantly, the maintenance job fits my schedule. Between calls to reboot thermostats, replace light bulbs, and fix air conditioners, I should be able to get most of my college assignments out of the way this semester.

Tonight isn't one of those nights. Tonight, there's a party, which means extra work for me.

The disastrous flavor of the day is a leak.

Loaded with my tool kit and wrench set, I knock on the semi-open door of the VIP suite.

Thumping bass pounds through the hallway of the twenty-third floor, and I wouldn't be surprised if the other guests are calling the front desk.

I knock again, but my louder attempt at getting someone to come to the door is drowned by a new song. I nudge the door open and enter the most lavish room I've ever stepped foot in.

The ceiling is at least twelve feet tall. The wall of windows in front of me offers an unobstructed view of LA at night. Bodies clad in tuxedoes and dresses cluster around tall tables. A collection of shimmering black, white, and transparent balloons float over gold tablecloths. The room is stuffed with pink roses and other white flowers I don't recognize. Empty wine glasses and plates with bite-sized food lie scattered, while raised arms and swaying hips writhe around the DJ.

The glances thrown my way are swift. Without words, the crowd parts around me, but the toolbox grows heavy in my hand. At the end of the hall, the door to the bedroom I need to access is shut. I bang on the wood, and it flies open.

"Use the bathroom in . . ."

The most beautiful girl I've ever seen in my life halts mid-sentence. Her eyes are a green-gray-gold pattern that forces me to peer closer to decipher the mystery of the color. The two triangles of her eyebrows lift. The cupid's bow of her mouth makes two more triangles, and her almost too-pointed chin gives me yet another triangle to admire. All these angles should make her face look sharp, yet the roundness of her lips, the ovals of her eyes, and the raised apples of her cheeks create the kind of balance old masters would kill to sculpt.

My eyes return to hers, and I hold her gaze. The sounds of the party fade as I discover her secret. Her eyes aren't gray or gold or even green. They're a complicated mosaic of each. All those colors create a stained-glass window that forms an illusion of cohesion.

The door creaks to reveal another girl, who wears a tiara of neon lights and a hot pink sash with BIRTHDAY GIRL in glittery gold letters that clash with her fancy dress. "You're the maintenance guy?" The smile she offers fails to cover her distress. "Please be the maintenance guy."

"Yes. There's an issue with the sink?" I say to the birthday girl, but my gaze remains glued to the beautiful woman who doesn't look away from my stare. Doesn't even flinch.

"It's not an issue," says the birthday girl. "It's a full-blown flood." She touches her friend's elbow. "Rose, are you okay?"

"Right this way." Rose unfreezes and tucks a nonexistent strand of hair behind her ear. Her back is a new challenge. The golden straps of her dress, which looked innocent on the front, create an elaborate lattice across her shoulder blades. I grind my molars and ball my fist around the handle of the toolkit to prevent myself from reaching out and tracing my finger along her skin.

Both girls stay outside as I enter a bathroom the size of the living room-kitchen combo in the off-campus duplex I share with four of my hockey teammates. I immediately locate the problem: a steady drip from the cabinet under the sink continues to feed the water pooled across the marble tile floor. An out-of-place collection of half-dead potted plants nearly floats by the large oval tub. Those won't need watering for a while.

"I'll call housekeeping to come and mop up." I crouch in the puddle beside the vanity, open the cabinet doors, and spot the cause of the leak—a loose pipe connection at the back. The seal's likely busted, and the water supply valve is still on. I reach for the shutoff, turn it tight, grab a wrench, and twist the nut back into place. I will need to check if we have replacement parts in the storeroom.

"Good thing he's not afraid of this mess," the birthday girl whispers from the doorway loudly enough for me to hear.

"Maybe I just like getting dirty," I mutter under my breath, then catch Rose's gaze. Yep, she heard me.

"So . . . what's your name, Mr. Handyman?" The birthday girl shouts.

"I shut off the water, so you can't use the sink until we come back to properly fix it." I stalk through two inches of water to the tub. "I suggest you direct your guests to the restroom on the rooftop by the sauna and fitness room." I wash my rough hands, which are familiar with barbells, hockey sticks, and most tools, but look utterly out of place under a high-end tub faucet. Instead of the fluffy white towels stacked on the counter, I use the rag I keep tucked into my pocket to wipe my fingers.

"I'm Olivia." The birthday girl smiles at me in a way that makes me wonder how much she's had to drink. "And this"—she gestures lazily—"is Rose."

Rose gives me a slow once-over that I feel from my jaw to below my belt. The interest crackles between us like electricity, making me question if the attraction is mutual. It must be.

"We think you're too cute to be a plumber." Olivia's voice snips our connection.

I drop my gaze, ignoring the birthday girl's flirting as I pick up my toolbox. I walk past them. "You can call reception if it leaks again."

In the time I've spent in the bathroom, the party has progressed to more grinding and further intoxication. If not for the clothes, decor, and expensive booze, it would seem like a frat party.

Fingers touch my exposed forearm, and a current shoots to my ribs. I glance down, and my heart rate accelerates at the sight of Rose's gold fingernails on me.

She steps closer than she needs to. Her flowery perfume hits me.

"Who should I ask for?" Her voice is low, like we're in on a secret together. She chews on her bottom lip, but her gaze is unwavering. "If it leaks again."

"Just tell them to contact maintenance. I'm the only one on duty until 5 a.m." I tear my eyes from the mosaic of hers and survey the party.

She follows my gaze, then looks back at me, and need purrs in my veins. "My mother taught me to know the names of staff who help you out."

Right. I'm only the help. "I'm Alek. Alek Orlov."

"Thank you, Alek." She says my name like it means something. Like maybe she notices me just as much as I've noticed her.

I walk to the elevator.

The metal doors reflect my face back at me. It looks tired, but somehow still lit up after meeting Rose. I shouldn't be thinking about her. I stab the down button. I shouldn't be feeling like this at all.

Was she flirting or just being polite? Was she just caught up in the thrill of the party?

I glance back. Just once.

The hallway is empty. My shoulders fall and I pinch the bridge of my nose. I need sleep.

With a ding, the elevator arrives.

"Wait!" a voice calls the moment the doors begin to close.

I prevent the doors from touching and push them aside. Rose runs barefoot down the hallway, heels in her hands. Her dress swishes against her thighs as she slows. She looks wild and windblown, her short honey-brown bob in disarray, like a beautiful storm.

"I needed some air," she says, slightly breathless. "Thought maybe you wouldn't mind sharing your escape."

I don't. I absolutely don't. I step aside and she slips into the elevator, her elbow grazing my stomach. The scent of her floral perfume wraps around me like a memory I haven't made yet.

We stand side by side, shoulder to shoulder, too close in all the right ways. The faint whir of the elevator motor is the only sound. Our hands brush once, then again. It's intentional now. My skin pulls to hers like a magnet to steel. The air is thick with possibility.

"Is sink fixing always this hot?" she asks. Her lips curve, teasing, and there's hunger behind her eyes.

"Only when the client is."

Our gazes lock, and the air between us sizzles. Her lips part as she twists to face me. I move backward as I look down at the work of art that is Rose.

"You think I'm hot." She inches closer.

The cool wall of the elevator hits my back. "I do."

"You're very honest, Alek Orlov."

"I know what I want, Rose . . ."

She doesn't offer her last name, but the tips of her breasts skim my torso. My abs contract.

I lean in just a little—she does too.

My breath catches. Now I'm the one who's breathless. She curls her hand into the top of my uniform, clutching the material, and tugs. I bend toward her, my mouth seeking the promise of her lips. Her chin lifts and her warm breath fans across my mouth.

"What do you want?" she whispers.

Everything.

For this elevator ride to never end.

To taste her. All of her.

To bury myself deep inside her.

Heat surges then banks as my conscience catches up with me. This is not me. I don't do this. I take women out on dates, hold doors open, buy them dinner. But Rose has me skating on unfamiliar ice. Doing, not thinking. My hand wraps around hers, our fingers stitching together. She inhales like my touch burns her.

The elevator dings and the doors open.

"Rose?" Melinda Haliday, owner of this hotel and the Haliday Hotels Group empire, stands on the other side. Perfect posture. Impeccable makeup. She inspects me from head to toe, and I feel the laser of her stare on every scuff on my shoes, the stains on my uniform, the calluses of my hands. Her gaze lands on my nametag and my stomach drops. Making out with hotel guests is certainly not part of my job description.

Rose stiffens and backs away. The most beautiful girl in the world meets my gaze for a fraction of a second. In her eyes, I see . . . shame? But also regret? Fear?

"Mr. Orlov. I see you've met my daughter," says Melinda.

Daughter? I shake off the lust coating my every thought. Synapses fire in my brain, connecting the dots.

"Yes, ma'am. There was a leak." I hold up my toolbox, like the small metal case can shield me from Melinda Haliday's disapproving stare.

"Thank you, Mr. Orlov. I'm sure you're expected back in maintenance." Relief at my dismissal mingles with the disappointment of what might have been.

I exit the elevator.

Melinda steps inside.

Now that Rose stands beside her mother, the resemblance is impossible to miss.

Metal grates against metal as the doors begin to close.

"Rose. I don't mind you being interested in someone who's blue-collar." Somehow, she makes "blue-collar" sound like a disease. She takes Rose's hand. The movement is smooth. Practiced. Possessive. "But we don't mix business with pleasure for a reason. The Haliday name is riding on us."

Rose's downcast face disappears between the elevator doors inch by inch, but the phantom warmth of her hand still burns in mine.

Three

ALEK

January

"No." I shove back my ergonomic chair, then stand and shake my head at my business partner.

"No?" Callum rolls his eyes at me from the seat across from my desk. "Why the fuck not?"

"You know why."

"The sales contract is perfect." Callum points to the document that has my body hurting more than when I overdo it at the gym. "A multibillion-dollar deal that adds an extra zero to the end of our net worth."

The logo of TRI etched into the pen on my desk, on my business card, and gleaming in steel on top of this office building are constant reminders of our company's success.

"It's the transition terms I would've negotiated," he insists. "You should be happy."

I'm anything but.

I bite my tongue as I look at the name on the buyer's signature line. Haliday. The name I've tried to erase from my mind over the last twelve years. The name that represents the worst rejection of my life.

The name of the girl with the mosaic eyes.

"Don't tell me you're still holding a grudge." Callum repositions his silk tie. "What happened to forgive and forget? With all this money on the line, who cares if our business goes to the Halidays? It's been over a decade since Rose threw you out of her life."

I wince. "You should have told me HH Group was behind the offer."

His hand falls to his lap. "We chose based on which buyer met our requirements."

I turn my back to him, the late afternoon sun glinting off the tall tower buildings in the financial district of Los Angeles miles away. "What's the next best bid?"

"A payout over twenty years instead of five. A three-year transition."

My gut roils. "The whole point was to sell quickly and get money for the next project."

"And HH Group offers us that and a mere six-month transition. Plus, they guarantee that they will take on the entire workforce with no layoffs." Callum comes to stand beside me as if he wants to enjoy the view. "A dream deal we never saw coming. We can't pass this up."

I glare at his reflection. "No."

"I can't believe you still have your panties in a twist." He slaps his palm on my shoulder. "Your priorities aren't straight."

"Insult me all you want, but we do not have a deal."

"You're a fucking asshole. Your goodie-two-shoes image is only for public consumption." His fingers dig into my trapezius muscle. "When your best friend and cofounder brings you a great deal, all you care about is your hurt pride."

I push his hand away. "Stop wasting our time and get your team to find a different buyer."

"You may be the CEO of this company, but you're not God. Things can't materialize just because you want them to. If we don't sell—"

"We'll sell." I set my jaw. "And we'll finally get to work on the projects we've always wanted, not just the ones that make us money."

Callum abandons his post beside me and resumes his seat. "Speak for yourself. I don't see anything wrong with just making money." He crosses his legs. "I could buy a better penthouse."

"Your priorities are clearly straight."

"At least I have priorities." He rises and throws a scrunched-up ball of paper at me like he did when we were freshmen at UCLA. Sometimes, I think his level of maturity stagnated at the age of nineteen.

Callum leaves, and I'm alone in my office. I scan the contract once again. The deal is good. I stare at the Haliday Hotels logo, and the bile in my stomach rises. Maybe that's because of the late hour and skipped dinner, but who am I kidding? Rose Haliday's face fills my mind, and my heart jumps into overdrive.

Unable to sit still, I open the door to the adjoining room, change out of my jeans and into my sweats, and start my warm-up routine. Exercise is supposed to distract me, but my thoughts are filled with Rose. All logic dictates I should have learned to deal with these feelings that have been a constant companion over the last twelve years. I've done everything—well, almost everything—to rid myself of the image that haunts my dreams and my waking hours. I tried to work her out of my head. But the hours at the gym, weekends at the rink, and hiking vacations in the Himalayas haven't excised the ghost.

I even tried Callum's suggestion of sleeping with women who look like her, and some who look nothing like her. Anything to purge Rose Haliday from my brain. But every experience was a total failure. Nothing or no one ever came close.

Most days, I manage to believe the lie that my feelings are less acute. But she's always there, lingering in the crevasses of my heart. Even when I resist searching for her online to see what her married life is like, if she covers the freckles across her nose with makeup, or if she has mini-versions of herself sitting primly in the famous annual Haliday Holiday cards.

The memory of how miserable I was runs in hot waves up my neck. Angry. Young. Dumb. And in love. I won't repeat those mistakes again.

I take the fifty-pound weights, assume the proper stance my personal trainer drilled into me, and start with bicep curls. Each rep redirects the flow of my emotions. I breathe and I curl until I fail on my twelfth rep. My heart beats confidently under my breastbone.

Across my office on my desk, my phone pings. I ignore the text and pump another rep. Another ping. Then there's a cacophony of bells I can't ignore. Weights on the floor, I pick up my phone and read the string of texts in the Fifth Line group, wincing at Callum's text narcing me out.

Soren:

> Fuck no. Not she who must not be named.

Of course my former college roommate, who's finishing his popular sci-fi book and accompanying streaming series, is the first to pick on me. He'll do anything to procrastinate writing the ending to the saga.

Linc:

> Who's Rose Haliday again?

Soren:

> THE girl.

Linc:

> Right. I tend to forget, what with all the women A dates these days.

Blake:

> Did you bump your head? Callum has a new girl warming his bed every night. Alek is attempting to regain his virginity.

Callum:

> Not every night.

I groan. These asses love to mock Callum's overflowing sex life and my lack thereof.

Me:

> Don't you nutballs have anything better to do?

Callum:

> Ah, the re-virgin crawls out of his cave to speak to us.

Linc:

> I'm in town next month. Pickup game?

Hockey is what brought the five of us together on the UCLA campus. Callum was there on a scholarship and would have made the NHL if it weren't for his accident. Linc made the big league and is making a play for the cup in what might be his final year. Blake, Soren, and I never had dreams of professional hockey. Still, when we can, we get out on the ice and take on the local kids down at The Cube.

Soren:

I'm in.

Blake:

Me too.

My thumbs move over the keyboard.

Me:

Last one with skates on buys the scotch.

Callum:

Maybe a few good checks will knock some sense into Alek.

I drop my phone on the desk. Despite Callum's needling, entertaining offers outside of HH Group is the way to go. I'm in control now. Circling the room, I count to sixty before the next rep. The wall by my desk is papered with the goals for Second Chance Events, where my attention has been for the last year. With the sale of TRI, I can finally be 100 percent focused on the charity.

There's only one hitch. I'm missing connections in high-end entertainment and party spaces.

Before me is my vision board for my new venture. The people, places, and things to bring my idea to life. In the center is the smiling photo of Ezra and Leanne Menken, my dream partners. Hollywood royalty who can make the final connections that I can't achieve on my own.

That fact frustrates me to no end. There are very few things I haven't been able to achieve on my own since Callum and

I started ORSN, our first company together, straight out of college We built that company up, sold it, and started TRI off the profits.

The next round of reps gets me into the brainstorming zone.

Goal 1: Find a buyer for TRI.

Goal 2: Find a way to sell the Menkens on Second Chance Events.

Goal 3: Don't think about Rose Haliday.

FOUR

TWELVE YEARS AGO

September

My senior year at UCLA is supposed to be the most specialized of my degree. With a major in Business Economics and a minor in Entrepreneurship, picking classes is like selecting the best dress for a party when every single one fits perfectly.

The smile on my face must be brighter than the shining September sun as I rush into the building that holds my victory. With this course, I'll prove to Mom I'm worthy of being the one to launch HH Group to a new level when she retires. She took risks when she was young, and even though she doesn't approve of me taking this course, I'll show Mom that our company is my priority, just like it has always been hers.

I straighten my shoulders and enter the small room, taking in the desks arranged in a circle. The only person in the room is Professor Patel. Getting accepted into his Applied Entrepreneurship seminar is like being selected for the Olympics. I'm one of ten lucky students out of hundreds of seniors who applied. Pride warms my chest.

He is fumbling with cords leading from his computer to the projector as he lifts his gaze to me. "You're early. We won't be starting for another half hour."

"Early bird gets the worm." I shrug and look at the desks. The knowledge that neither Mom's last name nor her influence were the reason for my acceptance makes the success exclusively mine. "Are they assigned, or do I pick one?"

"Pick a card from that bowl and park yourself anywhere."

I approach the bright yellow clay bowl that must've been made by a kid. I tip my fingers in, sift through the small yellow envelopes, and pick one. "Do I open it now?"

"You'll all open them at the same time. Part of the fun."

Fun? Isn't this class supposed to be serious? I frown, but I put the envelope on top of my journal and set my large cappuccino with two extra espresso shots on the desk closest to the podium. With no supply list, I brought a couple of my favorite notebooks, my laptop, and some pens and highlighters. Coming empty-handed felt unprepared. I open my sketchbook to the most recent drawing of the party decor for the Baby2Baby Gala in November.

Olivia's birthday party was a hit, and I'm confident I can bring the glitz and glamour to this charity event. I shade the tablecloths with the royal-blue theme of this year. Yellow sunflowers in crystal vases will brighten the room on the tables around the swag area and circling the dance floor.

Students trickle into the room, pick yellow envelopes, and choose their desks. Two girls and six guys take their seats. I offer each newcomer a smile, then get back to my design. The door opens again, and I prepare another polite smile for the final student. I lift my gaze, and my heart stutters.

What is he doing here?

Gone are the overalls I sunk my fingers into in the elevator. But I'd recognize those straight thick eyebrows and that square chin anywhere. The stubble featured in my dreams last night is gone, and his dark brown hair is trimmed shorter on the sides. My gut squeezes. No matter how cute the maintenance guy is, I won't mix business and pleasure. Mom's warning rings in my head. Does Alek work nights at the hotel and days for UCLA? No, not with that backpack slung over his shoulder. Maybe the staff get to audit courses as a perk of the job?

Professor Patel hands him the last yellow envelope, and Alek takes the last desk. I shift in my seat. He's one of the chosen ten.

"Welcome to the fall semester of Applied Entrepreneurship." Professor Patel walks to my desk and taps a thick finger on my yellow envelope. "As you must've noticed, there is no assigned reading material for this class. Any ideas why that is?" He looks around the room. A burly guy with a splotchy beard raises his hand. Professor Patel nods at him.

"I'm Rafael Sanches, and my friend's sister took your class two years ago. She said you prefer hands-on project-based activities more than theoretical principles."

"Bravo, Rafael. You've already applied a couple of the entrepreneurial principles I teach in this class: leverage those around you, ask previous students what to expect, and"—the professor pauses, and I lean forward— "exude confidence by being the first to speak."

The girl beside me writes down confidence and underlines the word, like she needs those three lines in order to remember.

Professor Patel takes my yellow envelope and circles behind the desks. "Each of you selected one of these. Think of this as your starting base. You all joined this class with prior knowledge and skills, but also with your financial background and your circle of friends. Inside the envelopes are the permissions and restrictions you will live by this semester." Professor Patel hands me the envelope. "Let's open them."

I rip the side, and a piece of paper the size of an index card falls out. In bold text are three bullet points that look like a set of instructions.

Rafael asks, "What's the catch?"

"Read your card aloud, please."

Rafael clears his throat. "I'm allowed to use the class bank for a sum of up to $10,000." A few whistles sound in the room. "I get to choose if I'm presenting or not, and I can pick any topic for my project."

"He gets a lot of money and can do whatever he wants? My card doesn't say that," a guy with a green beanie interjects.

Everyone looks at the professor. "Correct. Each card is different. You bring a lot of attributes into this classroom, but I'm here to change the playing field. Not all of you will have equal starting points. However, everyone will have the same time allotted for your final presentation. As an entrepreneur, you don't operate on a level playing field. Another principle of entrepreneurship: adaptability."

The girl beside me, her blond ponytail falling over her shoulder, looks put out. "My card says my project has to deal with food. I'm allowed to use personal funds with an unlimited budget, and I'm the lead presenter. Can we switch cards?"

Professor Patel perches on his desk. "You must work within your card's parameters."

I read the first bullet point on mine, and my shoulders fall. My financial parameter is no money. I'm allowed to fundraise with a cap of a hundred dollars per person. I can't throw money at my project, but there is no limit on the number of people I can have make a donation, so that's in my favor. Things get better when I read points two and three. My project area is app development, and I'm copresenting.

Alek rests his elbows on his desk. "You didn't answer the switch question."

"I did not. What does your card say?" the professor asks.

"I'm not allowed to use any direct money contributions. All parts of my project have to be based on donations of goods and services. My partner's project topic will become mine. My role during the presentation depends on them."

The professor asks the rest of the students to read their cards aloud. Some get to use their own funds, and others are limited, including the guy in the beanie. When the professor gets to me, I read mine aloud, then remark, "You still haven't answered about switching."

"No switching is allowed." The professor's gaze sweeps over everyone.

Beside me, the blond with the long ponytail groans.

"Don't worry. There'll be other opportunities to get advantages." Professor Patel's face hardens.

"Sounds like we're on a reality TV show." Alek taps his pen against his leg. "Are there elimination rounds?"

"I assure you this is more real than any reality show. However, as with any other class, you can choose to leave before the drop date."

The girl beside me huffs. "Does the number in the corner of the card mean anything?"

"Good eye." The professor holds up a finger. "That's the order in which you get to pick your partners."

The hairs rise on the back of my neck. I'm number ten.

"Who's number one?"

The girl next to me breaks into a wide smile. "I'm picking Rafael and his money."

With each number that I am not selected, dread chills my skin. Being number ten, I'm at the complete mercy of fate. The students around me make their picks, but it's like I'm invisible. I've never in my life not been chosen.

"That went fast. Thank you for being so decisive, everyone. We are down to our last two. Rose and Alek, am I correct?" Professor Patel looks between us.

Alek's almost-black eyes lock with mine. If I doubted he recognized me before, I'm one hundred percent sure he does now. I fold my card and plaster on my best smile-for-the-camera grin and face our professor. Not only do I have to rely on donations to ace this project, I have to work with the guy my mother specifically didn't want me around, whose full lips I fantasized about. I turn to Alek, and my stomach drops at the scowl on his face.

My dream class just turned into a nightmare.

FIVE

ALEK

TWELVE YEARS AGO

September

"I guess we'll have to work together." Rose scrunches her nose, and the freckles across the bridge make her snobby expression almost look cute. "Hopefully you have a good work ethic. I have to get an A in this class."

"You know my work ethic," I say. She raises her brow, and my chin lifts in response. "You do recognize me?"

"Alek, the maintenance man."

"Well, for a second, I thought all hotel personnel might look the same to you." Even I wince at the vinegar in my voice.

She leans back in her chair. "I know the names of all the managers and probably most of the front desk staff. How long have you been working at our Los Angeles location?"

"I started full-time in August." My palms feel sweaty, and I rub them on my jeans. "My dad has been in the maintenance department for over twenty years. He's the supervisor now."

"Gleb?" Her head tilts. "You don't look anything alike."

"Same height, but I take after Mama's side of the family."

"Well, as much as I love getting to know my hotels' staff, we need to strategize." She leans over my desk and snatches my card. A whiff of the same flowery perfume that left me breathless at the party lingers in the air around me. "Let's see what we have to work with. We're stuck with app development as the project topic. That's not something I've ever done. You?"

My lips twitch. There's a subject I studied that the hotel heiress didn't? "My degree is in software engineering, so you could say so."

The expression on her face lights up. "Maybe we're not in as bad a shape as I imagined. Shame we didn't get the unlimited personal funds one. Or even the food project theme. I could totally slay a project about hotel catering for events or room service. Although that's less sexy." She rattles on like she is the project leader and I'm just hired help. "Too bad Professor Patel said we couldn't switch."

The gall of this woman. I bite my lip. "Are you looking for a more influential partner? I'm not good enough?"

She blinks three times rapidly. "It's not you. It's the cards. Currently, you have very little to bring to the table, and if I had a choice, I'd definitely pick anyone's card but yours. Strategically, that is. You understand, don't you?"

Her mom's "blue-collar" comment sounds in my mind. I cross my arms. "Strategically, sure."

She places my card on top of hers on the desk. "Look. I'm going to be CEO one day. And CEOs can't be too soft. My goal is to ace the final presentation. How I get there is important, but the result is what people in the corporate world most care about. Your card is a setback."

"I thought that's the whole point." I lean forward. "Professor Patel wants to put us in a situation that removes us from our daily lives. The way the restrictions are set up allows him to see how we'd fare based on our own ingenuity and business smarts. Not just with what Mommy hands out."

A red blotch stains her cheeks. "I still don't have to be happy I got dealt the worst hand."

I look at my hands. The rough skin is a stark contrast to Rose's soft manicured fingers. My skin still remembers the electric current that ran from them into me. That was before she was ashamed of them. Of me. "Worst hand, huh."

"Metaphorically. You were hired by HH Group, so I'm sure you are one of the best when it comes to what you do for us."

"You would think that."

"Am I wrong? About you being good with your hands?"

She doesn't know anything about me, and instantly assumes manual labor is all I'm good for. Despite the fact that I'm also a student at UCLA. Or that I'm in this prestigious course. If she cared to ask, she'd find out I'm about to graduate a semester early at the top of my class. The back of my throat burns. I lean closer to her ear and whisper, "I'm very good with my hands." I sound entirely unlike myself, making the statement as low, sultry, and suggestive as I can.

Telling spots bloom on her cheeks as she twists and stares at me.

Instantly, I regret the remark. I'm smarter than this. Our harmless flirting when I thought she was just an interesting hotel guest was one thing, but antagonizing a fellow student with sexual innuendos is another. Getting in trouble when I'm so close to graduation is the last thing I need. My goal is to get to the middle of December. Then I can look for jobs that do not require fixing leaks in the stuck-up hotel heiress's VIP suite.

Rose's lips part as if she wants to speak, but then her blush spreads to her chest, which I should not be noticing. I shift my gaze to where the ends of her hair skim her chin. She narrows her eyes, moving her face close to mine. "Too bad this competition is for people who can use their brains."

My skin heats. This is not the reaction I imagined, neither from her nor myself. That becoming-CEO plan of hers unfolds in front of me. I can see the strength and determination in her eyes. Rose Haliday has what it takes to do whatever she wants. And that truth is somehow making me even more turned on. More than the view of her almost-naked back. I chew on the inside of my cheek. That image hasn't left my mind since the party.

I tell my cock to calm down and make myself give the girl whose lips I want to both kiss and bite a friendly smile. Our project has the potential to earn me a recommendation from Professor Patel, which I can present to future employers. In the past five years, this seminar has opened doors to several startups, and mine will be next, no matter what this girl thinks of me.

"I guess our first lesson is to use each other's strengths to get what we both want," I say.

Her gaze meets mine. "Or maybe it's how to work with the cards you've been dealt."

"Don't be so nice regarding your feelings about working with me."

"Nice doesn't get you anywhere. That's one of many things working under my mom taught me. As a woman managing her own empire, she learned early on if she depended on 'nice,' she'd still be a socialite relying on her parents' trust fund. Instead, she owns a network of twenty-three hotels and resorts and employs thousands of people, including maintenance workers. 'Nice' isn't a word used to describe my mother. But she's been called a visionary and was Entrepreneur of the Year twice in *Business World Magazine*. I don't want to be nice. I want to be like her. Or better."

Why am I hanging on her every syllable? I push back in my seat, creating some space and breathing room from the inferno that is Rose. She juts out her chin like Callum does after he's won a gruesome fight on the ice.

I place my palm on the cool plastic of my desk. "That will hold us back when we have to solicit donations and fundraise for this project."

A smile spreads across her face like I've complimented her biggest achievement. "I've attended hundreds of fundraisers. They are just glorified parties. I throw several of those a year."

"You mean your event planner does the work and you show up looking pretty?" Or gorgeous. The image of her in the dress creeps back into my brain. I shut it down, focusing on her personality instead. That should shove all the unreasonable attraction back into its place.

She glares at me. "Don't put words in my mouth."

Words are not what I want to put into your mouth springs to the tip of my tongue, but this time, I manage to hold back.

"By now, you should have worked out the basic logistics of how you will work together." Professor Patel's voice interrupts us.

"Give me your number, and I'll text you," she whispers out of the corner of her mouth, her attention on the professor.

"By our next class, I expect you to arrive with your project idea, description, and a preliminary timeline. Remember, you only have ten weeks before the final presentation." Professor Patel checks his watch. "See you next week."

As the students around us start packing up, a phone plops on the desk in front of me with a contact page open. The name is already filled in. Alek in the first name box. Handyman in the last name box. I clench my teeth, refusing to give her the satisfaction of a reaction. I refuse to believe she forgot my last name. Instead of typing my number, I enter the direct line to the maintenance department of the hotel and pass the device back to her.

I watch her face as she registers what I did. "Do you not own a phone?" She presses her lips in defiance, refusing to play by my rules.

This project might not go how I imagine. Still, one thing is for sure: the next three months will be interesting. I rarely get to engage in verbal sparring at this level. I'll have to sharpen my tools. A fizz of excitement pops in my veins. I'm up for the challenge, especially if I get to shatter the snobby nepo baby's illusion that she'll be running our partnership.

I meet her gaze. "If you'd like my number, you'll have to ask nicely."

Her eyes widen, and she shoots up from her chair. "Not happening. You can expect an email from me to your university email address. If you don't reply, I'll report you to Professor Patel."

I stand. At six foot one, I'm far from the tallest on the hockey team. But she's at least six inches shorter than me. I rarely use my height to intimidate, but apparently Rose is the exception for a lot of things. I lean over her. "Not happening. I'll email you. Working with me on this project is nonnegotiable, and if you don't want to play nice . . ." I lean down and lock my eyes with hers. "I know how to get my hands dirty, sweets."

"Don't call me that." The black of her pupils dilates. "I'm not sweet. And I'm not your pet."

"And I'm not your errand boy."

We square off. The heat of her gaze could burn a hole through my face. I should despise her, but the fire she meets me with only stokes my own.

Let the games begin.

Six

PRESENT DAY

January

What else might sway Alek to sell his company to us? Mom's offer met every ask. She overpaid, according to my advisers. With TRI's efficiency and forecasting tech, HH Group would get an edge over the competition and implement needed improvements.

I ignore my mother's incoming call, just like I ignored her three texts demanding to know where I am. I switch my phone to silent and shove the device in my purse. The guilt of not answering gnaws at me as I straighten my skirt and push against the door with TRI's logo etched into the glass. This gamble better be worth the lecture I'll endure when I return.

The low-level drone of voices from the rows of desks in the open space greets me like the polite applause of a golfer at the Masters. This cannot possibly be the entire company. A smiling guy in a hoodie with headphones around his neck stands up from the nearest desk. "Ms. Haliday?"

I raise my chin. One of the good things about having the same last name as my mother is that no one knows which one of us to expect.

"This way." He high-fives a woman with a bandanna wrapped around her head. "It's warm for January, isn't it?" he asks as he leads me out of the buzzing room down the hallway.

Two voices spill out from an open door.

"The Menkens only work with people they know."

"Well. How do I get to know them then?"

My escort doesn't knock and just looks in. "She's here." Without any introduction, he leads me across the threshold. "If you want a drink, I can show you what we have."

An assistant who's this casual with clients wouldn't last long around my mother. Maybe we shouldn't be paying billions for a company where I can't even get a proper offer of a cup of coffee. "No, thank you."

I instantly regret not asking for water as the man I haven't seen in person for twelve years rises from behind a black desk. I become the desert, hot and lost. Alek's square jaw hardens, and his dark eyes narrow. The mouth I remember to be soft and teasing doesn't offer me a smile.

The years have been good to him. At twenty-two, he was an irresistible combo of hockey muscles and clean-shaven youthful cheeks with his easy-to-grin brown eyes that, when he looked at me, turned into hot chocolate— the thick and extremely sweet European kind that makes me thirsty after one sip. Today I'm parched because this Alek is that boy and more. So much more. Everything is harder: his jaw, his cold stare, the pressed line of his lips, the shoulders under his shirt, and the way his arms cross over that broad chest of his. The chest I, once upon a time, laid my head against, falling asleep to the thumping lullaby of his heart.

"This is unexpected." Callum, whose face is regularly featured in celebrity gossip columns, rises from one of the two chairs in front of the desk. His gaze swings to Alek before he bridges the distance between us with his arm extended. The same genuine lopsided smile he charmed the girls with back when he and Alek were roommates at UCLA curves across his lips. "It's been what, a decade since we drank at The Devil's Martini?"

"Twelve years, actually." I stretch my lips into a matching smile, shake his hand, and turn to Alek.

No smile. No hand. Cold eyes assess me like I'm here to ruin his life instead of negotiate the best deal of his career.

"Hi," I manage to push past my clenched teeth.

He doesn't even nod, but a muscle does tick in his jaw. A tell of Alek's I learned when we were still friends. He is nervous. A real smile creeps over my lips as I hold his stare.

"Forgive Alek. He was expecting your mother." Callum gestures for me to sit.

Alek doesn't hide his huff at Callum's assessment but sits behind the desk with his arms still crossed.

I tear my gaze away from Alek and face Callum. "She doesn't know I'm here."

My mouth remains dry, but I'm here to do my job and not complain about lack of hydration. I'm here to prove to my mother I'm more than the figurehead she limits me to. Good enough to be the face of the company but not good enough to run my own division, never mind HH Group in its entirety. Securing this deal to get proprietary rights for the software Alek created will be undeniable proof to my mother that it's time to give me real responsibility in my family's company.

I straighten my shoulders. "I'm confident we can negotiate a deal that benefits HH Group and both of you."

"No need to persuade me," Callum says. "I'm on board."

Alek throws a glare at him that's even angrier than the one he greeted me with.

My lungs tighten. This is not about the contract. This is about our history. I toss away Plan A for these negotiations and skip right to Plan C. Alek is still upset about us. No, not us. Me. I lock my ankles together and angle them to the side in a position worthy of a British Royal portrait. Unthreatening, yet a pose of quiet power.

I raise my gaze back to Alek and pretend my blood isn't heating just from looking at him. "What can I do to persuade you to let bygones be bygones?"

"I'm sorry you had to waste a trip." Alek sets his palms on his desk. "I've already told Callum, and I'll tell you the same. Selling TRI to HH Group is not in our best interest."

I scoot to the front of my chair. "Is there anything I could offer to change your mind?" I place my hand on top of his. The heat of his skin warms my clammy palm, and the touch, that connection we once had, zings straight to my heart. If I jerk away, I'll be seen as weak. So I stay still, pretending to be patronizing, a gracious queen reassuring her subject. However, on the inside, I'm back to the twenty-two-year-old girl who just wants to touch a cute boy who has a tendency to stare at her too hard.

"No." Alek removes his hand from underneath mine, and the muscle in his jaw ticks with new intensity.

"Actually . . ." Callum leans back and watches us with a satisfied smile. "I have an idea that might persuade Alek to look favorably at the contract."

"As I said, I'm open to renegotiations. I'll get our lawyers on the line now, and we can hammer out the details."

A sly smirk graces Callum's lips. "No lawyers are needed for this particular . . . addendum."

I narrow my eyes. "I'm not embroiling myself or HH Group in any illegal activities."

The glee falls off Callum's face. "Whoa, whoa. Nothing illegal or unsavory." His gaze flits to Alek. "Just something neither of us would like to be public knowledge."

Alek tips forward. "What are you up to?"

"First, let me remind you, Rose, that your mother signed an NDA that forbids her or any of her emissaries to disclose information you learn about our companies in the process of this contract negotiation. That means you're bound to that as well."

I didn't know this, because my mother never lets me sit on these types of negotiations, but I nod in agreement.

"Excellent. You are aware one of the reasons we are selling TRI is to raise capital for another venture."

I have no idea about that either, but I smile as if I do. "Congratulations. I guess you're now officially serial entrepreneurs." I give a perfunctory clap. Our old professor would be proud of Alek. I let my hands fall to my lap. "Would you like HH Group to add the new company to the deal?"

"No." It comes from Alek quicker than Callum.

Alek glares at his friend. "We are not going to discuss the new venture with her."

"Have some faith." Callum turns to me and jerks a thumb at Alek. "This one has some trust issues." He ignores Alek's growl. "We are not looking for HH Group to purchase Alek's new venture. However, there's a service you can provide."

Unease slides down my throat. "Me? Not HH Group?"

"What are you trying to do?" Alek stares at Callum in angry disbelief. Either he's become an excellent actor, or this is the first time he's finding out about this proposition as well.

"Hear me out before either of you decide to throw me out the window." All teasing drains from Callum's face. "This is why you keep me around. I find unique ways to get the resources you need, all while making things work for each party involved. Let me do my job."

"Be quick about it," grumbles Alek.

"In order for the new company to get off the ground, Alek needs to rub elbows with some Hollywood and high-society types to make his new venture successful. Specifically, Ezra and Leanne Menken. And you, Rose, happen to be close to Ezra and Leanne Menken. Weren't they good friends with your father and his parents?"

Alek swears under his breath. "There has to be another way."

"But this way is here." Callum points to me. "Wanting to make a deal. It's a win-win."

Hope unfurls under my ribcage. This will be easy. I can see my mother's proud grin as I bring her the signed contract. I try to play it cool in the presence of Callum and Alek, though. "You want me to introduce you to the Menkens?"

"Something like that." Callum taps his mouth with his index finger. "The Menkens won't invest with a simple introduction. No, Rose, you need to present Alek as if he's . . . like family. Be seen with him at a few social events. Once the Menkens accept him, Alek can broach the idea of Second Chance Events."

Alek holds his head in his hands and mumbles, "This is ludi-crous."

I stare at Callum. "He can't be my date. Any time the tabloids clock me with an unattached man more than twice, they hear wedding bells."

"And what if they do?" Callum asks. "You haven't dated since your divorce, right?"

I can't deny his assumption. Walking away from Dean was the best decision I have made in years. I avoid looking at Alek. "That's correct."

"So, some people gossip." Callum shrugs. "Isn't that worth the price of getting our company?"

"Why don't you do it?" Alek asks Callum. "Like you said, you do this for a living. You'll get the Menkens on my side in a single visit."

Callum cocks his head. "I'm glad you think so highly of me, but I'll be training for my around-the-world regatta. And you know my romantic affairs don't last more than a week. Who would believe I'm actually dating someone?"

"No one." Alek's hands drop limply on his desk. "How would this even work?"

I gape at him. He's considering this preposterous scenario?

"That's up to you two. I suggest you set a time frame, figure out some photo ops to be seen together, and then find an event or two the Menkens will be attending. Make sure you're both there. Once they've accepted Alek into their inner circle, he gets to persuade them to join Second Chance Events. Then you two part ways."

I consider the terms. Not good enough. "'Until he persuades the Menkens' is not specific. That could take years. I need this sale to happen now."

"We'll throw a few more addenda into the actual contract, keep the lawyers busy for a few months until you can seal the other deal." Callum looks at Alek. "Any objections?"

"All of them," Alek says. "This is an outlandish idea only you, Callum, could've come up with."

"You're welcome."

The contract is on the table, a feat my mother couldn't manage. Alek seems to be considering the deal. So what if I have to spend some time with the one man I've never been able to get over? A man my ex-husband certainly couldn't hold a candle to.

Alek crosses his arms yet again. "I'm not pretending to be Rose's friend to get to the Menkens."

"Sounds like you'll be pretending to be Rose's *boy*friend." Callum cocks an eyebrow at Alek. "Isn't that a dream—"

"Shut up."

"Stop it." I cross my legs. "This isn't about dreams. This is about reality." I stare at Alek. "Are you in? Or do you hate me that much?"

Alek stands and rolls his lips. My stomach tightens. I'm sure he's about to tank the deal.

"I don't hate you." He leans across the desk and offers me his hand. "I'm in."

I press my palm against his. "Pleasure doing business with you," I say as my body betrays me. A stream of heat ignites where his skin touches mine, melting every cell on its way to my solar plexus.

I don't hate Alek Orlov, either. I don't hate him at all.

SEVEN

ALEK

PRESENT DAY

February

Across the wide white granite conference table, Melinda Haliday grins like the cat that caught the canary. This is quite different from the last time I was in the same room as her. She twists her pen. "I'm thrilled you've agreed to restart negotiations."

The six lawyers sitting on her side of the table nod in agreement. I refuse to glance at Rose, who's not sitting next to her mother as I expected. Instead, she's far on the right beside her mother's assistant, who is furiously writing notes like his life depends on capturing every statement with precision.

"Alek and I recently came to view your offer from a different perspective." Callum addresses Melinda. "Thanks to Rose."

I try not to glare at my best friend. After Rose left last week, our deal agreed upon, I had to swear Callum to secrecy and make him promise not to tattletale to the guys, and especially not to my family. Mama keeps sending me photos of her friends' single daughters and nieces, hoping I'll take one out on a date. Callum loves egging her on. He likes to push boundaries and always has, but there's no one else on this earth I would trust with this information. To the outside world, Callum is a fickle playboy who doesn't know the meaning of the word monogamy, but I know the true man. Loyalty is in his DNA.

"Yes." Melinda spins the single ring with a large rock on her finger. "Rose is certainly full of surprises."

Everyone turns to Rose, and at last I have the freedom to study her without causing suspicion. Her hair is extra straight today, and it caresses the tempting line of her long neck. My imagination goes awry at the memory of that soft skin against my mouth and the gasp she made as I ran my lips across her collarbone. I reposition myself, but the discomfort clings. The apples of her cheeks pink. I adore when she blushes. Just not when she might give us away.

Rose sits straighter. "This deal is advantageous to both of us. By adding the limited-time stock buyout, the employees of TRI all get a piece of the pie with this sale."

One of the lawyers asks for clarification, and we spend the next forty minutes hammering out the price the stock has to hit in order for the buyout to kick in. As with most of our business negotiations, Callum does all the talking, grinding the lawyers down one by one until he gets what he wants.

I'm here for Rose.

Well, not for her, specifically. Over the last week we've emailed a few times, trying to work out the details of our fake relationship without actually committing to what we're doing in writing. Emails can be hacked, and we don't need our arrangement to be the subject of online gossip. In the end, we agreed to meet in person to discuss.

When Callum suggested the meeting, I balked at first. His laugh filled the room. "If you can't spend an afternoon with Rose in an office, how will you survive a fake date? I know it's been years since you went on one, but you do know you might have to hold her hand. Among other things."

"We need to call this off," I protested, unsure I am able to pretend with Rose Haliday.

Callum sipped from his glass of scotch and met my panicked gaze. "Sure. But that means delaying the launch of Second Chance. The charities waiting for your promises will go another year without proper funding."

With my silence as consent, he continued, "Lighten up. Maybe try having a little fun. You never know. You might enjoy yourself."

"Alek?" Rose is standing beside me. I must have zoned out. "I have something I'd like to discuss with you."

Right. The other deal.

Everyone around me is leaving their seats or on their way out of the room. Callum winks at me. "See you at the office." He exits the conference room with Melinda and the lead lawyer.

I pop up from my chair. Rose's floral perfume tickles my nose and evokes memories I refuse to let surface. I step back and nod. "Right. Here, or . . ."

Rose swings her head left and right. "Let's go to my office. Less chance of being interrupted."

I follow her out of the conference room, down the long hall, and back to the reception area with a hammered sign welcoming guests to the executive floor. We enter another hallway and pass a door with a large brass plaque that reads MELINDA HALIDAY, CEO & PRESIDENT.

Around a corner, Rose presses her shoulder into another door, and we enter an office unlike the rooms with stuffy decor on the rest of this floor. Actual live plants soak up sunlight from west-facing windows: a mishmash of budding flowers, broken stalks, and new growth. The all-glass desk is cluttered with binders and brochures, what looks like swatches of cloth, and boards with color schemes and photos. On the hardwood floor lies an area rug that matches the two chairs and the couch. Unlike the furniture in the reception area, they almost look comfy. Inviting.

I did not expect this. But then again, Rose did always have a way of surprising me.

Rose places her laptop on her desk and points to the couch. "Mind if we sit there? I'm sick of boardrooms today."

I follow her. "This isn't what I expected."

"No?" She shoves off her shoes and plops onto the couch.

I gesture to the cozy ambiance of the room. "I saw the spread in *Business World* on your mother last year. This is nothing like her office."

Her nose wrinkles. "Why would it be?"

"The girl I knew wanted to be exactly like Melinda Haliday."

"Not exactly. The plan is to be the next CEO." She swallows. "Your plans changed, I see."

"I haven't changed all that much."

"Let's agree to disagree." Her gaze travels up and down my body, and I wonder what differences she's seeing.

"We were always good at that." The claim comes with images of Rose and me from years ago that I've locked up and guarded myself from—not very successfully, might I add. "You've definitely changed."

"You're not supposed to point out when a woman's aged."

"Not at all what I was referring to." I gesture to my ring finger. "You got married."

"As the gossip sites have reported ad nauseam, it took me longer to get a divorce than the years we were together."

I ease into the chair opposite her. "I'm not much into high society or Hollywood gossip. Not my crowd."

"Lucky me." She rolls her wrists like she's warming up for a game. "If you were, you wouldn't need me."

"I don't need you." The knee-jerk reaction jettisons from me like a slapshot.

"So, you are backing out already?"

"I'm here, aren't I?" I can't help but stare at her. How did we get here? "Thanks to Callum," I add.

"Callum has that ability."

"To irritate me?"

"To make connections and network." She massages her neck. "It's uncanny how well he can read a room, a person."

"That's why he's the face of TRI."

She peers sideways. "And you're the brains?"

"I'm more of a team captain. If I want something, I do what it takes to help my team score."

"That's what's happening with your new venture? Second Chance Events?"

"If all goes well." I jab a thumb at the collection of things on her desk. "What's all this for?"

The defensive Rose falls away, and her face lights up. "A ball I'm preparing for Valentine's Day for local kids with physical disabilities. I arrange personal shoppers and stylists, and they can just eat, dance, and be kids. Everything is covered for them and their caregivers, so the only thing they need to do is show up and enjoy the day."

"An HH Group project?"

"Not exactly." She pushes her hair behind her ear. "I try to put together several charity events a year at no charge."

I stand and walk over to the messy desk, unable to suppress my grin. "You found a way to satisfy your event-planning kink."

Her lips twitch. "It's not a kink. It's a hobby. I believe there's a difference."

The implications of her hobby spin in my mind. "That must take thousands of dollars to maintain."

"Hundreds of thousands. Thus, it's a hobby." She crosses her arms. "Would you recommend I get a private island instead?"

I meet her glare. "I'd never tell you how you spend your money."

"Outside of purchasing TRI."

"That's your decision. As I recall, I could never change your mind once you made a decision." I look down at the desk, inspecting the index cards pinned alongside the boards, her loopy handwriting adorning each. "And I'm starting to think maybe you haven't changed that much either. Looks like you still prefer physical boards to digital ones? There are some top-of-the-line apps I can recommend."

"You switched to digital boards then?"

I pick up a board with a collection of famous artworks in funky frames alongside pictures of clowns and rainbows. "I have not. Old dog, new tricks and all that."

"Please do not say that when you try to promote your company to Leanne and Ezra. You're supposed to be the innovator, not the late adopter."

I abandon the boards to cross the room. "Old doesn't mean bad. Plenty of older technology is still useful."

"Hard to call attaching stuff to a board 'technology.'"

With a sigh, I unzip my hoodie and take my seat again. "Are you going to police my vocabulary? We're not preparing a presentation we have to deliver together."

The sparkle in her eyes sputters and dulls. "But we are. The moment you and I are seen in public together, everything you do or say is a reflection on me."

"This is not 'My Fair Lady.' You don't have to teach me how to properly speak to the upper class."

"Debatable."

I edge to the front of my seat. "Maybe this was a bad idea. No one will ever believe we actually like each other if you correct every sentence I utter and look at me like that."

"Like what?"

I hold my hands out. "Like I haven't taken a shower in a week."

"It's your clothes."

Today, to toy with Melinda Haliday, I dressed down in my Silicon Valley uniform of a hoodie and jeans. Foolish me didn't think Rose, who's seen me in sweats and a ripped T-shirt, would care. "What's wrong with my clothes?"

"You'll have to up your wardrobe. The press commented on Dean's attire constantly."

My neck heats at Rose's mention of her ex-husband. If she was my wife, I'd do anything to make her happy. I ball my fists. "I didn't think I needed to wear my custom tux for this meeting."

"I'm not talking about the black-tie galas. We'll be in plenty of casual situations, and you can't look like that." Rose's hand pans in my direction.

"What's wrong with the way I look?"

Rose rotates the bracelet on her wrist. "Where did you buy these clothes?"

"Mama bought them for me at Macy's."

Her gaze flies to the office ceiling. "Oh, dear lord. You still let your mother buy your clothes?"

"She's done a great job. I give her a budget, and she makes sure the stuff that doesn't fit gets exchanged."

"Alek," she groans. Her saying my name makes my body react, which should not be happening, especially since she's berating me. "You're a grown man. An owner of a multi-billion-dollar company. You cannot be dressed by your mother." She shakes her head. "At least this isn't Target."

"My socks probably are."

Seeing her flustered makes my insides heat, reminding me of one of the things that attracted me to her in the first place. My Rose was always determined, opinionated, and stubborn. She held steadfast to her beliefs. Challenging those ideals was half the fun. Breaking her composure was another of our games.

"I'll get you the number of my stylist." She pulls out her phone. "I made a list of potential events over the next months." She taps on her screen. "Do you play tennis?"

"No."

Her mouth twists. "Poker?"

"No."

"How about polo?"

"No."

"Smoke cigars?"

I chuckle. She's clearly grasping at straws. "Definitely not."

"Fine. Do you belong to any clubs?"

"I go to Mars Gym."

"That's not a club. That's a gym. So a 'no' there as well."

"Name the club, and I'll join."

She exhales hard. "It's not that simple. You need recommendations, and the applications take months or sometimes even years. What about squash?"

I push my hand through my hair. "I assume you mean the sport, not the vegetable."

Seemingly unimpressed, she shoots me an icy glare. What wouldn't I do to get another hit of her fieriness, the intensity I've craved since seeing Rose again?

"I still play hockey." There, I can remind her of who I used to be. The man she knew before. Good idea? Probably not, but it's too late now. "I won't drown at the pool, and Callum makes me visit a golf course once a year." He closed more deals in the clubhouse of the three golf courses he's a member of than he does in boardrooms.

"That could work." She continues tapping the screen. "The Menkens are huge golf players. We belong to the same golf club, and we usually watch the Masters Tournament together." She flips through her screen. "That's almost two months away. We need an earlier occasion. Oh, the Oscars. They never miss the show."

"I could do an Oscars watch party."

"Not a party. The actual Oscars. You know, at the Dolby Theatre."

"Isn't there another option?" I press my palm onto my bouncing knee. Fancy parties were never my scene. Overdressed crowds and I do not mix.

Her face lifts to me. "Maybe I should back out. You sound like you have no idea who Ezra and Leanne Menken even are."

"I've researched them extensively," I snap. "I know their investments, the key events of their careers, and I know they're looking for an investment opportunity. Get me into that party, and I'll impress them."

Her phone falls to her lap. "I remember why we argued so much at the beginning of our entrepreneurship class."

"Because you thought you were in charge and I was useless?"

"Because you try to solve everything with hard work when there are other solutions."

I bite back my smile. How can it be this easy to fall into old patterns? Worse, why is my chest burning at the familiarity? Like I would give anything to do this for the rest of my life with Rose? Quibble over the most efficient way to do things. Watch her eyes spark with the fire of defiance, interest, and maybe desire.

I'm creating illusions. Rose doesn't desire me. But there's no denying twelve years hasn't dampened my desire for her.

All of her. I meant what I said to Callum in my office when he proposed fake dating Rose. But damn if my friend hasn't opened a door that I'm desperate to walk through.

Maybe, just maybe, if I don't rush things this time, I could make Rose love me again . . .

Eight

TWELVE YEARS AGO

September

How did I lose our first battle? I didn't want our first project prep meeting to be at his place. Yet, when his email showed up in my inbox with the time options, nothing else fit our schedules. All the rooms with doors at the library were booked. I suggested we meet at my hotel suite before his shift, but he isn't on until the weekend, which would leave us with no time to prepare. So here I stand, outside his duplex, walking distance from campus, staring at the steps leading to the front door.

I put my hand into my pocket, clutch my phone, and climb the stairs. Next time, we're meeting on my turf.

Before I can knock, the door swings open, and a tall guy stands there in electric-blue basketball shorts. They have a stripe of sunny yellow on the sides and hang low on his hips. He does a double take, scratches his bare chest, and leans against the doorframe. "Prettiest pizza delivery person yet. I should leave a Yelp review. What's your name?"

Did Alek give me the wrong address? Is this a prank? Payback for me insisting I take the lead on our project? My spine straightens. Basketball Shorts doesn't get to make fun of me. I scrunch my nose, narrow my eyes, and deliver the look Mom gives when she's pissed off at a vendor. "Where's Alek?"

"Whoa." He backs away. "You must be Rose, now that I think about it." His gaze drifts down my body. I glare back at his naked torso, tall frame, and lanky arms. He steps aside, gesturing for me to enter. "Alek warned us you're feisty."

Feisty? Mr. I'm-good-with-my-hands called me feisty . . . I seethe inside, but step over the threshold into a living-dining-kitchen space that's half the size of my bedroom.

"Alek, your date is here," the half-naked guy shouts.

"I'm not—" I start as Alek's voice says louder, "She's not my date."

"Does this mean you finally joined the dark side and invited a girl over? That's a new move." The guy smirks at me. "I see the appeal. She is gorgeous."

"She is standing right here, and she would urge you to refer to her in the first person."

His face breaks into the pretty-boy grin of a preppy model. "I like you." He stretches his hand to me. "I'm Callum."

"Stop hitting on her." Alek's damp hair flaps over his eyebrows as he shoves Callum with his still-outstretched hand to the side. "You have practice, and Rose and I have a study session."

Callum crosses his long arms. "Is that what you nerds call it? I'm just used to the good old-fashioned name."

"What's that?" Alek rocks on his heels as he moves his hair off his face and his bicep flexes. I shouldn't be looking at his biceps or any part of him. My neck heats.

I return my gaze to Callum, whose wolf-in-sheep's-clothing smile comes back.

"A hookup."

Alek punches Callum's shoulder. "For fuck's sake, man. Get your gear and leave. If you're late, Coach will make you do extra burpees."

"I'll do a hundred of those to stay and watch this show." Callum laughs at our matching scowls. "I'm just joking." He backpaddles to the stairs Alek just descended. "Don't study too hard. This one's already too smart for his own good. All that brain is going to get too heavy, and he won't be able to walk straight."

"Better that than fumbling because your ego is too large," growls Alek.

"Do you mean my ego or my di—" Callum ducks the Nerf ball Alek chucks at him.

Callum continues climbing and calls from the second floor, "You know it's very large too. We've shared locker rooms for three years."

Alek shoves his hands in his pockets. "He and the guys were supposed to be gone by now."

"He's varsity?"

Alek nods once. "Hockey."

I shift the bag with my laptop on my shoulder. "Explains the abs."

"You noticed." Alek drags the toe of his shoe across the worn linoleum.

"It was difficult not to when they were more eye-level to me than his face was."

"Will you program his name in your phone as Mr. Abs?"

"I'm not planning on programming his name into my phone at all because I'm not planning on seeing him again. And because I'm not planning on spending any more time here than necessary."

Callum bounds down the stairs, this time wearing a T-shirt. "You can save me under Mr. Dick. I would be honored." There are three other muscled guys behind him, and each has a giant blue-and-yellow duffel bag over the shoulder. I've never watched a hockey game in my life, but if this is what's under those bulky uniforms, maybe I should.

"I'm game if you don't want to exchange phone numbers at all," he adds. "I love an independent sex-positive woman who doesn't need to be cuddled after the deed."

"You're such an asshole." The tall blond says with a tinge of an accent. Maybe European. "I'm Soren. This is Blake and Linc." He shoves Callum out the front door.

Blake nods at me, and Linc winks at Alek. "You two be responsible."

Alek slams the door behind them. "My computer is over there." He gestures to the coffee table that's pressed against the too-large-for-the-room sectional. I'm not certain how all five guys could possibly fit into this space that seems tiny even for the two of us. I can smell Alek's woodsy aftershave all the way from here.

I put my laptop bag on the coffee table and remind my tingling skin that Alek is my project partner and technically my company's employee. More importantly, I am not here for a hookup. "Who decorated?"

He rubs his clean-shaven jaw. "It's mostly hand-me-downs or garage sale finds."

"Forgot the measuring tape when you went to pick up the sectional?"

"My mama found it."

I dust crumbs from the couch before sitting. "Of course. You're a momma's boy. That makes so much sense."

"If you're implying that me having a good relationship with my parents is somehow a bad thing, you'll change your mind when you meet my mama and papa. Russian immigrant parents are a force of nature."

How does he manage to spin everything around, including my attempts at insulting him?

Alek sits on the couch, his knees around one corner of the coffee table. "I put together some ideas for our project."

"I have ideas too." I take my computer out of my bag and set it as far away from Alek as possible, which means I have to take the opposite corner of the sectional. Even my much smaller frame has a problem finding enough space between the couch and the coffee table.

"I thought we could start by agreeing on what kind of app to create."

I boot up my laptop, but I can't help but look back at him as I suggest, "Maybe in the hotel industry? We have that in common."

"Hmm." Liquid chocolate eyes meet mine. "Is that the only thing you think we have in common?"

"No." I swallow my embarrassment. "We're both college students. We are both in Mr. Patel's class. We both live in LA."

"And . . ."

"That's all I know about you."

He leans back. "What do you want to know?"

"I know everything I need. This is not a date." I shake my head to dislodge the what-if-this-were-a-date thought that snuck in.

"No?" he says, faking confusion.

"We—"

"We what?" Eyebrows raised, he leans back and puts his bent arms behind his head. The T-shirt that was already stretched across his broad chest rides up to expose a strip of taught abs.

I lick my lips. Is he attempting to egg me on? Indignation burns in me. He grins in my direction and forces me to unearth my mother's getting-down-to-business expression. "We need to work together. We're not here to get to know each other."

"Ah, that's interesting," he says. I almost ask him why, but I hold myself back. It doesn't matter, though, because he offers, "For a moment there, I thought you were almost curious." I ignore that laughable remark, and he continues. "Seems to me that's exactly what Professor Patel wants." He crosses his foot over his knee. "For us, his brilliant students, to discover our strengths and weaknesses and form a team. To use the best qualities we have and bolster each other's deficiencies."

Heat crawls up my neck. "I don't have any deficiencies."

He tosses his head back in a laugh. The sound is loud and boisterous—the first pop of champagne that marks the start of a celebration. His amusement is the fizz spilling over the lip of the bottle. A giggle bubbles up and my lips stretch into a smile before I can contain it. His laughter is honest, real, unlike the performative laughter at the golf club or my mother's board-room. The sound fades as he puts his elbows on his knees and says, "Only an heiress would claim she is perfect at everything."

"I didn't say I was perfect."

"The definition of deficiency is a shortcoming or a lack of something. If you don't have any of those, you must be perfect."

"What are you, a walking dictionary?"

His mouth splits into a grin. "Just a kid who got perfect grades in public school, only missed one question on the SATs, was valedictorian, got into UCLA on a hockey scholarship, and is on track for early graduation."

I cross my arms. "Message received. You are smart. Your mother must be very proud."

"She is. But I'm also telling you about myself. Sharing my strengths." He refuses to drop my gaze, comfortable and capable. So much like my mother. Like how I wish she would see me. My heart rate quickens.

"But I'm not perfect. I'm a decent defenseman, but not good enough to go pro. Quitting hockey and focusing on graduating a semester early cost me my scholarship. I filled that deficiency by working nights and weekends at the hotel. I know what I want, and I will not stop until I get it. With or without you, I will ace Professor Patel's class."

Embarrassment floods my veins. "I hit a hole in one last week," I blurt.

His lips twitch. "Good for you."

I clear my throat. "I attended Windsor Academy, a private school, and earned a 4.5 GPA. I was class president for two years running and coordinated my prom, pairing it with a fundraising event that raised over $100,000 for the Baby2Baby charity. This year, I'm part of their decoration committee for the November gala. I also aced my SATs and am on the dean's list. Oh, and I started working for my mother's company at the ripe old age of twelve."

"So, you care about others," he says.

"I do. And I care about this class. It's also vital that I impress Professor Patel."

He cocks his head. "Why? According to every article I read, you're all set to inherit your mother's company someday."

I push my hair behind my ear. "Who's making assumptions now? My mother won't just hand over her company. She expects me to work twice as hard as her to earn my place at HH Group. This class will prove to her that I'm ready for real responsibility."

"Seems we have a lot more in common than one of us assumed." He steeples his fingers. "You still haven't mentioned any deficiencies."

I roll my eyes. "I can't cook to save my life. Happy?"

"I might be." Those warm eyes stare at me.

"Great. Can we work on the project now?"

"Let me show you my app idea. It's about hotels," he says, his attention turning to his laptop. "My concept is to create an app guests can use to open hotel rooms without plastic keys or keys of any kind. That eliminates waste, costs less to maintain, and saves time at check in and check out."

He launches into the explanation. Where hotels are concerned, we might have come from completely different perspectives, but we both have an innate understanding of that world, and its players and challenges. We speak the same language. I get what he's envisioning, and he puts together the pieces including app design, programming, and internal user perspectives—areas I do not have expertise in myself.

The buzz of a true, solid plan forming zaps in my veins. Flutters form in my stomach with the seductive whisper of success.

"That could work. Can you code it?"

"I can program the back end, but it'll be a push to complete the user experience in ten weeks. That means hiring others. We need to have a minimal viable product, where people can log in and activate the door, and it has to be—"

"Perfect." I finish his sentence.

We smile at each other. His grin is like the first glass of champagne after too little food. I'm lightheaded but want to snatch another flute off the tray. More of Alek. Maybe I didn't get the short end of the stick after all.

I turn my laptop his way and scoot closer. My blood turns from champagne to Irish cream. Finally, it feels like we're getting somewhere. "I can put together a loose timeline."

"I'd expect nothing less." He moves my way.

"Once we have more details, I can start building our presentation."

"Good. I kinda suck at PowerPoint."

"Another one of your deficiencies."

He rubs his lips. "I guess."

"I can't code." I nudge his upper arm. Warm, solid muscle meets my exposed skin, and goosebumps run across my arm. "Do you know any coders for hire?"

"There're plenty of kids on this campus hungry for money. But we need cash to pay them. We could do a car wash?"

I frown. "Maybe something a bit grander. I can ask my mom if we can use the ballroom in the hotel. How about a costume party for Halloween?"

"Will there be beer?"

"I imagined champagne and signature cocktails."

He runs his hands through his dark brown hair. "The hockey team likes beer. A lot. Add that to the drinks list, and Callum alone will bring a dozen girls. Never mind the other guys."

"Let me guess. Your girlfriend drinks beer too?" I say, then inwardly groan. Why on earth did I just ask that?

Alek glances down at his clasped hands. "I'm single."

"Right." I tap on the spreadsheet. "Me too." Crap. I sound like I'm flirting again.

"That's hard to believe."

"My mother had two kids at this age."

"She's that eager for grandkids?"

I run my finger in circles on the mousepad. "Not grandkids yet, but in a perfect world, she'd have me married to her friend's son."

"And you don't like him?"

"Dean?" I shrug. "We get along. He has different goals. He's happy to live off his trust fund."

"And you want a guy who . . ."

"I want a guy who's curious and smart. Someone who can keep me on my toes."

"I know what you mean," Alek mumbles. He clears his throat. "What about your dad? What are his dreams for you?"

"My father died before I was born."

"I'm sorry. I didn't know."

"You really need to do better research." I spin the tennis bracelet on my wrist. The only tangible thing that connects me to my father. "I've seen photos and some videos of him, of course, but it's so hard to imagine what our relationship would've been like. Everyone talks about the daddy-daughter bond and . . . I don't know. It would be nice to experience that."

"I get it. I love my dad; he's the best." Alek's face softens. "Back in Russia, he was a hockey player, and that's what helped him emigrate to the US before I was born. He put me on the ice at three and drove me to every practice and away game. When I was fifteen, he got me the job at HH Group part-time. Since then, I picked up shifts when I could. He's always made work almost fun."

"So both our parents dragged us into their careers."

"See?" He smiles. "Not that different."

"Is that a deficiency?" I try not to smile back, but my gut tells me he can see right through me.

NINE

PRESENT DAY

February

Pink is the "it" color of the event, and the hydrangeas, tulips, and lilies I selected have turned the ballroom at the LA Haliday Hotel into a romantic blooming paradise. Even if spring isn't officially here for another six weeks. In the corner, a photographer snaps a group of kids posing like superheroes in front of a fuchsia backdrop. Heart-shaped lights float around the room, reminding everyone that today is Valentine's Day.

Olivia dunks a strawberry into the chocolate fountain and pops it into her mouth. My half-sister's dark eyes—her father's eyes—survey the room. Three years younger than me, Olivia is the product of a six-month fling my mother refuses to talk about, let alone acknowledge. As kids, we never spent much time together, but working at HH Group has naturally made us closer in the last decade. "Your events are awesome. Too bad Mom refuses to attend."

"You know this is a difficult holiday for her." Today's the anniversary of my father's car accident. Life support kept him alive for another three months, but Mom insists her love life died the day the drunk driver caused my father's limo to go over a cliff.

"Still, she should see what you've accomplished." Olivia licks chocolate off her finger.

I don't remind Olivia that Mom doesn't consider charity events to be worthy achievements. She only respects what happens in the boardroom. Which is why, again, the deal for TRI is crucial.

"Well, I wish I could stay longer, but I have an occupancy report due in the morning. Back to the office for me."

I hug my sister and tell her not to stay up too late. While I have too much of Mom's attention, Olivia scrapes by with much too little. I wish Mom would recognize the amazing talent and intelligence Olivia possesses. Never mind her passion for the hotel business. Sometimes, I think Olivia would make a better CEO than me. I know she wants the role. But it'll never happen. I'm the heir apparent, and Olivia isn't even the spare. When I'm in charge, my first order of business will be to promote Olivia to a position that reflects her savvy and dedication. Olivia is my family and integral to HH Group. I'll never let her forget that.

The party is full of kids dressed to the nines in dark suits, silk ties, and dresses in every color of the rainbow. I smile at a girl in a shimmering gold dress complete with tiara as she rolls her decorated wheelchair to the middle of the ballroom, joining a group of kids already dancing.

I make a note on my phone to tell Zoe that she outdid herself with the kids' outfits. The updos, haircuts, nails, and shoes varnish the gathering in an upscale vibe, but the best part of the evening has to be the smiles. There are some anxious smiles, some radiant ones, and some that are a bit unsure. But all their faces, the expressions that reflect this experience, make the flutters under my breastbone intensify. Seeing the results of weeks and sometimes months of planning still manages to catch me off guard.

When the people I'm doing this for get to relax, celebrate, see their friends and family gathered without having to worry about money or how to organize it all . . . that is the reward.

"You sure do know how to plan a party." Warm breath tickles my ear, and I whirl to face Alek, his torso clad in an . . . apron?

The years have taken the fresh boyish look off his cheeks and added more stubble to his face. His sleeves are rolled up, exposing forearms which are more defined than when we first met. I thought then they were too seductive to expose willy-nilly to the world. What does the rest of his body look like under his clothes? My gaze trails down his torso, and my core heats. I catch myself before my interest drifts any lower. I shake the ambush of his presence off.

"Are you back to working at the hotel until the deal comes through?"

He stuffs his hands in his pockets, the dark material accenting veins in those defined forearms. "I'm volunteering."

My stomach drops. "Do you have a community service sentence that wasn't disclosed in the acquisition documents?"

"Rose, take a breath." Unlike in the office, where Alek looked like every inhale he took was painful, he's different here. It's not just the soft lighting. He's more . . . relaxed. Gone are the stern jaw and weary eyes. Flutters whir in my chest. He shakes his head. "Not everything I do has an ulterior motive. You know that's not who I am."

Has he been taking suck-up lessons from Callum? The only thing I know is that he's here to get to my friends. "You've wasted your time. The Menkens won't be here tonight. They're in Venezuela until the end of February."

A soft sigh escapes his lips, which I know for a fact taste better than the chocolate fountain behind him. "I investigated the organization this event is supporting, and they were looking for donations and volunteers. I did both. Part of my research."

"Into what, exactly?"

"Charity event planning and what's done with the items remaining afterward. For Second Chance Events." He steps closer. "See? Nothing for you to worry about."

I inch away from the woodsy aroma of his aftershave. "Who said I'm worried?"

"Your eyes are wider than usual." Alek inhales too close to me. "And I do know you and your sweet heart."

"That's an oldie. I'm not that person anymore."

"Too bad." He shuffles his feet like he wants to ask me to dance. "I liked that person."

I stare at him. "You hated that person."

The smile falls off his face. "I thought I made my feelings very clear."

Heat pricks the back of my neck. The memory of our last night together is locked behind a row of doors, and I'm not opening them up. "I thought you made it even clearer that you hate working with me again."

"We are not working together."

"No? What do you call it?"

"Mutual—"

"Satisfaction?" I shouldn't have said that, but the surprise in his eyes is too much fun to see. I shouldn't go back to our typical games, but with every conversation, the once-forgotten rush resurfaces. The thrill wakes feelings in me I hoped were buried under layers of media training. How long has it been since I could be myself and let my snarky remarks loose? The memories of our last night together scrapes at the door.

Somehow, we've gravitated closer together, and even in the semidarkness of the ballroom, I see the familiar flame of passion in his eyes. "That's one way to put it. I scratch your itch, and you scratch mine."

"Let me be clear. There'll be no scratching." We discussed where and when to show up, but I haven't set boundaries around our fake relationship. Time to set the story straight. "This is all pretend. We need to sell our relationship to Leanne and Ezra, so I'll be nice when we're in public. But when it's just you and me, I'm not going to pretend."

Even though pretending would be easy. Pretending the last twelve years didn't happen. Pretending we are back in his room in that tiny duplex or curled on the couch. Pretending I still get to watch him chop strawberries and pop sweet slices onto my tongue. Pretending his calloused fingers can linger on my mouth or his lips rest against my forehead. Pretending I'm still safe and loved.

"Dance with me." He holds out a hand.

I glance around the room, searching for an excuse to say no to the man in the apron.

Like he reads my mind, he says, "Stop looking for a deficiency. Everyone's enjoying themselves. You can afford yourself one dance."

The DJ melts one slow song into another and, with lyrics circling the ballroom about second chances at love, I am out of reasons to say no. No reason aside from the butterflies in my chest and the tingling in my fingertips at the fantasy of touching him. I slip my hand into his, the movement more steady than my words. "One dance. Then I need to check on the caterers. I'm here to work, not play nice with you."

Alek leads us onto the dance floor, his other hand settling on my waist in a barely-there touch. Yet my heart rate spikes, and I attempt to keep a few inches between our bodies. We sway in time to the beat, and I concentrate on the bulge of his bicep, fighting the image of the last time I was in his arms.

He leans in and whispers in my ear, "I don't need you to be nice. No one will believe we're actually dating if you're nice to me all the time."

I look up at him. "I'm not that impulsive, wide-eyed college kid. I grew up. I pretended for a year to be nice to my disinterested husband because that's what the public expected. I can pretend you are my boyfriend, but that's as far as this will ever go."

"First, that man didn't deserve you."

I swallow the lump in my throat. Olivia is the only person who's ever said anything similar. Mom constantly hints that we need to give our marriage another shot. She insists Dean is my perfect match because we have money, we're second-generation Hollywood royalty, our families are friends, and he's not a bad guy. But not a single time when we were together did Dean make me laugh, or dream, or my skin tingle. He never made me feel alive.

"Second, I understand the rules of this deal. You don't have to pretend when it's just us."

"We'll minimize the 'just us' time. My responsibilities come first. I'm sure you agree."

Alek straightens, and his shoulder muscles flex under my palms. "Sure."

I barrel on. "We only see each other at the events I specified, and I'll tell my publicist we're guarding our privacy."

"I've no objections."

"No PDA."

His grip on my hand tightens. "Rose, be serious. You're trying to persuade the world we're dating without PDA? You might as well say no to the whole charade. No one will believe it."

"Dean and I never touched each other in public." Or that much in private, but Alek doesn't need to know that.

"Dean is a fucking loser," Alek growls.

"He's not a bad guy."

His eyebrows quirk. "Whether you like it or not, this is supposed to be a rekindling of an old flame. PDA is the best way to sell it."

I feel his gaze. His argument, as usual, makes too much sense. My body betrays me as the beginning of another flush pulses between my breasts. I'm not sure I can endure PDA with Alek. The heat creeps up my skin. His thumb skims the back of my palm, and the spot between my legs aches. What parts of me can survive his touch without transmitting my feelings like a billboard? I turn away and watch a group of kids dancing in a circle. The girl in the golden dress smiles up at a boy's beaming face illuminated by the flashing LEDs in her casters.

"Fine." I sigh. "You can put your arm around me from time to time. We can hug. You can hold my hand. We can dance if necessary. No kissing. Just follow my lead, and don't make me regret agreeing to this."

His shoulders relax, and he twists further, his hip brushing against mine. I jump, and a frustrated breath rushes past his lips. "Are you going to hire an intimacy coordinator to choreograph where and how I'm supposed to touch you in public? What are you afraid of?"

Dying of internal combustion? Heat creeps up my spine.

His lips, his words, find my ear again. "Do you have a reason not to trust me?"

I almost tremble in his embrace, a scatter of goosebumps rivaling the lava swirling in my abdomen. *It's not you I don't trust. It's me.* I swallow. "Not currently. But if you take this too far, the deal is off."

His chin nuzzles into my hair ever so slightly, making me wish I could close my eyes and sink into him. "I promise not to stray from the outline. If your plan is to be a good girl, then I'll be a good boy. I won't do anything you don't ask me to do. And I won't ask anything of you."

The relief washes over me as my shoulders drop. Even though this is a charade, I somehow have faith in Alek. Unlike my mother, who seems to forget I'm a capable person and not a mere tool to achieve her goals.

Well, I'm making my own decision right now, aren't I? I'm fake dating Alek Orlov, and I'll prove to her that not only is it time to give me real responsibility, but that I deserve it.

"Do you have any requests?" I ask.

His gaze jumps from my neck and meets mine. "Act like you believe in Second Chance Events. If my girlfriend is excited, it could help, especially if my girlfriend is the future CEO of Haliday Hotel Group. Your endorsement might sway the Menkens more than my mediocre networking skills."

"I can't agree to that unless you explain your plans. I can't, in good conscience, endorse an enterprise I don't know anything about."

His lips twitch. "As I just said, I'd never ask you to do something you don't feel comfortable with. You sign an NDA, and I'll share my proposal."

The last beats of the song are replaced by an upbeat tempo. Alek loosens his hold on me and steps away.

I immediately miss the heat of him and the firmness of his body. The way I felt grounded without even realizing it.

"Well?" he presses.

"Are there any other conditions?" I ask, trying to bring myself back into this life that involves us suddenly not dancing together.

"Let me think." Alek takes in the ballroom. "You did a great job. The kids are loving this." A crack of the boy I knew shines through the CEO facade. It's right there in his grin. "You have a knack for event planning. You always did."

"So now it's a knack and not a kink?"

Alek cocks his head. "Can't it be both?"

"It's neither. It's a hobby. A way to de-stress from the pressures of life."

He exhales. "Only you would consider organizing charity events a way to de-stress, sweets."

"Stop calling me that."

"Then I have one more request."

I turn to face him. "What annoying thing do you want me to do now?"

"Not you. Us." He gestures between us. "We need to agree on pet names."

My stomach drops. "No."

"Do you have a favorite pet name?"

"Everyone calls me Ms. Haliday or Rose."

He rubs his chin. "How about honey?"

"No."

"Babydoll?"

"Absolutely not."

"Shnookums?"

I glance skyward. "Do you want me to call you something ridiculous?" My gaze lands on his impossibly toned forearms and large hands. "Mr. Handy?"

Alek's gaze snaps to mine, all casualness gone from his face. "Do you still have me as Mr. Handyman in your phone?"

"No," I scoff. "I changed it to 'Boyfriend,' but I'll change it back if you don't stop using a ridiculous pet name for me."

His eyes dance with mischief. "You can change it to whatever you'd like. But pet name stays."

I throw my hands in the air in half amusement, half frustration. "I forgot how much you love to object my objections."

"I told you, once a defenseman, always a defenseman." He rolls down the sleeves of his shirt, and I try not to drool. He buttons a cuff. "If I have a goal to score, I will figure out a way to do it, even if it's through an assist."

What a way for him to remind me exactly what place I occupy in his world.

TEN

ALEK

TWELVE YEARS AGO

October

Rose and I leave Professor Patel's class together this time. Smiling.

"He actually liked our plan." Rose glows with delight. "We were the only ones he said that to, weren't we?"

After a few battles, we decided to narrow our app down to an online check-in and check-out system that allows hotel guests to use it instead of the plastic keys and thus bypass the long lines at the front desk. Or it could, of course, simply cater to introverts who prefer to avoid talking to the hotel staff.

"We were the only ones," I reassure her. Warmth swells under my sternum. Her happiness is contagious, vibrating in my ribs like streaming down the ice at full speed. Seeing the joy on her face makes me want to do or say anything to keep it there.

"We're so winning this." She would probably be skipping if it wasn't for the rest of our classmates trailing behind us. There's a fizz beneath my skin, a quiet satisfaction of shared success. I can feel it in the way our footsteps fall in sync and her shoulder brushes mine, like we're a team already. She leans closer and half-whispers. "How does it feel to be on top?"

My mind and cock instantly go to the sex position, featuring the image of Rose's short hair fanned across my pillow.

I place the folder in my hand in front of my insta-erection. When was the last time I even got laid? In high school, I dated Tara for nearly a year. We were serious until I stayed in LA for college and she left for New York. In junior year, Anya, a psych major with an easy smile, tried to make it work for two years, but we wanted different futures. Since then, sex fell onto the back burner. I've never been the hookup type.

"Where did you go just now?" Rose's voice brings me back to the painful erection tenting my jeans.

Before I can answer, Rose's backpack trills. "Hold that thought. It's Mom."

We step onto the grass to let other students pass as Rose digs through her bag and pulls out her phone. I breathe slowly and think of cold showers, algorithms, and leaking sinks. I recall anything that's not sexy to get my body under control.

"Shit." A crinkle forms between Rose's expertly sculpted eyebrows.

The look of distress kills my boner instantly. "Everything okay?"

"No." Her shoulders drop. "My mother is refusing to give us the ballroom for our project's Halloween fundraiser."

"You're kidding?"

The phone in her hand trembles. "I wish. She says I need to prove I can figure out a location without her help."

That doesn't make sense. Our cards didn't say we couldn't have help from friends and family. If my family had a space to hold our fundraiser, they'd jump at the chance to be of use. But the backyard of their bungalow is too small for the event Rose and I have been dreaming up.

Rose shoves her phone in her pocket. "This is her way of punishing me for taking this class instead of the business management course she picked."

"She picked?"

"My mom is very . . . involved in my education. In everything, really." Rose squints at the sun. "She thought I'd learn more in the other class and didn't see the value of an entrepreneurial course since I won't be starting a new business. The plan is to take over HH Group when she retires."

"So why did you take Applied Entrepreneurship?" I ask.

"Partly to prove to myself and my mother I have what it takes to run my own business, not to simply maintain the company she created. And maybe to prove to her that I have good ideas."

I stare at the girl who I assumed a week ago was a hotel heiress riding the coattails of her mother's legacy and expecting me to do all the heavy lifting. Maybe I was wrong. Maybe there is more to Rose Haliday. The pull in the pit of my stomach says yes, dumbass, about time.

"Anyhow, we have less than a month to find somewhere to house Blatantly Subtle, the live band I booked."

"Wait, you got a band?"

A grin flickers on her lips. The sight hits me square in the chest. It's not just that the combination of her features and smattering of cute freckles steals my breath every time I look at her. It's that her sureness lights up a side of me no one has had access to before, a side that whispers that this is a face I want to see smile for the rest of my life.

A beat pulses under my ribcage. "How do you know them?"

"The lead singers, Carlee Waters and Landon Beau, are performing at the Baby2Baby Gala in November. But I discovered them at this dive bar just off campus. The Devil's Martini. Ever heard of it?"

"You go to regular bars?" I tease.

She punches my arm. "Don't be a jerk."

"Do they serve champagne there?"

"No." Her eyes sparkle. "But they do make a mean lemontini. Why don't we meet there on Saturday night, and you can watch the band play?"

"Are you asking me out on a date?" What if she is? Do I wish she was? But she's not. She can't be. This isn't even close to flirting. We're partners, and she's a Haliday. We have less in common than I had with Anya. Still, my chest tightens like a fist, and low in my stomach, an ache sweeps in at the thought of dating her.

A wave of red crests across Rose's skin, her glow undeniably adorable. "No." Her voice is a squeak. "I mean, for research. Bring your roommates. I'll bring my sister."

"Okay. But do me a favor. Warn her about Callum."

She laughs and starts walking away. "Their set starts at 8 p.m. See you Saturday."

CALLUM, BLAKE, SOREN, LINC, and I stroll into The Devil's Martini at a quarter to eight on Saturday. The place is brimming with people, all packed into dark tables and chairs on a black floor or standing by the bar running along the right side of the room. Up front, a spotlight shines on a small stage.

Blake clicks his tongue. "How have we never been here before?"

"Because we drink for free at home." Callum grins. Unlike Blake, who comes from a long line of actual English dukes, the rest of us came to UCLA on hockey scholarships and tend to hang out in places where free food and drink are the norm.

"This place looks like the beers aren't that expensive." Soren rubs his hands. Born and bred in Norway, he's still astounded at how cheap most things are here in the States. Especially fruits and vegetables. He eats oranges and avocados like they are going out of style.

We scan the room and spot Rose waving from a table near the stage. Callum's grin widens. "There's your girl."

I hit him on the shoulder. "She's not my girl," I say as I wind a path through the tables. At least not yet. My pulse kicks up. There's this impossible hope lingering in my gut that she could be. Maybe someday when I'm successful, rich, and respected enough, she could be. I shove the thought down, bury it under casual words and a mask of cool.

Rose gestures to the five empty chairs. "I was beginning to think you weren't coming."

Linc takes a seat. "Show doesn't start until eight. We're early."

Soren and Blake snag spots on either side of him, and Callum rounds the table to sit on the other side of Rose, leaving the only open spot beside her.

I slide into the seat. "Forgive Linc. He's a tad cranky. Girlfriend troubles."

Callum frowns. "Speaking of girls, I was promised I'd be meeting your sister."

"My sister bailed. So, you're stuck with me."

"Guess only Alek is scoring tonight." Blake taps his signet ring on the table.

I kick his shin even though my gut clenches at the possibility. "Don't be an ass. Rose and I are partners for a class."

He leans forward, flashing his pearly whites. "Then you won't mind if I ask the girl out?"

"He might not, but I would." Rose's eyes sparkle with amusement, but the teasing tone of her voice is warm.

"He shoots, but he does not score," Soren says like the announcer at our hockey games.

Blake stands up. "I'm buying the first round. Pitchers."

"I'll help carry," Linc stands too. Soren trails them to the bar.

I turn to Rose. "Do you want a lemontini?"

"No, no. Beer's fine."

I peer at her. "You don't drink beer."

"I said I prefer champagne. And that they make a mean lemontini here. I also drink beer. Tonight, I feel like having a beer."

Her eyes sparkle in the low light. She looks different than all the other times we've met. There's some shimmery stuff around her eyes, and she's wearing lipstick a shade darker than her natural lip color. Her hair is pulled away from her ears in small clips. Combined with the strapless top, they leave her long neck exposed. The piece of clothing is a work of art. My need for that beer intensifies as my mouth goes dry.

"Bad news on the gym at my private school. They don't want their students interacting with university students in an unofficial capacity. So, that's another no for a party location."

Callum leans into our conversation. "Party? What party?"

"The fundraiser on Halloween for our project."

"I thought that was at her hotel?"

"That fell through, remember?" I turn to Rose. "You'll have to forgive him. He got hit in the head by a puck last week and hasn't been the same since."

Rose smiles and runs her nails down the curve of her neck, and my blood simmers. I lick my lips to ease the urge to kiss that delicate skin. I glance at the bar. Where is that beer? I need a drink now.

"Why don't you use The Cube?" Callum turns my attention back to the table.

"The hockey rink? Won't that be expensive to rent?" Rose asks.

"We don't have any games that weekend. I can talk to Coach."

I start brainstorming. "Turn the party into an activity as well. We could charge extra to use the ice." My leg starts to bounce. This might work. I turn to Rose. "What do you think?"

"Halloween on ice?" Rose pulls out a pen and scrunches her face as she scribbles on the back of her coaster. I hold off the desire to kiss her adorable nose right here in the middle of the bar.

I most definitely need to do something about this. Out of the entire UCLA student population, Rose is in the top 1 percent of the people I should not imagine kissing or being on top of. I shove my hands into my armpits in an attempt to regain control over myself.

"Is there a place to set up a bar and dance floor?" Rose asks Callum.

"Sure. We can use the concession stand as the bar." I demand Rose's attention. "And the reception area is huge. We hold award dinners there at the end of every hockey season. Tons of people attend."

Rose's smile is brighter than the spotlight on the stage. "This could work. Can I see the space?"

"Sure," I say. "Are you free tomorrow?"

"Come on." Blake sets a pitcher in the center of the table. "Isn't seeing your girl tonight enough?"

"She's—"

"Not your girl," Callum, Blake, Soren, and Linc say in unison.

Callum reaches for the first pitcher and starts pouring.

Rose slides closer to me and twirls the coaster with her notes in her fingers. "I need to talk to you."

My stomach drops. The lines of her face go from soft to pinched. "You don't like the Halloween on Ice idea?"

"What? No. I actually like it very much. It's smart." She chews on her bottom lip, and I wipe my palm on my jeans. She sets the coaster down and sucks in a breath. "I sort of want to apologize for our first class."

"Apology accepted."

Her eyes narrow. "Don't you want to know what exactly I'm apologizing for?"

"There were so many things."

She hits me lightly on my pec. "Don't make me out to be a complete bitch, I just get competitive."

"Competitive is good. I like competitive."

"That's one thing I also like about you." She raises her chin. "You're very much like me. You want to win."

"There's just one thing you like about me, then?"

"Last week, you had 1000 negative points, and today, I'm telling you you're in the positive, and you want more?"

Oh, I want more. But I shouldn't. "If I gained 1000 points in one week, let's see what the other eight weeks will get me."

Her knee bumps against mine. "They will get you an actual punch in the gut if you don't stop making fun of me."

"Go ahead, punch me." I flex my abs and puff out my torso. "I'm ready."

Without hesitation, she balls her fist and punches my bicep, then my abs. She winces and shakes her wrist as if it stings. "You are hard everywhere."

If only she knew. What would she say if she knew? I grasp her hand, pull it under the table, and gently massage her knuckles. "Any other confessions you want to share?"

Rose's eyes dart to her hand in mine, and for a second, I think she'll demand I let go. Instead, she opens her palm, allowing me to deepen the massage. Her hand is so much smaller than mine, and the skin is soft across her palm. Is she that soft everywhere? My cock is screaming at me from its prison of denim, begging to get involved in the action. I keep massaging Rose's palm, enjoying the faster cadence of her breath and the light quiver of her lowered lashes as she watches my thumb travel across the bottom of hers.

"Is your non-girlfriend coming with us?" Callum's voice jolts me out of the sensation of Rose as he slams a beer down in front of me.

"Sorry?" I ask.

"To the party at Alpha Theta tonight?" Callum grins, his eyes darting to where I'm still holding Rose's palm.

I flinch and drop her hand.

"No." Rose wraps her fingers around the glass. "I have plans with my friend Dean."

I open my mouth to ask what plans, but the lights turn down and a woman taps the mic on stage. "Ladies and Gentlemen, welcome to The Devil's Martini."

For the next forty minutes, a blond with a spectacular voice and a man dressed in head-to-toe black have the attention of everyone in the crowd.

Everyone but me, because I can't take my eyes off Rose.

ELEVEN

TWELVE YEARS AGO

October

With my legs tucked beneath me, I sit in front of a repotting mat. Olivia sprawls across one half of the L-shaped couch across the room, flipping between shows on the TV. As a freshman, she could've stayed in the dorms on campus, but after four years of an all-girls finishing school in Switzerland, she said she'd rather live at the hotel. With the three-year difference between us and Mom having sent her to boarding schools since she was nine, we didn't spend much time together growing up. Her curly hair is pushed back by a headband, and she bites a hunk of her licorice. "What do you want to watch?"

"Can't tonight. I have to work on the Halloween party."

With two weeks left until the Halloween on Ice fundraiser and only six classes until our final presentation, Alek and I are almost halfway to the end of this course and not close to halfway done. I stare at the project plan we created, the yellow and red blocks far outweighing the green completed blocks. I rub tired eyes. Everything seems to be falling apart with every new challenge that rears its ugly head.

I return to the only thing keeping me calm these days. Taking a deep breath, I pull the Thai constellation monstera I rescued from the lobby out of the tight pot. The roots are pot-bound, and the soil is rock-hard. I dip it into a large pot of cool water, letting it gently swirl until the air bubbles stop rising, then lift it and slowly release the roots, making sure not to damage the frail plant.

Alek and the guys loved the band, and when I toured the rink the next day, the idea of turning the space into a haunted house jumped at me. The walk from reception to the rink is perfect for a darkened tunnel full of fun and creepy decorations, and the concession stand can double as a cash bar since it already has a liquor license. Not to mention, with their fridges I can easily keep our event food from spoiling since they're letting me bring items in the day before. The food will mostly be donated, meeting Professor Patel's criteria. Callum charmed someone into giving us credit to buy the alcohol. The online payment system is set up, and our bank account is live and in the black with hundreds of dollars of donations from Olivia and Blake's trust funds.

The number of calls I've made to restaurants and caterers has almost made me lose my voice. When I can't throw around the Haliday name or promise a discount if they agree to donate, the most frequent answer I'm hearing is "No." My fears about the limitations on the cards Professor Patel gave us are coming true. Maybe our smarts and dedication won't get us to the top.

And that's just the fundraiser. The actual project list seems to grow each day.

At the knock on the door, Olivia jumps up. "I'll get it. I ordered ice cream."

I sweep my hair out of my face with my wrist and stretch. Grabbing the new larger pot, I pour a generous layer of the chunky soil mix I made. I love the feel of soil in my hands.

I roll the planting pad out of the way, gently place the Thai con into the pot, secure it to a moss pole to keep it upright, and find a spot for it on the windowsill beside my desk. House-keeping knows to leave the plants and piles of notebooks as is, and they never touch my laptop. The rest of the room looks as pristine as it did in the morning when they did their job.

Olivia giggles after opening the door. "No maintenance issues today."

I pop up and rush to the door. "Olivia, Alek is here to work on the project. He's my partner."

Olivia's eyes widen. "Is that what you old folk call hookups these days?"

Alek's mouth quirks. "She sounds just like Callum."

He drops a bag off his shoulder and sets it by the entrance. "I brought my tools and told reception to ring your room if there is a call." He sets his backpack next to the scuffed satchel. "And I'll leave my stuff here until we're done. You're still okay with this?"

"Is this a sleepover situation?" Olivia's grin is wide.

I shove her to the door. "This is a work situation. I'll send room service to your suite."

"Don't have too much fun," Olivia teases as I close the door on her.

Against the warm caramels and creams of my suite, Alek looks uncomfortable in his navy-blue maintenance uniform. "When we were assigned as partners, I never would have bet on you being so busy that I'd have to adjust my schedule to yours," I say.

His brown eyes lack the light that always toys with my body. "That's what I get for having six classes and two jobs."

"When do you sleep?"

"Don't tell the owner." His mouth curls. "Between calls. Perks of working the night shift, it's usually quieter. There's a cot in the office. Some nights, we never get a maintenance request, so I do my homework and sleep."

"Let's hope today is that day." I push off the door and lead him into the living room. "If you need a nap, I have a second bedroom here."

His head jerks back. "Really?"

"That cot can't be comfortable."

"When we were assigned partners, I never would have bet on you inviting me to sleep in your hotel room."

I bark out a laugh. "Who sounds like Callum now?" I place my hands on my hips. "I like to think I'm a good person."

He cocks his head, and his mouth opens and closes as if he wants to speak. I step nearer, desperate for his response, desperate to know if he thinks I'm a good person. He points to my laptop on the coffee table. "Any progress?"

Disappointment cakes my throat. I swallow away the taste. "I have the qualitative and quantitative data collected based on our interviews with the reservation manager and housekeeping. I also spoke with the head of logistics at HH Group." He crosses his arms. "Don't look at me like that. I was in Mom's office, and she walked into the break room. I couldn't miss the shot." I pull out my phone. "I recorded the entire interview so you can listen."

Alek stares at my phone. "Maybe later."

"When you're sleeping?" I arch an eyebrow.

"Not planning on sleeping tonight."

I plop onto my couch and beckon him to join me. "Aren't you afraid of burnout?"

"I'm afraid of missing out." He plants himself beside me and opens his laptop. The model is years older than mine, and some of the letters on the keyboard are worn off. "What did the head of logistics say?"

"She was pretty impressed. She hasn't seen anything like what we are proposing and doesn't think we have any direct competitors. Some indirect ones offer apps to check in, but nothing that offers guests the option to check in *and* open their rooms with their phones. She confirmed what you and I assumed. The app should lead to less waiting, and if you can have fewer front desk staff, the hotels will save a lot of money on hourly wages." I point to the graphs I'm working on for the presentation. "I'll demonstrate our benefits using these."

His elbow brushes mine as he enlarges the graphic. The contact is slight, fleeting, just a whisper of pressure, but my body reacts like he's touched a live wire. A tremor of awareness rolls through me, quick and hot, blossoming in my core. A flashback to the feel of his hand on mine after the party before we almost kissed. I wanted more then. I still want more. My breath stutters, and I pretend to adjust a pillow to hide my trembling fingers.

"What we need to figure out next is the logic of use interactions. Who will be looking at this every day? The hotel manager? The head of the department? What kind of interfaces do we need with the systems that track occupancy and housekeeping turning over rooms." His speech is feverish, so fast I can't catch everything he's saying. He rubs his chin, his forefinger tracing the line of his bottom lip. How would it feel against my mouth that's eager for that new sensation? I shake the thought away. He's here to work. I'm here to work. I just need to not be next to him for a second.

"Do you want something to drink?" I stand to give myself space. "I have water, cranberry juice, and a few sodas. Olivia is a root beer addict."

"Do you have any energy drinks?"

"Those things are dangerous."

His eyes dance with amusement as he sits back on the couch, stuffing his hands behind his head. "I've seen you bring an extra-large coffee to every class. I don't think you can lecture me on healthy."

"Coffee is not in the same league as energy drinks. How many of those have you had already?"

"Define already?"

"In the last twenty-four hours?"

"Maybe three. No, four."

"Is it even allowed?"

"The better question is, is it necessary?" Alek yawns. "I'll sleep during the Thanksgiving break. Until then, my choices are energy drinks or failing one of my classes."

I truly look at him. Underneath the slightly messy brown hair, his eyelids are heavy, hanging low over tired eyes. Below which are puffy bluish circles. There's a shift in the confused feelings in my body. The attraction doesn't vanish; it deepens and folds in on itself, transforming into a softer, more dangerous emotion. I've seen those dark circles before, but not on Alek. I saw them on Mom before she hired an army of makeup artists. Before she was the all-powerful CEO. I feel that familiar tug in my gut that urges me to protect, to nurture, and to fix, like I do with my plants. I want to give him water and a warm comforter. I want to take care of him. "Look. Why don't you take a power nap? I'll type up my notes on the meeting while you sleep, and then we can start working?"

"You don't have to coddle me. I'm a big boy. I can keep up." The last phrase is distorted by another giant yawn.

"I don't doubt that. But I need you alert and productive." I point to my second bedroom, hoping he'll say yes. "Nap, then work."

He bites his lower lip. "You know, you are very bossy."

"One of my most redeeming qualities." I nudge his knee. "The guest bedroom is the one with the broken sink. Do you remember?"

"Oh, I remember." He stands, towering over me, and I have to look up to see his face. His fingers grip the collar of his maintenance uniform. "Not sure I should sully your bed with this. Even on the covers."

"The sheets are fresh. And soft." The heat from his torso seeps into me. "You can take your clothes off."

"If you want a striptease, Rose, I'm out of energy at the moment."

Our faces inch closer. I can smell mint and orange on his breath. "If I wanted a striptease, I would've asked for one. I'm bossy, remember?"

The air between us switches to a new wave. From him being tired and me trying to help him to him studying my mouth and me imagining him out of his clothes, bound in the sheets on my bed.

I want to invite him to my bedroom.

Finding someone who wanted to sleep with me has never been difficult, but the desire to do so has never been such a primal longing. Mom gave me the birds-and-bees talk when I was thirteen because she wanted to be sure I didn't follow in her footsteps and get pregnant at seventeen. Her version of that talk also included a definition of what boys I was allowed to have fun with versus who I was allowed to date. A maintenance man from our hotel doesn't fall into any of the allowed categories.

I cannot have sex with Alek.

But if I could, if I asked him, would he say yes?

Alek's gaze meanders from my mouth to the hollow below my neck, and my skin burns.

Goosebumps run across my collarbone. I tug the panels of my sweater closed because I can't ask, so he won't answer. There's a reason why business and pleasure never mix well.

My decision made, I sneak under Alek's arm and escape to the other side of the coffee table. "I'll wake you in an hour."

Two hours later, I creep inside the darkened guest bedroom and allow myself three breaths to appreciate the slow rise and fall of his naked chest. So tempting, but I know better than to give in. After one more inhale, I shake his shoulder gently. "Alek, wake up."

His eyes flutter open, unfocused at first, then his hand reaches out and traces my cheek. "Rose?"

It's all I can do not to fall into him. His finger is tender and light, and I very much want it to trace other parts of my anatomy. More, I want to lean forward and see if his kiss is as gentle as this touch. His thumb drags across my bottom lip like he might be thinking the same thing, and the tingle transforms into a craving. An ache. Just like in the elevator the first day we met: the heat in his eyes, the tension stretching between our hands like a held breath, the electric possibility—

In the other room, the phone rings again.

"Hey." I pry his hand from my cheek. "The front desk called. A flooded toilet in room 304."

All softness flees his face, and he bolts upright. "I'm on it."

He pops off the bed, pulls up his half-undone overalls, and races for the front door. I follow, fighting my desire to make him stay, my mind looking for excuses. If I called the front desk right now and said I had a flooding toilet, they'd make him fix my problem first.

And I definitely have a problem. My growing attraction to Alek.

"Thanks for letting me sleep." Halfway out the door, he turns back, his hand on the doorframe. "You're not what I expected."

"In a good way?" My stomach floats, caught somewhere between my ribs and throat. My pulse, wild and hopeful, skitters, searching his face for confirmation. I need to know I'm not the only one feeling this pull.

"A very good way." He squeezes my shoulder, and then he's off, heading for the stairwell.

My skin hums where he touches me. Should I follow him, grab his hand, and pull him back inside? My fingers brush the spot where his were, like maybe I can recreate the sensation. My heartbeats are slow and fast all at once.

I push myself back into my room, close the door, lean against it, and whisper into the dark, "You're not what I expected either."

Twelve

ALEK

"Looks like our plan is working." Callum exits the showers, grabs a towel, and rubs his hair.

"What are you talking about?" Linc's head snaps up from pulling up his socks. I don't know if it's because he played professional hockey for over a decade or if the rest of us are just slow, but Linc is always first off the ice, first to the locker room, and first in the shower after a game. I can't believe next season could be his last.

Callum, who's always the last off the ice as if he doesn't want to leave the frozen arena, swings his locker open, wraps the towel around his hips, and pulls out his phone. "'Hotel heiress Rose Haliday was spotted whispering sweet nothings into the ear of a new man.'" He moves to the middle of the room and rotates his phone so the guys can read the article. "You can't see Alek's face exactly, but it most definitely looks like she's having a good time."

The photo of us surrounded by the kids on Valentine's Day, her in a black cocktail dress, me in my apron, is grainy and must've been taken with a zoom lens. But there's a smile on Rose's face. The thought that I put it there makes my heart beat a little faster.

Soren snatches the phone and scans the text. "So phase one of Operation Win Her Back was a success. First date complete." He high-fives Blake.

I snap my damp towel at the pair. "It wasn't technically a date. I volunteered at an event she organized."

"This picture shows you dancing. That's First Date 101," Soren says, then grins at Blake. "Maybe even second date material."

Linc, all too pleased, remarks, "I want a status update when he gets to the third date."

"Whoa. Guys." Callum leans against a locker. "Let's not get ahead of ourselves. One non-date" —he winks at me, and I groan— "is a good start. There's more work to do." He slings an arm over my shoulder. "What's next?"

I sigh.

"That bad?" Blake sits on the bench before me.

Soren plops down beside him. "Do you have to walk a red carpet?"

"Should I tell Yanna you'll be on TV?" Linc leans in, placing his hands on Soren and Blake's shoulders. His daughter is obsessed with award shows, especially if music is involved.

Callum shimmies into his boxers. "Is she dragging you to a fashion show? Or to a spa?"

All the guys groan as if those scenarios are more painful than an elbow to the nose.

"Worse." The top button of my jeans slips into place. "She's taking me shopping."

Linc lets out a low whistle. "You're gonna have to carry her bag. I miss doing that."

It's been a few years since we all stood around the grave, but my heart still pinches at the reminder of his wife's untimely death. I clench my jaw, push the sadness aside, and pop my head through the neckline of my henley. "Actually, I'll be carrying my own. The shopping is for me. Apparently, my wardrobe isn't fancy enough."

When the expected howls of laughter don't appear, I whirl on the guys who are looking at the ceiling, the floor, and even the exit to avoid my gaze.

"Yeah, she may have a point." Callum takes one for the team. "You're either in jeans and a hoodie or a hockey jersey. Might be time to man up."

"Or suit up, rather." Soren hides his laugh behind his hand.

"Fuck off." I wish we were still on the ice and I could legally body check one of them.

"Maybe I should come with." Callum shakes his bespoke suit pants. "I could help."

"I'll be humiliated enough with just her there. I do not need your snide remarks."

Callum puffs out his chest. "Come on, I'm fun. Rose likes me."

"Too much."

"There's no such thing." He smirks. "You need to take pointers."

"Like what?"

"Talk less. Smile more."

I slam my locker shut. "You're quoting *Hamilton* now?"

"It's timeless advice," Blake agrees, standing and picking up his jacket.

Soren follows suit. "Yeah, but I've never seen pretty boy here take the first part of it."

Instead of looking offended, Callum stands tall. "I'm an exception. My tongue is my tool, and please get your mind out of the gutter." He points a finger at each of the guys, landing on me last. "Although, yes, it is a tool there too. I'm multitalented, and I own my strengths. Abs. Tongue. Talk. I'd like a word that starts with a T instead of abs, and I'd have myself a sweet alliteration. Trunk? Tease?"

"Turd?" I suggest.

"Your abysmal sense of humor never disappoints." He shoves on his shoes and shuts his locker. "Talking about sweet, when are you meeting sweet Rose?"

I glare at him. "Don't call her that."

"Wasn't that your nickname for her in college?" Linc interjects as he strolls out of the locker room with Soren and Blake.

I ignore his jab and shove my phone and wallet in my pocket. "Right now, if you must know. She's picking me up in five."

"What a refreshing reversal of roles." Callum's eyebrows waggle. "She's showing you who wears the pants in the relationship, and you're rolling with it. How progressive of you." He holds the exit door open. "Hurry your ass up. Let's not make the lady wait."

I push past him out into the hallway. Soren, Blake, and Linc are already laughing in the lobby. "More like convenient," I argue. "She has a limo and a driver and arranged the whole thing."

"Is she paying for your Cinderella moment too?"

"I'm paying for everything." The laughter ahead quiets, and there's a quiver in my stomach. I round the corner, and there's Rose standing in the center of a circle of my friends. I admire the dark navy pants and intricately designed blouse that looks casual but still showcases her gorgeous figure.

"You see? Pants," Callum half whispers.

I glare at him.

Blake hugs my fake girlfriend. "Glad you're giving Alek a second shot. But if this doesn't work out, I'm still single." His gaze finds mine, and he squeezes her a little harder.

The green-eyed monster in me rages. The duke-in-waiting did always have a thing for Rose, but he never pursued anything after I called dibs. That insecurity still lives in me and is one of the reasons I insisted Callum couldn't tell the guys about the fake dating deal. Instead, I'm running with the ploy of trying to win Rose back. I trust them, but loose lips sink ships. The fewer people who know, the better.

"They've made remarkable advances in AI girlfriends." Rose untangles herself from Blake's grip.

"Snap." Callum slaps his thigh. "Woman scores in the first five seconds."

Rose grins, gives him a quick peck on the cheek, and graces me with the most polite hug known to man. The sweet scent of her shampoo knocks me senseless, and I can't form thoughts. When she wrapped her arms around my neck at the charity event, I had trouble concentrating on the conditions of our arrangement as her scent teased and played with my head. I inhale one final lungful and release her.

"I can't believe you still all play hockey." Rose spins to the group.

"We should go." I place my hand on the small of Rose's back and steer her to the exit. When I glance over my shoulder, the guys are making kissy faces. I give them the finger behind my back.

THE LIMO STOPS IN front of what looks like an old ware-house-turned-private studio. Cream-colored brick is punctuated by tall windows curved at the top, all trimmed in white. A brass plaque beside the door reads, "By Appointment Only."

I hold my hand for Rose to help her out of the limo. "So, my custom tux didn't meet your specifications?"

"It's fine for a New Year's Eve party at TRI, but the Oscars is about looking extra, not like a penguin."

"I trust you."

She pulls her hand from mine. "So you are okay with wearing a bright pink sleeveless blouse to the Oscars?"

"If it impresses the Menkens. I'll wear a burlap sack."

Inside, the space is airy. The white windows stream sunlight onto ivory furniture, glass tables, and racks of clothes that line one wall. The tall woman whose face blooms into a smile at the sight of Rose is close to my height. Her green eyes stand out against the tan of her skin, her hair styled in long waves with a thick fringe across her forehead. Her white jumpsuit seems part of the studio's decor.

The two women air kiss, and Rose gestures to her. "Alek, this is Zoe Yilmaz. One of LA's hottest designers and my personal stylist."

I shake Zoe's hand, and she meticulously studies my physique from my toes to my ears.

"What a treat to meet and dress Rose's new man." Her gaze flits to Rose. "Apart from Dean, you've never brought anyone to the Oscars." Zoe turns me around. "Goodness, lots to work with here." She makes a clucking noise, and I feel like a piece of meat being inspected before it's placed on a barbeque. "Proper tailoring will be required, but I have some options for us to try."

"She's a magician." Rose places her purse on one of the small glass tables by a long leather couch. "Zoe organized the rentals and donations for the clothes the kids were wearing at the Valentine's dance."

"You can keep flattering me as much as you like, but even though I owe you, all I have for this session is an hour." Zoe threads her arm through mine and leads me further into the studio. "Then I'm off to finalize the tailoring for one of the nominees, and I can't be late. Even for you, Rose."

We pause by a rack of men's clothes. I thought Rose was kidding when she mentioned a pink sleeveless blouse as an option, but she was not far off. Instead of a sea of black and white, there are greens, yellows, blues, and purples. There's even a navy jacket with lapels studded in silver.

"You like that one?" Zoe asks.

My eyes grow wider.

"Don't judge until you put it on." She removes a silver shirt from underneath the jacket and hands it to me.

I search the space. "The dressing room?"

Zoe raises a brow. "I can have a privacy divider brought in, if that'd make you more comfortable, but think of me more like a fashion doctor."

My apprehension isn't about Zoe's professional evaluation.

"Are you worried your girlfriend will disapprove?" Zoe continues.

The term "girlfriend" cuts deep. A bittersweet feeling I don't have the time right now to fully decipher. Us dating is what we want everyone to believe, and I suppose asking Rose to leave the room would appear weird. Rose stops her perusal of the other outfits. I meet her gaze. "I'm sure Pooky won't mind."

Rose's face hardens at the absurd nickname.

With a smile, I tug the tails of my shirt out of my jeans and undo the top button. It's not like I haven't spent years changing in front of dozens of men or I'm ashamed of my body. Getting my arms into the sleeves of the silver button-down is a bit of a struggle as the material strains around my shoulders without any give.

"You can stop there. This is supposed to be tight, but we don't want the main story at the Oscars to be about a starlet being injured by a flying button to the eye. Right, Rose?"

Rose doesn't answer. Her hand is at the base of her neck as her gaze drags along my exposed pecs and abdomen instead of my shoulders, which are supposedly causing the problem. Is her chest rising and falling a little faster, or is that just my wishful thinking? Twelve years ago, she liked me physically. I want her to want me again, but this time I want her to want all of me. My attraction to her has never changed, but is her attraction still there too?

To test my theory, I take my time peeling the silver sleeves off, not looking at Rose directly but acutely feeling those gray-blue-green eyes of hers on my skin. I catch her reflection in the mirror across the room. Her stare brushes across my body as if she's painting me. I wish it were her fingers, not just her gaze. My cock agrees with me, but this is not the place for me to lose control and revert to adolescence.

I think of Second Chances, the deal to launch the venture, the dollar figures, the freedom to do what I really want to do next, and the mountains of documents I still need to go through to prepare my next proposal. I consider the charities depending on me to save their budgets next year. The bureaucracy of running a business, the search for a new office location with a loading dock, the employees who depend on me, and the lawyers hammering out the sale of TRI right now.

"How about the black one?" Zoe dangles a shirt in front of my waist with a smirk that suggests she might have noticed my rather large problem.

This time, I have no trouble feeding my arms through the sleeves. The material is more elastic and giving. I button the shirt and let the tails cover my still-recovering groin.

"This is too loose around the torso, but we can fix that. I suggest we use this as our base. Do you agree?" she asks Rose.

I look at my fake girlfriend, and I don't need an answer. She likes what she sees. Although there's no massive erection for her on display, her neck is flushed and her eyes have a liquid quality to them that shouts, "I like, I like." The hairs on my forearms tingle, and my chest puffs up.

That damn blush kills me every single time.

Rose rolls her lips. "Good basics." Her voice is hoarser than when we talked in the car.

The corners of my mouth tip up. Even though she doesn't want me to know I can still affect her, her body just spilled the secret.

Thirteen

PRESENT DAY

February

The black shirt Zoe has Alek in is simple, but the material's quiet luxury speaks volumes. The way it effortlessly skims his frame draws attention to the breadth of his shoulders, the bulge of his upper arms, and the toned strength in his forearms. The color deepens the brown of his eyes to almost black, and my stomach twists. I need to redirect my focus, away from Alek's body, which my traitorous fingers itch to touch.

Yet I can't stop staring at my fake boyfriend. My heart shutters against my ribs when I catch the subtle movement of his throat as he swallows. His shirt collar is undone just enough to tease and the black fabric is tailored perfectly. It's maddening the way every detail seems to draw me closer, like a tide pulling at my resolve, washing up over and over again. A guy's torso shouldn't be affecting me, yet heat ignites between my legs.

The tendons in his neck flex, his jaw tightening as if in reaction to something. Or is it someone? Who's he thinking about?

Is it Zoe?

She's sunshine wrapped in a gorgeous package. The opposite of me, vivacious and untroubled, she currently has her hands all over Alek's torso, pinning the shirt to his molded abs.

I grind my teeth, envious of Zoe, who's able to touch him in such a carefree way. The feeling that rises is hot and fast, burning my solar plexus like acid. My skin prickles and flushes with heat that doesn't belong to desire but the sharp sting of jealousy. It pulses behind my sternum.

In desperation, I turn and try to concentrate on the rack of clothes in front of me, but the intensity between Alek and me is palpable. I last two seconds and swing back to ogle. When his gaze catches mine, it's like a tether snapping taut. His tongue flicks over his bottom lip, slow and deliberate, and the corner of his mouth goes up as if he knows exactly what he's doing. My heart stumbles, and my fingers grip the fabric of a random shirt in front of me like a lifeline. What am I doing? My breath is shaky as I break the connection, determined to regain control of myself. Of this whole situation.

Alek is a better actor than I give him credit for. Back in college, he seemed incapable of putting on a show. What you saw with Alek was what you got. I loved that about him. But if he puts the same effort into shmoozing Leanne and Ezra as he is right now in convincing Zoe we're dating, they'll be eating out of the palm of his hand.

Zoe, either oblivious to the pheromones floating in the air or trying to be polite, which is not a quality she's known for, steps back to stand beside me with a pair of pants in hand. "What do we think about the combo of that shirt and these pants?"

Free to look at Alek, I stare greedily. But now it's his lower half, and if I thought I caught a hint of arousal there before, I'm no longer able to judge because he's pushed both of his hands into the pockets of his jeans.

"Should we do jackets first?" he suggests.

"Jackets are very"—Zoe chews the side of her nail—"intricate. This is so last minute that I'm hyperventilating thinking about the alterations needed for you to walk the red carpet in one of my designs and who I'd have to bribe to get it all done on time." Zoe thrusts a pair of pants to Alek. "Try these first. I'm going to excuse myself and grab a glass of water. It's hot in here. You two need anything?"

"Water," both of us say at the same time.

"Three waters, then." Zoe's gaze ping-pongs between Alek and me. "No defiling my space while I'm out. Get whatever this is out of your systems somewhere else. Understood?" She saunters out of the room without waiting for my response. "The pants better be on before I come back," she tosses over her shoulder as she exits the back of the studio.

Alek stares at me as he unbuttons his jeans. With his hands out of his pockets, his hard length is unmistakable. He undoes the zipper, and I should look away or turn my back to him to give him his privacy, but he doesn't seem to be searching for any. He tugs on the waistband and lets the material glide down his legs. The boxer briefs underneath are tight and stretchy, meaning I can see so much more. Memories dragged up in the middle of the night when I can't sleep remind me there is a lot to see. A quake of heat rolls across my abdomen as my brain fires warning bells to look away. Responsible, reasonable Rose has left the building. My throat almost closes up as I watch the muscles of his back ripple when he steps out of his jeans and into the pants Zoe gave him.

Everyone knows a striptease can be sexy, but I can honestly say this is the first time in my life someone putting their clothes on has made me so aroused. His gaze is on me, steady and unaffected. I press my cooler palm against the side of my heated neck. Can he read the state of frenzy he's driving me into? He adjusts himself as he zips the pants up and closes the button. The pants fit. They clad him in the armor of high fashion while both of us know what hides underneath.

With the way he's looking at me, those penetrating eyes the color of 90 percent chocolate, my desire tells me to have a little fun. To let myself play the game he's playing. Maybe I should. Getting something out of this deal besides TRI is not the worst idea. I can scratch the itch that's been just below my skin for ages. The itch that I'm growing to accept only Alek can satisfy.

But a voice deep down insists I don't compromise the deal just because I'm horny and haven't had sex since well before my divorce. That the past is the past, and I can't afford to be distracted. I can't let Alek affect my decisions like he did twelve years ago.

OLIVIA IS CHATTING WITH Helen at the reception desk when I step off the elevator on the executive floor of HH Group. My sister gapes at me. "Well, hello you. Did you go to a new aesthetician? You are positively glowing."

I grip the strap of my purse. "Just met with Zoe to pick outfits for the Oscars."

"Aren't you wearing the dress we bought in Miami?" Olivia follows me down the hall to my office.

I divert into the kitchen, my mouth still parched even after the water I had at Zoe's and in the limo. Maybe I need to add more electrolytes to my drinks? "I am. This was for Alek."

Olivia folds her arms and leans against the doorway. "Since when are you taking anyone, never mind Alek, out in public?"

Her inference is loud and clear. The moment I step onto the red carpet with Alek, the world will officially call us a couple. Us dancing in the photo from the charity event already started the rumor mill, and being seen at the Oscars together will cement things. Zoe was easy to convince since I was practically salivating over him. If I do this, there will be no turning back. My blood races beneath my skin where it touches my bracelet. Am I really doing this? A spurt of panic crests in my throat, yet underneath it, warmth unfurls. Maybe everyone believing we are together wouldn't be so terrible. My mother wouldn't approve, logic agrees, but my body . . . my body is all in.

I should grab a bottle of water, but my tired brain craves coffee. I flip the switch on the coffee maker to heat the water, then I grab a bag of beans and pour them into the machine. Should I tell Olivia the truth about the deal with Alek? My fingers pause on the lid. The heaviness of guilt and fear drag me down. What if Olivia looks at me differently? What if I lose the way she trusts me? No, I shouldn't. I don't need one more person to think less of me.

"It's new. We reconnected over selling TRI, and, I don't know." I turn to face Olivia. "There's a spark there."

Not a lie. This afternoon, the physical connection we had twelve years ago hung in the air like steam in a sauna. Wet and hot. I squeeze my thighs together. I'll need to grab a change of underwear before I attend any meetings today. I push the button for a double espresso.

I certainly wasn't lying about there being a spark. But the physical was never our problem. Everything that surrounded us back then . . . our circumstances, that's what got in the way.

Things are different now. Alek is no longer the cute maintenance boy I craved to touch. He's a wealthy, extremely attractive, fully grown man who only sees me as his meal ticket to impress Ezra and Leanne. No matter how much I was considering it, now that I'm not in his immediate presence, the idea of hooking up with him because I'm horny is foolish.

Olivia tilts her head. "After the shit show you went through with Dean, if anything makes you happy, you go for it. If that's reconnecting with Alek, you have my support. You were into him back then."

Tears immediately prick my eyes. I don't know why. Not once during my divorce did I shed a tear. I broke things, yes, but never broke down. I've been a fortress and confident businessperson whose only goal is to grow HH Group. I take a shaky breath. Maybe it's the relief of someone telling me it's okay to feel things again, or maybe it's the weight of deceiving my little sister. If lying to her is this hard, how am I ever going to handle months of lying to everyone else? To the world?

I grip the handle of my mug and order my tears to retreat. "That means a lot."

"Just don't ask me to double-date with his business partner." Olivia rushes off, presumably to her next meeting.

I finish making coffee and head to my office. When I open the door, my mother is sitting at my desk typing away on my computer. The needles of irritation join the assembly of words ready to jump off my tongue. All sharp, and none of which I can actually say to her. I take a gulp of the bitter brew and rustle up a smile to put on my face. "Mom. Did we have a meeting?"

She doesn't look up from my laptop. "No. I wanted to check on the seating arrangements for the HH Group thirty-fifth anniversary reception." She nods at the board hanging on my wall with thirty tables mapped out, names of the people who have RSVP'd pinned next to them. "I moved some things around."

The angry comments I almost swallowed when entering my office rise like a medieval armory. The urge to hurl the coffee cup across the room is so strong that I place what's left of my coffee on the nearest surface and stomp to the board. A frustrated exhale erupts out of me. "Mom, you can't sit Dean beside me." I pluck the pin with his name. "Not at our table."

"He's family." Her makeup is leaning toward the dramatic today, which means she's been on camera. Another interview or a negotiation she hasn't filled me in on yet. Would I have even been told about the deal with TRI if she hadn't blurted it out in a moment of frustration when Alek was refusing to sell? She knew I knew him. She knew I was in charge of innovation at HH Group. Mom knows a lot, but she doesn't always care. She keeps typing on my keyboard.

"He *was* family." I jab the pin back where I originally had it, on the other side of the room from our table. "We're divorced, remember?"

"Still family."

"What does that mean?"

At last, she drags her gaze away from my laptop. "You two have so much history together. You grew up together. You're from the same circle. He always wanted to marry you. Besides, he has his own trust fund. He's not into you for the money. He doesn't want anything from you."

Exactly. I cross my arms. He doesn't want anything from me because he doesn't want *me*. I only appeal to him because I fit the parameters of a suitable wife.

Elbows on my desk, Mom steeples her fingers. "Are you sure you can't find a way to reconcile?" She breathes out the loud sigh she used to employ every time I disappointed her as a child. "The clock is ticking. I had all my children by the time I was twenty-three. You're thirty-five and not even pregnant. Do you have time to start over and still have a family?" She waves her hand around my office. "An heir to pass all this down to?"

I twist Dad's bracelet on my wrist. The usually calming scratches of the diamonds aren't bringing any relief. Mom's plans for me always included being a businesswoman and also having the traditional family she never had a chance of with my father. His death not only killed the love of her life, it robbed her of the wedding and the marriage, raising me with a responsible partner, and the dreams of growing old with him. Mom would never admit it, but she threw herself into building HH Group not just because she had something to prove to the world as a single mother, but because it was the easiest way to stave off grief before it swallowed her whole. The grief she still carries hidden inside.

An orchestra of emotions chokes me. The heartbreak over never knowing my father. The sadness for what my mother lost. The never-ending anxiety over not meeting expectations. My vision blurs. The guilt of letting my mother down. The bitterness over divorcing Dean. My heart drums in my ears. But those are familiar and long-living ones. The pulse vibrates my temples. Today, the loudest emotion is anger. I clench my jaw. The frustration of her thinking she can tell me what to do with my life. Will she ever stand by my decisions? Will she ever accept I'm an adult and that I know what I don't want? Dean is most definitely a person I don't want in my life. I pull my crossed arms so tight they almost hurt.

"Let me be clear." I'm not shouting, but my voice isn't calm or pleasing. "Dean and I are never, ever getting back together."

Mom goes back to her sigh. "Shame. You would have had beautiful babies." She pushes my laptop away. "If you insist on not getting back together with Dean, we'll have to find someone who's suitable husband material. I haven't given up the last thirty-five years to watch it all go to your second cousins."

"I'm perfectly capable of finding my own dates, thank you." I sidle closer to the desk. Anger swirls hot in my gut, but curiosity flares as I catch the glint in her eye. What is she using my laptop for?

"I appreciate you duping Mr. Orlov into thinking you're interested in him so he sells us TRI, but by dating"— she air-quotes the term dating—"him, you're delaying finding your real match. Let me screen a few candidates so once the deal is signed and you drop that man, you have options."

That man. My blood boils. That man, as she calls Alek, showed up at the fundraising event I put together and volunteered. He accepted my boundaries when we agreed on what our fake dating would look like for the world. He didn't refuse to change his wardrobe. But the biggest difference between that man and Dean is that Alek listens to me. He cares about my ideas.

I round the corner of my desk, and the screen of my laptop comes into view. My project plan for the anniversary reception sits there. "Did you change caterers?"

"The new company isn't tested. Ample has been providing the food for years, so I canceled the other contract."

My fingernails dig into my palms. "That was the point. Ample's quality was not up to par at the last event. People commented. I thought we agreed to try a new vendor."

Mom slams the laptop shut. "I said I'd consider it, and I've decided to go with Ample." She stands and brushes off her skirt, like the soil from my flowers somehow got onto her. "I'm due for a conference call. Let's talk about this later." She sweeps out of the room.

Calling after her is futile. I sit down, open my laptop, and review the document from the top, looking for other changes. The ones we won't talk about later because we never talk. I always bend to her will. I drop my head into my hands and press my thumbs into my aching temples.

This has to stop. I need to show her I'm in control. I can do things without her. I'm just as capable of making the right decisions for myself and for the company. I pull up my emails and find the latest replies from the lawyers about what changes we need to make to the contract with TRI. All are minor. The only thing that stands between me and the signed contract is getting Leanne and Ezra to accept Alek. I find my contact at the Oscars and send them a message to ensure they have my plus

one and sit us next to the couple that have been my surrogate
grandparents.

Let's get this thing signed.

Fourteen

ALEK

TWELVE YEARS AGO

October

The usually drab hall at the entrance to the rink is spooky, and what looked like grime and poor maintenance fits the grungy haunted house theme Rose came up with. "If we don't have the money to make this event high-end and chic, let's give it the vibes of a post-apocalyptic dystopia." The original idea did not inspire confidence. Who'd want to pay money to come to a Dystopian Halloween Skating party?

"That's why you are not in charge of party planning." Callum, dressed in shorts, suspenders, and a bow tie he borrowed from Blake, collects another hundred from a couple wearing matching zombie costumes. "Food and drinks are behind us.

Skating begins momentarily, and the afterparty starts when everyone is off the ice."

The couple joins the sixty or so people that have showed up to the party.

The space allows for more, but the flow of people has dwindled in the past twenty minutes.

The slit in the torn skirt of Rose's corpse-bride outfit reveals her thigh as she rushes over. I drink in each rip and tear that exposes tiny strips of her flawless skin.

"How much have we raised so far?" she asks.

"With the presales and current in-person numbers, we're almost at our goal." I show her the tablet we are using to collect digital payments. "But Callum has some cash as well. So, we're probably over."

"And you doubted me." Rose claps and smiles like a delighted child, which doesn't really go with her gruesome makeup. My heart leaps with her delight.

"I didn't doubt you. I just wasn't your target audience."

"That's the best apology you'll get from him," says Callum. "You take over while I get the bar set up."

"No skating and drinking," Rose shouts after him.

"Yes ma'am." Callum struts through the partygoers like he's in charge. But I can't look a gift horse in the mouth. Any volunteer is help I take. He got us the rink for free, which would've easily eaten half our profits, and he agreed to bartend the afterparty.

"When's your sister coming?" I ask. "I want to close the doors and open the skate rental window. It'll take some time for everyone to get their sizes and lace up."

Rose consults her phone. "Olivia texted that she parked ten minutes ago." Rose takes a dead-looking rose from the bodice of her dress and tucks it into her hair, then glances at the door. "It doesn't take that long—"

"Next time you need a valet. I'm parked in the boonies." Olivia waltzes into the party room, and I avert my eyes to avoid seeing way too much.

"What are you wearing? Or, should I say, not wearing?" Rose snags Olivia by the elbow and drags her into a dark corner.

"You said dystopian Halloween, so . . ." She gestures at the dirty gauze strategically wrapped around her breasts and thighs. I step away and close the door.

"Olivia." Rose's voice is commanding. "Two dirty rags smaller than underwear are not a costume."

"It's my first Halloween not at an all-girls high school. I wanted some boys to pay attention to me. Sue me."

"All of them will pay attention," I mumble.

"Not helping." Rose almost bites off my head. She turns to Olivia. "We need to cover you up."

"Don't be such a wuss. I'm nineteen. I saw a picture of the sexy nurse costume you wore your first year in college."

My need to see that photo is visceral.

"My skirt was almost to my knees in that outfit. And you couldn't see my nipples through the material." Rose scans the room. "Plus, I hired a photographer to document this event. If they take your picture, you know where they'll end up. All over the front page. Then it's not about you being nineteen and wearing a skimpy party dress but an HH Group scandal. Families will cancel their reservations because Melinda's daughter refuses to wear clothes." Rose presses her fingers to the space between her eyebrows, exhaling through her teeth as if she has a headache. "You know how Mom is. She'll yank you out of UCLA and send you to a convent. Is that want you want?"

Olivia crosses her arms, and the strip of gauze over her breast slips. "Typical Rose. Sucking all the fun out of life."

"Typical Rose or not, you are either going home, or we're finding you a different outfit."

"You have a spare costume in your pocket?"

Rose looks at her dress, then at my bright yellow hazmat suit with a matching hood and gloves. "What are you wearing under that?"

"Nothing."

"Great." Rose winces.

"I think there was a lost and found in the room with all the skates," I say.

"Genius," Rose says as she shields Olivia from view and pushes her to the door. "Cover her from the other side, let's go."

Rose and I form a human cocoon around Olivia until we get into the room with shelves of skates.

"Guard the door," Rose orders as she beelines for the box and pulls out a scarf, several hats, mismatched gloves, and a wad of socks in various colors and sizes.

I turn my back to them and catch sight of Blake and Soren, one dressed as Batman, the other as Superman, talking to a girl in a Cleopatra costume.

"You are not serious. I will not be wearing this childish thing," says Olivia.

"It's either this, or you go home."

There's the sound of Velcro and a few grunts. Callum waves at me from behind the bar, giving me the thumbs up that he's ready to party. I tap on my watch, indicating he has to wait another hour, and he gives me two thumbs down.

"Does this meet your dress code requirements?" Olivia asks.

I turn to Olivia, who's stuffed into what must be a kid-sized pumpkin costume. The curves that were on display earlier are covered by an orange cloth stuffed to look rounded. A small orange skirt peeks from the bottom.

"Don't forget this." Rose plunks a green felt hat that looks like a leaf on Olivia's head.

"No man will even look at me in this thing," Olivia pouts, and I lift my hand to my mouth to stifle a laugh.

"We should start handing out skates." I shove the gate over the counter up.

"I can see why she gets along with you." Olivia adjusts the leaf on her head. "You're also all business and no pleasure."

"You can help us hand out the skates." I nod to the line forming in front of the desk.

"No thanks. I need to use the bathroom." Olivia escapes out the side door, leaving me alone with Rose and a line of anxious partygoers.

For the next hour, Rose and I ask for skate sizes and hand them out. When the line slows, I lean on the counter. Across the room, Olivia is talking to one of the band members setting up for their set.

"She's nothing like you," I say to Rose, who hands a pair of skates to a witch.

"Olivia's like her dad: tall, dark-haired, and always looking for fun."

I spin to face Rose. "Are you like your mom?"

"Everyone likes to point out that I have Mom's height, her freckles, and her organizational skills."

"Are you and your mom close?"

Rose shrugs. "Growing up, she played both mom and dad. I don't think I'll ever have anyone closer than her in my life. You?"

"Me and my mama?" I tap the spot above my sternum. "Like you, Callum calls me a momma's boy. But he shows up every Thanksgiving for her blini."

"What's blini?"

"Russian crepes. Mama has this family recipe Callum says are orgasmic. His words, not mine." I wave at the bar area where a small crowd is catching every one of my best friend's utterances.

"Mama's very involved in my life, but it's more like she wants to take care of me and sometimes forgets I'm an adult."

"I get that." Rose takes a sip from her water bottle. "My mom forgets I'm an adult too, but mostly by refusing to let me make my own decisions or give me any real responsibility. From one side, she insists I'm the future CEO of HH Group, but when I bring up an idea about improvements, she tells me I haven't spent enough time in the business to advise." The blue hair from the wig of her costume sticks to the fake blue cut on her cheek. I run my finger along her jawline to rectify it. The contact with her skin sends a shiver up my arm. Rose halts her speech and looks at my hand.

"Just some hair got stuck. Keep going." I should be listening and not thinking of touching her again. I dig my fists into my pockets. "You were talking about your mom."

"Mom, right. All I want is to ace this semester and prove to her I have viable ideas. I can be a successful leader of HH Group."

"I can't see a world where Rose Haliday is not a success."

She twists her mouth. "Are you mocking me?"

I inch closer, taking the water bottle from her hand and quenching part of my thirst. "I'm admiring your drive. And your belief in yourself."

"Lots of people consider me too driven. Too self-assured." Rose plays with the bracelet on her wrist. "One thing Mom made sure I knew as a child. She's always told me I can do anything I want. I may not have gotten hugs from her, but she's never been short of praise when it's earned. And I made sure to do the things that earn her praise."

"No hugs from your mom?"

"That's what you take from that?"

I hand her the bottle back. "I think my mama would do nothing but hug, feed, and clothe me if she could. Hugs are her love language."

"My mom prefers handshakes."

"Don't you miss full-body contact with other humans?"

Her multicolored eyes meet mine. "Well. For that, there's sex. I'd take praise over it any day."

Tingles run along my neck. How did we get to this topic, and should I be discussing sex with Rose? In public? I scan the benches, but the closest people are out on the rink drowning in a trendy playlist. Still, I lower my voice. "You equate sex with hugs?"

Rose shrugs her naked shoulder. "Are you one of those people who thinks sex is a big deal?"

Under my yellow jumpsuit, my body's on full alert, paying very close attention to the conversation. "Bigger deal than a hug."

"How so?" She angles her face, her gaze glued to me.

"I'd hug a person I've just met if I like them. I won't have sex with them."

Her overdrawn black eyebrow climbs. "No one night stands for you?"

I consider what a one-night stand with Rose would be like. Would we have had one the night we met before I knew who she was? The scenarios of what I could do with Rose as a partner rush in and pump blood straight to my cock. What is she into? Does she like to control everything in the bedroom as much as in real life, or does she want to be told what to do? How sensitive is she? What does she taste like, everywhere? I don't think one night with her would ever be enough.

"That's Callum's domain." I glance across the room, but my best friend isn't behind the bar. "I'm more of a relationship guy."

"I think you need to rethink sex. It's just a thing you do when you are interested, and the other party is also. It's not a big deal. Just be responsible about contraception."

My cock takes her statement as an invitation, which my brain acknowledges is misguided. I look at the skating rink again to make sure Rose can't read every horny thought of me peeling her out of the white dress and kissing her pink lipstick off. I turn and pretend to ready the shelves for when the skaters return, wishing she was anyone other than a Haliday—or my project partner.

FIFTEEN

TWELVE YEARS AGO

October

I'm not staring at Alek's backside. The hazmat suit isn't much of a departure from the baggy material of the weird jumpsuit the maintenance people wear at the hotel, but it's thinner and wraps tighter around everything below his waistline. As a person who's never really thought about male butts or thighs, what with all the ab propaganda in advertising, I might be discovering new things about myself. I might be an ass and thighs person. Or at least an Alek's ass and thighs person.

"I think that's the last one." Alek sprays the skates with antiseptic, the job he's taken over after my sneeze attack. "You wanna go hit the ice before we join the party? What's your shoe size?" He grabs a pair of large skates. "I should've brought my own, but with the prep, I totally forgot. It's been a really, really long time since I've worn loaners."

"You go ahead. I'll follow everyone to the bar and see if Callum needs anything." And I'll make sure Olivia didn't remove her pumpkin outfit, because the photographer has been snapping pictures left and right. A photo of a mostly naked Olivia Haliday would pay ten times the amount he donated today.

Alek places the skates on the counter. "Relax. Even you must have fun at some point."

I glare at him. "We met at a party."

"And you weren't having any fun." His eyebrow shoots up. "Unless supervising people who fix your sink is your kink."

"I don't have a kink. I do have fun, but not when our final grade is on the line."

"I can't see how skating for a bit would ruin the fundraiser. Everything is running smoothly. Callum has the bar covered. He may look like he has shit for brains, but that's just a facade. He's a smart and capable guy, and I'm not just saying that because he's my best friend." Alek looks at my feet. "We can take a break. Size six?"

"Seven." My stomach twists like the peel in a lemontini when Alek grabs another pair of skates. "It's not that I don't want to skate." I pick at the strategic rip in my corpse-bride gown. "I can't."

"Do you have a medical condition?" Alek's tone is concerned.

"I'm perfectly healthy, I . . . It's just . . ."

His melted chocolate gaze promises comfort and care. "Just tell me, Rose. I won't tell anyone."

"I can't skate." I cover my face with my hands.

"Is that all? Lots of people are bad at it. You saw what was happening out there." He points to the ice. "Besides, everyone's at the bar."

"I have never skated in my entire life," I whisper.

He shrugs. "So what? I'll teach you."

"I'm not six years old." I stomp my foot. "I don't need to learn how to skate. It's not a survival skill. I managed for twenty-two years, and I will be fine for the rest of my life."

A trace of a smile plays on his lips. "Don't tell me Rose Haliday won't try something new because she's afraid to look bad."

"Don't be an asshole. You skate, enjoy a break, and I'll go check on Callum." I back toward the exit.

Alek extends the smaller skates my way. "Come on, Rose. I promise you'll have fun."

I shake my head.

"Just spend fifteen minutes on the ice with me and see what it feels like. Then you'll be able to add another notch to your I-can-learn-anything belt."

My chin ticks up. "I *can* learn anything."

"So you've told me. Many times." He gives me a teasing smile.

"Fifteen minutes." I snatch the skates and head to the benches. "But if I fall, you aren't allowed to laugh."

"I wouldn't dream of it."

The laces are long and thin, and they hurt my hands when I pull to tighten them.

"Let me." Alek gets on one knee and takes the laces. Our fingers graze, and my heart beats faster. I pull back and admire his strong hands as he tugs and pulls, locking me into the boot. I feel cared for, but I also feel other sensations I should not be having around my project partner. I watch his nimble fingers with their practiced movements, and a spark flickers in my belly. My mind betrays me, thinking of how those long, lean digits could be put to other uses. He wraps the longer laces around the top of the skate before tying them off and moving to the other skate.

"Looks like you've done this before."

"I helped with the younger kids when I was in high school, and some of them didn't know how to tie their normal shoes. The skates were an even bigger challenge." Alek surveys his work. "Looking good." He glances up, and, for the first time since we've met, his head is lower than mine.

From this angle, he looks more boyish. The slope of his nose and curve of his dark eyelashes paint a portrait, no longer a boy but not quite a man. His mouth is right there, and if I leaned in a few inches . . . I bolt to my feet. I don't even finish straightening when I wobble, and Alek catches me, his hands firmly around my waist.

"Woah." He wraps my arm around his elbow. "Wait until we get on the ice before you start losing your balance on me."

His bicep is solid and strong as I tighten my grip with every step. We cross the threshold to the ice, and my feet flounder, almost toppling me again. I clutch his jacket. "Maybe I should go back."

"I've got you." Alek untangles my grip, settling my palms on his shoulders as he faces me, and his large hands gently but firmly grasp my waist. He widens his stance. "Move your feet toward me."

"You're in the way," I argue.

"I'll skate backward. Don't worry about me."

"I'm not worried about you." My fingernails dig into the plastic of his costume. "I'm worried about me."

Alek twists me to the side and sets my hand on the rink's railing. "Hold on to this for a sec."

"Don't—"

He glides away without looking back like it's the easiest thing ever, then turns and speeds to the other side. Then he breaks sharply into a turn, runs even faster toward me, and stops with a flourish right in my personal space. Wow.

"Do you trust me now?" he asks. How is he not even out of breath?

"I do" is on the tip of my tongue. I bite it back. "You won't let me fall?"

He offers me both of his hands. "Let's go skate, sweets."

I take them and slip forward. Alek sets his palms back on my waist and guides us into the middle of the rink. My grip on him is steady, and the torturous first circle around the ice is made better by Alek's goofy smiles and encouraging words.

"You're doing so much better than the six-year-olds."

"Is this supposed to be a compliment?" I study my feet, concentrating on keeping my skates straight.

"Yes, actually." His laughing voice is near my ear. "They are tinier than you are, so it's easier for them to move on ice."

"Moving on ice is a perfect description of what I'm doing."

"You're skating, Rose."

"I'm being pulled along while you prevent me from falling."

"Fine." Alek loosens his grip, and my stomach drops. Before I can protest, he holds out a palm. "For this round, I'll hold only one of your hands."

The sight of our entwined fingers accelerates my pulse faster than the terror of our first round.

"I've got you." Alek skates closer, his body curving around mine like a shield. "Breathe in." He demonstrates and waits until I follow. "Breathe out." We do it together. "One more time." We repeat the motion, and although my pulse is not slowing, my fingers are a lot warmer. "Let's skate."

And we do.

I do.

It's awkward at first, but, after a few rounds, my muscles comply. Alek says I'm some kind of a skating genius, which I know isn't true because I barely stay upright. But I lose count of the circles as we pick up speed. I hear myself laughing with

Alek when he lets go of my hand and I skate on my own beside him.

"I'm doing it."

"Like you said, there isn't anything you can't learn." Alek says behind me. "You'll be a pro skater in no time."

"I'll never be a pro skater, not because I can't but because I don't have the time." I speed up. "But I might do this again sometime."

"Text me, and I'll be happy to take you."

I risk tumbling and look back at him. "You don't think I can do it on my own?"

He catches up and skates sideways beside me. "I know you can. You're one of the smartest, most capable, determined people I've ever met. But I love seeing you have fun with a skill I taught you."

"Just lording it over me?"

"No, sweets. Enjoying seeing you happy." He takes a blue, dead-looking rose from my hair.

I swat at his gesture and his overly sentimental statement and immediately lose my balance. My arms flail, my skates shoot out, and I'm suddenly falling through the air.

Right into strong, sturdy arms that catch me before I hit the ice.

"Got you." The words are barely a whisper.

Our chests are pressed together, and my thigh is between his legs. Heat invades me and crawls along my skin. "You didn't let me fall."

His gaze crawls to my mouth. "I promised I wouldn't. I keep my promises."

Bubbles fizz and pop in my veins as I stare into Alek's ever-darkening eyes, sweet and exciting like my favorite champagne. My fingers curl into the collar of his jacket, pulling him closer. I know I shouldn't—I know this is a bad idea, but my responsible brain has taken a back seat. Other parts of me are driving now. I need to taste his lips and to see if they live up to the hype my overactive imagination has been busy conjuring.

Alek's head dips. Our lips are inches apart. So close that I smell the familiar woodsy scent of his cologne and feel the whoosh of his breath. I lift my chin to breach the distance, but instead of getting closer, we rush to the ground.

He twists us so he hits the ice first, and I land on him, gasping for air.

My hair creates a curtain between me and the rink. "I guess we both fell."

The world narrows to the two of us. My ribs press to his, my breath trapped between us stuck on a setting of panicked exhilaration. Alek's hands are still holding me firmly, steadily, safely. For a long second, I don't move. I just let the heat of his body seep into mine through our costumes. My lips part as the pulse in his neck quickens under my gaze. The scent of him, the solidness of him under my hip, the way his thigh slots between mine, holding me in place, our closeness overwhelms me. My liquid desire, still fragile but already dizzying, takes root. If I lean just a little, I could kiss him right now.

He moves my hair out of the way, and his fingers linger on the curve of my cheek. "I sure did."

Sixteen

ALEK

PRESENT DAY

February

My mama is probably glued to her TV screen right now, searching for Rose and me among the actual celebrities entering the Oscars. Photographers shout as new limos arrive and stars we can't see begin their red carpet walk. I'm not on the red carpet, though. The stream of ultra-famous people merges with our mostly famous one and their non-famous dates like me in the bowels of the Dolby Theatre. Rose is beside me in an emerald dress that accentuates the shards of green in her irises, the color of rolling Irish hills. My fake girlfriend walks like this is a normal day in LA as we follow other equally overdressed people.

A celebrity in her own way, Rose waves and smiles, acknowledging glammed-up actors, directors, and others who are definitely big names in this business. She casually loops her arm into mine like it's the most natural thing. My heart swells with awe. For a moment, I can imagine I really belong here, belong with her. A tight grin tugs at the corners of my lips, one I can't quite shake because I've never been prouder to stand next to someone in my life. The stares of a few people make my teeth ache as they scan me from head to toe. I ignore them and focus on Rose, which is easy considering she's the most beautiful woman in the room. She renders me breathless, and it's not just because I could use a little more room in the slim-fit suit Zoe delivered this morning.

Rose's honey-brown hair is in light waves that expose more of her neck, as if she chose the style because she knows her effect on me. I long to press my lips against her exposed skin. I clench my jaw and look away, forcing my gaze to the chandelier above us. It takes every bit of restraint I have to remind myself why I'm here today.

The Menkens. I'm here for the Menkens.

We work our way into the auditorium and she leads us to a pair of seats that contain large white signs with our names and faces. My picture is from an interview I did three years ago when Callum had the flu and I had to step in. Next to my seat are placards with images of an elderly couple labeled Ezra and Leanne Menken.

"Shouldn't you sit next to them?" I ask, hovering between the assigned seats.

Rose arches an eyebrow. "The whole point was to place you there."

"Do I just sit down, then?"

An usher removes the pictures, and Rose adjusts the sleeve of her one-shoulder dress. She leaves enough of her collarbone exposed for my gaze to keep being drawn back to it.

"My friends are good people." Even in her high heels, Rose's mouth is still just about the level of my shoulder, and I bend to hear her among the chatter surrounding us. Her perfume—warm and floral—wraps around me. The scent is dizzying, and I force myself to focus not on the way she smells or how close her lips are, but on the pitch I've practiced a hundred times. Her fingers brush the lapels of my white crushed velvet jacket. "I'll fulfill my part of the deal and introduce you, but I'm not selling them on your idea. That's your job."

Rose doesn't seem to have a problem remembering I'm not simply here as her date. But it's not like anything has ever been simple between us.

"That's the deal." I nod.

My research on the Menkens filled the vision board on my office wall. My web browser is teeming with bookmarks on their involvement in both businesses and charities. I roll my shoulders back and exhale slowly, telling myself I've got this. Pitching to potential partners is not completely new. I haven't done it alone in years, but I know this is my best idea yet.

In terms of financial details, I can quote down to the penny what they donated through their charitable foundation over the last twenty years. Their prospectus for this year included a plan to work in a new direction, and I can do exactly that for them. I've prepared talking points on how our philosophies align. It's not just about impressing them; it's about proving my company deserves a shot. That they'll make a smart investment with their time and money. Once I regale them with how Second Chance combines green initiatives, the newest tech, and helping charities with their annual budgets, they'll see the potential and sign on as partners.

I just need a chance.

The music swells, and the announcer welcomes the audience to this year's Academy Awards as Rose lowers into her seat. I scan the filling auditorium for the older couple one more time and follow suit.

A man and woman remove the place cards with Ezra and Leanne's faces and sit beside me.

"Who are they?" I ask Rose.

"Seat fillers," she whispers, her breath tickling my cheek.

The lights lower, and the chatter in the audience dulls to a murmur. The host takes center stage, and the spectacle I've only ever seen on TV begins.

"Leanne and Ezra are probably just late." Rose presses her shoulder into mine. Nerves quicken in my throat—half about them showing up, half about how good it feels to have Rose leaning into me like we belong to each other. I nod, watching the stage, but my thoughts are tangled by her nearness. She places her palm on my elbow. "Don't worry."

I SHOULD'VE WORRIED.

The line of limos we're behind slowly moves to the entrance of the Vanity Fair afterparty. The Menkens were a no-show. Who misses the Oscars? I twist the button that's holding my jacket closed. "Are you sure the Menkens are here?"

Rose reapplies her lipstick and tucks the tube into the green clutch that matches her dress. "I'm not, but if they are in town or were delayed, they wouldn't miss this event. Lots of business deals happen at this afterparty. I don't want you to say the day was a waste or that I didn't try to fill my end of our bargain."

I do want to talk to the Menkens, but sitting with Rose the whole evening, talking and laughing with her, was most definitely not a waste.

"If they aren't here—"

"We turn around and head out." She watches through the darkened limo window. "Isn't Second Chance all about supporting parties and events? How can you be a party hater?"

"I don't hate parties if they are entertaining, like your Valentine's Day fundraiser. Parties full of small talk aren't my idea of fun. Thus why I need to partner with a celebrity who likes the party scene. Usually that's Callum's role, and that's why we've worked so well together all these years. That's why I need the Menkens."

Rose twists my way. "Too bad Callum's going on his regatta thing."

"He's always chasing new adventures." The disappointment of not having my best friend beside me as usual stirs in my gut. "New venture. New women. This around-the-world trip on a sailboat is a thrill he's been eyeing for years. Once TRI is sold, he's off to sail the high seas."

"Isn't that dangerous?"

"Challenging is more like it. After twelve years in the corporate world, he wants a new venture."

"You haven't considered joining him?"

"Boats are not my thing. My challenge is Second Chance Events. If I can get this off the ground and do some good in the world with the money and the opportunities I've been given, I'll be challenging myself too."

The door beside Rose opens. "Time to put your money where your mouth is. Let's go find Leanne and Ezra."

I maneuver across the seat and exit the limo behind Rose. The curve of her bare shoulder, framed by emerald silk, holds my gaze longer than I mean it to. Her walk's all confidence and grace. I square my shoulders and follow. The red carpet into the afterparty stretches before us.

"Smile for the cameras, but don't stop and talk to the reporters." Rose adjusts her dress and takes my hand. Her skin is warm, and her grip is tight. Heat sparks up my arm like static.

My heart stutters, caught off guard by how a gesture so small can feel like so much. People shout questions, trying to engage Rose, but she keeps a casual pace, waving to the reporters while I focus on not tripping, blinded by the camera flashes.

Inside the venue, the lights are muted except for the camera crew that follows a reporter interviewing the guests.

"Remember, everything here is being recorded." She side-eyes me. "Try not to grimace."

In case I'm grimacing, I rearrange my face into what I hope portrays calm confidence. She drags me toward a long line of low plush couches. As a server passes, she plucks a flute of champagne off a tray and takes a long sip. "If you want to get out of here quickly, we should divide and conquer. Meet back here in fifteen? I'll text you if I find them."

"And if we don't?"

"We move to Plan B."

"I thought this was Plan B."

She sets down her drink. "This is Plan A, Point 1. Plan B is to accidentally stumble upon them at my golf club. You golf, right?"

I whisper into Rose's ear. "I don't know how to play. Callum is the golfer."

"Let's hope they're here because if they're not, I guess I'll have to give you some pointers." She heads away from me.

Alone in the semidarkness filled with music and conversations, I pass clusters of drunk people shouting a little too loudly as they sway, gorging on booze, food, and entertainment. I spot faces I can put a name to and the ones that create an itch in the back of my mind, telling me I've seen them somewhere. None of them are the Menkens. I unbutton the jacket that was snug at the beginning of the evening and has escalated to suffocating me. This will all be worth it, I remind myself.

A clap on my back makes me flinch. I twist around to find a tuxedo-clad Callum.

"What are you doing at a party?" My business partner's I-love-surprising-the-shit-out-of-people smile breaks across his face.

"Working, why are you here?" I reply.

"Not working." He raises two tumblers of amber liquid in one hand. "I thought you were just going to the Oscars."

I run my palm up my face and over my hair. "The Menkens didn't show."

"Fuck." My friend shoves one of the tumblers my way. "You look like you need this."

I take the drink and scan the partygoers as I take a sip. The scotch burns my throat.

"So, is the deal over?"

"I'm not giving up yet." I peer into the faces around me one more time and take another swig of my drink. "But if they aren't here, I will need your help."

He shakes his head. "I told you I'm not joining Second Chance."

I meet his eye. "I know. I promised I wouldn't ask again." My fingers tighten on the tumbler. "Can you teach me how to play golf this week?"

Callum almost spits out his scotch. "I tried to drag you to golf courses for years, and now you want to learn?"

"The Menkens are big fans."

"Of course they are." His gaze shoots skyward. "Everyone in this fucking town loves golf."

"So you'll help me?"

"Oh, sure. Let me see." He pulls out an imaginary phone. "Yeah, I'll just drop everything and turn you into a pro golfer. How's tomorrow at 5 a.m.? Should take about an hour."

"Stop being an ass. I can't look like a fool in front of these people." I glance around the room, feeling more out of place than usual. "Rose said she would give me pointers, but what use are they when I don't know the basics?"

Callum clinks his glass to mine. "Problem solved. Get Rose to teach you and take the occasion to convince her about Second Chance. If she's on your side, she'll help you sell the venture."

Per usual, Callum sees the social context I've completely missed. Why didn't I think of that? I go to sip my scotch and find the glass empty.

"Besides, I think you'd enjoy a little one-on-one time with sweet Rose." He swings his hips suggestively. "Admit it, despite everything that happened, you still have a thing for her."

I do, but I'm not telling him or anyone else what I really feel for this woman. I glance away, trying to hide the way my chest constricts. If I admit how much I still want her and my intent to get her back falls apart, I'll look like a complete love-smitten fool. "I don't—"

"Cut the shit, Alek. It's me. I know you."

"Stop trying to play matchmaker." I make my voice sound bored. "I'm here for Second Chance Events. That's it."

"They'll let anyone into this party. Even Callum." Rose sweeps in behind us.

My friend grins at her. "The woman of the hour."

Rose gives him a peck on the cheek. "What are you doing here?"

Callum swings his glass to the corner of the room where Soren is talking with a woman I don't know. "Soren's publicist got us in."

"Publicist?" Rose says.

"Apparently Soren has to schmooze this crowd. The studio is hinting at a spin-off feature movie."

Rose's nose crinkles. "Of what?"

"Star Blazers." Callum raises his glass to his lips. "You have seen the show, right?"

"I'm too busy to stream anything. Hotel empire to run, remember?"

"You didn't read the books?" I ask.

"There are books?" Rose's gaze wanders to Soren, as if seeing him in a new light.

"Star Blazers is a best-selling sci-fi series. Soren started writing the series in college and sold the first one after graduation."

Someone bumps into my back and I step closer to Rose. "He's a main-stage event at Comic-Con. They just wrapped another season of the show."

Callum leans in. "Everyone's dying to know what happens next. Including Soren."

"Wasn't he writing over the holidays?" I watch Soren, looking uncomfortable in an ill-fitting penguin suit. I should send him to Zoe. My jacket is too slim for my liking, but it's a giant leap from anything I own. I also appreciate the capsule wardrobe she sent me.

"Nope. Writer's block." Callum tips his glass at Rose. "Careful there. Wouldn't want to lose that pretty piece of jewelry."

Rose and I glance down at her tennis bracelet, which is hanging loose on her wrist.

"Darn." Rose tries to put it back on but fails. "The clasp keeps opening."

I take the tiny ends of the bracelet and thread them back together. My thumb lingers over the delicate veins of her wrist where her pulse beats below the soft skin. A jolt of affection pulses through me, so quick and unexpected it leaves me breathless. I'm pretending this is nothing, but my body knows I'm lying. I want to do this for real, every day, like I have the right. I raise her wrist and place a kiss where my thumb was. Our eyes meet, and Rose inhales sharply.

"Ms. Haliday." A woman with a camera steps in front of us. "May I take a picture of you and your date?"

Rose jerks her head to the intruder, her breaths quick and shallow. I take her hand and draw her into me, away from the reporter. Her fingers curl around mine, and a quiet truth settles in my bones. I was made for being by her side, supporting her. Our fingers intertwine and we fit together like two Lego pieces.

"Sure." Rose smiles and leans into me.

After what feels like a thousand clicks, the woman lowers her camera. "Is the reclusive Aleksander Orlov really at a party?"

My chest rises. "I wouldn't abandon my girlfriend. Right, babydoll?"

"Right, honey."

The photographer's eyebrows jump. "Oh, really?" She looks at Rose as if I can't be trusted. "How long have you two been dating?"

The lie is simple, the act agreed upon, but my nerves spike anyway. What if Rose doesn't go along with the plan? What if she denies we are together? Laughs us off?

Rose brings our clasped hands forward. "It's new."

Seventeen

TWELVE YEARS AGO

November

Preparing for Rose's arrival, I set the bag of chips and the brand-name container of salsa on the counter in the kitchen. Does she even eat chips and salsa, or does her personal chef prepare some delicacy I can't fathom?

I scrub my hand over my face and let out a low grunt, annoyed with myself. What the hell am I doing, playing as if it were a date? This was a foolish idea. I didn't have snacks the first time she was here.

"What are we celebrating?" Callum pulls the bottle of champagne out of the fridge. "Are the gossip rags correct about you sleeping with sweet Rose?"

"Stop fucking calling her that." I snatch the champagne out of his hands and set the bottle back into the fridge. "And what are you talking about, anyway?"

"Your ignorance over gossip is commendable, but when you date a hotel heiress, your mug gets in the papers." Callum rips the bag of chips open, and several spill onto the countertop. He grabs some and stuffs them in his mouth, then dives back into the bag for more.

I snag the bag. "These are not for you, and now I need a bowl."

"Champagne. A bowl for the chips. Is her fancy rubbing off on you?" Callum shoves another chip into his mouth. "Of course, if the press is right and you are doing the dirty, all that rubbing is inevitable."

I slam the cabinet door and pour the chips into the giant bowl we used for spiked punch during our last party. The wood reverberates with the force of it, and my jaw locks. I'm two seconds away from shoving my friend out of the kitchen. "You will lose some of those pretty teeth if you don't stop talking about Rose that way."

"I'm mostly talking about you that way." Callum takes my laptop from the coffee table, types up a storm, and turns the screen my way. "See for yourself."

HOTEL HEIRESS PLAYING BLUE COLLAR AT THE HOCKEY RINK?

Photos of Rose and me accompany the headline. It's us on the skating rink, holding hands as she smiles like she's actually enjoying herself. I look like I'm enjoying myself too, but I know the grin on my face is genuine. Callum says I'm the best to play poker with because I suck at hiding what I think or feel. Doing so around Rose is harder because all I want to do is make her smile. Then I want to kiss the smile off her face.

I close my eyes and shake my head. I'm not going there. She is my project partner. I can not screw this up. I can not fall for her.

Even if it's too late.

I grip the edge of the counter until my knuckles go white. The damage is already done, and I'm the fool still pretending I've got control of this situation. This is a disaster.

A knock at the door drags me out of the swirl of possible doomsday scenarios these photos might lead to. Callum beats me to the entry and swings the door wide open.

"Callum, are you feeling okay? You're wearing a T-shirt." Rose's voice is cheery.

"I wouldn't want you photographed with me naked after all the pics of you and Alek googly-eyed."

The memory hits me hard: the sound of her laughter echoing in the rink. Her breath fanning my lips. I was so close to kissing her. Too close. It's good that I didn't. The camera would've caught that too. But for fuck's sake did I want to kiss her. Still do. My gaze drops to her mouth before I drag it away.

Rose's gaze shoots to me. "You saw?"

I try to swallow past the lump forming in my throat. I hope she can't read what must be written all over my face.

"Just now." I spin the laptop her way. "I'm sorry."

"You have nothing to be sorry about," she says with a sigh. "I invited the photographer. It was my fault for thinking he was trustworthy. Guess the payout for pics of me was too high. Lesson learned. Don't trust paparazzi ever again."

"No pictures of Olivia, though," I say.

"Apparently, her in a pumpkin outfit isn't what sells." She produces an envelope. "At least we made a hefty profit."

"You get all the credit for that."

"I'll take the positive with the negative, then." Rose walks to the bowl of chips. "Is this your dinner? Should I order a more substantial meal?"

"I ate already. I thought you might like a snack." I stumble over my words.

She picks up a chip. "Thanks."

The lump in my throat shrinks, releasing the constriction on my airway. My heart tumbles. This is just a snack. I should stop imagining a hidden meaning.

Callum opens the fridge and takes out the champagne again. "He was ready to celebrate before I told him the paparazzi news."

"We did beat our goal by 50 percent." I grab the bottle and hide it back in the fridge. "Now we can afford the two coders I contracted and splurge for a UX designer. That puts us ahead of schedule, which means I might get some sleep this month." My cheeks heat at the memory of waking up in Rose's bedroom and mistaking her for a dream. I almost kissed her that day too. Almost kissing my project partner is becoming a problem. I hover with the door to the fridge between Rose and me, hoping the cold air cools my growing attraction. "We should have a decent prototype for the presentation that people can actually download and play around with."

Callum pulls the chip bowl his way. "What he means is he's peeing his pants due to the excitement of seeing an idea of his becoming a semi-real thing." He waves the crispy triangle at Rose as he pushes me away from the fridge. "You are a huge part of making that real. He wants to thank you with this cheap-ass champagne he bought." Callum hefts the bottle back out.

What's wrong with my best friend? He should not be here in the first place, nor should he voice what I told him in private.

Rose bites her lip and grins at me. "We are sort of rocking this project." She wipes chip dust off her hands. "Where are the flutes?" She looks around the counter.

My jaw clenches. "We don't own those."

Ever-helpful Callum opens the cabinet with the mismatched glasses and mugs and picks the first three. "Let's drink to the day when we'll have the money for proper champagne and perfect glasses to down bubbly from." Callum releases the cork with a pop and pours foaming liquid into the garage-sale finds.

Rose picks the mug that says "Welcome to Los Angeles" with a faded depiction of the Hollywood sign. Callum takes the cup advertising our hockey team, and I grab the mason jar with as much dignity as I can muster.

"To the success of this project and whatever projects the future may bring," says Rose, and we clink glasses. She tips her mug and downs the champagne as if it's a shot. She cringes but smiles. "I think this is the first non-champagne champagne I've ever tasted. It's not that bad."

I take a sip of the fizzy liquid and the sweetness tickles the roof of my mouth. I set the jar down, giving Callum a not-so-subtle get-your-ass-out-of-here look.

"Well, that's my cue to go." He tops the cup with more non-champagne then shuffles to the door and picks up his back-pack. "I'm meeting the guys for wings and beer, so please don't behave well while you have the place to yourselves. Give the paparazzi the gossip to really talk about." He slams the door behind him.

"He's always this way, right? It's not a facade for my sake?" Rose pours more bubbly into her mug.

"Callum?" I stall because my heart aches from her question. During our time at the rink, I almost felt like Rose and I could have a future beyond this project. Her interest in Callum leaves a sour taste on my tongue. I've never been jealous of the attention my best friend gets from women, but I was sure Rose had no interest in him. "He's always like that."

"I guess some girls go for his type." She twists the sparkling bracelet on her wrist. "Listen, we might have another problem. I mapped out the presentation and ran through it three times. I'm eight minutes over."

"So? We'll just cut some fluff."

She stares at me. "There is no fluff. I pared the competitive analysis down to three slides and created an at-a-glance benefit chart to summarize the savings." She sets her laptop on the stool. "There's not enough time."

"Let's sit." I point to the couch, which has become our default workstation. "I'll show you what I've coded so far, and then you can walk me through the presentation. We'll figure this out."

"Thank you for the champagne." She takes a sip and smiles at me over the rim. Callum and any worry I may have is forgotten when she looks at me like that. Having her so close and comfortable makes it seem like we have a special thing. Our thing. For this moment, it's easy to pretend we're more than project partners. "I don't remember a time when I celebrated such a small thing."

"Funding our project is not a small thing. You're amazing." The remark escapes before I can stop. I return the alcohol to my lips before I say something even more inappropriate.

"The money part worked out, but . . ." Rose picks up my laptop and scrolls through the article about us. "Mom sent me several texts this morning, and I'll be meeting with our publicist tomorrow."

"Damage control over you skating at your own party?"

"Skating is not the problem." She rubs her arms, almost like she's hugging herself. "It's the dating rumors."

"You are not allowed to date?" That seems wild.

She stares at the laptop screen. "I'm allowed to date. I'm just . . . well, it doesn't matter."

The implication hits me like a bad check against the boards. Of course she can date. She had plans with that guy the other night who's a friend of her mother's. "You're not allowed to date me, you mean? I thought we were past your mother's comment in the elevator about what I'm good for."

"We aren't dating." Rose looks at me, her expression almost angry. I don't want to believe she agrees with what her mother said. She sits up straighter. "We're working on a school project together and making sure we deliver a superior product to Professor Patel. To be the best in our class." She shoves the laptop my way. "Will you just show me the final wireframes?"

Her mother was right. Rose Haliday could never be interested in someone like me. I'm no more than a schoolmate she was forced to partner with. No matter what I think keeps sparking between us, my wishful thinking is not an actuality. Just like the night at her hotel suite. I woke up from that dream, and I need to wake up from this one as well.

I steady my breath and let the silence cover the sting. If I act unfazed, maybe I'll eventually feel that way too. I walk her through what I have so far and focus on what I can control. Acing this project. Once that's over, I can leave the beautiful hotel heiress behind and live my life. The one without her.

Eighteen

PRESENT DAY

March

I thought the best view of Alek was in his outfit for the Oscars. Or, rather, of him trying on that outfit in Zoe's studio. Every time I open my toys drawer beside my bed and select my special friend of the day, that image is the first thing that pops unbidden into my brain. What I use varies depending on what fantasy about Alek I'm hyper-fixating on, but the memory of his shoulders, pecks, abs, ass, and the things I didn't see clearly enough get me over the edge every time.

Today adds another image to my collection.

"Am I wearing something I shouldn't?" Alek adjusts the waistline of his white shorts that showcase drool-worthy calves. The form-fitting golf shirt is tucked tight enough to see the outline of his muscles. My core clenches, which is not what should happen in the middle of a golf course. He lifts his eyebrow. "Don't tell me Callum pranked me again, and I need to go buy a new shirt at the pro shop."

My gaze meets his, and I hope he chucks my overheated cheeks up to the exceptionally sunny LA March morning. "Callum did well."

"Why do I feel like you are taking pleasure in making me dress up for each occasion you drag me to?"

"I'm not dragging you anywhere. We have a deal, remember?"

"Right. The deal." Alek hides his eyes behind sunglasses and stares at the path to the first hole. "How far are we walking?" He reaches for my golf bag and hoists the strap over his shoulder.

"Oh no, we're not starting with the actual golf course." I head to the driving range, where a handful of the club members line up in a row, whacking golf balls over and over. "We begin at the beginning." The sound of clubs slicing through the air accompanies us as I lead Alek to an empty stall far from everyone else. I hand him a driver. "There's a saying in golf. Swing for show, putt for dough. Let's see your swing."

Alek grasps the club with both hands. "The videos I watched weren't very helpful."

"Luckily, I know what I'm doing." I take a 7-iron out and stand in front of Alek, demonstrating the grip.

Alek attempts to mimic me. "Like this?"

"It's not a hockey stick." I tap his club with mine. "Relax your fingers."

Said fingers wiggle, and my mind skips to last night's session with my vibrator. I straighten my shoulders. "Better. Now, take a swing."

The club wheels back a foot and Alek slaps the ball, which shoots out of the stall at an almost horizontal angle.

"You're worse than I thought." I show a complete swing. "Engage your entire body."

I repeat the move twice more and gesture for him to try. Alek's attempt is almost robotic. I shake my head.

He halts. "What's wrong?"

"A good swing is not only arms. Use your hips." The heat that was firmly in my cheeks now invades every part of my body as Alek watches me take a swing. I remind myself he's trying to understand how I'm moving.

"So the hips help with the thrust?"

The word "thrust" should not be triggering any kind of a reaction from me, but my temperature rises even higher, and the sun is not the culprit. "Essentially."

"Okay. I'm good at that."

"Are you flirting with me?" I put my free hand on my hip and cock it.

"Just practicing. For the Menkens."

"You often talk about thrusting hips with your girlfriends?"

His lips twitch. "It's more of a show than a tell situation."

As if I'm twelve again, my ears just about burst into flames. I shove my club back into my bag. "If you're not going to take this seriously—"

"Wait." Alek's fingers land on my forearm. His skin is hot against mine, a single point of contact that sends a tingle racing up my arm and down my throat. My breath stutters. My whole body feels like it's on the precipice of a dangerous yet delicious time. The smirk falls off his face. "I want to learn."

"Then try again."

Unfortunately, the next three swings do not improve. But he *is* trying.

I move closer, my palms reaching out. "Is it okay if I touch you and show you the hip action?"

A muscle in his jaw ticks as he nods.

I position myself as far away from him as I can while still placing my hands on the space below his waistband. His taught muscles resist my effort to move him. "You need to relax."

He clears his throat and adjusts his stance. I begin with a gentle sway and move the right hip out more.

"Can you feel it?" I say into the space between his shoulder blades that is somehow a lot closer now.

"You don't have to be gentle with me. Feel free to do anything you need," he delivers in a gravelly voice that shoots down my spine, igniting the last part of me that's not already on fire.

My fingers sink into the fine material of his shorts. With the mantra "we have a deal" repeating on silent, I rotate his pelvis over and over. I shove the images of him in my bed away because my confused body is mixing my imagination with reality.

I step to the side. "Try again."

He does. The hip movement is better and more fluid, but the top of his body looks like a mannequin.

"Why are you frowning?" he asks as I rub the wrinkles off my forehead. "What?" he continues. "Are my hips really that bad?"

"No. Much better." I make the mistake of looking at his pants and what must be spare golf balls in his pocket. "But your shoulders, your arms . . ."

"You standing behind me helped."

"You're too tall for me to direct your shoulders and arms."

He offers me the club. "What if we switch? I stand behind you, and you do it so I can . . . feel."

This seems like a very, very bad idea. My hands on his body have already overloaded my senses and almost gave me a heat stroke. His hands on *my* body might be disastrous. My body that loves nothing more than to react to Alek's remarks, his presence, and his touch.

My lips must be disconnected from my brain because "Let's try it" escapes even though my brain insists I run away.

The sun is momentarily blocked as Alek positions himself behind me. The cool lasts for a millisecond before his heat meets my back.

"Put your hand on my hands." Did that come out like a command?

Thick arms encompass me, and his palms drop onto my hands. Scorching hot. I can barely sense the handle of the golf club in my grip. This is a very, very bad idea. If I lean backward ever so slightly, I could press into him to feel those pecs and abs I dreamed about.

I do a slow swing, and his body curves around mine like a pliable yet solid sheet of muscle. A slightly woodsy scent envelopes me, and I stop mid-swing. Alek reminds me what his hand on my body feels like. What yielding to Alek's magnetic pull does to me. A shiver runs down my neck. My pulse is louder than the clicks of Louboutin heels on a marble floor. My fingers tighten on the handle of the club.

"Rose?" Alek's low rumble shoots straight to my core. There isn't enough air in this open space.

I need to focus on what we are doing here. This is about golf. This is about Leanne and Ezra. This is about the sale of TRI. This is about proving to my mother I can close a deal. I run my tongue over my teeth.

With a long breath, I move back to the starting position. "Let's try that again."

I do a slow swing, and his hands fall away mid-arc. I instantly miss his fingers on mine.

"You need to keep a hold of me," I tell Alek.

"Are you sure?"

"Very sure," I say, despite the voice in my head that insists I need to step away. I should just hire him a coach who doesn't have full-body heat waves around my fake boyfriend.

Alek's chest brushes my shoulders, and the uneven rhythm of his breath tickles my ear. Once again his arms wrap around mine. His hips are inches away from my lower back. If I step back, I'll be flush against his body.

I drag myself out of the trance and swing. As my arms go to the top left, his right arm presses into my breast. I linger in the final position entirely too long.

"Did you get it?" I whisper.

"Maybe one more time?" His voice is velvet.

Alek doesn't loosen his grip as we repeat the tandem swing. This time, my cheek brushes his bicep, and his thumbs hold my wrists. I close my eyes, enjoying the closeness of him.

"Rose?" Mom's voice shocks better than a cold shower.

I make to step out of Alek's grasp, but he possessively wraps his arm around my waist and turns us to the woman who built an empire and dominates every boardroom she walks into.

Beside her stands a tall blond man in a bright teal outfit.

"I'm glad you're here." A ridge forms between Mom's eyebrows when her gaze finds Alek. "What are you doing at the driving range?"

"Rose is teaching me how to golf." Alek erases the inch separating our bodies.

"Do you belong to this club?" The almost imperceptible narrowing of Mom's eyes might go unnoticed by others, but I've been around her my entire life. When she zeros in on a target, there's no protecting it. And Alek is, for some reason, her target today.

I set my hand on Alek's and wrap it tighter around my waist, stepping in front of him a little. Mom's other victims didn't have me to defend them.

"I'm Rose's guest. Is there something wrong?" Alek's voice is polite but firm.

"I just don't like when people mix business with pleasure." A flash of annoyance swipes across my mother's face, and her gaze bores into mine like she's trying to talk to me telepathically. But I don't have a clue what she is implying. Mom sets her hand on the tall guy's elbow and smiles at me. "Chad's a partner at the biggest corporate law firm in LA."

Is Mom thinking about changing law firms? I squint at her. Yet another thing she hasn't shared?

"He's thinking about joining, and I was hoping you can show him around." Mom nudges Chad forward.

Alek's body turns to steel. "She's a little busy right now."

"Rose knows how to juggle many tasks." My mother takes off the glove on her right hand.

"Who are you?" Chad's stare sharpens on Alek.

Alek's lips graze the top of my hair as his hold on me tightens. His finger draws a pattern on the back of my hand. "I'm her boyfriend."

Chad cocks his head. "I was told Rose is single."

I straighten in Alek's embrace. You have got to be shitting me. My mother is trying to set me up with this man after I told her to stop meddling in my dating life? My blood boils, though for a different reason. Once again my mother has made up her mind and acted without consulting me. When will she realize that this is not her protecting me, but smothering me, and treating me like I don't have a say in any of this?

I stare straight into my mother's eyes, lean back into Alek's solid warmth, and stroke his forearm. "Not anymore."

Mom's face freezes. "I didn't realize you were exclusive," she says through gritted teeth.

Alek entwines our fingers. "I don't share."

Her gaze darts between our fingers, Chad's face, and the nearest occupied driving lane.

"Rose." My mother leans on her golf club and gives me her media-darling smile. "Would you be a dear and show Chad the clubhouse." Her gaze shifts to Alek. "Mr. Orlov and I need to talk business."

Did she just dismiss me from my own boyfriend's embrace? Is she treating me like a child once again? As if the adults need to talk and my role is to be a good girl and go do what my mother tells me? Rage fills my lungs. I'm tired of being treated like a doll. I clench my jaw. I don't want to be that good girl anymore. It's time she knows I'm done being manipulated. That I make my own decisions, starting with who I want to fucking date.

"No." I turn on my heel, yank Alek down by his golf shirt, and press my mouth to his. My head swims, probably from turning too sharply, but maybe also from the heat of his lips on mine.

Alek's eyebrows quirk, questioning.

What am I doing? Using Alek to prove to Mom that she should stop setting me up with other men? Dizzy heat floods me and I start moving away. Alek's lips do what his body did when Mom and Chad showed up—they erase any distance separating us. He covers my mouth with his tentatively, like he's testing if this is okay, or asking for my permission.

My heart melts at the gesture and at the care that I long for. I melt into Alek. I slink my arm around his neck as if to say, "Yes, please."

Alek makes a noise that's between a low sigh and a quiet growl. His other hand catches the back of my head, and his mouth descends on mine in a not-at-all-gentle kiss. His lips open to mine, and his teeth nip my lower lip. I'm dizzy again. So, it's definitely his lips, then. I grab the sleeve of his shirt, and I dive into the kiss, not because I want to prove my worth to my mother but because more of Alek's mouth on mine is precisely what I need.

Nineteen

ALEK

March

I can't stop kissing Rose. Her jasmine scent has scattered my brain as my mouth finds hers again. Her lips part, and my greedy tongue dips inside. I'm rewarded by a small sigh as her chest presses into mine. I nip her bottom lip, sinking into the sensation of what it's like to kiss someone you want, someone you need, and someone you crave. There's no more pecks and no more pretend because everything my body is doing right now is raw and unrestrained.

No longer in control, I kiss the woman in my arms. I can't find it within myself to care who sees us or what they think. If she's willing to kiss me, I'm stealing every second, because the way she arches into me, seeks my lips if I separate to take a breath, and the way she melts into my arms shows, without words, that she is entirely in this with me.

The sound that escapes me at the realization is too close to a growl as I crash back into the sweetness of her. I thought I forgot what it's like to kiss Rose. I was certain I erased the memory etched into each nerve ending of my body that had the privilege of kissing her years ago. I thought I nuked every recollection and built impenetrable walls between me and the zone of devastation of what she tasted like, how she felt, and how her pulse reacted when I traced my fingers along her fine, delicate neck.

I was wrong.

She is and always has been impossible to forget. This truth—my devastating reality—chased me in my dreams and appeared ghost-like in my mind every time I saw her since the day she stepped into my office.

And now? Now, I will carry the feel of her lips on mine because, even though her mouth is separate, it's also forever mine.

Rose stills and her hesitation yanks me out of my worshipping trance. She puts her finger on my cheek. I remove my lips from hers but can't quite keep myself completely away, so they hover over hers, far enough to hear what she's about to say, close enough to resume kissing her the moment she is done.

"Are they still there?" she whispers.

"What?" The rasp in my voice betrays what I want to keep doing instead of talking.

"Are Chad and Mom still watching?"

I jerk back. She might as well have elbowed me in the nose and drawn blood. The worst open-ice hit never hurt this much. My ribcage caves in, and my lips lock. The heat of embarrassment flushes through me.

I'm wrong again.

My muscles constrict and I pull away, straightening myself and my emotions. At least, I attempt to do the latter. Rose wasn't into the kiss. This stunt was for the benefit of her mother. Not for her. Definitely not for me.

I remove both of my hands from her soft skin and she shivers. In this almost ninety-degree heat, she wraps her arms around herself as if there's a chill.

"I think you scared them away." My voice is still hoarse, but whatever chill that's freezing her body has seeped into my tone. "I need a drink." I scan for the clubhouse. "Is there a bar here?"

Rose tugs her skirt down, adjusting her outfit. "Every golf club has a nineteenth hole. Follow me."

We walk in silence out of the bright, humid March day into the cool dark of the lounge. Rose bypasses the overstuffed leather couches and wing-backed chairs, taking a seat at the end of a long mahogany bar. I sit beside her as she orders a lemontini for her and a scotch for me.

"Sorry I did that." She looks at the tennis bracelet she twists on her wrist, unwilling to meet my eyes.

"Kissed me?"

"Yes. I told you that was off the table, but Mom and her attempts to set me up with Chad pissed me off. But I shouldn't have kissed you."

"I'm not sorry you kissed me." I want to step back to her and put my hands where they were before, but I ball them into fists instead. "And if this arrangement can help you stand up to your mother, sign me up."

"Really?" She chews on her lower lip, where my teeth were a minute ago. It's also where I want them to be now, despite any anger I might be harboring about her intentions behind that kiss.

"Thank you," she says. "First she set up my marriage with Dean. Now she brings in his lookalike replacement."

I dislike Chad, but I detest Dean. And I fucking despise Melinda Haliday.

The drinks arrive and Rose finally looks at me as if she's not afraid to do so anymore. "If I can't satisfy my mother by being married and producing an heir, I can at least prove to her that I'm capable of landing the TRI contract."

At the mention of her mother, the single last shred of hope that Rose was into that kiss extinguishes completely. As if that hope wasn't already lost the moment we broke apart. "You're brokering the deal to buy my company because you want to prove yourself to your mother?"

The blue shards in her eyes fill me with icy bitterness. "The deal is what's good for the future of HH Group. Without your tech, we'll fall even further behind. Exclusive rights through your company will give us an advantage over other luxury hotels and resorts, plus a new stream of revenue. We need to get to the next level. I'll prove I'm more than a pawn and that I have a vision. That I am the future of HH Group, not just because of my last name."

How did I not recognize this when she came to renegotiate the deal? Fuck. How could I have been so oblivious? The signs were there. I just didn't want to see them. A jagged claw drags across my ribs, hooking into them. All it took was me seeing her face to immediately become distracted by what I lost and what I wanted to get back.

"But why the pretending? Isn't there another way to show your mother how brilliant you are?"

The ice in her irises cracks. "I've grown up pretending in one way or another. I faked my marriage for years. I play into the illusion that I'm useful at HH Group with my parties and fundraisers when Mom questions their value." She sips her lemontini. "I'll fake anything until I get what I want, and that's doing what I actually want in my career. In my life."

I thought it hurt when I realized our kiss was for show. Now, everything about my mindset shifts. "I didn't know," I say, with regret in my voice.

"Don't do that." She sets her glass down on the bar, harder than appropriate. "Don't pity me, Alek. I haven't lied to you this time. You knew from the beginning I had an ulterior motive."

I knew she wanted my company and not me. I hold my palms up in surrender.

"Have you lied to me?" she asks, a rare hint of vulnerability in her eyes.

That look she gives me makes me drop my hands. Because I have lied. Maybe she already knows that too.

I told Callum the day she walked into my office that I was over her. I've lied for twelve years to my friends and to myself, but I can't tell her that. Yet. So for now, I offer another truth. "The point of our bargain, my motive, was to launch Second Chance Events with the Menkens."

"And I set the plan in motion. Every year, I stay at their house in Georgia for the Masters, and I asked if my new boyfriend could come this time."

"When is that?"

"You don't know when the Masters are?"

"Do you know when the Stanley Cup playoffs start?"

"Point taken." Rose takes another sip. "The Masters are the second week of April."

A weight drops behind my navel. Of course there's a conflict. Nothing in this arrangement can go smoothly. "I'm in Boston then."

"Can't you cancel?"

"I'm leading the workshop with Professor Patel at MIT. He got tenure there five years ago." I spread my hands, caught between two worlds I care about. "So no, but Boston is what, two, three hours from Georgia? I'll fly down for the weekend."

"Say hi to Professor Patel." She fiddles with the clasp on the diamond bracelet she always wears. "Does he know about Second Chance Events?"

"I'm pitching it to him while I'm there."

"Use the proposal you gave me. It's convincing." Her shoulders drop, as if she is relieved we're back on more familiar ground. "Although, if I were running the show, I'd make a few improvements to your logistics."

My phone rings in my pocket and I quickly reach to silence it, not wanting to be interrupted as Rose gears up to reveal a piece of that brilliant mind of hers. "Really? What would you change?"

"From my perspective, a high-end event coordinator will not spend time taking pictures of all their stuff and categorizing it. That's unrealistic. You could tap into the vendors themselves since they already have a product list and know the quantities delivered. Maybe you could hire staff to take pictures either there or, most likely, at the warehouse where the items are stored. The latter has the advantage of real-time analysis of any potential waste. Items get damaged, people take flowers home, etc."

Kissing Rose earlier revealed how much I've always loved the taste of her. Talking to Rose, however, reminds me how much I loved working on our project together back in school. The way Rose's brain works might still be the sexiest thing about her. A buzz begins in my veins at the memory of her pivoting mid-fundraiser, trading the ballroom setting for the

Halloween-on-Ice idea, because she knew how to work magic with whatever she had.

"Or maybe the drivers can also take photos. I don't really have that fleshed out." She twirls the lemon peel in her martini. "Then there's the perishable conundrum."

"I accounted for a two-day timeline before they become useless."

"See, that's where I think you miss out. Most flowers won't last long, but others have the potential for weeks if stored properly. Potted plants, small trees, and things like that can create an inviting space. Think of the Vanity Fair afterparty at the Oscars. Yes, there was a good portion of freshly cut flowers, but they used boxwoods and mini evergreens in the big room to create smaller areas, a cozier but chic ambiance designed especially for people to mingle. People often miss the potential of giving plants second chances."

"You're right," I say.

"I usually am." A genuine smile takes over Rose's features as she winks at me. "And other items can be reused multiple times. After a few uses, will you severely discount them, or could you offer that permanent inventory to charities for free? And how will charities select the items? You saw my office. Sometimes you need tangible samples for clients to touch and compare."

"My current idea is to have a store, similar to the reuse ones like Goodwill. But it would be online so we don't have to keep a retail space." I squeeze the nape of my neck. "But you bring up a good point. As always."

She looks down at her almost empty glass, but I swear I see the shadow of pink on her cheeks. Damn it, I love it when she blushes. An invisible cord draws me taller, and pride unfurls behind my sternum, instant and shamefully satisfying, because I'm the one who put that look on her face. For once, I'm the reason she let her guard down.

"Of course, to start all this, you need capital." She's back to business. "And assets."

"That's part of why the Menkens are perfect. They can talk their friends into donating. With celebrities and famous people involved, we can auction off items like memorabilia from a wrap party or a wedding. All proceeds will go to the operations capital."

"Not every celebrity will give you permission to do that."

"But if enough do, it could work. The cost analysis shows we will be able to scale up over the next five years." The charge I get talking about my company stirs in my gut, even more so because I'm discussing it with Rose. My hand trembles, and I stuff it in my pocket. "Would you want to see the numbers? Maybe consult?"

"It's a definite maybe. The concept of reusing materials from events is pure genius. Pure Alek Orlov. At least the Alek I once knew. It's such a win-win-win."

She still sees me, the real me. A quiet ease wraps around me, soothing the bruised memories of what we used to be like that I've kept hidden. "That means a lot, coming from the only competition in Professor Patel's class." My phone rings yet again. I silence it.

A hint of a smile graces lips that I swear are still puffy from our kiss. Then again, maybe that's just the way her lips are permanently burned into my memory. Will it take another twelve years to forget them?

Her hand reaches for me, then retracts. Comes back.

"But I genuinely think you've got a winning proposal."

"You do?" Why does Rose's praise feel better than any A+ I ever received in school?

"I do," she says. "And so will my friends."

My phone rings again, and I excuse myself to check who's calling. Callum's face comes onto the screen. "At last. We thought you fell into a hole. Is Rose still with you?"

I pan the phone so he can see Rose.

Callum winks at me. "I get your priorities," he says. Then he turns his head and shouts, "Yup, he's still on his date. Clearly more important than our pickup game."

"Shit. Did you start already?" I say.

Blake, Linc, and Soren's faces fight for space around Callum's head.

"We're still here," says Soren. "Rink's free for another two hours. Swing by."

Blake pushes forward. "Bring Rose." He waves. "Hi, Rose."

Rose leans in, her shoulder brushing mine. "He needs to learn how to loosen his hips, or he'll never hit the ball into the hole."

The guys roar in laughter.

Callum regains control of the phone. "Now you have to come, Rose. We need to hear about Alek's technique. And you did promise to watch us play, remember?"

"I don't have other plans." Rose glances at me. "Would I mess up your day?"

"Never."

"She's coming, boys. Better lace up," Callum hoots.

Twenty

TWELVE YEARS AGO

November

Today, the desks are set up in a circle like they were in our first class. Professor Patel stands in the middle, slowly clapping as he turns around. "You've made it to week nine." He stops his applause and grabs a stack of envelopes from his desk. Beside me, Alek lifts in his seat, and I feed off his interest.

Something is about to change. We can smell opportunity.

Unlike the yellow ones from two months ago, these envelopes are orange and standard business-letter size. The man definitely enjoys his dramatic elements. "As I won't see you next week when you are hopefully stuffing yourself with whatever your family's favorite Thanksgiving meal is, I would hate if you forgot about what being an entrepreneur is."

"Are you going to give us extra homework because entrepreneurs never get time off?" I ask.

Growing up in the hotel business, I'm all too familiar with working holidays and weekends. They are our busiest times. Our company holiday party is held in January, which is typically the quietest month of the year.

Professor Patel hands me the envelope. "That can be true. Startups require more effort than you might think. But today's lesson is more important. The thing about running your own business is you *are* that business, and if you do not take care of yourself, you are not taking care of your business. Just like you need to pay yourself, as we discussed during our first class on profits, you also need to be your own caretaker and cheerleader. You should be the kind of boss you'd like to have, which means giving yourself a chance to rest."

I hold back my scoff. I'm not sure my mother has had time off since the day she started HH Group. There are photos of her signing the contract for our Miami property between contractions while giving birth to Olivia.

The professor drops the final envelope with the last pair of partners. "I also want you to understand that, as a boss, when you create the kind of company that helps employees, you attract good employees."

"Is it okay with you if I open it?" I ask Alek, who's staring at the envelope in my hand.

"Go for it." His voice is polite, but I miss the Alek from before the paparazzi leaked the photos and I had to have the dating conversation with him. Before this tension stretched like a taut rubber band.

In the three weeks since the pictures of Alek and me skating came out, we've relentlessly used every possible free hour to work on the project. I've seen him more than any other person in my life, between sitting next to him here and curling on the couch in his house as we tore apart each slide of our presentation. Not to mention when he sat on the chair across from me, tirelessly coding the actual app. Our progress on both fronts is way slower than we planned, but I can see Alek's vision coming to life. My presentation is still far too long and I can't figure out how to finish everything in two weeks when we couldn't manage to stick to our plan these past eight weeks.

We are making progress, but why does this level of interaction get under my skin? This is what professionals do. I'm proud I didn't give in to my desire, and I stuck to the clear and logical path of keeping this situation about the project and only about the project.

But still.

I rip the envelope and pull out a piece of paper that's . . . blank. I look up and see equally confused faces of the other students.

"Is it written in invisible ink?" asks Rafael.

"Very clever, but no." The professor crosses his ankles. "This is not an exercise in spy methods. The paper is for you to write down two things you want to do with your project partner over the upcoming break that's not part of your project. Each activity must be what one of you does that the other has never done and vice versa."

"What's the purpose?" says Alek.

"Teambuilding. Nowadays, it's become synonymous with a meaningless waste of time, but the core goal is sound. By spending time together outside of your project, you'll get to know each other on a human level and make your business relationship stronger."

"We've been working together for weeks," I mumble. "Shouldn't we spend the extra time on polishing our presentations instead? Haven't we learned everything helpful by now?"

The professor shrugs. "Maybe you did. But what if you haven't? What if by just hanging out, you gain not only a project partner, but a friend and collaborator for future ventures? Someone who'll be part of your network. When you come up with a new idea, they might be someone you can run the concept by for honest feedback. Or maybe they will be someone you can call for a round of axe throwing to unwind. Making connections is work, but the results are entirely worth the effort in the long run." He taps his temple. "Of course, you could choose to ignore this task. It's not graded or mandatory . . ."

"I sense a but," I say.

Professor Patel's grin is mischievous. "But each complete task gets you an extra three minutes for the presentation. Go ahead and see what you can come up with before the class is over."

I cross my arms and face Alek. "Six extra minutes is not worth spending hours galivanting across town together."

"I didn't take you for a quitter." Alek crosses his arms too.

That rubber band snaps against my skin. "Knowing when to put all my effort forward and when to not participate is a skill. Professor Patel said this is not even graded."

"Not everything in life is about grades." He glares at me. "He clearly stated this is about what happens when class ends."

"You know what happens." My fingers curl around the envelope.

Alek's jaw hardens. "Do I?"

"We are from very different walks of life, and I can't imagine you calling me up to vent or to work on a project together."

His nostrils flare. "Because?"

"Because I will be the CEO of HH Group. My life is charted, and my group of peers is predefined. It's not your crowd."

"Because I'm not a nepo baby."

"That's how you see me?"

He raises his chin. "As if you don't see me in a certain way."

"Fine." The paper creaks in my hands. "If that's what you're getting out of this conversation, that's even more of a reason to skip this optional and time-consuming task."

His eyes darken. "The more you try to get out of doing this, the more it sounds like you're afraid."

"Afraid of what?"

"That's a good question. Does hanging out with me scare you?"

A laugh barks out of me. "We spend hours together every week."

"In this classroom or my living room. You cross the street if you see me on campus. Is it because the paparazzi might photograph us together again? More photos for your mom to disapprove of?"

"Why are you so eager to do them?" I throw the question back.

"First." He holds up a finger. "I agree with Professor Patel. We can learn from each other. Second. I always take the extra credit. And third. Our presentation will be stronger with extra time."

We both glare at each other, our chests rising and falling.

"Fine." I break the standoff. The extra time would let me keep several slides I've been agonizing over. "What do you propose we do?"

"Let's figure out when. I'm at my parents' place for Thanksgiving next week, and you said you're in France with your family."

"Mom's the one in France. Supervising the final touches on the chalet renovations in Courchevel. My plan was to finalize the presentation and help Olivia study for her poli-sci test."

A divot forms between his eyebrows. "Wait, you aren't doing Thanksgiving this year?"

"We're not a Thanksgiving family. Suffering through Christmas is usually enough family time, so we pretend the holiday before doesn't exist."

"Suffering through Christmas? Christmas is the best holiday ever. Thanksgiving is a close second."

"You obviously don't know my family," I huff.

"Then you should come to Thanksgiving."

"I . . ." He can't be serious. "You are not inviting me to dinner with your parents."

"It's not just my parents. We invite some neighbors and friends of the family too." Alek gives me a shy look. "Callum will be there. And Soren. You should bring Olivia. It's loud and full of homemade food that my mama will pile onto your plate." He points to the blank paper in my hand. "And it's what I do that you've never done."

"If I were to potentially agree, what should I wear?"

It's his turn to laugh. "Whatever you want. You can dress up as fancy as you'd like. But I suggest a comfortable outfit since you'll be eating a lot of food and doing silly dances."

I lean back in my chair and contemplate a homecooked meal. The chef at the hotel used to work in a Michelin star restaurant, and Mom's personal chef is sought after. But I'm curious about Russian food cooked by a Russian immigrant. "Will there be turkey and gravy?"

"And sweet potato pie with marshmallows."

"That sounds disgusting."

"Don't knock it until you try it." Alek pulls out his phone.

"What are you doing?"

"I'm texting Mama and telling her to expect two more guests."

"I haven't said yes." My pulse stampedes in my skull. I want to say yes, to see the world that made Alek into the guy I'm liking too much. But the thrill and panic of being seen there sets off alarm bells inside my mind.

He shrugs. "Come or don't come. Either way, you are welcome." He holds up his phone to display the three heart emojis his mother texted back. "Now that we have one item on the list taken care of, what things do you do I've never experienced?"

"Opera? Concert hall?"

"Of course, you'd think of those." He shakes his head. "My parents are both huge fans. I've seen *Tosca* too many times to count, and I take my parents to the symphony once a year."

My eyebrows fly up, trying to picture Alek sitting still in a velvet seat while sopranos echo off the ornate ceiling. It's oddly entertaining imagining him with his parents entranced as a string quartet plays Vivaldi.

"I'm shattering your expectations," he says.

"How about a gala event?"

Alek squints one eye and pulls air through his teeth.

A grin spreads across my face. "Not taking your parents to those once a year?"

"We're not into tuxedos and fancy dresses."

"Sounds like we found a thing you've never done." Finally, something he hasn't already done with his picture-perfect family. "Are you free tomorrow night?"

Twenty-One

ALEK

TWELVE YEARS AGO

November

Callum stands in the doorway to the bathroom with a bowl of cereal in his hand. "The seams across the back are a bit tight. Might not want to make any sudden movements."

"I should've just worn the suit Mama bought at the outlet mall." How would these people know where it came from?

"You'd stick out like a sore thumb."

I fumble with the bow tie, rewind the instructional video on my phone, and try again. "Can I just lose this thing?"

"Wear the fucking bow tie. This charity event is a huge deal, and I can't believe you even scored an invite."

"It's for extra credit for our project. You know that."

"What I know is that you two come up with the most inventive excuses to spend time together." Callum's spoon drops into the bowl. "She could just stop pretending she doesn't like you and ask you out. Or, better yet, you could ask her out, and you could stop pretending you aren't into her."

"She'd never say yes."

"I noticed you didn't deny you like her. That's progress, I guess." He grins. "Remember, nothing ventured means nothing gained."

"I'm not you." I lose track of what to do with the second loop and the bow unwinds. "I don't need to go out with every attractive, intelligent woman I meet."

"So Rose is attractive and intelligent?"

"Of course she's attractive, intelligent, and—"

"Sweet."

"Callum, I will seriously punch you in the mouth if you keep up with that joke. It's not funny." I manage to create a knot that still looks nothing like the one on the video but is at least not complete shit.

The doorbell rings. "Ah, here's the lady now."

I exit the bathroom, jog down the stairs, and swing open the door. As I do, I decide I'm going to this event, tie or not, ripped jacket or not. Because with Rose in that dress, I'm not missing a moment. The light pink fabric highlights her shimmering skin and, as if to torture me, her hair is woven with tiny flowers, exposing her graceful neck. My chest aches with more and more fierceness the longer I look at her.

"Am I early?" She ducks under my arm. Why does the sight of her bare back turn my mouth into a desert?

"You can close it," Callum shouts at me from the entryway into the living room.

I shut the door.

"And your mouth as well." He smirks.

I glare at him, and he waves at Rose. "Have fun, you two. Enjoy your sweet evening."

I double-glare as he winks and climbs the stairs.

Rose walks around me. "Not your size, but you are neither presenting nor receiving any awards tonight, so I approve."

She smiles at me. "We need to take a picture. For Professor Patel." Rose takes my phone from my hand, stands in front of me, and extends the phone for a selfie. "I figure if we document tonight and your Thanksgiving meal, that will be enough proof to earn those extra six minutes for our presentation."

She hands me my phone to show me the picture. My tie looks decent, but Rose looks better than perfect, her eyes sparkling and happy. Just this once, I don't seem like an impostor by her side.

"Well," I start, shoving my phone into my pocket. "Let's see what your life is like."

This is the world of Rose Haliday.

I step into the display of high-end everything—clothes, smiles, hair, and attitudes. Maybe Blake's tuxedo makes me appear like I belong, but the scratchy feeling underneath my sternum insists otherwise. I'm more invisible than when I cross the lobby of the Haliday Hotel in my maintenance uniform. Every gaze lands and remains on Rose, who stuns. I make sure my mouth remains closed and walk by her side, which is harder than I imagined. People stop to ask questions or just chat, surrounding her like she's the host.

I thank yet also curse Professor Patel for making tonight possible.

After the latest wave of faces, some I even recognize, float away, I bend and whisper, "How do you know them?"

"I help organize this event. I've been doing it the last three years."

I give the opulence that surrounds me another glance. "You mean, you did all of this?"

"Oh, no. I assist with general decor. This event is way too big for one person, and we hire companies for most of it." The tasteful shadow of makeup on her eyelids glimmers in the low light. "But I love this. Planning events is fun, and planning events for charities, specifically, offers me the option to give back."

"They probably would appreciate if you donated money."

"I do that every year too." Her fingers fall on the tennis bracelet on her wrist. "I have a long list of nonprofits I work with, but when I'm an integral part of the process, it hits differently."

"Olivia's birthday party, our fundraising event, this gala. Are you sure you want to be the future CEO of HH Group? Not an event planner?"

She laughs, and her hand lands on my elbow as she smiles at me. "You are too funny. I'm the eldest Haliday and, thus, I'm inevitably the future CEO. It's nonnegotiable."

"What if it was?"

Her eyes dim, smile evaporating. "There are tons of event planners. There's only one CEO of HH Group. Besides, I can't betray my mother. I've been training my entire life. I'll be very good at it."

I blow out a breath. "I don't doubt that part. I was just wondering if being the CEO is truly what you want."

"What else could I possibly want?" She narrows her eyes as if I insulted her. "Do you know what you want?"

"I do," I say, and she lifts an eyebrow. "I want to develop apps to help people and be in charge of my own company. I want to earn enough money to make sure my parents never need for anything."

Rose opens her mouth to reply, but a man in a tuxedo that proclaims money, even to my untrained eye, gives Rose a one-sided hug and a couple-second-too-long kiss on her cheek.

"Rose, you look gorgeous, as always." His gaze rakes over her dress and his hand lands on the small of her back. I have no right to, but I want to rip his hand away and plant mine there instead. "Melinda told me you were coming. I'm a little disappointed you didn't call me to pick you up."

Rose steps out of his touch and wraps her fingers around my bicep. "I came with Alek." Her smile is formal and forced. "Dean is a friend of the family." Rose inches closer to me. "Dean, this is Alek. We're working on a school project together."

Dean looks at me as if I just materialized next to Rose. His eyes have an unpleasant glint as his smile widens. "Ah, so he's here for your project?"

"Correct," Rose beats me to the answer. "I promised to show him behind the scenes before the stage gets busy." She pushes me forward. "Keep going," she whispers.

I let her steer me in the direction of the stage, where she shows security a badge she pulls out of her tiny purse. We're waved backstage. Rose continues to drag-push me to a corner, where we stand between two thick black curtains. She glances behind me. "I don't think he followed us."

"Why would he?" Even as I ask it, I'm not sure I actually want the answer.

"He wants to be more than my friend." She sighs, and I hold in a sigh of my own. My jaw clenches and I shift my weight, trying to swallow the resentment clawing up my throat. I can see why her mom wants her with someone like him. He looks like he owns champagne flutes. Rose glanced sideways at me, her fingers toying with the clasp of her bracelet, a nervous tell I'm starting to recognize. "I don't know. Mom says he's husband material, but I just don't see him that way, you know? There's no spark. No . . ." She looks up at me, and her hand flies to my tie. "Can I?"

"Did I screw it up?"

"For someone who doesn't wear bow ties, you did a fine job, but I think I can do better." She lifts her hands. Her floral scent surrounds me and my pulse beats in my ear. I should say no because the thought of her touching me is causing heart palpitations. Yet, for some reason, I nod in agreement.

Her hands almost touch the top of my collarbone. Almost. It might be easier if they actually did touch, or even better, if they were a full room away. Makeup creates a glow on her face with slightly rosy cheeks, glossed lips, and black lashes, but her freckles still peek through. When she lifts her gaze to me, her eyes catch mine.

"Lift your chin," she says. "I know what I'm doing."

I do as she says, and she steps closer. I hold my breath, trying not to look at her. The ruffling of her hands under my chin makes my own pulse the only noise in my ears. This knot must win a Guinness World Record because the torture lasts so much longer than even I imagined possible.

"All done." Rose's voice barely breaks through the chaos of my senses. I breathe out and nod, my voice lost somewhere between my heart and my throat. Even in the dim light backstage, her eyes shine as she peers up at me. Are her cheeks even pinker? Did the stage crew shift the lights? She chews on her glossy bottom lip, and I wish I could ask what she's thinking.

My hand develops a mind of its own and lifts to her face. Tentatively, my forefinger frees her bottom lip from the tight pinch of her teeth. I shouldn't have done that, but now it's as if I can't stop. Every rational part of me warns me to back off, but the feeling parts beg me to stay in this moment. I place my palm on her cheek, half expecting her to step back like she did with Dean.

Instead, she licks her lips, keeping her stare glued to mine. We breathe in tandem. Our inhales come faster and faster.

Am I misreading this? Am I reading too much into this moment?

She's just angry with a guy she doesn't like. Angry with the expectations set on her, maybe, even if she doesn't want to admit it. Since we met our attraction has hung around us like a badly held secret. But she made it clear she didn't want me to act on the pull. Not then. Not now.

Or is Callum right, and we are both pretending? I lower my head, watching her pupils dilate. I run my thumb along the top of her cheekbone and take satisfaction in how her eyelashes flutter. The real kicker, though, is when her mouth opens ever-so-slightly and she arches into me. It wrecks me, how her body seeks mine, how badly I want to give in. I'm desperate to taste every breath she exhales and claim every inch she offers.

Maybe she does want me to act? Her hand moves from my tie to the back of my neck with the tiniest of tugs. I give up, give in, and close the distance, letting my tongue taste the sweetness of her lip gloss as my mouth covers hers. One second I'm upright, the next—the ice gives way. No kiss has made me feel like I'm standing at the threshold of a change I'll never recover from. One more step and I'm a goner. I nip at the corner of her mouth. I'll just have to show her just how interested I am.

Her lips move under mine and she wraps her other hand around my neck, pulling me lower. I go willingly, sinking into her mouth as our tongues meet. Desire surges through my blood, confident and absolute. I want to memorize the way she fits against me and the sound she makes when I kiss her like this. My fingers hold the back of her head, and my hand wraps around her waist as I'm finally allowed to touch her exactly how I want to. It's not just a spark, but an electrical current that's sure to leave us both charred if one of us doesn't pull away. I should be the one to do it, but how could I?

I pull her body closer, press her into mine, and groan when her other hand runs into my hair. She kisses me like she feels this too, urgent yet so fucking sweet. Completely, beautifully undone. Maybe I held off admitting to myself I wanted this, but there is no more pretense to spare in regard to her.

I want Rose Haliday.

Her brilliant brain, her kind heart, her sweet lips, and especially her smart mouth.

All of her.

More of her.

For as long as I can have her.

"You can't be here." A rumbling voice reaches my brain as Rose's warmth disappears from my arms.

I face whoever interrupted us, shielding Rose with my back.

An older man dressed in all black, wearing a headset with his arms crossed, glares at me. "Do I need to call security?"

Rose steps from behind my back, and the expression on the man's face changes from indignation, to surprise, then to admiration. "Ms. Haliday, I didn't realize—"

"It's okay, Austin. We shouldn't be interfering with your work. We'll leave, and you pretend you didn't see us here?" Rose's voice is firm, and although the sentences she said formed a question, the intonation was clear that it was more of a command.

"Understood." The man gives me another passing glance as he disappears behind the curtains.

Rose steps in front of me, her face back to the polite, casual expression she wears most days. But her swollen, no-longer-glossed lips tell the truth. The truth that still pounds my heartbeat in my ears and beneath my ribs.

She can't resist our attraction either.

My self-destructive streak continues and I step closer, brushing my thumb along the bottom of her lip. The same gesture that started this. "The spark you were talking about, the one you don't have with Dean? I felt it."

"A spark?" she says. "Is that what you felt?"

"A whole storm of sparks." Am I a fool for admitting it? I'm standing here, fully clothed, but I somehow feel more naked than I've ever been in a locker room.

Rose's eyes watch me in a silent assessment. My heartbeat hammers in my ears to a dangerous song. I've faced bigger risks before, but none that ever left me this defenseless.

"Tell me you feel it too?" My voice cracks on the last word.

Her gaze flits over my mouth, then back to my eyes. She shakes her head, lifting her hands to move mine off her lip.

Of course.

I should've held back and played it cool. Now, I've scared her from whatever this is. Or maybe what it could have been.

Rose intertwines her fingers with mine and tugs me back the way we came. "I like you, Alek," she says over her shoulder, not looking at me. "I like you more than I should. But what I feel is not important. I shouldn't have kissed you back." The conviction in her tone scares me. "I can't mix work and pleasure. Us dating will cause a scandal, and neither of us has the option to mess up our futures."

Twenty-Two

PRESENT DAY

March

Olivia tosses our empty lunch containers from her favorite Thai restaurant into the trash can. Then she props her feet on the arm of the sofa that stretches along the window of my office. "You really sat in a rink and watched Alek play hockey?"

"And the guys from college. They still hang out."

Olivia plays with the tassels on her skirt. "What do Alek's friends look like now?"

I focus on Olivia's shifty eyes. "Why are you so interested in Alek's hockey buddies?"

"Can't I be curious? Some men age well, while others . . ."

"They haven't aged really. At least, not in a bad way." Heat rises up my neck at the image my brain immediately offers of

Alek in Zoe's studio and the feel of his body close to mine at the golf course. I peek at Olivia from my desk, catching the rise of her eyebrows as she studies me.

I send her a group selfie of the guys and me from the rink. Alek's serious face stares at my cheek on the left, and Callum grins straight into the camera on my right. Blake, Soren, and Linc photobomb us in the back row with rabbit ears and goofy faces.

Olivia's phone pings. She opens the files and grins. "He's so in love with you."

"He's not."

"The sex must be amazing." She moans. "I would love some amazing sex right now."

"Then start dating again. Your dry spell has been more like dry millennia."

"It hasn't been that long. And anyway, I'm all for sex, but I don't have time to meet anyone. The vibrator you bought me for my birthday is doing the job just fine. Still, I'm allowed to be envious of what you and Alek have. I mean, who wouldn't be? Look at you two."

What we have is a mess. My finger drags across my naked wrist where my bracelet usually sits. I should've taken it to the jeweler the moment the clasp started acting up.

"What? Is he bad in bed?" Olivia sits up. "Don't tell me he can't find a clit or doesn't care about your orgasms."

"As much as I love that we are now close enough to discuss our intimate anatomy, that's not the problem. At least, I don't think it is."

"You don't think . . . you haven't had sex with him yet?" Olivia gapes. "Why on earth have you not slept with that fine specimen?"

I can't keep lying to my sister. The truth corrodes me from the inside. Can I risk telling Olivia the truth? She'll never talk to Mom, and lately, it feels like if I don't talk to someone, I'll combust. Can't I have one person who I can talk to about the absurd situation I got myself in? Someone who is not Camp Alek? I set my elbows on my desk and catch Olivia's eye.

"What is it?" she asks with clear caution.

"You have to promise you won't say anything. To anyone. I mean *anyone*, you understand?"

Olivia's finger drags an invisible zipper across her mouth, and the truth spills from me. "We haven't had sex because we aren't actually dating."

The relief is instant, just as I imagined it would be.

Olivia reels back. "Wha . . . what did you just say?"

"Alek and I made a deal. I pretend to date Alek so he can get chummy with Ezra and Leanne for a new company he's launching. And, in return, he agreed to sell his company to Mom."

"You sly devil. Shit, my sister is a fantastic actress. You'll get an Oscar next." Her eyebrows scrunch. "Mom doesn't know?"

"She thinks I'm leading Alek on. When he signs, I'm supposed to break up with him."

"So you are lying to . . . basically everyone."

"I'm not lying to Alek. He doesn't need to know what Mom thinks." My stomach cramps with the discomfort I've been trying to avoid. One that screeches with guilt. "I didn't tell you to judge me. I need help figuring out this mess."

Olivia nods and lowers to the couch. "Tell me about the mess."

"Like I said, he's in this for access to my friends, and I need his company." I stare at the board with the tables for the upcoming anniversary party. "My body has other ideas. As if because we pretend we are dating, we are actually dating. I have not had such a reaction to a man touching me since . . ." I shut my eyes. Since Alek touched me in college. I squeeze my thighs together. "This shouldn't be happening."

"You forget I was there at UCLA. I saw how he affected you. It makes total sense that your feelings for him are back."

"I'm not talking about feelings. There are no feelings." I slump in my chair. "If I could only have sex with him to get him out of my system and then pretend it never happened. That would put an end to this silly attraction."

"So, have sex."

My eyes sting as I stare at the ceiling. "He has to want sex with me for that to happen. And if you missed the earlier part of the conversation, what he wants is the Menkens. The lie I told Mom is that he's interested in me."

"Oh, he is interested. The photo." Olivia brandishes her phone in the air like the key piece of evidence in a major trial. "I'll bet next year's marketing budget he says yes the moment the offer comes out of your mouth."

The phone on my desk comes to life with an incoming call. I hold up my finger and mouth "Menkens" to Olivia before hitting answer. "Leanne, hello. How's Venezuela?"

"We're having a blast. Sorry I've been so long getting back to you, but Ezra's two-line cameo has turned into a three-day shoot. He'll deny it, but he loves being back in front of the camera," Leanne purrs. "But yes, we'd absolutely love for Alek to join us in Georgia. We can't wait to meet him in two weeks."

I thank her and confirm our arrival plans. When she hangs up, I do a happy dance in my chair. Now that I know more about Second Chance, I'm convinced my father's godparents are the perfect partners to launch Alek's new venture.

The desk phone beeps. Leanne hasn't changed her mind already, has she? I push the speakerphone.

"Mr. Alek Orlov is here for you, Ms. Haliday," says Helen, my executive assistant.

My skin tingles, and I glance at the door as if he's about to walk through. I clear my throat. "Let him in."

The moment I hang up, Olivia stands and grins. "I'll let myself out. But you should really think about asking him. No man who looks at you like he does is going to say no." She leaves me alone with my thoughts, in my office that feels ten degrees warmer than the thermostat shows.

I take a compact out of my bag, check to make sure I don't have anything in my teeth from lunch, and apply a fresh layer of lip gloss. But then I wipe the gloss off because I'm not preparing for Alek, and this is what I look like if he decides to ambush me in my office. This is not a date, of course, and I'm definitely not trying to seduce him.

The knock on the door pulls me back to my feet. Alek stands in the doorway, a large pot of slightly wilted miniature roses in his hands. "I didn't mean to show up unannounced, but I'm leaving for Boston tonight, and I thought you might miss this."

I stare at the roses. With a consistent watering regime and some pruning, they'll be back to their glory in no time. "Miss the roses?"

Alek approaches my desk, sets down the pot of roses, and opens his palm. "Your tennis bracelet. I found it on the seat in my car. I drove straight here."

Tears prick at the back of my eyes. "I made the entire golf club search with metal detectors. I was certain I lost it there."

My hand covers his palm, and I should take the bracelet back, but like a person starved for touch, I linger on the calloused pads of his fingers. His thumb grazes my pinkie and my breath hitches, reminding me this is the last thing I should be doing.

I meet his gaze, the chocolate color of his eyes melted and gooey today. My "thank you" snags at the end.

"You never take it off. Is it important to you?"

"My father bought it when the ultrasound showed they were having a girl." Tenderness glazes the cracks in my heart from the pain of love I know but have never felt. "My mom insists he couldn't wait to meet me and said it was the first of many gifts he wanted to shower me with." I run my finger over the inscription that says, "I love you, Rose. Dad." Like this bracelet, the loss I carry never leaves. I blink away a tear. I won't cry, not now. "He loved my mom, but he already loved me too."

I try to close the clasp around my wrist. My hands shake, and I curse under my breath. Alek's long fingers catch the side of the bracelet with the clasp, and together, we attach the loop. He gently twists and settles the diamonds along my wrist.

His fingers run against the tips of mine, across the oversensitive skin where my pulse betrays the escalating beats of my heart. It's too much. The heat that grows when Alek is near ignites my chest. Because, once again, my body wants more. It wants what I can't have and what I definitely shouldn't want. This is only a physical reaction to an objectively attractive man, not my reaction to this particular man.

"Thanks," I muster as I lower my wrist and watch the familiar glint of the bracelet that's been saying "I love you" in a voice I never got to hear in person. My father's voice. The words he whispered to Mom on their prom video that I caught her rewatching. The words I long for someone to say to me again, and mean it.

Alek's hand drops to his side as softness flits over his face as if he's in awe of this side of me, the part I don't share with anyone. Quietly, as if not to disturb the moment, Alek points to the pale pink roses. "I saw these at the flower shop on the corner, and I thought they might be a good fit for your collection." He nods to the array of mismatched plants stretching to the sunlight on my windowsill.

"You remembered." I tear my gaze away and cross the room as his steps trail me. I place the pot in the middle, turn, and grip the windowsill behind me. "Thank you. You've made my day. Maybe I'll make yours?"

"It's been a great day already."

My lips twitch. "Leanne Menken called. You're officially invited to spend the weekend for the Masters. They can't wait to meet my boyfriend."

"Oh yeah?" He regards me as if I'm a puzzle and he's itching to put all the pieces together. No judgment. Just . . . appreciation? Heat spreads from my ribs up my neck. Him looking at me like this is sending a line of shivers down my torso as my body reminds me how close we are. It also reminds me of how much I enjoyed yesterday at the golf course when he was even closer.

Anticipation charges the space around us, creating a tension that pools low between my thighs. I have no excuse to kiss Alek again. I straighten and let my chin follow, and Alek's gaze unmistakably drops to my mouth. My gaze is glued to his slightly parted lips, so close I just need to stand on my tiptoes in order to breach the gap.

"Rose." My door flies open and Mom strides in as if this is her office, as if she didn't drill the importance of knocking into me since I was a toddler. "We need to discuss . . . Oh, Mr. Orlov. I didn't know you were on-site." Something about the way she says the phrase, a little too polished, makes me think she absolutely knew he was here. In my office.

"Do you have news about the contract?" She assesses the lack of distance from me to Alek. "Or is this visit all . . . pleasure?"

"Mom." I shove off the window and stand between her and Alek. She shouldn't be asking us that. "We're at work."

"Do you think it's a smart idea to have sex in your office?" Mom crosses her arms, making me feel like I'm a teenager.

Alek faces Mom. "She's an adult, and she's capable of deciding what to do or what not to do in her own office. With her boyfriend, might I add."

The corners of Mom's lips tighten. "Well, Mr. Orlov. If you don't mind, my daughter and I were about to have a meeting. In her office. In my company. Where I'm the CEO. I hope next time I get the pleasure of seeing you in person, you are ready to sign a contract."

"Ms. Haliday, if you insist on this level of unprofessionalism, I can find another buyer from the several offers for my company, despite my feelings for Rose."

My heart leaps to my throat. I know this is an act for my mother, but no one has ever defended me like this.

"Rose." Alek traces my lower lip with his thumb. "I'll call you to iron out the details." He leans in and places the barest of kisses on my mouth, then nods to Mom. "Melinda."

My mother glares at Alek as he strolls out of the office. "Good riddance." She takes a seat behind my desk. "My only consolation is this is all for show."

Is this for show? Yes, we've kissed twice now, and both times were in front of an audience. But before Mom arrived, I could have sworn Alek was about to kiss me for real. The promise almost clings to my skin, like a reassurance I don't want to lose. Hope crackles where it shouldn't, tangling with the simmering desire low in my belly. Maybe Olivia is right. Maybe Alek is interested.

"Did you hear me?"

My mother's demand snaps me back to the room. "What was that?"

"I said, the minute he signs the deal, you break up this farce. Chad and I had a long conversation yesterday."

"I'm not going to marry Chad."

"No, of course not. Not yet." She waves a hand. "I only promised to maybe interfere on his behalf, invite him over so the two of you can talk again."

I sink into the guest chair across from her. "I won't see him again either. I'm not interested in Dean 2.0."

She sighs, like I've brought shame on the family. "Is it so selfish of me to expect an heir to the Haliday empire? I haven't worked to build all this," she spreads her arms wide, "for my legacy to disappear."

"Why not focus on Olivia? She's single."

Mom raises her upper lip. "Olivia is not my heir. You are. You will be CEO, and all I'm asking for is grandkids."

"That's a lot to ask."

Her face hardens. Her fingers click against the glass of my desk. "Becoming the next CEO of HH Group is a lot to ask as well."

We eye each other. At a standstill. Mom has the upper hand, and she knows it. I want to flop on the floor, throw a temper tantrum, and shout that I refuse. Mom straightens. "So, should I tell Helen to find some dates for your dinner with Chad?"

"Fine. After we sign with TRI." The heaviness in my heart envelops me. A deal is a deal. And I'm juggling too many of them.

Twenty-Three

TWELVE YEARS AGO

November

The driver drops Olivia and me in front of a tiny front yard with a well-tended succulent-scaped border surrounding a beige bungalow, almost identical to the other green, blue, yellow, and orange ones along this street. The palm tree in the yard next door rustles unkept dry leaves so hard that I step away from that side of the driveway.

"Is it even safe here?" Olivia looks up and down the sidewalk lined with cars, indicating which houses are hosting Thanksgiving.

"It's a perfectly safe, working-class neighborhood." I make sure I sound calm, even though my stomach flipped so many times on the drive here I'm afraid any food I attempt to eat today will be coming right back up. "Do you have the dessert?"

Olivia holds up a paper bag from the caterer HH Group uses. A cascade of laughter spills from behind the fence that stretches between Alek's parents' bungalow and the one with the in-need-of-care palm tree. The side gate is open and a hand-written sign in orange permanent marker says: Orlov's Thanksgiving This Way.

"We go in and I get the proof for Professor Patel to earn the extra three minutes. I have an alarm set on my phone. When that goes off, we'll come up with an emergency at the hotel, and we'll leave."

The image of him kissing me at the gala, of me responding, without an ulterior motive to his kiss . . . My lips tingled for hours after, and my lungs squeeze every time I thought about the way he looked at me. This kiss was a mistake, I know it was, but the memory doesn't feel like one. We're supposed to be project partners, not more, which is exactly why I need to spend as little time around him as possible. I tuck my least fancy-looking long-sleeved shirt into my jeans and hope Alek wasn't joking that casual-casual is what most people will be wearing.

"But if it's fun, we can stay, right?" Olivia's eyes shine with excitement as we cross the cracked and discolored concrete of the driveway, the sounds of a party mere yards away growing unmistakable. Laughter seems to be a constant element, because once one enthusiastic bout ends, another begins. A tightness coils in my belly, my steps faltering as we get closer. What if I don't belong here? What if this whole thing is a mistake?

"We'll see," I say, not wanting to commit and get her hopes up. My sister has a tendency to get carried away, even when it's not what's best for anyone involved.

A small panel building juts off a cement patio surrounding the back of the bungalow and a path stretches along one of the fences. I spin the diamond bracelet on my wrist. My smile feels brittle, my stance too upright, too formal for a space like this. The gathering is a collection of tables with platters of food, clusters of chairs where young kids play, and people standing around, drinking beer from bottles.

The sounds and smells are overwhelming, and they're a far cry from the quiet demureness of one of my galas. Maybe the extra minutes aren't worth this. My chest feels too tight, my breath too shallow, and I swear my ears are ringing. My skin prickles with the urge to escape, to bolt before anyone notices me. I can turn around and run.

"Well, hello there you two," Callum's voice snatches my attention. Relief spreads through my shoulders, loosening the tension. Callum is familiar, a tether to something known and safe. I wave at the same time as Olivia's hand rises.

"This is Alek's roommate, Callum," I whisper to her.

"I know. I met him at the Halloween party."

Right. I take the bag from Olivia's hand. "Where should we put dessert?"

"On the deck. Alek just went to get his Mom's signature bli-ni." Callum points to a low rectangular table covered in a plastic orange tablecloth. The late November weather is mild and the likelihood of the cake melting is minimal, even for the flourless dairy-free chocolate ganache vegan masterpiece I chose.

I leave Olivia to Callum, who asks if she's thirsty. I take the few steps up to a deck that's smaller than the balcony of my suite. Alek's eyes widen as he walks through the glass door and sees me. A plate with what looks like rolled stuffed crepes wob-bles in his hand.

The sight of Alek hits me like a blast of hot air. He's not in a suit, but somehow the way the fabric of his shirt clings to his torso makes him even more lethal. I set the cake on the table among the desserts that look like they multiplied through some kind of sugar-fueled magic, including slices of what must be pumpkin pie and a bowl of strawberries so ripe they look like they might bruise if you breathe on them wrong.

"You came?" Alek asks, bringing my attention to him. He's in soft jeans and a plain long-sleeved shirt, pushed up on strong forearms, and his hair is slightly mussed like he's run a hand through it one too many times this evening.

"That was the deal."

"Good," Alek rasps as he hovers between the door and me. There's an ease in the way he holds his weight on one leg, but his eyes—those eyes—make my heart speed up.

He looks like comfort wrapped in heat. Like someone you could lean into . . . or get burned by. I shove my hands into the pockets of my jeans, my heart speeding up. What do I do now?

I look anywhere but at his mouth. Because if I look at his mouth, I'll remember how it felt on mine, and if I remember that, I'll forget all the reasons I shouldn't want his lips against mine again. And I do. I need to focus on literally anything else.

From the higher ground of the deck, I watch another person walk into the yard. Like a pebble thrown into a lake, the surface of guests ripples with hugs and greetings. They didn't do it for me because I'm not part of this world. This is just for the project.

I nod to a table with drinks, where Callum is mixing a cocktail that better be nonalcoholic, but I'm certain isn't, into a glass for Olivia. "I brought Olivia. Who else is here?"

"Soren's around somewhere, and Blake might pop in later after his family dinner. We're going to The Devil's Martini once we're done. Do you want to come?"

"Unlikely," I say, with the slightest hint of regret in my tone that surprises even me. I risk a glance back at him. "I still need to finish the presentation. Are you done with the code?"

"Finished the registration page this morning." He lifts his chin, his eyes locked on me. "How much do you have left to do?"

"With the six extra minutes we will now have, I want to expand the benefits analysis section. Maybe a couple of days to polish everything up? I'll be ready."

"I don't doubt you will." The gravel in his voice sends a wave of chills through me.

I drop my gaze and slip my phone out of my back pocket. "Photo? For Professor Patel?"

"Right." Alek holds up the tray of blini and gestures with his free arm to come in close.

I should be stepping farther away from him, not closer. But this is for the project. I can stand by him for a quick picture. I steel myself and step into the Alek zone, my hip hitting his. I raise my phone.

"Say cheese." It's too easy to smile with his arm over my shoulder. His body radiates warmth, and I catch the subtle woodsy scent that makes my knees waver. He's just close enough that I can feel heat from his skin through my shirt. I pry myself from under his forearm and check to make sure the image is good. My pulse thrums in my ears. "Got it."

Alek's gaze follows the trail of flush that must be spreading across my neck based on how hot it feels. His study ends on my mouth. I bite my bottom lip. My heart is now in my head, chest, and throat. Alek swallows hard.

He drops the tray on the dessert table and picks up one of the blini. "Would you like a bite?"

I shut down the "yes, please." My stomach, which was threatening to explode earlier, changes its mind and fills with fire that's now engulfing my entire body. This is a bad idea. I have the picture. I should turn around and flee. I press my thighs together. But the deprived girl in me rejects the panicky thoughts. I stare straight into Alek's eyes and take one step closer to the delicious treat I've been denying myself.

"I haven't washed my hands yet." I trace the heel of my palm with my index finger.

"There's a solution." He arches his eyebrow, his stare heated, and brings the food to my mouth. "My hands are very clean."

I lean forward, my lips hovering over his fingers holding the morsel. "I thought you like getting dirty."

"I might. Is that how you like it?"

"Depends."

"Would you like to find out?"

"Yes, please," finally escapes.

Under his laser focus on my every move, I stretch my neck, open my mouth, and take a bite.

Of the crepe concoction.

The combination of jam with the soft, sweet shell of the dough explodes on my tongue. A whole storm of sparks almost as good as the kiss we shared. I moan.

Alek's gaze is locked on my lips as I lick them. His stare travels down my throat as I swallow, and when his eyes meet mine again, the expression I read is hungry. The kiss I've been pretending did not happen reignites over my lips just from the fever in Alek's gaze.

I lean forward and take another bite, my lips grazing his fingers. His nostrils flare, and he places the final bite into his mouth, licking the fingers my lips were just on.

"Delicious," he says, and anyone listening would assume he's referring to the blini. To me, with the memory of the gala as vivid as if it happened moments ago, I know he's not. And I wholeheartedly agree.

Alek lifts another and one eyebrow, then he brings the food to my mouth. The palpable tension around us tightens, and breathing is difficult. It's as if the whole backyard is lacking oxygen. I want to open my mouth and take a bite. But not of the dessert. I want to bite Alek's lip. Right here in front of everyone instead of behind backstage curtains. I sway, and my head inches to Alek as my body craves him. His gaze drops to my lips again, and I don't know what's going through his mind, but I want his thoughts to be as needy and urgent as mine are. I want him to desire me. Is that so bad?

"Where are the blini?' Callum walks up the steps and I back away from Alek. "Olivia has never had a Russian pancake."

"Here." Alek shoves the tray at Callum, which he barely grabs without the blini falling. "Rose needs to wash her hands. I'm showing her the bathroom."

Alek wraps his fingers around mine and tugs me around Callum, across the wooden deck, our bodies frantic, our breaths labored. In seconds, he ushers me into the room with pink vintage tile and a plastic pink curtain hanging around the tub. He locks the door behind us and takes two steps across the room to the other door, which I assume leads to another room or a hallway. The click of that lock is almost louder than the first.

It's not as loud, though, as the pounding of my heart in my ears or my own inhale.

If the backyard lacked oxygen, the bathroom must contain none at all because my breaths are short and almost painful when Alek pushes me against the door and sucks my lower lip into his mouth. My vision swims, and my confused stomach clenches as my entire body tightens. I reach for Alek's shirt, fisting the material as my wrist grazes the skin on his stomach.

With a sharper inhale, Alek freezes, then he finds both of my hands and holds them above my head. His lips are back on mine, and, without the ability to touch him, I bow my back to meet his body. He moans as our mouths bite and tease and roughhouse, tackling each other in fast, hot exchanges, fighting for dominance and submission, eager to give and to receive.

My hips buck and the ridge of Alek's hard length is unmistakable beneath the zipper of his jeans. I grind against him, happy the material of my jeans is stiff enough for friction to press against my underwear in just the right way. The rub of the hard seam on my clit is almost enough. He moves his hips, finding the rhythm I can only imagine would be even more delicious if our jeans were out of the way.

Alek's stomach presses into mine as I wrap one leg around him, looking for a better angle, for more friction, for the release my body is screaming for. With a groan, he releases my hands to find my butt and pins me exactly where the bulge in his pants fits perfectly against me. I squeeze my legs as Alek kneads my ass and sucks on my neck as if he can get closer than we already are.

After an almost-too-hard thrust of his hips, I grab onto his shoulders tightly, hungrily kissing him with my sore lips. I'm chasing my release as if he's my personal highway to orgasm, and I don't care what it takes to get the climax teetering my body on the edge of bliss. One of his hands leaves my ass and trails up my side, underneath the lacy cup of my bralette. His moan vibrates against my tongue, and my skin burns icy-hot where his palm touches the partially exposed skin of my breast.

"So close," I moan into his mouth.

Alek's finger drags over my nipple. I gasp. He pinches the stiff peak lightly, then a little harder, and I'm there. My body clenches, then releases as wave after wave of sharp pleasure washes over my stomach and chest. I throw back my head, absorbing the aftershocks that empty my lungs of tension. Everything is still. Our hips, hands, and chests are locked in our bliss.

I open my eyes to find Alek's scorching gaze roaming my face. His cheeks are flushed, and his lips may need several treatments at the salon to undo the damage of my chewing on them. His hair is mussed and the bulge in his jeans that brought me so much delicious friction is most definitely still there. I came, but he didn't. I attempt to wiggle down his body but Alek doesn't let go. He kisses me lightly. I rock my hips.

"Don't." His voice is low and thick. "I don't have much control left."

"That was control?" I don't want to tease him because, to me, what we did in this bathroom demonstrated an utter lack of control. I've never in my life behaved like this wild girl, wanting and needing. My control disappeared the second both locks clicked. Or maybe it was earlier on the deck. My usual, measured attitude during sex vanished, and I don't want it back.

"What are you like when you're out of control?" I whisper.

His gaze darkens. I fear his answer yet also need to hear it.

"No jeans," he says quietly, as if he's afraid to break the moment. "You, bent over that sink. Me, buried deep inside you."

I don't care about reconciling this bluntly speaking about sex guy with the competitive but nice guy I've gotten to know. He paints a picture of us naked and sweaty, him pressed against me. The need I thought the orgasm sated is back with a vengeance. I want the out-of-control side of Alek. I want him right now.

I repeat the rocking motions with my hips and reach for his fly. "It's my turn."

He catches my hand. "I need a second."

"To do what?"

A low laugh rumbles through him. "To get myself together and not actually fuck you in a bathroom."

"What if I want you to fuck me in this bathroom?"

"I don't think you want our first time to be me bending you over the sink."

"You keep promising that." I unzip my jeans and peel them off.

His low "fuck" crushes into me. He clasps his hands behind his neck, his jaw ticking. "No matter how much I want you, I don't have a condom. I didn't exactly plan for this to happen."

"You're still a nice guy." I run my fingers below my navel. "I have an IUD. And I'm clean." The chocolate in his eyes is as molten as my core. I want him to find out how wet he made me. I tug at the lace of my underwear and meet his eyes. "I had my annual before the start of the semester."

He stares back at me. "That was four months ago."

"I haven't slept with anyone since." I pull my underwear down and step out.

Alek's eyes widen. His greedy stare roams my exposed skin. He licks his lips and shakes his head. I fan my hands over the soft hill of my stomach, dip my finger into the wetness I need him to taste.

He grips the corner of the counter, and his knuckles go white.

"I had my physical in May," Alek grumbles. "And I haven't been with anyone, either. I couldn't even notice anyone with you around." He doesn't move.

I lift my finger to my mouth and suck.

"You win." His hands fly off the counter and land on my hips.

A possessive pride I don't have any right to feel fills me. I grind into him. "The moment you're inside me, I need you to forget how nice you can be. Do you understand?"

"Just tell me what you want, and I'll do it." He traces the long line of my neck. "But if you ever need me to stop, tell me."

He spins me to face the mirror, places each of my palms on the counter, and runs his hand along my spine, settling his fingers on my ass. He presses his hard length along the still-aching part of me.

His body arches over mine, and he whispers into my ear. "Do you still want me to fuck you right here? To bend you over like this?"

I nod.

"I'll need a verbal confirmation on this one."

"Yes." Never before has this reckless desire burned in me. To do exactly what Alek said. I need the feel of him inside me like I need oxygen.

"Good girl."

Twenty-Four

ALEK

TWELVE YEARS AGO

November

I turn Rose to face the mirror, place each of her hands on the counter, and run my right hand along her spine, settling it on her ass that's inches away from my painfully hard cock. The dream of our first time being gentle and proper on her soft and perfect bed flies out the window. I grin. When do Rose and I ever do anything the easy way?

My body arches over hers, and I whisper into her ear. "Do you still want me to fuck you right here? To bend you over like this?"

She nods.

"I'll need a verbal confirmation on this one."

She licks her lips. "Yes."

"Good girl." I straighten.

I should go slow. I should acquaint myself with every inch of her, but I want to know if she's wet. If she wants this as much as I want her to want me.

My fingers skim over the curve of her hip and dip down below her navel, cupping the spot I'm after. I press my chest into her back and hiss into her neck when my finger parts her seam and sinks into her drenched warmth. My cock begs to be where my finger is. I could plunge myself into her right now, but this isn't the time. I nip her jaw, testing if I need to stop or if she's reconsidering. But she moves her hips, sinking my finger deeper inside her.

Her palms drag along the bathroom countertop. I hold still, offering the knuckle of my thumb to grind against. Two of my fingers are inside her now. Rose moves and finds a rhythm I match, thrusting my hand up as she lowers herself faster and deeper. Her head falls back against my shoulder, and I allow myself to kiss and bite the arc of her neck as she loses herself. With her eyes closed and her cheeks and neck flushed, she digs her fingers into my thigh and stills. Rose's orgasm spasms around my fingers, a contradiction of pulsing muscles inside her to the frozen grasp on the outside. She breathes a long sigh of satisfaction and relaxes under me.

I bring my slippery fingers to my mouth. I wanted my first taste of her to be my tongue licking her folds, but I'll take anything I can get. The salty-sweet tang of Rose hits the back of my throat. Now that I know how wet and sleek she is, my cock jerks, aching to slide into her. I grind my erection into Rose's parted thighs.

Her eyes flutter open and in the mirror I watch her as I suck my fingers. Her already large pupils expand to cover the mosaic of colors in her eyes. She knows exactly where those fingers have been and what I'm tasting. She twists in my arms and licks the base of my fingers not inside my mouth, then sweeps her tongue up to meet mine. The messy dance of us kissing and licking her climax off my fingers is hotter than any kiss we've shared before.

Seeing her mouth around my fingers heightens my need for those lips to be wrapped around my cock. I want that. I want everything.

Her mouth sucking me into delirium.

My cock deep inside her, wet and wanting and hot.

My fingers back into her as she grinds against me, pleasure etched in her face.

All of these. Right now. In a row. Never to end. She consumes me inside and out.

We rock into each other, my hard-on still trapped inside my jeans. "You like that?"

She wiggles below me. "It's a start."

I bite off the groan at her breathless voice. "What else do you want me to give you?"

"You know."

"Maybe. But I need to hear you say it." I find the shell of her ear. "Here's another promise—whatever you tell me to do, I'll do." I nip her earlobe. "All you need to do is ask."

"You promised to bury yourself deep inside me."

My vow coming out of her mouth is too perfect. I raise my hand and show her my glistening fingers while undoing the button of my jeans with the other.

"Yes, but," she pants. "Not just your finger." Her palm brushes against my crotch.

"What then?" I curve over her back and remind her, "You say it, and I'll do it."

"Fuck, Alek. Your cock." She palms me again. "Please."

I'm gone. Control out the window. Brain off, dick on. A low "fuck" rumbles out of me as I pull my cock out of my boxers. Teasing her was almost too much foreplay, but hearing her say the words was so much hotter than I anticipated.

A wiggle of the bathroom door handle freezes both of us in place.

"Someone in there?" A voice sounds from the deck-side door.

"Just a second," I say, my throat constricting.

Rose is fumbling to put her underwear back on, her fingers refusing to cooperate. I push her hands aside, help her back into her jeans, and shake my leg in an attempt to lessen the pressure in my own pants.

The handle twists again. "My daughter really needs to go."

"I'll be right out."

With my hand on her elbow, I drag Rose to the other door, unlock it, and push her into the bedroom. My body yells to not let her go. Before my brain loses another battle, I instruct, "Go into the hallway, all the way to the end, then take a right and another right."

I close the door on her beautiful face.

I cross the room, unlock the other door, and push past my cousin. "All yours."

Fresh air pours into my lungs on a deep inhale, my eyes scanning for Rose as I stand on the deck. Soren jogs up the stairs and stands beside me. "You seen Callum? He has my keys, and I need to pick up Blake."

My nails dig into the wood railing. "Nope."

Soren eyes me. "You okay, buddy? You got that look on your face you get when the ref calls an unfair penalty for high sticking."

"I need to find Rose."

"Ah." Soren backs up. "Now I get it. I think I saw her out on the driveway, texting."

"What?" I abandon Soren, run down the stairs, dodging guests like opposing team members, and spill out onto the driveway.

It's empty.

I yank on my hair. "Fuck."

EVEN WITH MAMA AND Papa buying my half-baked, "She had a work emergency," explanation, Rose disappearing from my parents' party was bad. I stab the elevator button for the twenty-third floor. Her ignoring my texts for the rest of the night is a bigger sign than the DO NOT ENTER I hung on my door as a teenager.

But we aren't teenagers, and although kissing her was not the plan, especially not in my parents' bathroom, I know she was on board with what happened. Her running away and this silent treatment makes no sense.

Right now, I need sense.

I step out of the elevator on Rose's floor. My heartbeat pulses in my neck as I knock on the door of her suite.

"Just leave the food outside," Rose shouts.

I knock louder.

"Leave it outside." Rose's voice is closer.

I want to kick the door. Instead, I knock again, trying to keep my irritation in check. Seems she didn't read my texts. If she did, she'd know it's me. I knock with all the anger I cannot push into a kick.

The door barely opens. A sliver of Rose in a silky robe appears, her hair damp and her face freshly clean. Through the narrow opening, her gaze lands on me. "Why are you here?"

"Why are you here instead of eating the chocolate cake you brought to my parents' house?"

Her face hardens. "This is where I live."

"Well, I'm here because this is where you are."

"So you're stalking me?"

"I'm checking in on you to make sure you're okay. That I didn't mess us up." I grip the doorframe. "That I didn't misread the signals."

"What us?" She opens the door a little wider. "And what signals?"

My fingers squeeze the metal of the doorframe. "You grinding on my cock in my parents' bathroom?"

Rose opens the door wide, drags me in, and looks around the hallway. She slams the door shut. "There are guests in both of the other suites, so please refrain from shouting about . . . your parents' bathroom."

"You think the guests have never heard the word bathroom before?"

"They probably have never heard about me," she starts with a swallow, then whispers, "grinding on your cock before."

I clench my jaw. Her lips talking about my cock makes the fool in my pants react. Getting hard is not what I currently need, though. I shove my hands into my pockets. "You asked me a question, and I answered it. Although you were in that bathroom with me, and unless I imagined everything, you were very much into it."

She crosses her arms, the robe she's wearing gaping slightly over her breasts. "I was until you shoved me out of there."

"I didn't shove—okay, I did, but it was only to make sure no one saw us together."

Her head tilts. "I suppose you didn't want to get caught slumming it with a Haliday?"

"What?" I glare at her. She raises her chin, and I suck air in through my teeth. "I didn't want us to get caught hooking up at the party, especially the first time my family was meeting you. I wanted to introduce you properly. I pushed you out of the bathroom for your sake." I pinch the bridge of my nose. "We got caught backstage and you said kissing was a mistake." I push my fingers through the mess of my hair. "If it were up to me, I'd kiss you everywhere, and I'd do it in front of anyone. I would scream from the hilltops that you're my girlfriend."

She rocks backward. "I'm not your girlfriend."

I gawk at her. If a label is the problem, I can solve it right now. I explained to her, all she needs to do is tell me. I clear my throat and catch her gaze. My heart drums strong and certain.

"Rose Adeline Orson Haliday." I lower myself to one knee in front of her. "The first time I met you here in this room, I thought you were the most beautiful woman I'd ever seen. The more I got to know you, the more I learned you are so much more than your beauty. You are smart and kind, driven and competitive, but also generous." I take her hand. "All of which makes you so easy to love. My heart has been yours for a while, but I'd like to offer you all of me." I draw my thumb over her palm. "Be my girlfriend?"

Tears well in her eyes, but she doesn't say anything. The silence stretches and my confidence wanes. My hands go clammy, and I let go of hers. Maybe I shouldn't have come here. Maybe I should've given her space. I rise. "You don't want to be together?" My voice croaks with disbelief.

A tear runs down her cheek and drips onto the collar of her white robe, leaving a gray spot, then another. Her chin wobbles as she brushes past me and runs into her bedroom.

My chest implodes, and I drag my heavy limbs toward the door. I should leave, but the fact that I made her cry kills me inside. I need to make sure she's okay.

The California king in her bedroom is undisturbed. I step in further and see Rose's reflection in the mirror through the gaping bathroom door.

Rose wipes her eyes with a tissue but stops the moment she sees me. She drops her hand and turns.

"Are you okay?" I approach, unsure if I'm crossing a boundary, or where the boundary even is.

"Why are you still here?"

"I need to make sure you're okay."

"I'm not okay." She slams her palms on my torso, and the physical pain is nothing in comparison to how shitty I feel for upsetting her. She clutches my shirt. "I'm not sure I'll ever be okay."

"What can I do?" I put my hand on top of her fist.

She pushes me away. "You've done enough."

"Tell me." My voice cracks. "You know I'll do anything you want. I promised."

"I need to not like you. I need to *not* forget about my responsibilities. I need to not have this feeling in my chest like you're the only person I want to be around. I need to remember I'm a Haliday."

"You can be a Haliday and like me. Those are not mutually exclusive." My brain is failing to comprehend what Rose is telling me. "I don't understand."

"That's exactly it. You don't understand. In my world, I don't have the freedom you do. My life is prearranged. Every step I take is a new domino in a long line leading to my goal: CEO of HH Group. Meeting you threw me off balance. I'm out of control. I kissed you at the gala. I almost fucked you in the bathroom. I want to drag you into my bed and peel your clothes off and do"—she wipes her hands over her face—"everything."

"I want that too."

Her eyes plead with me. "It's not that easy. Sex has always been simple, but with you, it's not. Because I know with you it won't be just sex. If we go there, it will mean more." She wipes her eyes with her sleeve. "More will set off a chain reaction that'll alter both our lives." Rose pulls the sides of her robe together. "I don't think I can do it."

"You can't, or your mom doesn't want you to?"

"Why can't it be both?"

"Is it your mom?" I bargain.

"No, it's about what *I* want."

"From everything I've learned about you, you crave freedom, and you crave making decisions of your own." My limbs turn to concrete, unwilling to move, but I have to go or I'll be the asshole who pushes her to do what *I* want. I take a step back. "The entrepreneurship class, making the fundraiser work at the ice rink, and coming to my house just to get three minutes for our presentation. You always find ways." We're back at the entrance. "If you decide to be with me." I open the door and step over the threshold. "If you decide you want more. Come find me."

Rose's quiet tears me apart.

No answer. But that is the answer.

She looks at her bare feet, sighs, and slams the door.

Just like on the elevator the day we met, her face disappears behind another door, showing me exactly what boundary lies between us. Solid and definite.

I stumble to the elevator button and look over my shoulder, waiting for her to run after me.

The hallway is empty and quiet.

The elevator dings.

I step in. Still alone. Still waiting. Still in love with the woman who refuses to love me back.

TWENTY-FIVE

ALEK

PRESENT DAY

April

The house the Menkens apparently rent every year to attend the Masters Golf Tournament is a newer building with a guard at gates followed by a winding road shrouded by trees that must have been meticulously planted when this place was built. I drive my rental SUV to the front door, per Rose's instructions, and am pulling out my phone to text her when the door opens.

There she is.

My lungs fill at the sight as she steps out, fresh and smiling. I regret not coming sooner. Mentoring future CEOs and innovators for two weeks with Professor Patel has reminded me of all the good they can do in the world. But not seeing Rose for that long created a crater in my world only her presence can fill.

She extends her hand, and I happily take hold. I could get used to this.

"You made it." She brushes my lips with a faint kiss that mirrors the one I gave her in her office the last time I saw her. I know the gesture is for show and the Menkens must be watching, but my heart still thrills at her touch. She points to the man who exits the house. "Keller will take your bag and park your car."

The man behind her extends his hand. "Good morning, sir," he says, and I fish the car fob out of my pocket.

As he retreats to my SUV, Rose leads me into the house. We go up a wide modern staircase, then walk to the end of a long corridor.

"Our room is the only one that faces the pool, so it gets noisy when there are events, but the balcony makes up for it."

"Our room?" I ask, wondering if I heard her right or if that was my brain wishfully thinking.

We enter through the double doors and into a room that rivals my condo's main floor. A giant low-to-the-floor bed takes up one wall while a door leading to what I assume is the bathroom is on the same wall we just entered. Opposite us is a massive sliding door with a view of the pool and green lawn beyond. The room is beautifully decorated, but it has one enormous problem. There's no sofa. The only place to sleep is the bed.

The anxious question in my chest bursts out. "We're sharing the room?"

Rose peers at me like I'm not making sense. "To the rest of the world, we are practically engaged." Like that explains everything. "I'm a divorced thirty-five-year-old woman. I won't pretend I don't have sex before marriage. Requesting separate rooms is cause for suspicion."

"I might snore."

"Do you?" Rose narrows her eyes.

"No. But you could use that as an excuse."

"Alek, be serious."

"I guess we can ask for an extra comforter," I say. "I'll sleep on the floor."

"Don't be ridiculous. This bed can sleep a family of four, and I promise I don't snore. You won't even know I'm here."

Impossible. I know she's in my presence if she's standing on the other side of the room. I can feel her around me with people everywhere. Besides, it's not her that I'm worried about. I look down at my pants as if my dick might betray me. Rose being in my bed means I'll be taking multiple cold showers. And that might not even be enough.

I shrug. "I was trying to be a gentleman."

"No need for that. Be yourself. That's plenty." Her naked shoulder presses into my arm below the short sleeve of my shirt. The brush of her skin on mine siphons my attention from lingering worries about the bed. She's not wearing any makeup today. Or, if she is, I can't see any. Her freckles brighten the bridge of her nose and her lips.

"What?" Her eyebrows furrow. "Do I have something on my nose?" She rubs her slightly upturned nose tip.

I gather my wits and hope my face is not transmitting every desire I've been staving off where Rose is concerned. "I was admiring your freckles."

As close to the truth as I can get without embarrassing myself and telling her things she's not interested in hearing.

"Oh, I played eighteen holes yesterday with sunblock and a hat, and yet, here they are." She rubs the bridge of her nose this time, as if the freckles are only drawn on and can be wiped off with a finger.

"I love your freckles." Another truth slips out, and I know I should be more careful. This weekend will be tough, and I need to not let my guard down.

Rose smiles. "You're in luck. With the amount of time we'll be spending outside tomorrow, you'll see even more of them. Take your fill." She glances up at me, and I do.

I look for any other changes in her face. My finger grazes the side of her cheek, and as she swallows, I run my fingers lower over the column of her neck, then down to her nape. In tennis shoes and a white dress with a pleated skirt and a block of light blue along the side, she could be a golf apparel model—pristine and bright like a fresh spring day. I inhale the familiar sweet scent of her hair as I bend down.

Rose exhales and steps away. "You need to change into your golf outfit." She backs toward the door. "Ezra and Leanne are waiting. I told them you needed to freshen up. Your bags should be here any minute." Her hand is on the knob. "I'll see you downstairs."

I take the time to brainstorm my plan of attack for the next two days. Talking about the project with the Menkens can't be a hard sell. I need them to see the impact the app will make on charitable companies, how they can affect change, and find the angle they'd respond to.

"Here you are, sir," Keller says as he drops off the bags. "I'll unpack and hang them up for you when you're done."

"Thank you," I say, immediately grabbing the main one with my clothes.

The Menkens affection for Rose got me here, but that sentiment will not persuade them to join me. Resolute and ready to represent Second Chance Events, I change into appropriate golf attire and make my way through the house, following the sound of voices. I spot Rose in the kitchen and head to her like she's true north.

"What do you think?"

Rose spins to face me and her eyes widen. "You look presentable."

"Presentable good or presentable bad?"

"You look good. You look very good." She leans in and whispers, "Ready to see if we can talk Ezra and Leanne into partnering with you?"

My fingers find her warm, sun-kissed skin. Envy of the star creeps into my veins. "What's the plan? We haven't really discussed what we're doing."

"We eat breakfast." She holds up her coffee cup. "And I introduce you to my friends. Then we watch golf, come back here for dinner, and repeat the same thing tomorrow. I emailed you the details."

"I got that. I mean, what are we," I start, gesturing at the gap separating us, "doing?" I indicate the other room where I assume our hosts are sitting.

Her eyes shine up at me. "We play like we've been away from each other for two weeks and can't get enough of being back together in the same place. Can you do that?"

My hand skims down her forearm, I interlace our fingers, and then I lean down to gently peck her temple. "I think I might be able to do that, yes."

I should wait until there is an audience to our show, but I can't seem to keep my hands to myself. As much as I am trying not to get distracted or lose sight of why we are here, I have a whole weekend of being able to freely touch her, and maybe even to kiss her. A slow, almost disbelieving smile pulls at my mouth as warmth expands to my heart. The joy of the prospect overpowers the anticipation of talking to the Menkens.

I follow her lead as we enter a bright sunroom, where two people wearing white sip on flutes of mimosas.

Rose pokes my side and I see her smile at the elderly couple. My abs tighten, and it's a similar feeling to when the puck slips across the ice in my direction. Even though this is their house and Rose has been staying with them for most of the week, some part of me was preparing for another shutout. A fluke that would make them cancel. Or a sign I should stick to the things that worked before and stop pretending I'm a philanthropist.

"Leanne, Ezra, I'd like you to meet my boyfriend. This is Alek." Rose gently pushes me forward.

"Honor to meet you," I say, flinching internally. Is honor too strong a term? Should I just have said it's nice to meet them? This is wrong. Callum should be here, talking and knowing what to say to butter these people up. I'm a straight shooter with bullet points and business proposals. My collar feels too tight, like I'm suffocating in a shirt tailored just for me. My gut knots as if bracing for a punch I can't dodge. I have no idea how to ply them with platitudes, how to make them like me.

Mrs. Menken rises and, instead of giving me a handshake, she moves in for a hug. I have no choice but to reciprocate. Her embrace is brief and warm, loosening the worry stuffed behind my ribs. Maybe this won't be as formal as I feared. When she lets me go, she looks between Rose and me. "Remind me how you two met again?"

Rose tightens her grip on my elbow and draws closer. The flowery scent I could recognize in a crowd calms my ratcheting nerves enough for my smile to hopefully appear genuine.

"Alek and I went to UCLA together, and we recently reconnected over HH Group's purchase of his latest company, TRI." Rose's introduction of me is factual and what we agreed upon, but it's also bland and could be applied to anyone from college who she's crossed paths with professionally.

I slip my arm out of hers, set my hand firmly on her lower back, and look at Rose like the two weeks apart from her were devoid of sunshine. "I suppose fate gave us a second chance."

"I see," says Leanne in a way that indicates she more than gets my intention.

Ezra points to two empty chairs. "We're just glad Rose is back on the dating scene." He butters a piece of toast. "Our girl is such a treasure, and only someone special deserves her. Not just for her business qualities, but someone who appreciates her kind heart."

I hate letting go of Rose's body. To keep the connection when we sit, I press my knee against hers under the table. "Her kind heart is what reconnected us. I attended her Valentine's Day dance. She helped make those kids incredibly happy."

"Alek volunteered in the food line. Apron and everything." Rose's mischievous smile sends a different kind of electricity to my heart than the touch of my fingers on her lower back. I don't know which I like better. I'd love to keep both. If I can.

"Are you involved in any charities?" There's an unsaid challenge in Ezra's tone. Maybe he's sizing me up, but I don't feel the pressure. At least not from him.

"Actually, his next company will be," Rose says, when I don't volunteer anything.

"Can't wait to hear more, but I'm afraid we have a call. We shouldn't be too long." Leanne pushes back her chair and stands. "Have the chef bring up some breakfast for you, and we'll see you at Amen Corner."

Ezra shakes my hand while Leanne hugs Rose. His grip is a bit too hard. "Rose's father was our godson. So, if you hurt her in any way, we will come after you." The tone is joking, but there's an underlying menace that makes the hairs on the back of my neck rise.

"Stop it, Ezra. You'll scare the young man." Leanne tsks at her husband's underhanded threat.

"I appreciate his defense of Rose." I meet Leanne's gaze and hold it. "But you don't have to worry. She's the best thing that's ever happened to me. I won't hurt her. I promise."

Another truth slips from me.

I don't want my time with Rose to end.

Ever.

Twenty-Six

PRESENT DAY

April

On our way to Amen Corner, Alek's hand lands on the small of my back. I allow myself to relax into his touch and enjoy not just the green landscape around us, but also the solid arm around me and the calm satisfaction it produces in my chest.

Because I can.

Because Alek touching me is all part of the show.

Because I want to.

A few acquaintances intercept Alek and me, but when he shakes hands with them, his other never leaves my back. Like his hand has a right to be there. Is it calming Alek too? I introduce him to some former schoolmates who run their own corporations now, my former neighbors who complain about newcomers that were let into their gated neighborhood, former and current business associates, and friends of friends whose names I've memorized from one function or another.

One person tries to part us, but Alek pulls me closer to his side. He finds other little ways to touch me, brushing hair out of my face, pressing his lips to my cheek, my temple, my nose, and completely convincing everyone on our fancy promenade that we are together and not a couple of con artists.

We arrive at Amen Corner, where three of the most treacherous holes on the course cluster together. Despite its difficulty level, this part of the golf course is serene and picturesque. Nelson Bridge looks like a fairy-tale stone structure spanning the clear babbling creek as the backdrop of tall pines swing in the breeze. Heavily trimmed shrubbery and borders of colorful flowers paint the image of calm.

Ezra stands beside Leanne, and he's the first one to spot us. They are behind a row of chairs in front of a thin wire that separates golfers from spectators. Every year, I suggest we get chairs. They are not getting any younger, not that I tell that to my friends. But they insist they have plenty of stamina for watching the best players in the world.

"You've found us." Ezra gives me a quick hug, his eyes on the swing of this year's projected winner. He shakes Alek's hand. "What do you think of the view?"

Alek glances at me and presses me into his hip, a slow smile painting his lips. "Best view on the course."

"Couldn't agree more." Ezra kisses Leanne on the cheek. "The golf isn't bad either."

Leanne smiles and puts her head on Ezra's shoulder. "Aren't I lucky?"

"You are," I say.

There have been times when I wished my marriage had a chance to be like Ezra and Leanne's. They both came from the same circle, met when they were rising stars in the film industry, married young, and have never wavered in their love for each other. I glance at Alek and allow myself to live in an alternative universe where we didn't break up. One where I didn't spend years in a loveless marriage with Dean. Where instead, Alek and I were about to celebrate our twelfth anniversary. My heart aches for what could have been. I could have been happy with Alek. I know because I'm happy right now. Even in this fake situation where I can't find the line between truth and pretend.

Alek makes me happy.

"We had to see for ourselves if the man who captured Rose's heart is good enough for our sweet girl," Leanne says as I pull myself out of my daydream. "She insists you commit as much time to your charities as we do. Still, I was certain you were one of those tech billionaires who spend their money and time on new technology."

"Both things can be true." Alek's hand on my waist tightens, and I lay my fingers on the spot above his heart, signaling this is the time to start discussing Second Chance Events. He drags in a breath. "My current goal is to combine my interests."

"Give away your money to charities?" Leanne asks.

"Better. I'd like to help charities use the money on their causes, not on overhead." The people around us clap politely as a player on the green sinks a put. "I'm launching a new app where charities can organize events by reusing supplies and decor from high-profile parties."

The excitement on the green over, Ezra turns to Alek. "Aren't similar initiatives already happening?"

"Not in the events industry. At least not on a large scale. Every day, parties, weddings, and galas throw a lot of their decor, flowers, and food out after the event is over. My app will allow charities to be matched with events and plan in advance to pick up any reusable items. Second Chance Events—that's the name of the app—will facilitate software, temporary storage in a warehouse, and even transportation and delivery. Our ultimate goal is to lower the costs of putting together fundraisers for charities and reduce waste."

"That sounds like a lot of logistics." Ezra squints into the sun. "It'll have to be local, or else shipping costs would eat all the profits."

"My algorithms will allow matching across zip codes for certain things. That technology is already proven with stores that sell leftover perishables at the end of the day or donate them to the local food banks. We'll transfer that learning and apply the process to event materials."

The crowd oohs, and Ezra's attention returns to the course.

Leanne pats Alek's shoulder. "Fascinating idea. We'll be watching to see where you go with that. Maybe you could use one of our charities as a beta case."

Alek opens his mouth, but he doesn't say anything. The door is wide open to ask my friends to invest, and he's frozen.

I turn to Leanne. "I thought you might like to partner with Alek? Be the high-end face of Second Chance Events?"

"Yes," stumbles Alek. "With your connections and your stellar reputation, you can champion Second Chance to the families and companies that regularly do large-scale events."

Another wave of ahhs followed by a round of applause drowns the end of Alek's plea.

"How about we go to the side where it's a bit quieter," Ezra says, then leads Alek away to a shady spot under a nearby tree.

Instead of the golf, I watch the two men talk. Alek's face transforms from the usual stoic mask to a warm, engaged expression, and I don't need to hear what he's saying because I can see the passion and belief he has in his idea. He shouldn't doubt himself. Yes, he needed a little push from me, but once he starts, his conviction is compelling. Plus, Alek's ace-up-his-sleeve is his genuine interest in helping people combined with his in-depth knowledge of the technology needed.

Leanne threads her arm through my elbow. "You really are in love this time, huh."

"I . . ." It's my turn to stumble. My stomach does a somersault. What was I doing with my face for Leanne to think I'm in love? I hate lying to the woman who's been like a grandmother to me, but it feels less and less like a lie. I wish us being together were the truth. My shoulders drop. I like him. I've always liked him. "Alek's the best man I've ever met," I say.

"Your dad would've approved of your choice," Leanne whispers.

I stare at her. "You never once said that about Dean."

"Nothing against Dean, but he was never the right person for you. Your mother felt that marriage was advantageous, and I won't pretend I don't understand why. But the way you look at Alek and the way he looks at you reminds me of what I have with Ezra."

"Alek is nothing like Dean." The words are so true. My feelings for Dean never came close to how I feel around Alek. The way I felt around him twelve years ago. These past few months have been like those years never happened and we are just picking up where we left off. My heart aches.

"He's a keeper. I look forward to more time with you two back in LA."

"In LA?" I stare at her. "What about tonight's dinner?"

She sighs. "The call this morning was not a good one. We have a flight booked for 2 p.m."

"Anything I can do to help?"

"I wish. Our daughter-in-law got in a spot of trouble, and we need to smooth things over. Family defending family and all." She squeezes my arm. "But at least you get the house to yourself. I told the staff it'll be just the two of you for dinner."

Alek and Ezra return. "My assistant will call yours. Once we've reviewed the documents, we'll schedule an official business meeting." Ezra shakes Alek's hand. He then throws an arm around Leanne. "I thought I liked him before, but now I know."

Leanne and I exchange glances. I try to rein in my smile. "I like him too."

After we say our goodbyes, Alek pinches the bridge of his nose. "I should've rehearsed more. I don't remember half the stuff I told him."

"That's a good thing."

He shoots me a pained look.

"It is. You looked passionate, and Ezra is clearly interested. You'll talk more in LA."

"Your confidence is impressive."

"Your idea is impressive." I step closer, hoping for his hand to settle in the now familiar spot. Alek doesn't disappoint, his fingers landing on the small of my back. The contact rushes quiet bliss through me. My spine relaxes, and my breaths are easy. I feel safe and cared for. "I've done this sort of thing many times before for projects that are decidedly less interesting."

Alek takes a deep breath. "Will you come to the meeting with me?"

"Would you like me to?"

Eyes the color of hot chocolate peer into me. "I'd love for you to be there. You make me fall in love with Second Chance Events all over again when we talk."

"Then I'll be there." With the introductions to Ezra and Leanne over, I've done my part, but softness spreads through my rib cage at the thought of spending more time together. "You've done all you can today. Maybe we should enjoy this beautiful place and watch some golf."

His gaze never leaves mine. "I'm not sure I can enjoy golf, but I'll enjoy your company."

There aren't people within earshot, so I'm not sure for whose benefit he said this. I turn my attention to the action on the green, but can still feel Alek's gaze on me. The lead player backs away once, twice, then taps the golf ball. The guests in the crowd hold their breath as the ball rolls toward the hole. And keeps on rolling right past. The audience groans.

"Doesn't sound like that went well." Both of Alek's hands are on my waist as I stand in front of him, trying to peer through the taller crowd.

"This is where most of the winners of the Masters are decided. No matter how skilled you are, the winds are unpredictable. Not the most difficult hole of the tournament, but it's maybe the hardest to forecast." A gust of wind rushes by, and I shiver.

"Are you cold?"

I shrug, but Alek's arms wrap around me as a protective shield. "I'd give you my shirt, but I don't think we'd be allowed to stay and watch."

I giggle. His warmth surrounds me, intermingled with whiffs of deodorant or aftershave mixed with the distinct woodsy scent that is all Alek. Not overpowering, but drifting around me in a perfect accompaniment to the heat of him against my back and the warm skin of his forearms that encircle me like a gentle, supportive corset. Innocent but also frightening. Secure yet vulnerable.

My giggle fades. The knowledge that Alek touches me in public just for show used to keep my heart sheltered behind a wall. Now, the cement blocks that guarded me are nowhere to be found. I relax into his arms, letting myself believe this is real. I bask in the feeling and the delusion as the golfers in front of us change and the sun travels across the sky. I don't talk or even move, mesmerized by the meditation of this place and the freedom to be in the confines of Alek's embrace.

TWENTY-SEVEN

TWELVE YEARS AGO

November

I stare at the door I just shut on Alek's face.

This was the right thing to do. The Haliday thing to do. I draw back my shoulders. Everything I told him was the truth. I lift my chin. I won't apologize for who I am. My jaw tightens.

The elevator down the hall dings.

I close my eyes. He's leaving. Why did I think he would wait for me to reopen the door? I shake my head. He's actually leaving. I mash the heels of my palms into my eyes. He's doing what I asked, so why can't I breathe? Why does his absence strangle me, wrapping tighter around my chest and squeezing? I lurch forward. My palms thud against the barrier separating me from Alek. I dig my fingers into the wood so they don't go around the handle and open the stupid door, then I press my forehead against the cool surface. The tightness around my chest snaps, but there's no relief. My hands shake, and the vibrations rush up my arms, into my heart and my head.

My lips now tremble too. I press my fingers to them, attempting to push everything back. I know I did the right thing. I open my eyes. Nothing in my body feels right. I hurt. Everything hurts. The years of training should take hold, but my heart refuses to cooperate. Because it's too late. Because I've stepped over the threshold of safety and into the danger zone of falling for Alek. Tears leak from the corners of my eyes, silent at first, then the sobs join in. I have fallen for Alek, and I sent him away. My legs can't hold me any longer.

Through my tears, I stumble to my couch, grab a pillow, and throw it across the room. I shove the coffee table aside and throw every other pillow I find. I'm done holding everything in. The desire to wrap my arms around Alek. The fear of messing up everything I've worked for. I bury my face into the couch and scream.

Nothing feels right anymore.

Why can't things be simple? Why did he ask me to be his girlfriend when I can't accept? Every reason why we can't, shouldn't, and mustn't pulses in my temples. Every objection beats in my heart.

A knock on my door stops my thrashing. The chaos in my mind halts.

"I know you're there." Olivia's voice comes from the other side of the door.

I stop crying for a second. Alek may not have come back, but my sister's here for me.

Olivia knocks again. "You left me at the party. Alone."

I pull the bottom of my robe down, retie the sash, and go to the door. "Shouldn't you be having fun?" I usher my sister inside. "I wasn't going to rush you home from the party."

"I was worried about you. You ignored my texts." She surveys the destroyed living room. "What happened?"

"Nothing."

"This doesn't look like nothing. Are you okay?"

"People should really stop asking me that." I clutch my robe.

Olivia furrows her brows. "Who else asked you that?"

"Alek was just here," I say, unable to lie anymore. How much should I truly tell her? I'm not even sure how much I want to admit out loud. The truth feels too hurtful.

"Do I need to call the police?" Olivia's face shifts from concerned to pissed. "Did he do this? Did he hit you?"

It's clear she thinks I'm in danger. I'm afraid I am, just not the type she's assuming.

"No." I stare at the ceiling as if the plaster can find an excuse for my behavior. A reasonable explanation, maybe. "I did this. I fucked everything up."

"In the living room?"

"In the living room, sure. In my life." I meet her gaze, already fighting back tears. "With Alek," I admit.

"You fucked Alek?" she shouts.

"No," I groan, closing my eyes. If that bathroom door handle in Alek's parents' house wouldn't have wiggled like it did, I would have an entirely different answer to Olivia's question.

"Okay, okay." My sister gently pulls me to the couch, and sits me down. "It's okay. Tell me everything."

I scrunch my nose, then begin to explain. I gloss over the events in his parents' bathroom, and also what happened when Alek showed up here.

Olivia narrows her eyes as if trying to read a secret scribbled in fine print across my face. She crosses her legs and taps her fingers on her knee. "What are you not saying?" she asks.

Shaking my head, I debate if I want to say anything before the truth simply topples out of me.

"He asked me to be his girlfriend."

"Rose," she gasps. "Did you say yes?"

"No."

"You know, you really need to broaden your vocabulary." Olivia leans forward like she's about to witness a plot twist in her favorite show. "What did you do?" Her voice dips, wry and teasing.

"I told him I can't date him, then pushed him out the door." Alek's promise to do anything I want rings in my ears.

"I don't understand."

I dig my nails into my scalp. That's the point. No one understands me.

"Scratch that. It's written all over your face." Olivia circles the air, pointing in my direction. "How about you answer this—if you were in a perfect world where you could do anything you wanted, would you have said yes or no to him?"

"Yes," I say in a breath. Fireworks erupt under my sternum. The answer is so beyond clear that I didn't have to put a moment's thought into it.

"Then, hear me out. Why don't you?"

"Because this is not a perfect world. Because he and I are from different worlds. Mom would be furious if I actually date Alek. She told me off when I held his hand in the elevator, told me I shouldn't mix business and pleasure. Then she got upset that we were photographed simply working on a project together. Can you imagine what she'd say?"

Olivia sighs. "She'd insist you only date men approved by her."

"Thus the problem." Tears prick at my eyes. "Alek won't meet her approval standards. His last name doesn't have enough prestige. He's the son of the maintenance man."

"But he meets yours."

Her words are a statement, not a question. Emotion clogs my throat at the thought of hiding Alek away as if I'm ashamed of him. I'm anything but. He's gentle when it counts and ferocious when I need him to be. He's the real deal. "Alek is like no man I've ever been with."

"Isn't that a good thing?"

"I like him too much. What if I fall for him?" Who am I kidding? I've fallen for him already.

"What if you do?" Olivia squeezes my hand. "You're Mom's favorite. She can't stay mad at you."

"I don't know. She might. Over him."

"Look, you and Mom have this bond I'm not part of, and I know fulfilling your destiny and becoming CEO of HH Group and all that is what you've been driven toward since birth . . . But, Rose, at some point, you have to stop living Mom's life and live your own."

Defy Mom and date Alek? My desires and duties fight for dominance. Years of calculating my future against the short time I've known Alek. Choosing him, choosing us, counters everything I've grown up to believe. I'm destined to be CEO. That's my dream.

My heart slams against my ribs, chanting Alek, Alek, Alek.

Damn it. I want to follow my heart. To choose him. I kick a stray pillow onto the floor.

"You're twenty-two years old, and you behave like you're Mom's age. All work and no fun. Think of what Mom was doing at your age. Probably my father." Olivia's voice hardens.

I take in the differences between Olivia and me. Her curly hair compared to my straight locks. Her dark eyes and tanned skin. Her dad was just a fling for Mom, but we got Olivia out of the deal.

"Mom's a hypocrite," says my sister. "She's all 'do as I say and not as I do.' But trust me when I tell you that there's more to the world than Haliday Hotels. There's more to you than being Mom's heir."

"When did you get all wise in your not-so-old age?"

She shrugs. "Getting to really know you these last few months has opened my eyes to some things."

The back of my neck burns. "If I haven't said so already, you should know that I'm glad you came to LA. I'm glad we're in this together. Thank you for having my back."

Olivia's hand brushes over her forearm like she's smoothing away a thought. Her smile wavers for just a second before she finds her footing again. "You're family. Family comes first."

"I love you."

"I love you too." Olivia wraps her arms around me. "Now put on some clothes and go tell Alek how you actually feel."

THE STREET IS DESERTED at 1 a.m. as I knock at Alek's front door. I wish I were here to work on our project instead of to bare my heart. Maybe I should've texted and made sure he's here, but if I'd done that, my courage would've disappeared. If Alek's not home, then this isn't meant to be. I stare at the dent in the unmoving, silent door. The windows of the house are dark. Maybe he went back to his parents' place or out with the guys to The Devil's Martini. Maybe . . .

The door opens slowly.

"Rose?" Alek's voice is thick with sleep, and his T-shirt is wrinkled as if he rolled straight out of bed. His eyebrows pull together on his drawn face.

With the remains of my resolve, I step inside.

He runs his hands through his disheveled hair. "What—"

"Yes," I say before the courage leaves me.

Confusion and hope mix in his gaze. "Yes?"

"Yes, I want more."

He takes a deep breath, as if he hasn't been breathing since he opened the door. A slow smile stretches over his lips, and the vice around my ribs eases. Alek's fingers thread into my hair and my heart all but flatlines at the feel of his chest. His mouth slants over mine and draws us into a slow, deep, hot kiss. His hands drift to my waist, and he hikes me up as if knowing exactly what I want. My thighs gleefully wrap around him. I gasp for breath when he releases my lips, only to moan as he stamps my neck and collarbone with tender pecks.

Alek carries me up the stairs and sets me down onto the floor of a room I've never been to in this house . . . his bedroom.

Excitement ripples through me, too much to grasp, as his hand moves along my ribcage and back to my waist, his thumb resting on my hip. "I was worried you were just a dream."

"Did I wake you up?"

"I could wake up like this anytime." He cups my cheeks and kisses me quickly as if to make sure I'm real. "I was working on the app, but I guess I fell asleep on the couch."

"I had to tell you before I chickened out. You can keep working." My eyes drag to the blue comforter on his bed. "Or sleeping."

"I'd much rather kiss you than work." He drifts his lips over the corner of mine. "And I'd much rather touch you than sleep." His hand sneaks under my T-shirt, his fingers dragging my bralette up and over my breasts. "I'd rather be here with you than anywhere else in the world." Alek's head dips down, and his tongue drags across my nipple. Then his lips claim a stiff peak. The sound that leaves me is a sigh mixed with a moan.

My fingers dive into his dark hair, caressing his scalp. His thumb glides across my abdomen, and he plants his hand on my stomach possessively while he licks and devours my breasts like I'm his last meal. An electric pulse zips to my core, and I dig my nails into his shoulder. His hard length brushes against my thigh, and heat pools between my legs. I didn't come here to have sex with Alek, but with his bed inches away, my lust is back, demanding more. Demanding everything I was promised.

"Can you . . .?" I set my hand on his cock.

Alek's gaze shifts from hunger to curiosity. "What?"

"Can you finally bury your cock inside me?" I'm breathless and unashamed. My chest constricts at the desire simmering in his pupils.

"I'll do whatever you want."

He grabs the back of his T-shirt and tugs. As I shed my clothes, my gaze watches his toned body reveal itself. When he steps out of his boxers, it's like he's the statue of David come alive. A completely naked Alek is a sight I don't want to ever unsee. The main difference between the statue of David and Alek is his full erection. I bite my lower lip.

He strokes his cock that I haven't had a chance to investigate properly, and my mouth waters. I promise myself I'll get a taste. Soon.

Instead of reaching for me, Alek's gaze roams over my naked torso. Another slow smile sends butterflies through me. I could get used to him looking at me like that. As his. I could spend hours snapping images of his smiles and create a collage for my wall.

He sighs. "You're so beautiful."

I step forward, running my fingers from his pecs to his happy trail. "You're so beautiful," I echo.

I trace his happy trail and his abs contract. Alek's lips part, and his eyes get hazy like he's drunk. Totally drunk on my touch. My breasts swell with the heady feeling that I do this to him just like he does this to me. I wrap my fingers around his cock and pump him slowly.

His growled "fuck" reaches me at the same time as he nudges me back, nowhere to go but onto his bed. The mattress is hard but I couldn't care less as Alek pushes my knees apart and runs a finger up the inside of my leg to the apex of my thigh. His moan is indecent. "Tell me, Rose, were you ever wet like this for me in class?"

I let out a breathy, "Yes."

"Will you be a good girl and let me eat you out now?" He kisses the curve of my stomach under my navel.

"Next time." I grab his hand and pull him toward me. "I need you inside me. Now. Whatever I want, remember?"

The hard muscles of his body glide across my skin, setting it aflame. I'm still so tender from earlier, from his fast and furious and oh-so-satisfying fingers, that I don't need more foreplay. I want the home run. He kisses my neck and my shoulder. I arch up, unable to wait. A peck on my forehead, and he's leaning over me. "You're sure you don't want to use a condom?"

I wrap my hands around his cock and pump it, guiding him toward my entrance. "I'm sure."

He rubs the head of his cock against my clit, then lower, and slowly slips inside. Bracing on one elbow, his other hand cups my cheek, and he nips at my lower lip, giving me time to adjust to him. I moan at the delicious stretch. I'm ready for him, ready to feel full.

He entwines our fingers and rocks gently. I gasp, closing my eyes and surrendering to the sensation.

"Open your eyes, sweets." His nose brushes mine. "Look at me."

I do. My eyes fly open, and I look at Alek. I see Alek. I see the man who holds down multiple jobs and never gets enough sleep. I drink in the man who is as smart as me, if not smarter. The boy who infuriates me, challenges me, and makes my heart beat stronger than it ever has before. I see someone who loves his family and is loved in return. Someone who earns the loyalty of his friends. A person who is good and kind and hot as hell, but also compassionate and funny.

I see Alek.

He moves inside me, slow but not tentative, careful but with all the friction I crave in his strokes as he angles just the right way to still rub against my clit. I move with him, rotate my hips to meet his every thrust, and wring every millisecond of pleasure he promised and is delivering.

My fingers tighten around his as my ribcage heaves and fills with what I've never experienced. My heart overflows, and my eyes threaten to as well.

"It's okay, Rose." Alek kisses any sound off my lips. "I feel it too."

But he can't. This is just sex. It's just chemistry working its magic. "This is not possible."

"I agree. But . . ."

This can't be more. This can't be . . .

"I love you," he whispers.

I hold back a sob. Because I love him too.

Twenty-Eight

ALEK

PRESENT DAY

April

The path to the Menken's house winds between trees, and although no one is around, I don't let go of Rose's hand. I should end the contact, but she didn't let go either, and I'm not strong enough to stop touching her in whichever way I can.

"What did you think about your first golf tournament?" Small creases emphasize the languid smile that plays on her lips.

"It was a great day." I want to add more. I want to say it was a great day because I got to spend time with you and because I got to touch the parts of you only a boyfriend is allowed to touch in public. Even though I'd like to do more, so much more.

But I'm greedy, and I've already scared her off once. I'm not going to repeat my past mistakes. If she wants anything from me, she'll need to be the one to make it crystal clear.

"Do you officially feel part of my world now?" Rose's thumb trails up and down the back of my hand, and that slight motion shoots directly through my arm and down my spine.

"No."

Her instantly sobered gaze flies to mine. "Everyone loved meeting you. You did great. Even if it goes wrong with Ezra and Leanne, you now have other connections you can utilize."

A blanket of concern dampens my buzz. "Did Leanne say something to you?"

"Only that she liked you. Don't worry." Rose tugs on my hand, but she doesn't let go. "They are impressed, and I'm certain this will work. Still, it's always good to have backup options. Like applying to college."

"I only ever wanted to go to UCLA." Thank goodness I did.

"Trust me, they are practically family. If they weren't interested, they wouldn't drag things out. You'd have known when we brought up Second Chance Events."

We walk up the steps and onto the deck where a table is set for two with flowers, candles, and soft music coming out of a speaker.

Rose turns my way. "This is a bit over-the-top."

"I had this idea that talking to Ezra about surprising you with a romantic dinner would play into the . . ." I clear my throat. "The couple plan."

"Well, in honor of Second Chance, we shouldn't let this go to waste." She turns to the stairs. "I'll just pop up to our room and freshen up."

I can't take my eyes off Rose until she disappears. My feet want to follow her, to never let her out of my sight. Desperate to cool down, I pour a finger of scotch and pull out my phone that's been dinging all day. The Fifth Line chat has too many messages for me to catch up on. I scan the usual chatter until I see my name.

Blake:

> Alek, I found a warehouse to rent.

Me:

> I need one with a dock for trucks and refrigeration units to store perishables.

Blake:

> It's not officially on the market, but if you move quickly, you can get a two-year deal with a significant discount. The guys who originally signed the contract didn't receive the next level of funding and need to sublet.

Me:

> When do I need to decide?

Blake:

> Here's the details. I'll tell them you're interested.

I open the link Blake sends, and at first glance, the location seems perfect for Second Chance Events' LA operations and headquarters. There's enough parking for the trucks I'm set to purchase. I send emails to my real estate guy, to the construction company, and send a list of things needing research to my assistant. I also consult my financials. I wasn't planning on finding a space for my new office so soon, but if the Menkens are in, I can float the money from my personal funds.

"Are you hungry?" Rose's voice rings nearby.

I lift my gaze away from my phone and stop breathing. Rose's short hair is slicked back, and her strapless babydoll dress barely reaches mid-thigh. The vision sends desire coursing through my already simmering blood. Yet, it's her smiling lips that make me think I might need mouth-to-mouth. "Very."

The swig of scotch I take only stokes the fire. I'm very hungry, yes, but I'd give up eating forever for a taste of her lips. This sounds irrational, even in the privacy of my head, but it feels entirely too true. Today has been an exercise in patience. Touching her while knowing she's not actually mine makes me want to chuck aside this fake dating deal and tell Rose what's in my heart.

I want to go and place my hand on the small of her back, to draw her into me, to smell her perfume, to never let her go. What a fool I was to think I could ever get over her by burying myself in work and workouts. That made me richer and stronger, but it did nothing to cure me of whatever affliction it is to love Rose

Haliday. But I can't go to her. Can't touch her. And I can't even tell her the way she makes me feel, because that's not the deal.

The remains of my liquor drained, I set the empty glass on the drinks cart. I should've poured a double. Or I should've never arranged this dinner for just the two of us. What was I thinking? I am not as strong when Rose is around. I rock on the heels of my shoes, making myself stay in place. I need to not be near her right now. I need to cool my thoughts, take a cold shower, and reconstruct the wall I had around my heart the day I agreed to fake a relationship that is all too real for me.

"Good," says Rose. "The chef said the first course is ready."

I pull a chair out for her and shove my hand into my pockets to prevent myself from touching her. We're not in public, so there's no excuse to caress her skin. The hours we spent on the golf course with her in my arms made me feel like she belonged there. Part of me wants to imagine today was real and that I didn't let her slip out of my life twelve years ago. I could close my eyes and conjure an alternate universe where we did date, stayed together, and learned everything there is to know about each other over these years.

But that is not the universe I'm living in.

I sit across from her as the chef delivers the food. I hide behind eating seared sea bass over a bed of risotto with charred asparagus stacked like toy green ladders. The scent is fresh—lemon and rosemary—but I barely taste the dish. Each bite is mechanical, an excuse to drop my eyes to the plate instead of meeting hers.

Rose's posture is one of a princess at a royal ball, even though we're alone in the backyard of a private residence. Her confidence is so easy and natural that I'm sure she'd still be elegant and self-assured even if we were eating messy s'mores from a stick.

"This is nice." She lifts her gaze, catching mine in the process. "Just the two of us. We can finally be ourselves."

The fish gets stuck in my throat. I cough. So she hated today. It was all an act. I guess the day of touching didn't affect her the same way it did me. Her casual statement helps me cool down better than the cold shower. I resurrect my defenses and stab the last spear of asparagus. "You prefer not pretending?"

"Isn't not pretending always best?" Her fork hovers over her plate.

"Not if we want Leanne and Ezra to believe we're a couple." I fucking hate the statement as it leaves my mouth. I don't want to pretend anymore.

"Do you always have your hands all over your girlfriends in public?" Rose gulps her wine.

"You were my last girlfriend."

The air connecting us draws taut, like laces pulled too tight on a pair of skates. My remark hangs there, raw and exposed. For a second, I think maybe they reached her, and the defensiveness in her might soften. But instead of leaning in, she sinks back. The silence lingers heavy, ripe with everything we've never said and the years we lost. I brace for what's next.

"You now take lessons from Callum?" An irritated chuckle escapes her lips.

I focus too hard on the crunch of asparagus, chewing longer than necessary, as if it can shield me while her cool gaze tries to break me.

"Fuck them and leave them before the sheets get cold?" She takes a gulp of her wine.

"I tried that. But it only proved that I'm a relationship guy. I want everyone to know that I'm with the woman I love."

The corners of Rose's lips turn down, disappointment fleeting across her face. She clutches the stem of her wine glass. "I hope you find that woman. You deserve her." She reaches around our drinks and gently pats the top of my hand like a mother consoling her child.

Finally, she touches me first, but this is not the touch I want. The fresh air around me doesn't seem to reach my lungs. Being so close to her and not telling her how she affects me, not holding her or kissing her . . . I thought I could do this, but I can't hold on any longer.

There will never be another woman I love, because the only woman I'll ever love is Rose. I grind my teeth.

I'll never be over her.

I drop my napkin on my plate, yank my hand from under hers, and rise.

"I'm not hungry," I mutter, retreating from this table, this conversation, whatever this version of us is.

"Where are you going?" Rose's voice follows me.

"Bed." I race to the stairs, not looking back.

The choices I made twelve years ago claw at me as I strip off the golf shirt and shorts. I storm into the bathroom, slap my hand against the button to turn on the shower, and step under the stream.

Hot water cascades down my back, and the strong pressure is like a massage for my muscles. I need to turn this shower to cold if just sitting across the table from her fully dressed was too much. What will I do when we share a room? A bed? I scrub the washcloth roughly across my skin as if I can erase my thoughts of her. When that doesn't work, I do what I do best. I create a strategy. I brainstorm my plan of attack, which includes talking points to bring up with the Menkens. I think of what I can code on the app to create a quick prototype I can show them to highlight the power of Second Chance.

Ten minutes later, frustration no longer controls me. My pulse drops to a survivable rate. Resolute and ready to win, I step out of the shower and reach for the folded towel on the shelf when I hear a muted, "Oh."

My gaze flies to the sound. Rose stands with my underwear and pajamas in her hand, her wide eyes glued to my abs. I place the folded towel in front of me.

"Sorry," she blurts. "I knocked, but you didn't reply. You left these on the bed, so I thought I'd bring these in while you were in the shower. You take very quick showers." She sounds almost accusatory. "There's a rain head and a massage head, and you can produce steam if you enjoy that." Her cheeks grow pinker with every reprimand. "Steamy showers."

I catch myself before the corner of my mouth rises. "I'll make sure to enjoy a longer shower next time." I unravel the towel, careful not to expose anything, and wrap the material around my hips. "I'm sorry my showers are too economical. Sort of seared into my conscience as a Californian. Droughts and all."

"Well, we aren't in California." She shakes her head, pushes my clothes into my hands, and rushes out of the bathroom.

My body hates every step she takes away from me.

I brush my teeth and put on the asinine pajamas I never wear at home. The fabric is already sticking to my abs. Sleeping in this will be a nightmare. Sleeping in the same bed as Rose will be an even bigger one. Then I realize I don't have to. The Menkens aren't here. I don't need to pretend. I step into the bedroom. "I'm sleeping somewhere else. There has to be another room."

"No," she squeaks, and a bundle of silky pajamas almost falls out of her hands. "You have to sleep here."

I run my hands over my face. "Why, Rose? Your friends aren't here to care what the two of us are doing or not doing."

Her mouth opens and closes. "There's a house full of staff. They'd love to sell the story of Rose Haliday's boyfriend sleeping in a separate room from her. What if they tell Ezra and Leanne? You can't leave."

The most frustrating mixture of dread and misplaced excitement assembles in the space around my heart. "Well, we wouldn't want to cause a scandal." Watching the relief pour into her shoulders, I remind myself that it's true. I don't want to cause a scandal or create any more stress in her life. I want to make her happy, not that I will ever be able to do such a thing.

I yank the comforter off my side.

She nods and steps into the bathroom. "Turn off the light when you're ready. I'll be a while." She closes the door.

I lie down on my side of the bed and kill the light. Moonlight seeps through the spaces between the curtains, casting lines on the bed and the floor. Enough to slightly make out my surroundings, but not enough to fully see. In the bathroom, the water runs.

With a deep breath, I try to calm the thrum in my veins. I shut my eyes, and images of Rose taking off her clothes and stepping into the same shower I was just in materialize unbidden in front of me. I turn over onto one side, then onto the other. The scratchy cotton of this new pajama top is too tight. I unbutton the constricting piece and throw the useless thing onto the floor. Finally able to breathe with ease, I promise myself I'm going to sleep.

Twenty-Nine

PRESENT DAY

April

The silky shorts and top that looked modest when I was packing them now seem flimsy. My nipples, the traitors, poke through the thin material even though I'm in a very warm bathroom. What will happen when I'm in the air-conditioned bedroom? They'll be screaming, "Look at me."

Except Alek doesn't want to look at me. Him yanking his hand from under mine and running away, then wanting to sleep in another room, is all the proof I need for even my hungry imagination to understand that he is only here for the deal.

He made things very clear. He isn't into me anymore. This has always been about Second Chance Events, and I'm a means to an end.

Any feelings from twelve years ago are burned away. But my body still wants to believe there's more. I need to get the message through my head, and obviously also to my nipples.

I sit on the lid of the toilet with my head in my hands. Why didn't I think this through? In my mind, the room and the bed were plenty big enough yesterday. Now, sleeping next to him seems impossible. I massage my temples. There's another set of pillows on the top shelf in the closet and an extra blanket. The floor space in the walk-in closet is big enough for me to lie down and have a makeshift bed. Then Alek and I would be separated by an entire door.

Yes. That's the perfect plan. I turn off the light in the bathroom and enter our bedroom. The room is dark and quiet. Alek's breaths are even. Thankfully, my shower was long enough. I turn to the right, grab my phone, and open the door to the walk-in closet. If I turn on the light in here, even if I close the door, I'll risk waking Alek.

Closing the slatted door, I find the flashlight function on my phone and illuminate mine and Alek's outfits hanging in an orderly row. I angle the phone flashlight higher to the top shelf where two pillows and a blanket sit.

I stand on my tiptoes, attempting to reach them, but I'm several inches too short. The chest of drawers underneath one side of the clothes rack looks solid enough. If I climb onto it, I should be able to grab the pillows and the blanket.

With my phone on one of the shelves and the flashlight illuminating the closet, I set my foot on top of the dresser. The furniture holds. Thankfully. I grab one of the shelves and pull myself up, both feet on the dresser. It wobbles slightly, but it's fine because I don't need to stand on it too long. Keeping hold on the shelf, I lean to the side, grab one pillow, then pull. It lands on the floor with a soft plop.

Success. I repeat the maneuver, and the second pillow hits the ground.

This was a great idea. I smile and lean a little farther to snag the corner of the blanket. Instead of an easy glide, the blanket doesn't budge. How can a fluffy blanket be so heavy? Is it weighted? I lean to the side a bit more, yanking harder. The blanket moves, but so does the shelf, pulling me down with them.

I fly through the air, covering my head. I land on the pillows as the blanket and shelf crash next to me, the dresser leaning on my legs. "Ouch." The flashlight on my phone still shines to the ceiling.

The door to the walk-in closet flies open, and Alek's bare-chested figure appears. "Are you ok? What happened?" He paws on the wrong side of the door. "Where's the light switch?"

Wasn't he wearing a shirt before? I stare at him, forgetting the weight of the dresser currently tipped over on my legs.

"On the left." My voice sounds tinny as I struggle to swallow my embarrassment.

He flips the light switch and catches my gaze on his pecs. I shield my eyes, pretending the light is the problem and not him. My underwear, bras, and socks as well as the top two drawers of the dresser cover my shins. I pull one of my legs toward me, but wince in the process.

"Don't move." Alek crouches next to me and shoves the drawers back into the dresser. His quick fingers pick my under-garments off me and glide along the angry scratch on my shin. "Where are you hurt?"

My skin is oversensitive everywhere it makes contact with his. He taps lightly on my calf. "Can you bend your knee?"

"I think so." I do, then straighten my leg.

"Does it hurt?"

"The skin stings, but I don't think anything is broken."

"Let me test something."

Alek takes my leg and assesses it gently, his dark eyes studying my face for a reaction. If the reaction he's looking for is pain, I don't have it. But my chest and neck become hotter with Alek's every rotation.

"Did you get a medical degree as well as become a billionaire over the last decade?"

"No." He sets my leg down. "But I've broken bones and know the basic signs."

"I don't think I broke anything."

"No, I don't think so either." He looks at me, then at the mess around us. "What happened?"

Pondering how to break the embarrassing news, I chew on my lip. "I fell."

"I see that. But why were you climbing on the dresser? Or did it also just fall?"

"Because I wanted the extra pillow and blankets."

Alek looks unimpressed. "The bed is plenty warm."

"Well, I decided maybe you were right."

He peers sideways. "You know I love when you say that. Right about what, though?"

"We shouldn't be sleeping in the same bed."

Alek arches one eyebrow. "What changed your mind?"

"I don't know. Felt like it was not a good idea."

He sighs. "I promise you don't have to be afraid of me."

"I told you I'm not."

"Okay, let me rephrase. Let's just get some sleep." Alek offers me his hand. I roll my eyes, but wrap my fingers around his, and he gently pulls me up. Dizzy, I grab his forearms, and he steadies me. "Are you okay to walk?"

"I'm perfectly fine." I wobble.

Alek wraps one arm around my waist and the other beneath my knees as he scoops me into the air.

"Let me down, I'm—"

"Perfectly fine. I heard." He presses me into his naked chest, and I reluctantly hook my elbow around his neck. He looks at me with uncontained concern, his serious gaze focused on me. "I need you in one piece."

"So I can be around to sell you and your company. I'm well aware."

"Sure." He takes three annoyingly sturdy strides and sets me on my side of the bed. He turns on the light and reexamines me, starting with my head. "Why did you agree to introduce me to the Menkens, and why'd you go along with this whole charade?"

I stare at my knees. "You know why. I need you to sell your company to HH Group."

"Why?"

"Because I need to prove to my mother that I can be calculating and make deals. It's time for me to take on more responsibility and prepare to take over."

"Why didn't you tell her the details of our deal?" His fingers trace my cheek, and I shiver. "That our relationship is fake?"

"I told you already. Getting her off my back makes my life easier. She meddles."

"Lying to your mother and the world makes your life easier? I never took you for a liar." He retracts his hand, and I clutch my fingers not to pull his touch back to me. "You always tried to be good. Do good."

My eyes snap to him. "And look what that landed me. A loveless marriage and a useless position in my own family's company. Spinning my wheels for a decade. Mom always wants me to be more cunning. I'm trying to do things her way."

"Why? Do you like the life she built for herself?"

I cross my arms. "Don't tell me having billions of dollars is a detriment."

"I know only too well how money makes life easier." There's the lightest caress on my knee, and we both stare down at where he's touching me. He removes his finger. "But it also is not the answer."

"The answer to what?" I look back up at him.

"To a happy life."

"And your life is happy?" I exhale loudly. "All you do is work."

"You're right. I thought I was happy. I have my friends and my family. But spending these last few months with you has made me realize I got lost. That something is missing from my life."

My breath catches, nerves swarming in my stomach. "What's missing?"

"You." His whisper shimmers in the semidarkness.

Did I hit my head? Am I hallucinating? Maybe I'm just creating fantasies of what I want to hear from Alek.

"Callum was right," he says. "I wasn't as over you as I thought. When you walked into my office that day, those feelings I tucked away when you left came rushing back. I hoped if I spent time with you, I'd either find a way to get you to fall for me again, or get over you for good."

"Oh." My mouth is dry, and I'm afraid to move in case I wake from this dream. Alek is trying to get over me. He still has feelings for me. My heart thumps. "Did the plan work?"

Alek tucks my hair behind my ear. "Does it seem like it worked?"

I stare into his eyes. "You make it seem like I don't affect you."

"Guess I'm a much better actor than I thought." Alek takes my hand and presses my palm over the hot skin over his heart.

The fast beats are in sync with my own. "You affect me just as much, if not more, than when we were in college. I—"

"Don't." I put my hand over his mouth.

It's just pheromones. We've always been attracted to each other. That's all this is. But even as I try to convince myself, my fingers tremble against Alek's lips. What if he tells me what I'm not ready to hear? What if I admit my feelings too? What happens then?

I gave in twelve years ago, and we ended in disaster. The stakes are higher now. He needs Second Chance, and I need HH Group. Everything is harder and messier. Me doing what I want and making this selfish, reckless choice is a risk that could ruin everything we've both worked for.

I press my fingers harder into his lips as if that will stifle what wants to come out of my mouth.

Alek doesn't move, doesn't push. Just waits. That's the difference, isn't it? Alek has only ever given me the power to choose. Dean never listened. He never heard me. He didn't care. But Alek does. Just like he did twelve years ago when I asked the impossible of him—and he gave it to me.

Regret clogs at my throat. I thought I was protecting us both then. But what if I was just running? What if I'm doing it again? What if I let fear of what the world thinks of us win not once, but twice? His breath is warm against my palm, and his eyes lock on mine, steady and patient. He's waiting now too. Letting me decide. And suddenly, that restraint undoes me more than any words ever could.

My chest tightens. If I let fear win again, I might never know what we could be. I drop my hand, my pulse hammering in my ears. The only thing stronger than my hesitation is the absolute certainty that I want this man. The acceptance of that truth.

I tilt my chin up, my voice barely a whisper. "Kiss me."

THIRTY

ALEK

April

I'm a patient man. I've always known this about myself. As a teen, I spent years preparing to get into UCLA that felt like decades. Working while playing hockey and studying tested my patience. Many times I was tempted to give up, give myself a break. The years I struggled to get my first company off the ground solidified the concept of patience for me.

But what I've been waiting for the longest is the woman who sits in front of me, her multicolored eyes wide with a fear I'm desperate to eradicate.

Rose's hand slips off my mouth, and the sureness in her eyes tells me she's made a decision. Will this hurt me again, or is my wait over?

"Kiss me," Rose says, but it comes out more like a question.

Twelve years ago, I promised I'd do anything Rose asked. I've kept my promise, even when the oath ripped out my heart. My lips hover so close to hers that all it would take is the slightest move for me to taste her. The question is . . . can I survive kissing Rose again? Kissing her for real, without an audience. For us. For me? If I kiss Rose now, will I survive if she asks me to stop?

"Are you sure?" I rasp.

"Yes."

I erase any remaining distance and brush my lips against the corner of her mouth. A quick hit to fulfill my promise. A taste of the good stuff. I jerk back before I make a fool of myself. She knows now I'm not over her, but I doubt she understands the depth of my desire.

"That barely counts," she whispers.

Goosebumps cover my arms. I bend closer and kiss her cheekbone, then the hollow beneath her ear. "Is this where I should kiss you?" I say into her skin.

"Yes." Rose swallows. "No."

I push my luck, my lips having a mind of their own, and pepper kisses along her neck and collarbone, down to her breast. "Like this?"

Her "yes" is low and thick and zips straight to my cock. Fuck. What this woman does to me is supernatural. Cruel. Bliss.

"Where else should I kiss you?"

"Everywhere."

The boundaries set in place for our fake relationship crumble against the weight of my very real need for this frustrating, amazing woman. Something loosens in my chest, like breaking the glazed sugar crust on a crème brûlée. Any restraint I had left is strangled by her whimper when I place my mouth on the curve between her neck and her shoulder.

Her moan wraps around me like the softest towel. My blood bursts into flames, and I almost touch my lips to hers. But if I kiss her for real, I won't be able to stop. If she only wants a kiss, I should still have an ounce of power left to step away and leave. Pack my bags in the morning, fly back to LA, and try to learn again how to live without Rose. I did it once before, and I might have to again. I will survive, I lie to myself, because I can't stop. I don't want to.

My senses are full of Rose.

Sight.

My eyes lock on the shield of her short hair framing her face.

Hearing.

Her shallow breaths pant from of her parted lips.

Smell.

I inhale the sweet mix of her lotion and shampoo.

Touch.

I skim the pads of my fingers over her collarbone and slip the thin strap of her top over silky, soft skin.

Taste.

I nip her shoulder, licking the light marks away.

Her gaze rakes across my naked torso, but her fingers stay away. My lust and love for her mix and grow each second she looks at me this way. Carnal and defenseless. Sweet and defiant. That gooey custard in my chest heats. She's the right person for me. My person.

I kiss a trail from her bare shoulder to the hard peak of her nipple, painting the edge of her top with my tongue. She arches, pushing into me, but that's not enough.

"Take off your top," I demand.

Without complaint, Rose pulls it over her head. I'm frozen, basking in the glory of her on full display. I feel my pulse in every part of my body.

"Are you just going to stare at them?" She inches forward.

I run my tongue along the front of my teeth. My knees hit the floor and I separate her legs, placing myself between them. Rose breathes a small sigh. With one hand around her waist, I yank her to the edge of the bed and fix my mouth on her nipple. One quick taste there, I tell myself, and I move on. I suck her into my mouth, and she's so velvety good I can't stop. I can't pry myself away.

Rose squirms and hums. "Alek." Her voice melts every letter of my name, sending scorching need to my groin.

I grip the waistband of her shorts. The overwhelming command my body sends me is to slide my dick into her. But I can't. The only command she's given is to kiss her, and I promised.

Why the fuck did I promise?

My fingers grip the silk of her shorts. I promised to always listen to her.

Kissing. I'm only kissing her. That's all the permission she gave.

The hot poker of my desire burns with every breath, but I clench my jaw. If kissing is all Rose wants, then I'll kiss the ever-loving fuck out of her.

She hisses when I release her breast, and arches into me when I "kiss" her other breast, my thumb grazing the damp, swollen nub I left behind. Can fingers kiss too? According to Romeo and Juliet, this counts.

Rose turns liquid in my embrace, relying on me to keep her upright. "Yes, Alek. Yes."

Her hand slips into her waistband and I growl, livid she gets to plunge her fingers inside herself and I can't. But I can kiss her. Everywhere. My eyes find the apex of her thighs as I swallow audibly and tug at Rose's wrist, freeing her hand from her shorts and myself from her body. "Shorts off."

Rose shimmies out of the rest of her clothes, and saliva pools in my mouth. "I'm going to kiss you here." I run my finger over her folds. "Do you like being kissed here?"

Her face hardens. "Dean. He would never do it." She looks away. "Said he wasn't interested."

Anger rips through me at the fuckwit who had Rose in his bed for years and failed to satisfy her every desire. I graze my finger under her chin, silently asking her to look at me. She reluctantly does. "Your ex didn't deserve you."

She swallows.

"You deserve better. The best. Don't ever settle for anything less. Understand?"

Rose stares at me.

"Say it."

"I deserve the best."

"Fuck yes."

"Fuck yes," she echoes.

I can't help but grin. There's the woman I know and love. I raise our entwined hands. "Do you still trust me?"

She nods.

"You'll let me kiss you anywhere?"

She nods again.

"Ride my face."

Her lips part. "I . . . How?"

I bring her palm to my mouth and firmly lick from the middle to the gap between her index and middle finger.

"I'll use my tongue." I make the same motion again and stop at the apex of her fingers, capturing the soft hill under her index finger and sucking softly, then harder. I'm showing, but I also need her to want this, so she's wet and ready for me. "Then kiss your clit until it swells." I put the pad of her hand on my chin and rub the muscle against me. She doesn't pull away. Her eyes shine as I repeat the lick, suck, rub sequence. "You can rub yourself on my chin as I use my tongue."

Rose's mouth opens as her chest goes up and down, faster with every instruction.

"Can I kiss you like that?"

"Won't I hurt you?" she asks.

I shake my head. "No." I climb over her onto the bed, placing a quick kiss on the back of her shoulder, and lie in the center. She takes my hand, turns her bare back to me, and I help her straddle my chest as her knees settle alongside my head. I lift my palms, and as she grabs them, she lowers herself on me.

"Hold my hands," I say. "Or brace yourself on the bed. I'll use my fingers."

She drops my hands and arranges her palms next to my thighs.

"Good girl." I nudge her thighs. "Come closer."

If I was concerned she was not into this, the view of her glistening pussy reassures me that even if she is hesitant, she is also ready for me to teach her this lesson.

"This is your show. You can stop anytime." I lift my head and firmly lick between her folds. She clenches when my tongue reaches her center and makes a tentative thrust. "You taste just like I remember."

"You've thought about how I taste?"

Instead of answering, I repeat the maneuver with my tongue, firmer this time. Rose groans and moves back, closer to my mouth. I repeat the same thing, with her pushing down more every time. My lips close around her clit and I suck like I did with her palm. A moan escapes her.

We find our rhythm. The heat that's been quickly spreading from my face down and from my dick up engulfs my entire body.

Twelve years of wanting her crashes into me. Every sound she makes, every twitch of her hips, is a reward I've been starving for. I bury myself in the moment, in her, desperate to make up for every second we lost.

I've missed this. My imagination is nothing like the real thing. Like Rose. She bends and bows as I intensify my sucking. Her arms shake, and she moves forward, away from my mouth.

"You are doing beautifully," I say. "Do you want to keep going or—"

"Keep going." Her answer is instantaneous. "I want more."

With a soft chuckle, I raise my head and lick her again. I want more of the feeling of her pussy on me. More Rose.

I move and add my fingers to my tongue in an ever-intensifying massage. She gasps when I press one finger into her, continuing to suck. Her body trembles with every thrust of my finger as I work her clit. At the next thrust of my finger, she lowers herself to meet me. Then again, and again, I don't know how many times, but each one hardens my dick even more.

Her whimper is needy as I moan into her, encouraged by her reaction. I put a second finger in, and she spears herself on both. Her fingers curl into my thighs, and she pulses around me. I want to ring every ounce of pleasure out of her, so I don't stop. The sound she makes is a long, guttural exhale, unrestrained, my name sprinkled in.

This is what I want her to sound like every time we're in bed together, knowing I'm the one capable of doing this to her, with her. With a soft kiss on one cheek of her ass, I help her move her knee over as she collapses on the bed beside me.

I wipe the back of my hand over my face. "That wasn't that scary, was it?"

She gently rolls her eyes, props herself on an elbow, and sets her lips on mine. Her kiss is languid, a silent stamp of approval, and all I can think about is doing this again. My lips stretch in a smile as I kiss her back. "I'll take that as a yes."

"Yes," she whispers.

"Thank you for letting me kiss you."

"You are the best kisser." Her fingers search for my hand. "You are the best."

Thirty-One

PRESENT DAY

April

Mother nature is my alarm, chirping birds and soft light from open curtains. I stretch, feeling more relaxed than I have in . . . well, forever. My hand searches the bed for Alek, but he's too far away. Damn California kings. I scooch across the sheets, my hand roaming for hard muscle.

Nothing but cool cotton.

With the sheet clutched to cover my bare breasts, I sit up. The bed is empty. The room is quiet.

No Alek.

My heart constricts. Did he go back to LA? The last thing I remember is falling asleep wrapped in his arms. A hole opens under my breastbone. He wouldn't leave me, would he? My fingers bunch the sheet as I search for evidence to disprove my theory. My top is in the middle of the floor, the walk-in closet door is open, and a navy-blue jacket sits on a hanger.

The pounding in my chest slows at the sight of the suit Alek arrived in yesterday. He's not gone.

He's just not in this room.

I slip on my shorts from last night, grab Alek's pajama top off the floor, and go in search of its owner. I button the shirt as my bare feet stumble down the stairs. From the direction of the kitchen, I hear . . . singing? I pad silently down the marble hall and have to clamp my hand over my mouth when I enter the kitchen.

In his pajama bottoms, Alek stands before the stove with a spatula in hand as he sings along to "My Girl" by The Temptations. The classic song pours out of his phone. He's a little off-key, sure, but the delivery is determined and joyful. I lean against the doorframe, admiring his confidence. Admiring him. Last night, Alek oozed the sexual chemistry that drew us together twelve years ago. This morning, the pheromones are still here, but I also see the man he is now. There's a self-assurance there I think can only come with time. I bite my thumbnail. One thing I'm certain of is that I like what I see.

". . . w-a-a-a-y?" He flips something. "My Rose." He substitutes my name into the chorus. Alek spins and another line with my name is cut short as spots me.

I wave at him. "Morning."

He pauses the music. "Morning."

I push off the doorframe. "Whatcha doing?"

"Making food. Since the Menkens are gone, I gave the staff the day off." He places both hands against the counter, then points to the open laptop. "I also had to review a contract for a warehouse. Trying to decide if I want to rent for two years or make an offer to purchase."

I scan the page. My eyebrows fly up. "That's a lot of zeros in that selling price."

He lets out a slow breath. "Yeah." His gaze meets mine. "But sometimes you have to take a chance. Gamble for the outcome you want."

"You want this warehouse?"

"Among other things." He swallows. "I want a second chance."

My pulse quickens, a rush of heat creeping up my neck as his claim lands, and I avert my gaze to his forearms, clenching my fist around the doorframe to steady myself. "You cooked?"

"The plan was to surprise you with breakfast in bed."

"I'm still surprised."

"Good." A slow smile spreads across his face. A mixture of Alek from twelve years ago and current Alek is an all-too-rare sight. He twists back to the pan. "I'm a professional at blini. I still go over to my parents' for brunch on Sundays and help out." He fishes the finished product out of the pan and sets it on a stack with several others.

I peek over the island. "Are they difficult?" My neck heats. "To make, I mean."

He raises an eyebrow at me. "Have you never made pancakes? They are very similar."

"I've lived in hotels most of my life. They have chefs on site, which is kind of part of the deal." I shrug. "Dean insisted on a housekeeper and a cook. Since living on my own, I've just picked food up on the way to the office."

Alek holds out a hand. "I can teach you."

Learning things from Alek might just become my new favorite thing. To say I skip over to him would be an understatement. It's more floating.

He tucks me between him and the stove, his strong arms encasing me from behind. "This is the batter." He points to a glass container with a spout and white goo inside. "Pour some into the pan."

My fingers grip the handle, tip the bowl, and batter rushes into the pan.

"Whoa." Alek puts his hand over mine and rights the bowl. "That's a lot of batter."

I look at him over my shoulder. "Did I ruin it?"

He puts down the bowl and wraps his arms around my waist. With a kiss to my temple, he says, "Not at all. We can fix this." He picks up the pan and rotates it in the air until the batter reaches the sides.

A fizz fills my chest at Alek's use of "we." I lean into him. "Okay. Now what?"

He rocks me back and forth. "Now, we wait. See the little bubbles forming?"

I inspect the white circle, which takes up most of the pan, and see a bubble near the edge. I nod. The stubble on his jaw scratches my cheek.

"When the surface is covered with them, we know it's time to flip."

I lean into him, the slow back-and-forth motion like a dance. How far we've come from the night he showed up at the Valentine fundraiser. "How did you come up with the idea for Second Chance? You never told me."

His "Hmmmm" vibrates against my back. "One of the charities I'm a board member of spent 70 percent of their budget on a huge gala event to draw in some big donations."

"That's a lot of money. Whose idea was that?"

"I'm ashamed to say it was mine. I thought the more lavish the event, the more they would make." He picks up the spatula. "I was so very wrong." He hands the utensil to me. "Time to flip."

I shake my head. "I don't think I should."

"How about we do it together?"

The bubbles in my chest froth again. "Okay."

"Take the spatula." I do, and he wraps his big hand around my much smaller one. My spine tingles at the feel of his long fingers against my skin. Fingers that I ground against last night. Heat flushes across my collarbone, and he gives my hand a squeeze. "We've got this."

He guides the spatula under the pancake and quickly tosses it. I hold my breath as the circle rotates in the air, then splats into the pan.

I twist in his arms and plant a kiss on his chin.

Those chocolate eyes study me. "We make a great team." He backs away. "There's coffee ready." He points to the barista bar. "I didn't want to touch that thing, so I found a French press and some ground coffee."

"Do you still take milk?" At his yes, I reluctantly step away from him, open a cupboard, and take out two thick-rimmed mugs. "So, the idea of Second Chance Events was because your charity overspent?"

Alek nods, and I set myself to the task of filling our mugs. "Basically. I'd convinced the coordinator to spend money on these elaborate flowers, and when the event was over and we hadn't raised the capital I hoped for, I watched these expensive bouquets get tossed into the trash. I was horrified by the waste."

"So you figured out a way to fix it." I stir the milk into the first mug. "You are brilliant, Alek."

"Occasionally. But sometimes, I'm very stupid." He puts our blini on a separate plate. "I found butter and syrup. Do you want to eat out on the patio?"

I pull out a stool from the island. "Can we eat here?"

He pushes the plate across the granite, then the tray he set up with the utensils and toppings, and rounds the island to sit beside me. His coffee mug in hand, he clinks it against mine. "To your first batch of blini, sweets."

The first sip of coffee is calming, and I have a feeling it's more about the company than roasted beans. "Why did you join the board of that charity?"

Alek concentrates on buttering the lacy dough and pouring syrup over it. "I knew this girl in college who took me to a charity gala, and they raised funds for kids' causes. I saw the value." He cuts the circles into bite-sized pieces. "I promised when I was in a position to give back, I would."

The gala I took him to? The only thing I remember from that night is kissing him backstage. I know the importance of fundraising for charities, which is why my pro bono work is all about them. But maybe after more than a decade doing it, I became numb to the bigger idea behind nonprofits. How inspirational they can be when they work. When they help real people. "And did you?"

"I started just donating money, but that didn't seem the same, so I added volunteering. Giving my time. The feeling of doing good, really making a difference, filled a hole in my life I didn't realize was there until I got my hands dirty, so to speak."

He jabs the fork into the morsel and lifts it to my mouth. I lean forward, wrap my lips around the bite, and pull it off. Alek's pupils dilate as he watches me. I swallow. "Delicious."

"Agreed." His voice is a little hoarse. He grabs his coffee and gulps it down.

"If donating was working, why start Second Chance? Or why not do Second Chance and TRI? Why sell?"

"After we sell TRI, I'll have more money than I could spend in a lifetime. In my grandkids' lifetimes. I'm done looking for opportunities to make money. What's another zero on the end of my bank account?" He shrugs. "It's time to do what I'm really passionate about, like if I won the lottery."

"Won the lottery?" I nudge him for another bite.

"When I was a kid, my parents and I would play the what-would-you-do-if-you-won-the-lottery-and-didn't-have-to-worry-about-money game. That's where I'm at." He pops a piece in his mouth.

"And giving back to charities is what you chose as a kid?"

He offers me the fork. "No. Back then, I wanted a Lamborghini and a private jet."

He takes a slow breath, his eyes drifting to the ceiling as if recalling the memory. The weight of his words still lingers when he speaks again. "TRI owns two jets, and Lamborghinis aren't that much fun to drive in LA traffic. Little by little, my dream changed, and volunteering was part of me seeing the world and what people need in a different light." His voice falters, the shift in his emotions palpable.

"But three years ago, I was having lunch with Callum, and we played the game again. The answer was clear to me—most rich people don't care about the poor. The donations are tax deductions more often than not. Making charities rely on that uncertain motivation is not a secure way forward. I knew what I could do to effect change. I can use technology to help the charities help themselves."

The weight of his conviction leaves me speechless, a reminder how far off track I've drifted. The quiet unease refuses to fade.

We eat in quiet comfort until his knee knocks mine. "If you weren't a hotel heiress, what would you do?"

I sit back. "Doing anything else was never an option. All my mother's plans hinge on my continuing the family legacy. I could never disappoint her."

Alek looks around the room. "Your mother isn't here. Dream a little. What would you do?"

I bite my lip. "I don't know." The hotel business is the only thing I've ever worked on outside of the app Alek and I created in college. "Charities are important to me, like they are to you. That's always been my hobby, so maybe a career in that realm? I don't believe I've thought about what I do with the charities as deeply as you have. I enjoy setting up events, so I do that, and I do it free of charge. I don't know if there's some alternate scenario where I'm a head event coordinator for a major charity." My gaze finds Alek's. "My version of Second Chance Events."

"Why an alternate scenario? What's stopping you now?"

I huff. "Decades of hard work? If I give up everything I've sacrificed to be the CEO of HH Group, those years would be for nothing. It's like losing. And I don't like losing."

Alek picks up the empty plate and walks to the sink. He runs water over the dish, turns, and leans against the counter. "But what about all the other years you have to live? The life before you." He crosses his arms. "From my perspective, it's not losing. It's making a choice. Choices are hard, but they are up to us."

"Not up to me, though. Not that choice."

Alek dries his hands and wraps them around me. "How about this choice: do you want to watch some men hit a tiny ball with a stick, or do you prefer staying inside in this empty house with no one needing anything from us?"

I smile up at him. "That's easy." I kiss him on his chin. "I choose us."

THIRTY-TWO

ALEK

November

I'm hot. No, I'm not hot, but something hot is wrapped around me. On my chest, on my thighs. I move my hand and touch soft naked skin belonging to a body draped over me like a cloak. A small palm is pressed possessively against my hip. I want to tattoo it there. Thanksgiving has a whole new meaning to me now.

My room is dark, but even with the blinds closed, murky light streams in, which is a good indicator my girlfriend and I slept through the night.

My girlfriend.

I trace a finger over the forearm that holds me close, the gorgeously ruffled little spoon next to me. The freedom to touch

Rose makes me brave, and I slowly twist in her arms so I can continue my exploration of the marvel in my bed. Her eyelids flutter, and the pads of her fingers glide down too, dangerously close to my morning wood. I hover between being desperate for her to wake and hoping she'll sleep a little longer. Soon, her ribcage rises and falls in slow waves.

My hand drifts over her waist, to her ribs, and rests at the top of her shoulder. I reverse my hand's course, her warm skin smooth and perfect beneath my palm. Without those multicolored eyes staring at me, I take my time drinking in her heart-shaped face. Her hair is properly tousled from our almost-sleepless night, and the vision is adorable. I wonder if this counts for the project as an activity neither of us have ever done together before.

I'm not talking about sleeping with Rose, although we definitely checked that box. Everything physical Rose and I have done has been intense. And the most intimate sex I've ever had in my life has been with her. Rose is everything I've ever dreamed of in a partner. She trusts me by speaking her wants aloud, and my new primary occupation might be yielding to her desires. Her pleasure is my pleasure.

The truth that escaped me yesterday makes everything brand new. I've never made love with someone before. Never slept with someone I love.

Until now.

I run my knuckles down the bridge of her freckled nose, which scrunches when I irritate her. Her lips twitch into a ghost of a smile, and she shifts to her back with her eyes still closed.

"Are you awake?" I rise on my elbows.

"Do I need to be awake?" she mumbles.

"No. Sleep."

She always says I don't get enough sleep, but she's equally guilty. I hop out of my bed, pull gray sweatpants on, and creep downstairs. I enter the living room.

"Morning," Callum says around a mouthful of cereal he's crunching next to the still-open computer I left on the couch when I fell asleep, before Rose showed up on our doorstep. Callum sets his bowl down. "The sleeping princess is awake."

I halt mid-step. Did he hear Rose come in? Did he hear Rose and me not sleeping most of the night? No. He would've made a much more inappropriate comment, and if I don't get him out of here before Rose wakes up, he definitely will. I flip my laptop closed. "Any way you can find another place to stay this weekend?"

Callum's spoon stops midway between the bowl and his mouth. "Don't you love me anymore? Are we breaking up?"

I flip him the bird. "I'll ask the rest of the guys to disappear till Monday too."

"No need to worry about them. Linc made up with Maria. Blake was summoned by his mother again, and Soren went with him for moral support. Those Europeans are tight. Wouldn't expect any of them back until Sunday night." Callum throws his arm over the back of the couch. "But I'm supposed to study, not party."

"Can't you call up one of your conquests and crash at their place?"

The sounds of a shower running rattles in the flimsy walls of the house. Callum's mouth falls open. "You have someone up there?"

"Not someone."

He presses his fist to his mouth. "You finally bagged Rose?"

I wrap my arm around his neck in a chokehold, playing around but also serious. "Never say anything like that about my girlfriend again if you want to continue breathing."

"Girlfriend." Callum taps out and chuckles through a cough. "Took you long enough."

"Coming from a guy who's never had a girlfriend in his life."

"Different folks, different stro—"

"We can discuss your masturbation techniques another time." I snatch his cereal bowl away. "Can you leave now?"

He eases off the couch and heads for the kitchen. "Let me say hi to Rose. Make her coffee, maybe?"

"I'll be the one making her coffee. Until Monday." I twist him in the direction of the front door.

"Aww, my boy is in love." He ruffles my hair. "Call if you need any advice." He wiggles his eyebrows as he grabs his backpack off the floor. "Enjoy your honeymoon."

I shut and deadbolt the door. The sounds of the running shower remind me why I need the house to myself. Without another moment of hesitation, I run up the stairs to my girlfriend.

AT THE SIGHT OF Rose naked in the shower, I'm instantly hard. Water runs in rivulets down her breasts, stomach, and to the darker triangle of hair I am now a lot more familiar with but want to touch again and again today, tomorrow . . . The caveman in me demands to claim this woman as mine as soon as possible in every way possible.

Her gaze roams across my body, and my hunger is reflected in her eyes as they halt their exploration at my cock. Can a man come from just being looked at? In this moment, I'd answer yes. That is, if the woman looking at me is Rose. But I want more than her gaze. I want her hands on me, and I definitely want to touch her as well.

I open the shower door. "If you let me join, I promise you can do whatever you need to do with me."

"Are we trying to get clean or dirty?"

Invitation accepted, I close the door behind me, trapping us in the rising steam. "What would you prefer we do first?"

"Dirty." Her answer runs hotter than the spray of the shower across my skin. She wraps her hand around my erection and twists her wrist as she moves up and down. "Definitely want dirty first."

The anticipation that got me hard has nothing on the sensation of her palm on me. I brace myself against the wall above her head as she continues touching me. Desire sizzles under my skin, visceral and demanding. Her hand increases the already impossible high, and her mouth so close and tantalizing promises even higher peaks.

Rose's gaze meets mine. "Ask me what I need."

"What do you need, Rose?"

"I need to taste you."

My gaze glues itself to her mouth. "You don't have to."

"But I need to. Or do you not want to be inside my mouth?"

"I've been thinking about my dick in your mouth for entirely too long, but—"

"This is for me." Her mosaic eyes bore into me. "Let me."

"Fuck yes."

With a demure smile, she lowers to her knees, far enough from the shower that the water only hits her back. Her throat moves in a quick swallow as she runs her palm up and down my shaft one more time. My dick jerks when Rose's tongue darts out and licks off my pre-cum. Fuck. I wish I could dig my fingers into something, but the warm, sleek tile doesn't give me the satisfaction. If I knew I could trust myself, I'd plunge my hand into Rose's wet hair, but I don't. My unhinged desire to claim Rose won't be the reason I lose her trust.

Rose wraps her lips around my cock and sucks. I choke on the sound that escapes me. She moves her mouth down, taking more of me as her tongue swirls around the tip. One of my hands slips and I clench it into a fist. I want to move her head and set the rhythm, but I also want her to do what she needs. I promised her, and I keep my promises.

"It's fucking unreal how seeing my dick in your mouth makes me harder than I've ever been." Words finally make it past the thickness in my throat. "You're so fucking beautiful."

One hand around the base of my shaft, she bobs up and down, keeping up the pleasurable suction I don't think I can continue to resist. She increases the pressure when she gets to the tip, and then she goes as far down as she can until I hit the back of her throat.

I let out a gasp at the sound of Rose gagging a little. "Wait," I say, but it's followed by my groan that says otherwise.

Rose glances up. She keeps up the tempo, and my hips jerk to meet her every move, greedy for more. Drunk on the sight, the feel, and the realization this is happening, I unravel, putting one hand on her shoulder to get her mouth off me before I completely lose control.

"I can't hold on."

She doesn't stop. Fuck.

"I'm warning you, sweets, I'll come inside your mouth. Is that what you want?"

Her eyes meet mine and plead yes.

My palms meet the shower wall. I'm so deep already, but she grabs my thighs and urges me even deeper. I let go. My mouth opens in a growl as I spill into her. She drinks me in, then releases me, evidence of my desire dripping out of her mouth.

My breaths ragged, I shake my head at the sight of her—so far beyond what I imagined, and I love every second of this.

I bend to lift Rose up and kiss her lips, licking inside her mouth and tasting the evidence of myself coating her tongue. My rough kisses don't deter her. She answers back with equal fervor, and when my tongue licks the inside of her mouth clean, I don't stop. Moving us back under the water, I run my fingers over Rose's flushed face and body, removing any trace of what we just did and priming the canvas of her body for more things my imagination can't conjure yet, but I know we can make happen. She's perfect for me, and that knowledge calms the part of me set on ravaging.

"Sweet, sweet girl," I murmur against her mouth. "I'll clean you now, okay?"

She blinks in agreement through the beads of water on her eyelashes. I kiss her temples, grab the shampoo, and massage the liquid into her scalp, kissing her lips as I rinse her hair by smoothing it under the water. My body wash is not good enough for her skin, but it's all I have. I take every opening to learn her curves as I press soft kisses against her skin on every spot before washing away the suds. I lather her back, her breasts, her stomach, and gently clean between her legs.

"I like this part too," she whispers as I rinse her off. She turns me around, and her nails scrape across my back as she scrubs me clean. Her hands wrap around my waist, soap and tenderness swiping my stomach. With the lightest of touches, she makes quick work of me, her last task a soothing massage of shampoo in my hair.

"All clean." I kiss the top of her head, open the door, and retrieve a towel. I hug her in the material, securing it over her breasts.

DREAMS DO COME TRUE. I'm still in the living room-kitchen-combo of my duplex, but the sight in front of me is most definitely copied out of one of my wet dreams. Hair still damp, Rose stirs milk into her coffee, wearing nothing but my boxers that she rolled at the waist and my UCLA T-shirt that hangs to mid-thigh. She swallows another bite of the ham-and-cheese omelet I made for us and hums in appreciation. "Where did you learn to cook?"

"It's an omelet, toast, sliced strawberries, and French press coffee. I hardly call this cooking." Sitting into my favorite spot on the couch, I fork the first bite of my eggs into my mouth.

Rose picks up her plate, grabs her cup, and joins me in the living room. She sets the food next to mine on the coffee table, climbs into my lap, and perches on my leg. Her thighs on top of mine are a casual sight I didn't expect out of a hotel heiress, but I can imagine us sitting like this every morning. The swell of her breast presses into me, and warmth spreads from that contact into my heart. I wrap my arm around her waist and nestle her closer to me.

"Can I see the changes you made to the home and registration pages?"

I nod. "After you eat." I reach across the table, draw her plate closer, spear some strawberries on her fork, and hand the loaded utensil to her.

She bites the food off the fork while I hold it. I smile as a new-to-me feeling of contentment swells in the space around my heart. I could get used to this. As she chews, I get her another bite ready and bring my computer to life, wrap one hand around Rose's waist, and type in my password.

"I also merged the code for the login pages the other coders worked on." I open the shared project folder. "Their code was mostly clean, but it took me a couple of days to adjust—"

"I don't see a new version."

I gape at the screen. "My changes." I point to the date and time fields from four days ago. My breathing halts. Breakfast forgotten, I search the prototype for my other changes. Nothing is there. Days and days of work are now lost. I tilt my head back. "Fuck."

Rose cups my face. "Alek?"

"All the changes are gone." My chest empties. "They didn't save."

"Shit." Rose looks at the screen, then back at me. "All your work."

"Users won't be able to create profiles or log in." My stomach jumps into my throat. Without the changes I made this week, we don't have a usable interface. I rake my hand through my hair.

All my sleepless nights and all the roles Rose took on to get the prototype done on time and on budget were pointless. The few bites of egg I swallowed revolt in my stomach. If Professor Patel and the panelists can't interact with the app, we'll fail the class.

Yesterday, the app, which at the beginning of the semester was nothing more than an idea, was complete. Now I'm no better off than when my dog ate my homework in second grade. I raise my gaze to the project partner I failed. This time I'm not just ruining my work, I'm ruining Rose's too.

"We still have last week's files, right?" Rose asks, her voice calm and steady.

I nod, the mayhem in my head interrupted.

"Okay, we have three days before we need to present." Rose squints at the ceiling.

That look I know. That's Project Manager Rose, who can figure out how to get stuff done. My stomach stops swimming.

She gets off my lap and picks up her phone from the coffee table. "I'll call Olivia to bring me my laptop and a case of those awful energy drinks you like." She pecks my lips, and my mistake doesn't seem like such a nightmare anymore. "We can do this."

I open the last saved version of the prototype and listen to Rose form our plan of attack. The storm hasn't passed, but she's given me shelter. I'm not going to mess up again. I catch Rose's hand and give her my best smile, thankful yet again that I have her in my life.

Fuck, I love this woman.

Thirty-Three

TWELVE YEARS AGO

November

Alek's living room smells like three days worth of stale food, coffee, and frustration. I fail to stifle a yawn. My laptop whirs beside me, filled with perfectly formatted slides, yet my eyes keep drifting to Alek. With the extra six minutes we got, the entire scope of what the app will do is laid out, and each of us know our parts of the presentation. I'm proud of our creation, and we just need the prototype to actually work.

Next to me on the couch, Alek is all sharp focus, his sleeves pushed up and jaw set. His fingers move over the keys with practiced precision. I love watching him like this—completely in his element. I want to touch him, but I don't know if it would help or distract him. We've had a few stress releases these last three days, and I don't know which I like more . . . Alek working on the app or Alek working on my body. I bite my lip and instead just sit close enough that my thigh brushes his. It's a quiet reminder he's not alone. We'll nail this project.

Ten weeks ago, I thought Alek being my partner was a mistake. Three days ago, I thought being with Alek would be a mistake. Today, I'm certain meeting Alek has changed my entire life for the better. Because somewhere over the months of knowing him, I've fallen in love with someone I never thought would both challenge and support me.

"How close are you?" My voice's a whisper.

His sigh is sharp. "The loading time is still twice as long as it should be."

"As long as it loads, we'll be fine." I push my laptop closed and pull down the hem of Alek's shirt that's ridden up to reveal the third pair of his boxers I had to borrow this weekend.

"All the extra minutes we earned will be wasted on just loading if I don't fix this." He grinds his teeth, not taking his eyes off his screen, as if the delay personally offends him.

I rest my chin on his shoulder, peering at his screen. "This looks so real, though."

He lets out a dry chuckle. "We can go back to just the wireframes, but you know it won't get us the same grade as an app they can interact with."

"Is there anything I can do?"

"Just . . ." His voice halts, and for the first time in hours, he turns to look at me. His expression shifts. "Be here?"

The simple request hits somewhere deep. "I'm not going anywhere."

I press a quick, barely-there kiss to his cheek, ignoring the way my stomach flips. Another jaw-cracking yawn splits my mouth. Stretching my arms over my head, I dramatically collapse against Alek's side. My body is done with this all-nighter.

"I'll just . . . rest for a bit," I whisper.

"I'll wake you when it's working." His fingers hover over the keys.

Alek turns to look at me, and his gaze softens. He lifts a hand, hesitates, and tucks a loose strand of hair behind my ear. His touch is gentle and reverent, and it makes my lungs tighten. I shift closer, pressing my forehead against his shoulder, my frame curling into his like it's the most natural thing in the world. His eyes are tired, but there's relief in them. I don't know what possesses me, but I press a soft kiss just under his jaw. His breath catches. He lowers his head and kisses me slowly.

The kind of kiss that says more than words ever could.

"Rest," he murmurs. "I won't let you down."

And I believe him.

I WAKE WITH A START, my mind churning with anxiety I can't pinpoint. The living room around me is filled with light. Not my living room, though. It's Alek's. The warm press of his body is still against mine, and his arm is slung over my shoulder like it belongs there. His laptop sits open on the coffee table.

"What are you two still doing here?" Callum chucks his backpack by the door.

My gaze cuts to Alek's roommate as I jolt from the warm haze we'd been wrapped in. The tender bubble we were floating in all weekend bursts and disappointment rushes in, dragging the sharp point of anxiety through my abdomen. Callum's tone is casual, but there's tension in his stance. Something's off.

The front door slams and Alek's eyes fly open. His gaze finds me, and a smile crawls onto his lips as panic crawls into my mind.

Tumbling in, Blake nudges Soren. "Are we too early or too late?"

Linc walks in and looks at his watch. "Isn't your presentation in thirty minutes?"

"Shit. What time is it?" I scramble off the couch, grab the laptop, and choke out, "We won't make it."

Alek takes the laptop out of my hands. "It's ready. I got the loading down to three seconds. No glitches. No delays."

I want to celebrate, but I also want to scream. "It's Monday, Alek. We're up to present in—"

"Twenty-five minutes." Linc checks his watch again, and I'm running toward the front door.

"You might want to get dressed first," says Callum.

My clothes. I stare down at the T-shirt and boxers. The plan was to swing by my suite, change, and do my hair and makeup.

I redirect to the stairs. The pants I came here in might work, but the T-shirt? Tears well in my eyes.

"Callum, make coffee. Soren, nuke the breakfast sandwiches from the freezer." Alek is on my heels as he shouts out commands. "Linc, pack our laptops and all the papers from the coffee table."

"I'll stand here and look pretty," Blake offers.

I burst into Alek's room. "I have nothing to wear. No makeup. My hair." Crying is the last thing I need to do, but I can't stop the sob that burst out of me.

Strong hands frame my face, and soft lips kiss my tears away. "You look stunning no matter what you wear. I have plenty of shirts you can borrow, and maybe Olivia can meet us there and bring you makeup?"

"It's at least a thirty-minute drive, even if she left now." I wipe my eyes and find my pants on the floor. Wrinkled. "I don't want to be the reason our presentation is ruined."

"They won't dock us because you're not wearing makeup." Alek pulls on khakis and picks out two identical collared shirts. "One for you and one for me? We can play it off as if we're matching on purpose. Like we're a team."

My heart thuds as I yank one shirt out of his hands. "At least you got the prototype running. Let's hope that's more important than what I look like."

I CLICK ON THE profile tab of the app. "The customers can check in and get access to their room, bypassing the front desk. Without plastic keys we eliminate waste, save money, and modernize the customer check-in and check-out experience."

The last page loads without a hitch. Alek's shoulders relax. "The prototype we've presented today would allow hotels to streamline operations."

We come together in front of the screen, our presentation behind us, and smile at each other. "Thank you for considering adding our app to your technology suite."

The applause from Professor Patel is enthusiastic. "Well done. If I were a hotel mogul, I just might write you an offer."

My mother gives the professor a polite smile. The trembling I was barely controlling takes over my hands, and I push them behind me. Confronting my mom about why she showed up at my project presentation when Alek and I filed in the moment our turn started was not an option.

Even now, I'm not able to make eye contact with her. I smooth Alek's shirt over my pants and hope his belt that I used to cinch it looks like a fashion statement and not my last-minute attempt to avoid looking like a tent.

"Can I try the app?" Professor Patel points to Alek's laptop.

"Absolutely." Alek works the app back to the login screen.

Mom's perfume reaches me before she does. She loops her arms through mine and, with all the poise of a queen, leads me to the side of the room as far away as possible from the people clicking around.

"The app was indeed very promising." Mom tugs down the long tails of Alek's shirt. "You are not just sleeping with the guy. You got him to implement your idea."

How she can combine a compliment and a diss so seamlessly, I will never understand. "The app is actually Alek's idea. My role was to run the project and get funding."

"I'm certain our lawyers will be able to persuade him not to mention his involvement," says Mom.

My feet stick to the floor. "What are you talking about?"

"This is your project, Rose. Your app." Mom's eyes flick to the men and then back to me. "We aren't giving your intellectual property to the son of our maintenance manager. No matter how good he is in bed, he is not the creator here. You are the brains."

I glare at her. "That's not true. We did the project together, but the idea was totally his. If you like the app, why not offer to buy it from him?"

My mother's hand clasps my arm. "I don't buy what's already mine. You know how business works. If you can get a freebie, that's the way to go."

"I won't let you steal this from him." I disentangle myself from her grip and stomp back to where Alek and the professor are now surrounded by the rest of the panel.

The second I approach them, Alek takes my hand and draws me into the circle. "You have Rose to thank for that. Besides being the organizational genius, she insisted we have extra functionality on the dashboard. She refused to let the UX designer off the hook until it was to her specifications."

"Have you considered working in app development?" Professor Patel asks me.

His question is as alien as if he'd asked if I'd considered being the Queen of England.

"She's the future CEO of HH Group. She has bigger potential." Mom sets her hand on my shoulder. "But I'd love to talk about the option of buying the IP for the app from the two of you. 50/50 split between you and Rose?" She addresses Alek.

Professor Patel crosses his arms. "I have several investors I can introduce the two of you to if you'd like to actually make this app. You've got all the major ingredients, and I'll mentor you on how to approach the first round of funding. You have a real opportunity to make it big."

Alek threads his fingers through mine. "Rose and I will have to discuss, but creating my own company is one of the reasons I joined this class. I'd appreciate any introductions."

"Why bother with those?" Mom smiles her CEO smile. "I can guarantee a competitive payment for the intellectual property and recommend you to some of the tech companies who I'm sure are looking for junior coders."

Alek faces Mom. "Thank you. That's not what I'm after." He doesn't let go of my hand, even when Mom's gaze glues onto our fingers. "Being a business owner is my plan. This class and this app is a launching pad for my career as an entrepreneur. I'm not interested in fulfilling someone else's vision. I'm grateful for your interest in buying the app idea, but I have to decline."

Mom's eyes narrow as she attempts to cover her irritation with a smile. "I wish you all the best with your business endeavor." She re-threads her arm through mine, the one opposite of Alek. "I'm afraid I have to steal my daughter now. HH Group business. You understand."

My irritation with Mom boils inside my chest. I mouth, "I'll see you later," to Alek and follow the woman who's right now the CEO of HH Group and not my mother. I match her quick strides as she marches down the hallway.

Once outside, I turn to her. "I didn't realize you were coming today."

"I didn't realize you were in love with that boy."

Cold dread sprints down my spine. "What are you talking about?"

Without breaking her stride, she grabs my elbow and hisses into my ear. "You should know better than this. Mark my words, I will not let a boy like that ruin your future. And I certainly won't watch it happen."

Thirty-Four

ALEK

TWELVE YEARS AGO

November

Through the open windows, the crisp evening air carries the distant sounds of laughter and music from a frat house down the street. But inside my place, it's just warm light, soft music, and the quiet hum of anticipation.

Kicking the guys out of the house for another night cost me a month of house cleaning and cooking chores, but another night with Rose celebrating our win is worth a lot more. I adjust the two new champagne flutes on the coffee table, checking once more that everything is perfect for my first official date with my girlfriend.

My girlfriend. Fuck, I'll never get tired of calling her that.

The metal bucket isn't silver, but it still gleams in the candle-light with condensation beading along its rim as the champagne that cost more than a keg of beer chills inside. The steaks rest under foil on the counter, and a small dish of freshly cut straw-berries waits on a plate—just the way Rose likes them.

I check Rose's last text. She should be here any minute.

My stomach knots from excitement as I take the potted plant I rescued from the corner store off the counter and place it on the coffee table. That leaves no space for plates, though. I put it back onto the counter and am opening the cabinets when there's a knock at the door.

I don't walk. I rush to answer, a smile already forming on my face as I turn the knob. Mama's already asked me if I can bring Rose over for the New Year's get-together. Hopefully Rose agrees because I can't imagine spending a day, let alone a holiday, without her. I swing the door open, and my smile dies.

Rose looks wrecked. Eyes red. Skin blotchy. It's like she's been crying for hours.

"Rose." I step toward her, my arms ready to hold her and fix whatever's wrong.

Stone-faced, she thrusts a bag toward me and steps back.

A step *away* from me.

A slow-burning coil of confusion burns in my gut. I take the bag and peer inside. My shirt. My belt. Notebooks, folders, and three of my energy drinks.

"What's this?" My voice comes out uneven.

"All your stuff." She clasps her hands in front of her and takes another step back.

Another step away from me.

My chest constricts as if something vital is slipping, but I force a grin. I'm not sure what's going on, but there has to be some type of misunderstanding.

"Come in." I step aside, making room. She'll come in. We'll talk. We'll fix whatever this is. "I got the right kind of champagne. One you'll approve of."

At the word "approve" her head jerks up, eyes flashing.

"I can't." Her denial is sharp, like little needles across my skin. She angles her chin to me. "I'm leaving tonight."

The moment frays. What? She didn't mention a trip. Did I miss her saying she was leaving? Have I not paid attention? I've been so tired that it's possible, but I'm acutely aware of everything to do with Rose, and her leaving town would have stuck.

"Tonight?" My brain scrambles for context or a clue to help make sense of this. "Where are you going?"

"Miami." Her voice is cool and detached, which is a stark contrast to the storm raging in her eyes. "Mom's going back to oversee the hotel renovation. I'll shadow her and help organize everything."

Miami? She's leaving for Miami?

A weird hissing sound fills my head, drowning the street noise behind her.

"You're great at organizing." My own voice sounds distant and robotic. "When will you be back?" I cross my fingers that she'll say she will be gone for a few days or a week, tops.

Her lips press together. "I'm taking the next semester off."

No.

No, no, no. This can't be right. We have plans. We're building something together. We—

"The time change will make things interesting," I say quickly, already working through the logistics. "I'll make sure my shifts at the hotel are midnights so we can work online during the day. Or maybe I'll come to Miami too. Does the hotel need maintenance people—"

"No."

I frown. "They don't need maintenance people?"

"You are not coming to Miami." Her voice is steel. "Our project is over. We did what we set out to do. I told you my goal was not to build an app. I had to show Mom I can be an executive and that I know what the job requires. HH Group is my future, not app development. Or organizing the development of an app you created."

"You did more than organize." My hand stretches toward her. "You're as responsible for our app as I am."

She wraps her hands around her waist. "Your app. You can do whatever you want with it."

My pulse pounds in my ears. I don't want the app if it means losing her. Is that what's happening here? Am I losing her?

"I . . . Look, just come in." My voice cracks. "Have dinner? Talk this over with me."

"No."

She shakes her head. Once. Twice. Each movement shatters a part of me.

"No."

My world tilts. My feet carry me forward before I even realize, stepping onto the porch and closing the space separating her from me. "Come on, sweets, what's really going on?"

She steps back. "Stop."

Her command yanks me to a halt.

"What is wrong?" I sound desperate. "Did your mom say something? Are there more photos of us? Whatever happened, we can figure it out." I reach for her, clasping her fingers. She doesn't pull away. "I love you." I throw the words in the air like a lifeline. "You know that. I'll move to Miami. I'll sell the app to your mom. We'll come up with a new project. Together, we can handle anything."

Her eyes glisten. For a second, for one fucking second, I think she'll break. I think she'll tell me the truth. And that truth must be that this is some twisted plan forced onto her by her mother.

But then her fingers yank out of mine. "I'm sorry. I should not have come here last week. I made a mistake."

Her statement rips me apart. "A mistake?"

She nods, looking away.

My stomach drops. "That's a lie. Nothing about what we shared this weekend was a mistake. You and me together . . .

it was perfect. I wouldn't change a single moment of it for the world." I tap the spot over my heart. "You felt this too. Don't deny it. This isn't you."

Her gaze snaps back at me, and her throat works as she swallows hard. "When I said I wanted more, all I was after was to sleep with you." Each syllable may as well be its own individual bullet. "Don't confuse sex with something else. You don't fit into my life."

I flinch. Physically flinch. The burn in my chest turns into an inferno. "I could if you wanted me to."

"Things don't work that way." She wipes her eyes.

"What way?" I demand. "We're not in Regency England, where royalty can't marry a commoner. There are no real rules prohibiting us from being together."

"But there are." Her voice is not even a whisper. "I don't want to ruin our lives just because the sex was great." She stares at the spot above my heart. "Build the app, take Professor Patel's help, and become an entrepreneur."

"Not without you."

Her eyes find mine. "Pretend last semester didn't happen, okay? Forget I exist and live your best life."

I can't feel my body. "But I want you in my life."

"No, you don't." She wavers. "Trust me when I say this is the only way."

I shake my head as anger finally creeps beneath the numbness of my heartbreak. "It can't be. I won't accept this."

Her lips tremble, and her eyes fill with unshed tears. "I made my choice, Alek." Her voice hitches, and red splotches dot her cheeks. "In the bag, there's a folder with a signed document confirming you are the sole owner of the app. I'm refusing all rights." Her gaze flicks to the bag that's fallen to my feet. "My lawyers went over the contract—it's airtight. No one can claim I had anything to do with it."

Her lawyers. Her fucking lawyers. Is that where she's been all day?

Everything in me rebels. My spine locks, my shoulders stiffen, my jaw clenches hard enough to grind off the enamel as my pulse detonates throughout my limbs. My thoughts go from smoldering to explosion. I want to scream and kick, but all I do is stand there, tense with restraint.

She doesn't mean this. I know she doesn't. I want to pull her into my arms, hold her until she stops lying to herself, insist we will figure it out, and tell her we can face her mother and the entire world. I want to prove to her that we can live our lives how we want to.

"You need to let me go," she begs. "Please."

She begs me to let her leave. To act like she meant nothing. Like she never even existed.

"You said you'd do anything I ask. This is me asking you to live your life and never contact me again. Please, say that you—" She stuffs her knuckles between her teeth and closes her eyes. A sob erupts from her, and she turns to the stairs. She stalls on the top step. "Please, forget about me."

I shouldn't be happy this is difficult for her, because causing her pain is not what I want, even though my ribcage caves under the weight of this fucking unfairness.

"Is this what you really want?" I need her to say no.

"Yes." Her chin juts out. "Forget me. Follow your dreams. Promise me."

My knees tremble. I'm frozen in place, stuck between needing her to be with me and keeping my oath to do what she asks. I can't understand her side of this fucked-up situation, but I can't make it worse for her either. Every fiber in my being cries not to do this. Not to commit to giving her this one thing.

Still, I nod.

"You have to say the words," she pleads.

Breathing is harder than ever. The vow that was easy to say this morning, last night, and for the last ten weeks, takes all my effort to grind out.

"I promise." I shatter into an infinity of tiny pieces that slice at my heart.

Rose hovers at the side of the stairs. "Have a great life, Alek."

I ache to reach for her, take her hand, and convince her to stay, but she made her wishes abundantly clear, and I'd never force her into anything, especially not into being together.

She turns and runs down the street, away from me. Away from us. My heart leaves my chest, following her, where it wants to stay.

"I love you," I call out in my final attempt to open her eyes. "And you're in love with me too."

Rose falters with her back to me, her shoulders slumped. She stops running.

A spark of hope ignites in my head. We've been here before. Only four days ago, in her hotel room, she pushed me away. I thought all was lost that night. But she came back.

"I don't understand why you're doing this now, but when you change your mind, I'll be waiting for you," I say. "No matter what."

"I won't change my mind." She resumes walking and opens the door to the limo waiting at the sidewalk. One hand on the door, she turns to face me. Her mosaic eyes shine with tears under the glow of the street light. "There's not a chance."

I TOSS BACK MY third chaser. The cheap shot burns my throat. The throat that spilled the promise to forget Rose. I gulp the fresh pint of beer to wash away the bitterness and slam the empty glass next to the other two.

There isn't enough beer in the world to make me forget her.

"Thought I might find you here." Callum slips onto the barstool beside me and flags down The Devil's Martini bartender. "I'll have what he's having."

"Shouldn't you be heading to the airport?"

He picks up a coaster and spins it on one of the corners. "I have a few hours. Flights to Toronto aren't technically international." He squeezes my arm. "Sure you don't want to come with me? Mom, Dad, and my little sister Parker all want to meet you. Plus, it's the home of hockey. We could play a game on real frozen ice, the way it's meant to be played."

I shake off his hold on me. "If I had money for any flight, I'd be boarding a plane to Miami right now."

"Fuck, Alek. Blake would give you the fare for your flight anywhere. It's couch change to him. But you need to tell us what happened. It's been three weeks."

My lungs burn. How has the world marched on? How has my blood circulated for three whole weeks when my heart has been ripped out and currently resides in Miami? "She hasn't even texted."

"Did you have a fight?"

I hiccup. "I wish. Then I'd know what the problem was and we could figure it out together."

The bartender drops off Callum's shot and a pint. "I don't understand. We saw you that morning. You two were . . . I don't fucking know. Perfect together. In sync. In—"

"Love." I take his beer, guzzle it, and wave for another.

"Yeah." Callum downs his shot and winces. "Something like that."

I spin on him. "What did her sister say?" Last night, I was so desperate that I begged Callum to text Olivia and ask if she knew anything.

My friend hesitates long enough for a buzz of hope to rise into my throat.

"She . . . ah . . . didn't text me back."

The buzz dissolves into the dull ache I've carried around for weeks. I snatch the new glass of beer from the bartender and wave it at Callum. "Good riddance to the Haliday sisters." I slam my beer into his empty glass. "Here's to never dealing with rich snobs again."

Another gulp can't keep the regret at bay for broadcasting my anger.

"About the rich snobs," Callum starts. "Blake officially gets access to his trust fund in January, and we have an idea."

"Fuck ideas." I scrape my nails through the three-week stubble that's more like a beard on my chin. "Ideas are a dime a dozen. Pointless."

Callum takes the beer out of my hands and I growl at him. He holds his palms up in defense. "And you think sitting at this bar, providing The Devil's Martini with their entire evening's revenue, has a point?"

"She told me to forget. The point is to forget her, forget us . . . forget everything."

"You've tried for weeks, and you aren't any closer to forgetting. Maybe closer to cirrhosis, but you know what the definition of insanity is? Doing the same thing over and over and expecting a different result. You need to pour your frustration into something productive."

"Fixing rich people's sinks? I'm done with that. I'm done with working for other people."

"What about working for yourself? Starting a company? Professor Patel insists you need to build a business with your brilliant idea. You are the brains. Blake is the money."

"And what are you, the panty chaser?"

My friend falls silent beside me.

"Fuck. Callum, I'm sorry." I turn to him. "I didn't mean that. I'm . . . drunk. And mad, and upset, and . . ."

Callum's shoulders rise and fall. "I have ideas too, you know. I may not be as smart as Rose, but you and I were a pretty good team on the ice. I bet we could be great together off the ice as well."

"You really want to be my partner?"

He throws me a smile. One I know gets the ladies all hot and bothered. "I mean, I've never swung that way before, but if anyone could get me to try it—"

"Fuck off." I nearly shove him off the stool.

He climbs back on. "Yes, I really want to be your partner. In business." His voice is soft, and when I glance at him, a real smile greets me.

"You're serious." Even through my drunken haze, a plan forms. Not the dream vision I had with Rose, but someone reliable. Callum and I have been together since the day I walked into our shared dorm room and he charmed the RA into having a floor party. That was when he introduced me to everyone. He's always been my wingman, and he's always had my back. On and off the ice.

I can trust Callum.

My beer pushed aside, I hold out my hand to my best friend in earnest. "I'd love to create a company with you."

"Yeah?" Callum's smile widens. "Yeah," he shouts over the noise of the bar. "We're fucking doing this." He grabs and shakes my hand. "I'll be a star NHL player *and* a rich CEO asshole."

I wrap both arms around him and slam my palms into his back. For the first time in three weeks, I grasp something solid.

Thirty-Five

ALEK

PRESENT DAY

April

Our weekend at the Masters extended into a full week in Georgia with lazy mornings, long walks, lingering dinners, and exciting all-nighters. Endless conversations didn't make up for our years apart, but they gave us a second chance with each other: rediscovering the things we already knew and sharing new parts of ourselves. The real world waited, but it didn't stop.

Four hours on my private jet flew by while I held Rose's hand on the flight back to LA. Today, at the golf club where she kissed me, her fingers rest against mine under the table.

The server takes away the dessert plates as Ezra passes Leanne the promotional brochure I created to outline the benefits and opportunities of Second Chance Events. Rose laughed when

I showed her the glossy paper. "Old-school technique to sell a new-school idea."

Leanne nods while reading, and my chest zings with confidence. "This morning I purchased the warehouse in LA, which will act as both a storage facility and a home base for Phase One." I smile at Rose. "Rose's idea."

Rose's laugh is light, and it dances along my skin like her fingers when she's being playful. "Just glad you listen to my never-ending suggestions."

Leanne folds the pamphlet and sets it aside on the table. "Your core principle is noble. Nonprofits have a long-standing tradition of allotting too much of their budget to the social contract of fancy parties in return for our money. It's how the donations world functions."

"It doesn't have to." I tap my finger on the brochure. "With technology, we're on the horizon of new approaches. Charities can source what they need for their events from a warehouse of reusable items with ease and at less cost. When technology and charity come together, there are lots of benefits we can offer the world."

Leanne's gaze falls on Ezra. He takes her hand in his. "We're not saying technology is bad, just that this concept isn't in our area of expertise."

"Your enthusiasm for the nonprofit world is clear, and with a proper partner who is passionate about event recycling *and* technology, your idea has legs." Leanne swirls the wine, sniffs the liquid, then takes a tiny sip.

The statement from Leanne is not a no, but I brace myself. Maybe it's being at a golf resort, which is usually Callum's territory, that is throwing off my sense of things.

"Exactly why I thought of you." Rose shifts in her seat. "This is an amazing option to make a difference. Make a choice for change."

Her friend meets her gaze. "We'll definitely suggest using Second Chance Events to the charities we work with once it's up and running."

Through the glass accordion doors of the private room, the laughter of the groups of golfers gathered around their tables is almost impossible to hear. I wish for the ambient noise of that room so I could use it as an excuse to lean in and ask Leanne to repeat what she just said. But I heard her loud and clear. They are not interested in partnering with me.

I can't deny this no. It rings in my ears, and I don't hear Rose's plea for them to reconsider.

The wrench the Menkens just threw in my plans will halt all progress. Without their clout to make Second Chance Events a fashionable trend for the rich and famous, the warehouse will sit empty for months as I look for another partner. The charities I promised to help will lack resources. I gulp down my scotch and force a grin onto my face as we discuss booking a round of golf when our calendars next align.

"If you have another idea that focuses on supporting emerging artists or children, please reach out." Ezra shakes my hand and leads his wife out of the room.

The hush of failure seals us in as the doors close behind them.

It's not like this is my first failure, and I'd be a fool to think it will be my last. Yet, this round, I have no one to blame but myself. The sick feeling in my stomach points out my biggest mistake. "Callum should've been here."

"What would he have done differently?" Rose takes her seat beside me. "You had the numbers to prove your new venture has the potential to sustain itself and the admin staff. You demonstrated the growth opportunities and the benefits. This company will help many charities find more space in their budgets while solving the problem of senseless waste at events."

I take a deep breath, trying to calm my anxiety. I know my value and the value of what I'm offering, and yet . . . "Second Chance Events is a good idea."

Rose clasps my hand. "It's an excellent idea." She squeezes, her grip confident. "They just won't be the people on this path with you."

"I was so certain they'd agree." My heart sinks further into disappointment as I trace the fine lines of her beautiful face. Why do I feel like I failed Rose as well?

She offers me a sad smile. "I was too."

"They do say every loss is an opportunity to learn."

"What did you learn?"

"First," I say. "I learned that Callum's job is way more difficult than I thought. He makes everything look easy. I've never quite realized how much more he brings to the company by attending events and schmoozing clients. How he sells what we do by making TRI look like a hot deal investors can't resist. I'm definitely not the right person for the job."

"You should tell him. Of course, he'll probably have your words engraved on a plaque, but you're right. Selling is a skill."

"One I don't have."

Rose crosses her legs. "I didn't say that."

"You don't have to cushion the blow. This isn't new to me." I chuckle. "Maybe Callum can teach me. Or perhaps I need to hire a consultant to step in and do this part for me. I thought I was prepared, but I should've done more work on explaining the benefits and how fantastic the combination of charity and business can be. The next potential partner I pitch will have a much harder time rejecting me."

"Of course they will." Her gaze softens, a hint of admiration in her eyes as she speaks again. "When your mind is set, there's no stopping you. You made your first company happen straight out of college. Your idea for Optimized Response and Service Network was good enough for Callum and Blake to invest."

Our idea, my brain shouts, but I shove the correction down. The past is the past, and we can't undo our choices. I don't want to open old wounds when the very real and present wound cuts just below the surface.

"Every year, I saw ORSN grow. And when you sold, I was thrilled for you," she says. "You did what you set out to do. You became your own boss."

I can't help but let out a small smile, but there's still a tightness in my lungs. "Sweets, you read up on my company's progress?"

"I'm the reason my mother discovered TRI. HH Group is lagging behind, and we need the infusion of smart tech." She rests her hand on my knee. "Naturally, I checked in on the smartest man I know."

I feel another rush of warmth at her praise, but it's tempered, a deeper need catching fire in me.

"My mother saw my research on my computer, then made the bid without telling me. I only found out that you declined the sale when she was livid. She's used to getting what she wants."

"So, you decided to make the deal with me, then. You sign TRI, and you give her the one thing she couldn't achieve?"

Rose pulls away. "Essentially."

"At least one of us gets what they signed up for out of us fake dating." Because I will sell TRI to Rose. My decision is final, a closing door I can't stop. "TRI is yours."

"I'll tell Mom."

I meet her gaze and soak in what might be my last chance to look at her like this. I suck in a deep breath. "So is this when we stage a fight?"

Rose's lips part. "What are you talking about?"

"Your part of the deal is over." I wrap my fingers around my drink to keep from reaching for her. "The Menkens are out of the picture, and you can drop the charade of pretending I'm your boyfriend. You can get back to your normal life. Be the CEO."

"Is that what you want?" The passion in Rose's voice is gone.

"For you to be CEO? I want whatever you want."

"No. I mean, yes, I will be CEO." She licks her lips. "Do you want to stop pretending to be my boyfriend?"

I must try. If this is the end of the line for Rose and me, I can't let her go without a fight. I made that mistake twelve years ago. If there is even the slightest hope Rose will give us a chance, I'll pry the possibility open. I may not be capable of convincing the Menkens to buy into Second Chance, but I'll give every ounce of effort I have to convince Rose to stay with me this time.

"Yes. I don't want us to fake it anymore."

Her chin lifts. "I see."

Drink abandoned, I take both of Rose's hands in mine.

"Because I'm done pretending. I hated every minute of pretending the last three months," I say. She tries to pull her fingers away but I hold them tighter. "Hating the pretending, but not the pretending you are talking about."

"Stop talking in riddles."

"That's the point, Rose. I don't want there to be riddles, or games, or deals. I want honesty. Real honesty." I might send her running, but at this point, I don't have anything to lose apart from my fragile heart, which is hers either way. "The hardest thing over the last few months was pretending I hated not touching you every time we were in private. And pretending I didn't want to spend time with you. I could've gotten my own stylist. My own golf instructor. But any opening I had to be around you, even though I knew everything was a charade and there was a very definite end date, I took."

Rose opens her mouth, but this time, I put my hand over her lips. "Please, let me finish. I have to say this. Before you walked into my office, I persuaded myself I was over you. That the years apart did their job, and the memories of you were just my brain creating perfect pictures out of what might have been a far less perfect reality. Then you walked in and shattered my illusions. You touched my hand in my office, and my heart beat for the first time in twelve years."

A tear trickles down her cheek, and I remove my hand from her mouth to brush the drop away with my thumb.

"You are the sugar craving I'll never be able to control. You're the one I'll never be able to stop dreaming about, sweets." I cup her cheek. "So yes, I don't want to pretend anymore. I want to explore the future together. I want to make blini, brainstorm ideas, and lie on the couch together, talking about our dreams and making some of them come true. I want to wake up with you and kiss you goodnight. I want to live with you. I want to love you. I want a life with you so much that I'll wear anything Zoe designs, go to fancy parties, and I'll even learn how to play golf."

A laugh hiccups out of her, and my heart leaps for joy.

I feel the weight of every word, a truth finally spoken, and it burns through me, both terrifying and freeing. My whole body aches to bridge the gap between what I want and what I fear.

I am standing at the start of something beautiful and fragile, hoping she'll step forward with me. Hoping she'll take the risk for the love that only happens in a very few lucky people's lifetimes.

"I'm tired of pretending, Rose. Please, let me be your boyfriend. For real."

"Are you finished?" she whispers.

"I'll never be finished wanting to be by your side."

"Good."

Her answer is clear, but there's hesitation in her gaze, a flicker of uncertainty. I'm not sure if it's for me or for her, but it makes my heart skip. The space that separates us seems to stretch, but it also feels like it's pulling us closer.

"Because I want you to be there." She places her hand on mine and presses her cheek into my palm. "Because I want you to love me. Because I love you."

For the first time in twelve years, I lean forward and kiss Rose for real.

THIRTY-SIX

PRESENT DAY

April

Three months ago, I walked into Alek's office with a plan to buy his company. Today, I grin at him across the table as Mom passes the final page of the contract for TRI to me. She's already signed, and I scrawl my Rose Haliday next to her Melinda Haliday. It's the first document we've ever signed together. The first contract where I feel fully like a CEO and not just a figurehead. My fingers press into the cool metal of the pen. Even though by signing on the line I complete the plan, I came out with so much more in the end.

I got Alek.

The lawyer on my left adds the final paper to the stack. "Congratulations on closing the deal. TRI is officially under the umbrella of HH Group."

Mom rises, ushering the two lawyers and witnesses to the exit. "Give us a minute to celebrate."

On the other side of the room, Alek and Callum dismiss their staff and meet Mom and me in the middle.

Callum offers Mom his hand. "Pleasure doing business with you."

Instead of a handshake, Alek takes my fingers, pulls me to him, and wraps his arm around my side protectively. "You were too far away."

"The deal is done. Time to end this." Mom takes my hand.

Alek's grip on my waist tightens. I'm being tugged in two directions by the people I care for most.

"No," I say firmly, then free my fingers from Mom's grasp. "Enough."

"Exactly. Enough is enough." Mom waves a hand at Alek. "Tell him what's really going on. Time to end this farce."

"Farce?" says Alek.

"Did you think my daughter wouldn't tell me what was actually going on between you two?"

Alek turns to me, brows furrowed. "What is actually going on between us?"

"Go ahead, Rose. Tell him." Mom sets her hand on her hips, and an almost gleeful smile stretches across her lips.

"Let's not do this here, Mom." I try to show her with my eyes that now is neither the time nor the place. We're supposed to celebrate the purchase of Alek's company, the new path ahead for HH Group, and the fact that I've proven to Mom I have what it takes to be her.

Mom purses her lips. "If you're not telling him the truth, I will." She faces Alek. "This was a fake relationship."

Alek's eyebrows furrow further.

"We wanted TRI, and this was the only way you'd see reason. She's not actually into you. She never was." The smile on Mom's face when she looks at me for confirmation turns my blood cold.

Not because I'm afraid to tell her the truth. When Alek confessed he had feelings for me all these years, my excuses for denying my feelings for him melted under the heat of his declaration. My blood turns to ice because this is one aspect where I'm nothing like my mother. Should Alek and I ever have children, I'd want them to choose happiness over HH Group's interests, not the other way around. A wave of pity for her washes over me.

Yes, HH Group became her way to exist after Dad died, but what about the other men Mom discarded? Is Olivia's father really the terrible person Mom makes him out to be, or did she use him too?

I lean into Alek, my hand settling over his heart. "You're wrong, Mom."

In fact, I'm so into Alek that I go against every rule of business etiquette instilled in me for thirty-five years. I wrap my arms around Alek's neck and kiss him for everyone to see. With lips on lips, mouths parting, tongues touching, I kiss my boyfriend in front of my mother and Callum, and I'd kiss him in front of a dozen people, a hundred, or even the entire world, because I'm in love with this man and I no longer care who knows. The more the merrier.

Behind us, Callum whoops. "About fucking time."

"Rose," Mom yelps. "Stop this display. What did I teach you about mixing business with pleasure?"

The dos and don'ts she's drilled into me too many times are singed into the gray matter of my brain. Lessons on how to act, what choices are right or wrong, handling the press, avoiding controversy, and looking good while doing it all. Yet what she did with her life shouts in my mind, and for the first time, I give those thoughts a voice. "When I told you I'd seduce him so he would sell TRI to us, you had no problem with me mixing business and pleasure. You're such a hypocrite, Mom."

Her head jerks back. "How dare you say that to me?"

"I'm tired of pretending. And it's not just about me." I finally confront my mother. "Olivia, your daughter, is the physical proof of you mixing business and pleasure."

Alek's hand covers mine, calm and assuring.

Mom narrows her eyes. "That momentary pleasure was not worth the long-term pain."

"How can you say that?" I raise my voice in disbelief. "You got a great daughter out of it."

"I got three months of hot sex and a lifetime of her mooching father constantly knocking on my door for money." Her gaze sharpens. "I learned that hard lesson and made sure you wouldn't have to. I gave you Dean on a silver platter, and you—"

"And I didn't love him," I spit. "I'm not sure I ever even really liked him."

She narrows her eyes. "Are you going to tell me you love this . . . this app maker? That he's not just a rebound after your divorce?"

I'm suddenly aware of Callum's and Alek's eyes on us. "Mom, you're causing a scene. Can we talk about this later?"

"Fine." She hikes her purse onto her shoulder. "Let's go back to the office and talk." Mom offers me her hand.

"I can't. Alek and I have plans."

"Simple. Cancel the plans."

"Take the hint," Callum mumbles.

I shake my head. "No, Mom. I made a promise. I'll call you tomorrow, and we can talk then."

"Rose, stop being unreasonable. I won't let you embarrass yourself further. Don't you understand this man doesn't have your best interests at heart? Not like I do."

Alek steps in front of me. "My intentions regarding Rose are nothing but true."

Mom clenches her fists at her sides. "Of course you'd say that."

"I gave up caring what you thought of me years ago." He turns to me. "The guys and I had a whole coordinated plan.

There's a dress from Zoe, and strawberries, and real champagne, but I can't wait." Alek bends down on one knee with a little black box in his hand.

My pulse booms in my ears, and my hands fly to my mouth. This is too sudden. Too soon.

"Rose Adeline Orson Haliday." Alek's eyes shine with resolve and adoration, and I believe both emotions. "The first time I met you, I thought you were the most beautiful woman I had ever seen."

I know these words. I've heard those words before, and I've never forgotten them.

Alek smiles at me. "The more I got to know you, the more I realized what I like best about you is not your beauty, or how smart and driven you are, although those qualities do make me admire you. But no, the thing that made me fall for you then and what reminded me why you are so easy to love recently is your kindness. My heart has been yours for over a decade, but I'd like to offer you all of me, and I sincerely hope you say yes to this question. Will you marry me?" Alek takes out the ring, his face brimming with love as he watches me.

His offer is both unexpected and hoped for. Not consciously, not out loud, but in the hidden corner of my mind where I dreamed of a second chance at a life I messed up before. A second chance at a marriage full of love, not a business deal. A second chance at loving Alek, at being loved by Alek. I missed his care and his passion, and also how being with someone can feel as right as breathing.

"No." Mom's voice comes from my right. "Maybe he's rich enough now not to be after your money, but his nouveau riche wealth doesn't cover his lack of pedigree. He'll never be your equal, Rose." She steps closer, her hand landing on my arm. "We've discussed this. You can sleep with men like him, but you do not fall in love. And you definitely don't marry them. Don't let someone like him break your heart. Because no matter what he promised you, he will hurt you. The only sure thing you can rely on is HH Group. When I'm dead, our company will be your legacy. An achievement you can be proud of. The biggest accomplishment of your life."

My gaze that was locked on the ring in Alek's hand snaps to her.

"Believe me," she starts again, "business is a lot less fickle than love." Her voice is sharp, hard, and bitter. "You'll have money, respect, pride, and I swear to you that with such things comes staying power." Her fingernails dig through the fabric of my shirt. "Look at my life. Don't repeat my mistakes. I raised you to see the truth in people—what opportunities and advantages they're after when they see you. He's not here for your love. He's here for our empire. Never give that away."

I'd like to believe she says this out of love. But I'm not sure I want that brand of love anymore. The type with conditions. The type that's only given when you fit the mold, follow the rules, and meet expectations. When I run HH Group, things will be different. I'll pull Olivia out of the third floor, move her up to the executive suite, and utilize her talents instead of letting them waste away. Mom did the best she could, but things have to change.

Maybe if I hadn't listened to Mom back then, I'd have had this proposal from the man in front of me years ago. Rage rushes through my body, and my hand trembles as I free myself from her grip. "I don't want to be you."

My gaze falls on Alek, his chocolate brown eyes patient and understanding. Not telling me to do this. Offering me a partnership. Offering me a choice. All I see is Alek.

Surety sings in my veins.

This isn't too soon.

It's almost too late.

My breaths are quick but happy. I don't care about a traditional proposal with pomp and artifice. I had that, and I don't want a repeat. That was proper, and this is real. I want real. Joy pours out of my heart in a rush. I'm done waiting. I almost missed my chance with him, and I've learned my lesson.

Without hesitation, I extend my hand to Alek. "Yes. I will marry you."

Alek slips the ring on my finger, and unlike the grand spectacle Dean arranged, no cameras flash in my face, and the white gold doesn't feel like a chain.

The beautiful ring is a welcome symbol of what we promise to share.

He swoops off the floor and scoops me into his arms, and that's welcome too. There's no other place I'd rather be. My lips find his, and our kiss is the most welcome because it's real too.

Alek is real.

"I knew you two could do this," Callum says when we break apart.

Mom steps away. "Enjoy being husband number two," she says in a tone that suggests there'll be a husband number three. She glares at Alek. "I'll have my lawyers draw up a prenup. You won't get a penny of HH Group's money."

Callum steps before us like a knight sworn to protect. "We have our own lawyers."

Alek moves a hair that's fallen onto my face and gently brushes his lips against mine again, reassuring me that I can trust him. And I do. I trust him more than any person in my life. I don't need a prenup. This should feel scary and dangerous, but instead, I feel like I can breathe for the first time in years.

He speaks to my mother but looks at me as he says, "Draw up your prenup. I'll sign it. Because all I care about is being with Rose. Till death do us part."

Mom smirks. "Rose had that promise removed from her vows to Dean."

"Yet another difference between her ex and me. He was a means to an end. I'm endgame." Alek's gaze stays on me. "You all right?"

I nod even though I'm pretty sure I'm not even close to all right. I swallow tears of joy and let in the desire to run out of this room. With him. "Take me home."

"I thought you'd never ask."

Thirty-Seven

ALEK

PRESENT DAY

April

The wallpaper may have changed, but the walk down the hallway to Rose's VIP suite is like a recurring dream I've woken from too many times over the last twelve years. Me coming to her door, knocking, and her not answering because she wasn't there. Me breaking my promise to leave her alone, sitting by her door, begging her to let me in, and her ignoring me. Her never replying.

This walk down the corridor eradicates all those nightmares because I walk with Rose, her hand with my ring on her finger around my waist as mine rests on her shoulder. I'm walking down this hallway with my fiancée, my future wife. I can't wait for the day she walks down the aisle toward me, Callum standing beside me, Blake, Soren, and Linc flanking him, watching me marry the only woman I've ever loved.

"What are you smiling about?" Rose pokes me in the side as she opens the door to her suite.

"Our wedding."

Crinkles form at the corner of her eyes. "We haven't even been engaged for an hour, and you're already planning our wedding?"

"No. Okay, yes, I was thinking about calling the guys and giving them the good news. But you and I will plan our wedding together. Or do you want to elope? Fly to Las Vegas and have Elvis marry us?"

Rose angles her face toward me. "If you'd asked me this morning, I would have said I want to avoid the whole pomp and circumstance. But you know what? When I marry you," her finger traces the line of my tie and hooks into my waistband as she tugs and places her lips against mine, "we deserve the entire fairy-tale experience. Flowers, balloons, silk napkins, and even that little bride and groom that sit on top of the cake. All items Second Chance can inventory, stock, and use to help charities."

"Have I told you how much I love you?"

Rose pretends to check the time on her watch. "Not in the last five minutes."

"I love you, Rose. I intend to spend the next hundred years making up for the fact that I haven't told you every day for the past twelve."

"I like that plan." Rose takes my hand and leads me across the living room, which is eerily similar to how it was the first day I entered to fix her sink. The furniture is new because some of the decor has been updated, but the room is mostly the same—a mixture of opulence and lifelessness. A place to stay, not a place to call home. Even the plants she loves to bring back to life so much, the plants that used to decorate the windowsill, are no longer here.

"Move in with me?"

Rose nips at my earlobe. "Are you trying to get all these life-changing questions out just in case this is the day I'll say yes to everything you ask?"

"I didn't know this is my personal 'yes day.' As a child, I begged my parents for such a day, but I'd much rather have this one." I have other questions for Rose, but I try to focus. "Is that a yes to moving in with me?"

"Yes." She shuffles me deeper into the living room. "Although we should probably look for a bigger place that's close to your office and HH Group."

My fingers fumble on the buttons of her blouse, my body ravenous for other yeses. "Is there a yes to me undressing my fiancée?"

"Yes." She strips off my shirt while I make quick work of her skirt.

"Is there a yes to me stripping you naked?"

"Yes."

With an impatient growl, I unclasp her bra and strip her underwear off. My fingers run along her soft skin as she unzips me.

I step away from our discarded clothes. I should be cold, standing bare in the middle of her living room, but I'm burning up under her gaze that roams my body and stops at my cock. I give myself a stroke, wishing her hands were on me. "Can I fuck my fiancée?"

"Ye—"

Her agreement disappears in the kiss I impatiently plant on her lips as we step backward until the back of her knees bump into her couch. I catch her, spin, and sit on the couch. "You on top. I need to see you."

"Yes." She complies and climbs on my lap, straddling me.

I groan into her mouth when she moves her hips up the hard shaft of my cock. "You're so wet for me."

"Yes." She props herself up with one hand on my shoulder, and the other takes hold of me and lines up the head of my cock with her opening.

"Fuck yes." I thrust and glide inside her as she comes down. Her warmth envelopes me, and the distance between us, between the years, evaporates. She moves faster, and I stop her, my hands on her waist. "Give me a minute. To . . . to breathe."

Her lips find the shell of my ear. "We have a lifetime."

She shifts, and we find our rhythm. Language is forgotten as our bodies become reacquainted and find the right speed, angle, and intensity for the world around us to blur. She rides me freely and recklessly, mumbling yeses, so many yeses. I want to try everything with Rose. Her orgasm squeezes around my dick as she closes her eyes, and a surprised "Ahh" escapes her throat.

"I love having my cock inside you." I'm more than ready to come, but there's something I want even more. I intensify my thrusts. "I love having my fingers and my tongue inside you." I hold on to her hips, and she rotates them to meet my moves. "But I especially love to watch you come." My thumb finds her clit and starts a dance which brings new fire to Rose's eyes. "Can you come for me again?" The duet of my finger and my cock play her. "Come for me, sweets."

She shakes her head as if she's going to say no. I don't want to break my lucky streak of yeses. I angle her a bit more toward me to give her clit even more pressure and don't let off. I'm relentless in creating both kinds of friction. Rose's eyes close again, and she digs her fingers into my shoulder, freezing as the second climax rips another "Yes" out of her.

"Good girl." I let go and move for myself this time. The pressure spirals back up as I follow with a couple more thrusts and fall apart underneath her.

Rose slides off me, and we stretch out on the cushions of the couch. I snake my arm over her shoulder and bring her onto my chest. Once she's settled, I stroke my fingers over her back. "I love you, Rose."

She curls herself into me. "Yes."

I chuckle. "That wasn't a question."

"But my answer is still yes. I love you too, Alek. My love for you has been tucked away for the last twelve years. I want to answer your questions with a 'yes' for the rest of my life because I plan on loving you at least that long." She kisses the spot closest to her lips and smiles. "But probably longer."

My relaxed body stills. Did she say twelve years, not twelve weeks? I flip us over so her back is on the sofa and prop myself up on my arm. "You've loved me for twelve years?"

"Yes."

"Why didn't you come back then?" I ask. "I was waiting for you. I thought I made that clear."

Her fingers wrap around my bicep, the white gold of her ring cold against my skin. She squirms under me. "I couldn't."

I browse her face—too close yet not close enough for her to kiss me and shut down this conversation. "Why not?"

She turns her chin to the side to avoid looking at me. "Because I made a choice, and I had to live with the consequences."

My lust-hazed brain clicks through the ramifications of her remark. She loved me twelve years ago, and she had to make a choice. A choice between me and what? I push away from Rose and pick up my clothes, suddenly freezing. Knowing she loved me all these years should make me happy, should make me feel more loved. So then why do I feel like I've been kicked in the gut?

She made a choice and didn't choose me. The room spins. The past spins.

Rose sits up. "I choose you now. I will choose you again. Over and over. I just . . . I didn't know then what I know now."

I shrug on my shirt. "And what is that?"

She clutches the throw draped over the side of the couch and wraps it around her. "That HH Group isn't more important than living my life. I didn't know I should've listened to myself and not to my mother. I didn't know what really loving somebody meant. I didn't know how hard it would be to live without you."

I stare at her. "Living without you wasn't living."

"I know." Her fingers bunch the material of the blanket. "I thought I was doing the right thing. For both of us."

Her words barely get through the haze and confusion in my head, but her sadness washes over me. I don't want her to hurt. I crouch on my heels in front of her. My fingers find hers. "I believed you didn't feel the same way about me then—that I had to let you go. I had to stop myself from driving to Miami to see you and try to talk you into taking me back. I was a fool. I shouldn't have listened. I shouldn't have let you go. I should've proven that you and I are the real deal."

She brushes a speck off my cheek. "No, you did what you promised. You're not a stalker. You're not someone who would force themselves on someone else. You gave me time. You gave me space." Rose's fingers stroke my face. "Look how things turned out. The deal I made was worth protecting you. It was worth you getting to keep your idea."

My hand stills her fingers. "You made a deal to protect me?"

"Yes." She rolls her lips. "My mother saw the brilliance of your idea at our presentation that day."

"Our idea."

She shakes her head. "We both created the prototype, the presentation, and made things work, but the original idea was yours. Admit that, Alek. You've proven how smart you are over and over."

"I couldn't have done it without you."

"But you did. You created ORSN and sold the company for millions. My mother was right. She has good instincts."

"The deal, Rose. What was the deal?"

"I couldn't let her take your idea away from you."

"I know you wouldn't have."

"But my mother would have. She gets what she wants, and she would have found a way to steal your app. I begged her to walk away and leave you alone, but she refused. She saw us together, me in your shirt, and she knew I'd fallen in love with you. You were more of a threat to her plans for me than the possibilities your idea could bring to HH Group. So I made a deal."

This truth . . . My thoughts, my emotions, and logic spiral in my head. I'm not even sure I want an answer to the question I'm about to ask.

The hairs on the back of my neck rise.

"What did you do?" I whisper.

"I made a choice between me losing you or you losing your app. I chose for you to keep the app. I signed the rights to the idea to you and agreed to never see you again."

My hand falls from her face, and I rock back. "You walked away from us so your mother wouldn't take my ORSN idea?"

"It sounds more noble than it was. She was determined. There wasn't a winning hand for me. So, I picked a winning hand for you. I did the best I could with what I thought my options were."

My ears thrum, her confession competing with my pounding pulse. I stand and pace the room. "A winning hand." I squeeze the back of my neck. "A deal." I stop and stare at her. "I would've never agreed to such a deal. I wanted you and your love way more than any app."

"You have my love." She stands and steps toward me.

I back up. "For how long? What if your mother offers you another deal?" Bile rises in my throat. "Would you tell me this time? Or would you walk away again?"

"I'd never."

"But you did. You cut me out." I want to take her hand. I want to wrap my arms around her. I want to go back to ten minutes ago when I was inside her and didn't know how little faith in me, in us, she had. "If you'd explained, we would've come up with other ideas. Nothing was worth giving you up. There's only one you. You say you had no choice. I didn't even know there was a choice." My cheeks are hot again. My mind races as I wipe away the moisture my fingers find. "What am I to do with this information now that it's too late?"

"It's not too late."

I grab my head and squeeze my temples. Thoughts that aren't fully shaped fight in my brain, and I can't form any conclusions. It's like the logical part of my mind snapped and is no longer functional.

I grab my jacket.

She steps forward.

I open the door.

"Alek, where are you going?"

"I don't know. I . . . I just can't be here."

"What does that mean?" Her voice trembles.

"I need air. I need space. I need time to sort through this."

"Sort through what?"

"My thoughts. My feelings."

"You don't love me anymore?"

My fingers tighten on the door knob. "It's impossible for me not to love you, Rose. But maybe love isn't enough without trust."

Thirty-Eight

PRESENT DAY

April

On the couch in my office, my body curls in on itself. It's like maybe, if I fold small enough, the world will forget I exist. Even though I've been crying since Alek left last night, I haven't hit the bottom of my twelve-year reservoir of tears.

"I brought coffee, but maybe I should have brought tequila." Olivia's shadow falls over me, her gaze full of urgency. "What happened?"

"I told him." My voice is hoarse. I stare down at the loose belt of my dress, twisting the fabric in my hands like I can wring the regret out of me. "About the deal I made with Mom. When Alek got the app free and clear in exchange for me never seeing him again."

"Wait." Olivia's brows knit together, eyes darting across my face as if searching for some other meaning. "Back up." Her tone rises, sharper now. "You did what?"

I take a shaky breath. "Back in college, when I stopped seeing him . . . it wasn't because I moved to Miami. The truth is that I was protecting him. From Mom. From losing his dream. Mom would've buried him and poisoned everyone in the business against his venture. So, I took her deal and let him go."

Olivia's lips part. For a moment, she just stands there as if what I said hasn't fully registered. "You gave up Alek to save Alek?"

The disbelief in her voice slices me open, and my tears start again. "I thought I was doing the right thing."

"A debate we will unpack later." Olivia sinks into a chair. It's the same chair Alek sat on the day he came to the office to discuss our fake relationship deal.

My fingers dig into the cushion. Deals, negotiations, compromises, and never doing what I want. I'm so sick of living by these rules. Someone else's rules. Yesterday, I thought the past was behind us. I was so confident and happy.

"More to the point." Olivia crosses her ankles. "What did he do?"

"He left."

Her face twists in disbelief. "He left you? After everything he did to win you back? I don't understand."

"Neither do I? One minute we were . . ." The tears threaten to return again at the memory of him in my arms in my suite, at the rightness of us together after so long apart, at the future that lay before us. I was high on finally making the right choice and choosing him. "We were happy, and the next minute, he was gone."

"You must be missing something. Tell me exactly what he said."

I sit up straighter, abandoning the pillow. "He asked for time. To figure things out." I sniffle. "Have I ruined our second chance already?"

Olivia pops up and paces in front of the couch. "You can't think like that. If he needs time, fine—that's fair." Her hands dig into her hips. She's in full figure-this-shit-out mode. "Give him time. But don't pretend this is over. That's not what this is. The man is so in love with you that it's painful to witness."

"But what is there to figure out?" My voice catches. "I love him. He loves me. Why does what I did back then still matter?"

She stops in her tracks and turns to stare at me. "Don't you see?"

"No. I did the right thing. Then and now. I don't understand why I'm being punished for clearing the air."

"You aren't being punished. This isn't about you. Alek is in shock." She shakes her head. "I'm in shock too, and I'm not a besotted lover who'd do just about anything to see you smile."

"Why? Help me understand," I plead.

"I can't believe you don't see this. You are so like her sometimes that you scare me." Olivia takes a deep breath. "Rose, you didn't ask him what he wanted. You made a unilateral decision for him, just like Mom always does to us."

The argument hits like a slap. I flinch.

"How does Mom arranging your marriage, choosing who sits beside you at HH Group events, and undermining your power at every turn feel?"

My temples burn. "I hate it."

"Exactly." Olivia's voice softens. "Do you see what Alek might be feeling right now?"

I nod. I have a lifetime of experiences to compare to what Alek faced last night. My chest collapses with the hurt I caused. A vice of a headache wraps around my skull. "Sometimes I wish you were the firstborn."

Olivia huffs. "Mom would hate that."

I take her hand and pull her to the couch, the seed I've never allowed to sprout taking root in my mind. "What if you were?"

"This is silly."

I play Alek's game. "Mom's not here. If you could do anything, anything at all with your life, what would you do? What do you want more than anything?"

Olivia's throat bobs. She's silent for so long, I fear she might not answer. "I want to run HH Group." Her statement is so quiet that I barely hear. "I'm sorry." She yanks her hand from mine. "I shouldn't have said that. You're my sister, and the role is yours. I have no right."

I grab her hands and hold on. "Don't do that. You're allowed to have dreams. Crap, this company is big enough for both of us to run it if we want to. Mom has no life because she's so busy keeping our empire together. If you need more responsibility, I won't be the one to hold you back."

"Really?" Olivia's dark eyes, which are so much like her father's, widen. "You aren't mad?"

"I'm relieved." The truth spills from me.

"I've always wanted HH Group." There's a rawness in her voice, an honesty she's been holding back for years. "But Mom had never wavered from you as the heir and me as an embarrassment, an afterthought. That is, when she remembers I exist at all. I do everything I can to make her notice. I'm the first person here in the morning and the last to leave at night. I work weekends and support her every decision. Nothing is good enough for her."

"Aren't you fed up with constant expectations?" I know I sure am.

"Mom's only expectation for me is to not screw up in public. I'm capable of more than occupancy reports and sitting in on exit interviews with Human Resources. I want a chance to show what I can do for the company," she says. "To make the call and prove I can lead without having to beg for attention."

"Then we have to make her see you." I pick up one of the cups on the table, hand the coffee to her, and take the other for myself. "With the sale of TRI, I negotiated full control of the merger. Work with me. Side by side."

"Mom won't like that."

"Mom doesn't get a choice. You're the one who gets stuff done. And you care, Olivia. You care about HH Group in a way I never could." My speech rings so true that the hairs on the back of my neck rise. "HH Group might not be my future."

"You can't be serious."

The dam is broken, and I can't stop the words from flowing. "I am. This life I built, the perfect life you see, it's not perfect for me. The pressure. The fakeness. I've been living Mom's dream, not mine." The rush of honesty almost drowns me inside. I gasp for air. "I never had a dream of my own."

I exhale. The weight of what I just admitted to Olivia and to myself crushes me. My lottery-winner conversation with Alek in Georgia rings in my head, and my heart beats out the facts I'm now certain of. "I don't want to inherit a dynasty—I want to build something. Something real, honest, and kind. I want to do good, like Second Chance Events. I want to help people."

"You don't want HH Group?"

"No." I laugh. It's so freeing to admit this aloud. "I want to do what I like with people I like. And I like the way Alek thinks. His heart. His vision. I love his idea for Second Chance Events. If I could do that kind of work and build a company that changes lives, I'd finally be living the life I want to live."

She pulls her hands from mine and reclines. "So what's stopping you?"

I stare at the windowsill with my collection of imperfect plants. The struggling rosebush Alek gave me has two new buds, the soft pink promising future fortune. "Fear. And guilt. Mom will feel betrayed, like I'm another man who left her. Another person who walked out." I swallow. My voice shakes. "But I don't think I can be her perfect heir anymore."

We sit in the quiet for a long moment before she finally says, "You know . . . it's not your job to make sure Mom's happy."

"I'm starting to understand that." I take a full, long inhale and expand my lungs to their full capacity. My exhale gives me time to carefully phrase my new understanding. "Love isn't about fixing everything. It's not about orchestrating perfect endings for the people we love. It's about loving them while they figure things out."

"Does this mean you'll take time off from HH Group?"

"I need to. My passion is to work with nonprofits. To enhance lives, not my résumé. To work with someone who doesn't need me to obey to prove my love."

Olivia squeezes my knee. "Shit, Rose. I've never seen you like this. I want that for you too."

I bump my shoulder against hers. "You just want my job."

"I—"

"I don't mind. I think—no, I know you'll be great. You taking over for me while I figure out my life can show Mom what you are capable of."

"I won't fail you."

"You could never." I lean my head on her shoulder. "I know we haven't been as close as we should be, but your happiness is important to me. Take HH Group to new heights or fail trying. I'll love you either way."

Olivia's lower lip trembles. "I . . . I love you too."

For the first time in way too long, I wrap my arms around my sister. Olivia squeezes back.

"What will you tell Mom?"

I shrug. "The truth. I want a sabbatical so I can figure out who I am without HH Group."

"She won't be happy."

"I'm done making Mom happy. It's about time I found my own happiness."

Olivia runs her hands over my back. "He'll come back, you know. Alek loves you."

"He does." Another truth hits my gut. "If time is what he needs, I'll wait. I waited twelve years. What's a few more days? I'd wait forever for him."

Olivia shakes her head. "Lovesick Rose is a new look for you."

By the time Olivia leaves, the sun is glinting off the glass of the neighboring office buildings like a thousand tiny promises. I stand alone in my office, no longer crumpled and no longer hiding. I will talk to Mom. I will take a break from HH Group. I will give Alek the space he asked for—but I won't disappear this time. I'm determined to wait for him, not out of guilt or need, but out of hope. Hope that this time, my choice is right, and Alek will choose me too.

Thirty-Nine

ALEK

PRESENT DAY

April

I hip-check my opponent, and we both ram into the boards as the plexiglass clangs against the railing. The jolt pierces my body, sharp and stabbing. Light flashes behind my eyelids as my shoulder crunches against the impact. Pain erupts in my clavicle, radiating through my body, but it barely scratches the surface of the ache in my heart. That ache is deeper and more familiar. Bruised love. Shattered expectations.

With control of the puck, I race up the length of the ice, my calves burning from the effort. Each stride is an act of self-sabotage, and every breath is pulled through clenched teeth. The only one capable of keeping up with me is Callum. As fast as he is off the ice, he skates like lightning on the ice. Always by my side. Always close. Always helping.

The goalie crouches, prepared for my shot. I should pass to Callum since the left side is open. The logical play is obvious, but I can't think logically any longer. I'm thinking with my emotions. I raise my stick and take my rage out on the puck, slapping the wood against the round disk and aiming for the slot between the goalie's pads. With no control, the biscuit sails through the air, far too high, and dings off the crossbar. No goal.

The clang reverberates like a death knell.

A loud horn echoes through the arena, signaling the end of another twenty minutes. The end of the game. The chill of the ice rises into my skates. Winded and numb, I come to a slow stop.

Callum skates up beside me, spraying tiny ice shards with his sudden stop. "What the fuck? I was wide open."

"I thought I had the shot." I don't meet his eyes.

Yesterday, I thought I had a shot at everything. The woman I love agreed to be my wife. Today, I can't even score on a sub goalie we routinely trounce. I go through the motions, shaking the hands of each of the opponent players, and then I head for the bench. My limbs barely cooperate, and my gloves might as well be lead. "I need a shower."

My skates squeak against the vinyl floor as I throw open the locker-room door. The harsh fluorescent lights blind me from above. I drop my gloves, yank my jersey off, and sink onto the bench to untie my laces. The air is damp and thick with steam and glares from my teammates. Sweat drips down my face, like the tears I cried on the elevator ride down to the lobby of Rose's hotel.

She made a deal with her mother to cut me out of her life. My heart squeezes in horror that she was put in that position in the first place. Anger encircles my ribs, making it even harder to breathe.

Rose made a choice. But she didn't give me a choice. The back of my throat burns. I grab a bottle of water and guzzle it down.

Soren tosses his helmet into the corner of his locker. "Well, that sucked."

"So what if they win one game?" Blake pats him on the shoulder. "We're still 12–1 against them. Sometimes it's nice to let the other team win. It's good sportsmanship."

Callum flips him the bird. The guards on his skates clack as he moves past me. "I liked our perfect record."

"Speaking of records." Blake drums his fingers against the metal bench. "Linc scored two more goals. He's on fire. Too bad his team won't make the playoffs this year."

"Does that mean he's playing another year?" Soren asks.

Blake nods. "He wants that Cup ring. There's even talk of a trade. Our boy might be coming home next season."

"Seriously?" Callum lifts his head. A spark of excitement breaks through his frustration. "He's going to play for LA?"

"It's not a done deal yet, but it's looking likely."

I try to be happy for my friend. Linc has been stuck in Buffalo for years. I just can't seem to drag up an ounce of good spirit. I yank off my skate, my muscles complaining. When I couldn't sleep last night, my home gym took the brunt of my anger and disappointment. The pads below my fingers are still raw. I curl my hand into a fist to hide them.

"Is Rose meeting you here?" Soren says lightly, as if testing the waters.

"No," I say.

"Did you two have so much sex last night celebrating your engagement that she can't walk this morning?" Callum smirks, nudging Soren's shoulder. "I know your dick hasn't been in use for a while, but you gotta give the girl a break."

I don't answer my friend, unbuckling my elbow pads and stuffing them in my bag. My silence is loud. Even Callum hears it.

"Fuck me. Don't tell me there's trouble in paradise already." Callum scratches his head, the shift in his tone barely masked. "You two always burn hot."

"I don't want to talk about it."

"Oh, we're definitely talking about this. Did you and Rose fight? What did you do to piss her off?"

I jump to my feet and shove the locker door shut with a loud slam. "This is not my fault."

Callum holds up his hands. "Whoa. Cut the bullshit and tell us what happened."

My brain is foggy, and I can't hold in this hurt any longer. With my head against the locker door, I word vomit. "She made a deal." I spill the details that shifted my entire world last night.

"That's why she broke it off with you?" Soren asks.

Blake exhales. "It's pretty badass, actually. She's tougher than I thought."

I wait for Callum's verdict, desperate for the clarity only my best friend can offer. He's quiet, so I turn to him.

"You walked out on her?" His face is blank, unreadable.

Why is he confused? My certainty jostles. "I had to. She dropped this bombshell on me, and nothing made sense. How could she do that?"

"Are you upset about the deal? Or?" Callum's voice is clinical. I wasn't exactly expecting him to rage with me, but this behavior is off-putting.

I run my hand through my hair. "I don't know what I'm upset about. It's just that everything I've been thinking is incorrect, like my view of Rose was wrong. I never thought she'd do something like this . . . decide what's best for me and my life. I thought we were partners. I thought she knew me. How could she think I would have ever chosen the app over her? Part of me wishes she hadn't told me."

"So you're mad at her for coming clean? Giving you both a fresh start?"

I stare at my friend. "No. You're confusing things. If she'd just told me what was happening back then, we could have figured out a solution. But she took that choice away from me." The statement hurts more than squeezing the raw pads of my hands. "I thought the last three months were about her finally falling in love with me. Like I finally got my chance. Instead, it turns out we wasted twelve years of loving each other." I stand and glower at Callum. "This is your fault. If you didn't convince me to be in this fake relationship with Rose, I could've lived in ignorance."

Callum's fist slams into the locker beside me. "Rose is right there. I'd kill for a second chance with the woman I love."

"For a man who hasn't had a relationship last for more than a week, you have some pretty good advice." Blake plops down beside Soren.

"Good thing you don't love anyone. I'd have to bail you out of jail, pay for a good lawyer . . ." Soren's voice fades when Callum doesn't laugh.

He's glaring at me, his jaw tight. His silence smothers the oxygen in the room, and tension crackles between all of us.

Soren holds up a finger. "Can we back up a bit? Did you say fake relationship?"

"Callum thought it would be a good idea if Rose and I pretended to date so she could introduce me to the Menkens." I explain to the guys what's actually been going on between Rose and me over the last three months. "Apparently, she's good at pretending."

Callum spins away and kicks over the bench. He swears at the top of his lungs. His helmet crashes down and bounces off the wall. With his chest heaving, Callum turns to me. "She's not a piece of code you can write over and over again until you eradicate the flaw. She's human. From the moment you two met, you put her on a pedestal and made her this perfect thing. Rose is not perfect. She made a mistake. She was twenty-two.

What wouldn't we all do to go back to twenty-two and undo a mistake or ten?"

My eyes flick to Callum's wrist, to the career-ending hockey injury he suffered during our last year in college. I quickly look away. "We wasted all these years, and there's no getting them back."

"So you want to waste the rest of your life, why? To spite her?"

"It's not that easy. She cut me out of the most important decision of my life. How can I know that won't happen again? Maybe there was honorable intent, but that doesn't excuse the actions. What if she decides breaking up will be better for my career, or for some other reason I can't even imagine? Do we spend twelve more years apart?"

"There are no guarantees in life, and that's a risk you take when you love someone. Do you trust her?" Callum says.

"I thought I did."

"So you don't?"

"I do. I trust her. I just want to know we'll make these decisions together."

Callum steps closer. "If whether or not you can trust Rose isn't even a question, then you need to get this through your head." He taps my temple. "Rose is not perfect. We all make mistakes. She's gonna screw up again. The point is, she told you. She refused to hide anything from you. That time is over. Take her off the pedestal, accept she's just as human as you, and that she can make mistakes. People change, and yes, you'll both make mistakes. But you'll do so together. Isn't that what you were after to begin with?"

Blake leans back against the locker with a thoughtful sigh. "Listen. What Callum is trying to say is that it's easy to play ref and review the recording twelve years later. Look at it from her perspective. She made a choice. Yeah, maybe it was the wrong choice. Yeah, maybe she should've told you. Maybe things could have been different if she had. Put yourself in her shoes. If her happiness was on the line, what would you have done?"

Anything.

I would have done anything in the name of Rose's happiness.

Soren looks at me. "She asked you to stay away, and you did. We all saw the pain that caused you and how you shut yourself off from happiness for over a decade. You made a choice too. It was the right choice. You gave Rose what you thought she wanted. Can't you see how she did the same thing for you?"

My gaze falls on my three friends, landing on Soren last. Their faces are serious, their gazes steady. "I fucked up, didn't I?"

"Hallelujah!" Callum shouts at the ceiling. "Finally, the puck hits the back of the net."

Blake nods. "Yeah, you really fucked up."

Dread pools in my gut. "How do I fix this?"

"Quickly." Soren grins, clapping me on the shoulder. "And you go big. Us writers, we call this a grand gesture. Works every time."

FORTY

PRESENT DAY

April

The glass doors whisper shut behind me, muffling the office sounds. Mom's office is perched high above downtown, all clean lines and curated control. The room is expansive and intimidating in its precision. No clutter. The decorations are sparse and designer-picked. Mom doesn't allow any sentiment. Pale oak floors stretch across the space, accented by a thick, dove-gray rug beneath a monolithic desk made of smoked glass and brushed steel. A wall of matte-black bookshelves to the left of her desk hosts a selection of tastefully backlit neutral-toned books purchased for the color of the spines, not what's inside.

The air smells like Chanel No. 5 and old money.

Mom leans back in her ivory leather chair, the kind that signals bespoke Italian. The floor-to-ceiling windows behind her framing the skyline are another of her power moves.

"Are you ready to apologize for the scene you caused after we signed the contract?" Mom's voice is even, smooth as the glass of the table. She doesn't blink.

"I think you're the one who needs to apologize," I say, quieter than I intended. I sit, meeting her eye-to-eye, and twist my engagement ring, grounding myself. "I understand you love me and you want the best for me, but I don't think you know what that is anymore." My throat tightens, but I press on. "I'm not always sure I know what that is either, but I want to find out. I'm leaving on sabbatical and taking a year off to decide if working at HH Group is the career path I actually want."

Outside, a helicopter cuts across the horizon.

"You see, he's already whispering in your ear, alienating you from me." Mom narrows her eyes. "I saved you once, and I thought you were a quick learner. I didn't realize I'd have to repeat the lesson at the age you're at now."

I inhale roughly. "I don't need saving." That twelve-year hurt flares in me like a contusion I thought had healed. I push back my chair and place my palms flat on my thighs to keep them from trembling. "Why can't you just let me live my life instead of trying to make it an improved version of yours?"

Mom crosses her legs, manicured fingers steepled. That's all I get. That's all she gives me.

"I've tried to be like you for years, but I'm not." I barge on. No more holding in my thoughts. No more playing the perfect daughter. I'm not perfect, and I don't want to be. "You know I'm not. I don't care about making more money or creating a legacy. That's your dream."

"And what's yours?" Her question doesn't come from curiosity. It's a challenge.

I stare into the corner of the office, where an abstract sculpture sits atop a metal stand. It's a tangle of silver wire. Exclusive. Approved by Mom. Its sole purpose is to show off Mom's wealth and taste. I might as well be describing myself. A curated object rather than a person. "I don't know exactly, but I want to use my time for good. Working with charities is the only aspect of my life I've enjoyed recently, so I want to do more of that."

Mom lets out a bitter laugh. "So he's roping you in to help with his project again, like he did in college. You do all the grunt work, and he reaps the benefits."

The diss in her voice is familiar, but the tone doesn't stick like it used to. I straighten. "I know you are hurt, Mom, but I've made my decision—and it is mine. Alek has nothing to do with it."

Her expression hardens. She stands, smoothing the front of her tailored black dress as she circles the desk. "If you want to believe that, fine." She stops inches away, eyes glinting. "But I refuse to accept your sabbatical." Her gaze sharpens. "You are not leaving me now when I need you to supervise the merger. The whole point of buying TRI was for you to push HH Group past the level of technology of our competitors. You do that first, and then we can talk about what's next for you." She turns her back, facing the window, her silhouette a dark slash against the afternoon light. "Once that's done, I might move up my retirement or try part-time, and you can add the title of CEO to your resume."

The old temptations—recognition, approval, and power—beckon. But they don't attract me anymore. "You are not listening to me, Mom." I rise. "If I can't have a sabbatical, then I quit."

Mom whirls around. "You can't quit."

"I can."

"You are part of the family."

"I can cut you out of my life, like you made me do with Alek." I tip my chin up. "Or I can pretend everything is normal, show up to events, and the world will assume I'm taking on more of a role with the charities."

"And who on earth will deal with the merger?" Her question hangs like a lit match by a gas fireplace.

The air in the room is charged with my mounting anger. This time, not on my behalf, but on my sister's. I'm not the only child Mom has hurt.

"You have another daughter. She sits on the third floor. Bring Olivia up to the executive suite, give her my office, and give her a real chance. You might still get a CEO who has the Haliday name."

The waning rays of sunlight stream through the wall of windows, but they don't penetrate the darkness between Mom and me. My engagement ring catches the light as I tuck my hands into my pockets.

I don't wait for her to speak again.

I turn, walk toward the glass doors, and leave the empire that was my future to the past.

WHAT HAVE I DONE?

I text Olivia to come up to the public bathroom as soon as she can and splash water on my face. Cold droplets glide down my cheeks like the panic I can't swallow. I count my breaths. One. Two. Three is how far I get when they stutter in my throat again. Breathe. I need to remember how to breathe and how to make my feet walk out of here and back to my office, where I can collapse on the couch and understand what I just did.

Quitting HH Group was not a concept I could even imagine before. The walls of the bathroom inch closer, sterile beige tile trapping me in a box. The rapid rise and fall of my chest strains against the confines of my jacket, and I slip out of the linen material. I'm too hot and too unsteady, so I splash more water on my face and hope Olivia comes. I don't know what I should do next.

My life has never been open to possibilities like it is now. I grip the counter like the marble might hold me up. The idea of freedom fascinated me in the past, but it was even less of an option for me than growing wings and flying out of my office. HH Group has been my future. The only future I ever considered, a crystal-clear path forward. Now, everything is murky. I clutch the stifling collar of my shirt and rip the button open, urging air to enter my lungs and my bloodstream so I can think again.

It's not like I just need air. I need clarity. Direction. A map.

The woman who stares at me in the mirror looks the same on the outside, maybe a little paler, but I'm nothing like the me from this morning.

"Are you in there?" Olivia's voice comes from outside of the bathroom door.

I manage to walk over, snap the lever on the lock, and let her in.

She takes me in. "What did Alek do this time?"

My heart hurts at the mention of his name, but I can't think about that now. "I quit."

Olivia takes my shoulders into her hands. "Quit what?"

"HH Group."

"That was not the plan. What about the sabbatical?"

"I know it wasn't the plan, but when she said no, I didn't care anymore. Words left my mouth, and they felt right. I don't want to be here anymore. I quit, then I told her you can handle the merger."

"I can't believe this." Olivia steps back like the air's been knocked out of her, but then she pulls me into a tight hug, her cheek pressed against mine. "I'm proud of you."

My stomach pitches. "Don't be too proud. I might be having a breakdown, and I don't know what I'm supposed to do next."

"That's easy. We get you back to your office, then we figure out a plan. You like plans. You like organizing. Now you get to organize your life in whatever way you want."

Panic reenters my body. The tile beneath my shoes is no longer steady, like the world shifts on its axis. I drape myself over Olivia and shake, the enormity of what I've done finally setting in. I'm free. I'm terrified. I'm ready.

Olivia and I walk to my office, holding hands like we did when we were kids, before Mom sent her to boarding school. Having my sister by my side is the support I've never been more thankful for. If Mom doesn't understand what a treasure she has in Olivia, I'll figure out a way to help her shine. I'll always have her back.

I swing the door into my office open and stop in my tracks.

The earthy scent hits me first—soil and decay and something strangely alive. The room brims with potted plants. A monstera with browning edges. A desiccated jade plant. A begonia with powdery mildew. A spindly ficus. Rows and rows of them. On all the window sills, the tables, and the floor. All imperfect.

My pulse quickens. I survey the room for the only person who would do this.

"Why do you have a plant cemetery in your office?"

"Alek." My voice wobbles between disbelief and delight.

I cover my mouth with both hands, but laughter pours out of me. My joy is too giant for my body, gushing and uncontainable.

The uncertainty I've been carrying around all day clears because the questions I've been avoiding are answered. Everything clicks into place. A lightness surrounds my head. I rush to the box with a giant bow on my desk. My fingers struggle with the knot as adrenaline surges through me, urging me to go faster. I hope he didn't put another plant in there.

A smile twitches at the corner of my lips, even as nerves start to flutter again. I yank the lid open, and my heart sinks. The lightness cracks and evaporates from around me like it's been kicked. At the bottom of the box is a folder I shouldn't still recognize, but I do. The folder I put the contract I signed to give Alek all the rights to his app in. The old version of our HH Group symbol still shines in silver laminate. My hands go clammy. A knot tighter than the one I just untied on the box forms below my diaphragm.

Maybe I read this all wrong.

Maybe the plants don't mean what I think they mean.

Maybe this is him telling me he can't get past what I did.

The weight of such a possibility replaces the joy that filled me only a moment ago. With shaky fingers, I open the folder and read the top page of the document inside. My sight blurs before the words come into focus.

Rose Haliday, Adviser, Second Chance Events.

I squeeze my eyes shut, then force them open. My brain still refuses to process what I just read. The knot under my breastbone doesn't move, but I don't pass out.

It's a work contract? I take the pages, confusion coiling in my temples and settling into a mix of panic and possibility. Why is he sending me a job offer? My brain stutters. My heart thuds louder as I scan through the pages. On the last one, in Alek's handwriting, is a note:

GIVE US A SECOND CHANCE. PLEASE. COME HERE IF IT'S A YES.

I can't breathe again. I press the folder to my breasts, tears prickling the corners of my eyes. I type the address into my phone. Energy surges through me like a current, carrying me to the door.

"Where are you going?" Olivia trails behind me.

My thoughts are steady and hopeful, filled with the understanding I didn't know I was waiting for. A choice. "I'm going to say another yes."

Forty-One

ALEK

PRESENT DAY

April

The cavernous space with rows of empty shelves, dormant machinery, and closed doors to the delivery docks are gray and industrial—not particularly clean and not particularly romantic. A handful of flickering overhead bulbs buzz around the perimeter, casting blurry light over dusty shelves. The stained concrete floor smells of oil and metal.

Why did I think the Second Chance Events warehouse would be a perfect place for a grand gesture?

I rub my palms against my jeans for the millionth time, pacing in front of the shelf I set up as a makeshift start of this attempt. At least Rose texted that she's on her way, which hopefully means she liked the plants. Or maybe Callum is right and sending all the plants the flower shop had put aside to toss in the trash was the most bizarre idea I've ever had. To every other woman I know, sick plants probably would be, but I know Rose. She loves finding ways to coax life back into things others discount, because Rose sees their potential when others only see what is lacking.

This isn't the reenactment of the dinner I didn't get to have with her the night she left for Miami, but this *is* my way of showing her I remember everything. That I did disobey her order back then, because I never actually forgot.

The hairs on my forearms stand as the door at the side of the warehouse creaks open, its rusty hinges groaning with effort, and my heart clears right into my throat.

Rose steps inside, the graying light of an early evening behind her. Her figure is small against the vast warehouse, but she finds me instantly, like she always does. Her jacket hangs unbuttoned, the top of her shirt exposing the long line of the neck I love to kiss. Messy strands of hair frame her face, and in her arms is the folder. That folder. The one that once gutted me.

"I'm here." Her voice is clear and strong, even though her eyes shine with something brittle. She walks with confident strides across the stained concrete and crushes into me, her cheek pressing hard against my pecs as if she needs to feel the thud of my heart, and says, "Yes."

I know what the question is this time. I bury my face in her hair and breathe her in, jasmine and Rose. Home. My arms wrap around her, gripping her to me as hard as I can without hurting her.

"I was going to woo you first," I murmur into her hair. "I have a whole apology plan. Soren said you deserve a grand gesture, and he's right. You deserve one, and so much more."

Rose peers up at me with a smile that pushes every shred of doubt from my body. "I can't say no to a grand gesture."

"So it is another—"

"Yes." She laughs into my chest, and the vibration restarts my heart that has been terribly quiet without her.

I intertwine her cold, trembling fingers with mine and pull her behind me. "Come."

"Where exactly are you taking me?" The corner of her mouth lifts as she follows me past the towering shelves that echo with the hollow sounds of our footsteps.

"Think of it as apology number one." I lead us to a shelf with a box identical to the one I sent to her office.

"Do I open it?"

"Please."

She fights with the knot a little too long, her brows scrunching. When she finally opens the lid, her hand freezes midair.

"No way." She sets the lid on the shelf and takes out a yellow index card. "Professor Patel's assignment? You kept it?"

I nod and take her hand again, walking us to a new row, a new box.

"Hold this." She passes me the folder and the card like they're sacred objects and moves to the next box, her fingers quicker this time. She bites back a smile.

The lid flies off, and Rose closes her eyes. She shakes her head like she can't believe what's in front of her. "No, you didn't." She lifts the coaster from The Devil's Martini, her writing still visible on the beer-stained surface. "Halloween-on-Ice party planning."

Her eyes glisten, but her lips stretch into a smile that glows under the tired lighting of the warehouse. She hesitates but lets me hold the coaster. "Next."

We move down the rows of shelves like archaeologists of our own love story. Row by row, box by box, relic by relic. She unveils the rose from the corpse-bride outfit she wore at the skating fundraiser. The mug that says Welcome to Los Angeles with a faded depiction of the Hollywood sign she drank the celebratory champagne from, cracked but intact. The paper that lists the two things we did to get extra time. The belt she borrowed to wear during the presentation.

Each time she opens a lid, I get to watch her smile, and with every smile, I remember the moments that built my love for her. Her joy reminds me how much I love making this woman smile. I want nothing more than to make her smile for the rest of our lives.

"Last one," I say.

I lead her to the smallest box. The most important one. Not because it's the end of our memory lane, but because it's the beginning of our future.

Rose opens the box and takes out an even smaller black velvet box. She flicks her gaze to her left hand. The engagement ring I gave her glitters on her finger. "You already gave me a ring. I already said yes when you asked me to marry you."

"Open it, sweets."

Rose pops the lid and draws a shuddering breath. She raises a delicate tennis bracelet that's almost identical to the one she wears daily. A vintage style that Blake helped me find through his family jeweler.

She flips the diamonds over and reads the inscription on the back, her eyes tracing every letter. "I love you, sweets. Alek."

"I thought I'd give you one more bracelet from a man who loves you." Every part of me hums with so many feelings for her.

"Yes, please." She nods, her voice catching.

I set the pile of mementos on the shelf next to the open box, take the bracelet from her hands, and fasten it next to her father's. My fingers brush against the threads of her delicate veins. Her pulse is quick and strong.

Rose bites her lip. "There's one more gift you could give me."

I take her hand in mine, palm-to-palm, quelling the light tremble in her fingers, and squeeze in agreement. "Anything."

"Remember, it's your turn to decide."

"I—"

She presses a finger to my lips. "I'm not making this mistake again. Let me tell you what I want, and then you make your choice. You don't have to say yes, but I would love for you to do so."

"Tell me," I say against her finger.

"I don't know of a way to prove to you that you can trust me, but I do know one thing. I don't want to be my mother. I don't want to tell you what to do. I don't want to be CEO of HH Group. I quit."

"Quit?' I lean back in shock as she recounts the meeting with her mother.

"For the first time in my life, I'm officially unemployed." Rose lets go and reaches for the folder. She holds the file close, her fingertips tracing the HH Group logo. "I read the contract on the way here, and although I love Second Chance Events, I don't want to be your consultant."

My heart sinks. Cold seeps into my upper body. I shouldn't have led with the offer. With all the things she said about Second Chance, I thought us working together might be seen as a good sign, but I must've misread it. I open my mouth, scrambling to recover. "You don't have to—"

"Please let me finish."

I shut up and nod.

"I love Second Chance Events."

A but is clear in her tone.

"But I don't want to work for anyone anymore. I'm done with not being able to make decisions, and I'm done with not being in charge of a company I spend my days at."

I want to respond, but I don't breathe. I just watch her eyes, her mouth, the pulse in her neck, and all the things that tell me this moment isn't perfect, but it's honest, and we are doing the talking thing I wanted us to do the first time around. I don't say anything because I'm a patient man, and I want to know exactly what's happening in that brilliant mind of hers.

"I have a counteroffer for you. I didn't have time to prepare official papers, but you can consider this a verbal one." Rose breathes in, visibly bracing. "We couldn't close the Menkens, so you are without a partner. Let me be that partner. I can bring the clout you were looking for and help with the sales like Callum. I think we make a pretty good team. As a partner, I'll have the say I'm looking for. How about 49 percent ownership for me? That'll make me an integral part of Second Chance Events."

My lungs burst with the need for air. "No. I can't accept that."

Her face falls, her gaze wounded. I curse myself, cup her cheeks, and kiss her forehead. "I won't accept anything less than fifty-fifty."

Rose meets my eyes, tears glinting. "I can do that."

"Then—" I go down on one knee, my heart thundering like applause. If I hadn't already proposed to her, I would have done so right now. I take her hand, the one with my ring on her finger and two bracelets on her wrist. "Rose Adeline Orson Haliday, will you please be my equal partner in Second Chance Events?"

"Yes." Through the laughter that bubbles out of her mouth, Rose utters the word that is the only gift I crave. I don't need a box or a ribbon or contracts to know this is the second chance I've been asking for. This is the beginning of the rest of our lives.

EPILOGUE

ALEK

PRESENT DAY

June

With her hand in mine, Rose tugs me up the stairs to our office. I feed off her energy, my heart racing even more than it always does in her presence. Maybe one day the giddiness I feel around her will disappear, but I can't imagine that future.

"What's the rush?" I ask.

"You'll see."

The hallway smells like fresh paint and industrial floor polish. The glass in the door has gold letters spelling out Alek Orlov and Rose Haliday, Founders. We discussed Rose changing her name when we get married. I offered to change mine. After negotiations, we decided to compromise. Officially, we will both hyphenate our last names, but in business, we'll retain our individual personas. The best of both worlds.

I can't stop a grin from spreading across my lips as she cocks her head and reads our names.

She twists the knob and flings the door open.

I gasp. "A desk?"

In the middle of the room is an antique partners desk. The dark wood gleams in the light from the high warehouse windows, glinting off the brass fixtures. Both sides of the desk are identical, meeting in the middle. Rose and I will spend our days in the office facing each other.

"I found it in an auction of movie memorabilia," Rose whispers, like she's revealing the plot twist of a movie. "Turns out Ezra Menken sat at this desk when he filmed *One Night in Miami*."

"I love that one." My gaze meets hers.

We stumbled across the now-classic movie one night while taking a break from the kind of marathon I would participate in again and again. The one where it's me and Rose in our new house as we christen every surface for a whole weekend.

The delight in her expression sends an inkling of pride through me. My fingers brush the lines of the desk. I meet her gaze, her eyes reflecting more than this room. My heart jumps at the happiness in those mosaic eyes. A happiness I'm a little responsible for. A happiness I intend to make a permanent fixture.

"There's more." She bounces on her toes, clearly proud of herself as her smile dares me to guess what's inside. "Open the top drawer."

The wood slides smoothly to reveal a folded piece of paper. The logo of the LA Icelines is imprinted on the top. "Hockey tickets?"

"I asked your mom, and you don't even have season tickets." She leans against my arm. "Hockey is growing on me, so I got you a box."

"I love it."

"I thought we could auction off some of the tickets for games we don't go to. To help our charities."

"Rose, this is perfect." I kiss her temple. "You are perfect."

Her laugh is light and carefree. "I'm far from perfect, but at least my deficiencies are diminishing."

"I like your deficiencies."

"I also bought a pair of skates. I was hoping your offer to continue our skating lessons might still be good. It's been"—she squints— "about twelve years since my last lesson, so I might be a bit rusty."

This time, my laugh fills our office. "I hope they won't become a once-every-twelve-years tradition."

"No, maybe a monthly one?" Rose holds up her index finger. "About traditions. How about we start another one? Say have an annual Second Chance Halloween-on-Ice event. What if, in addition to the Valentine's Ball, we get the kids on the rink?"

My heart swells. "I once volunteered at the Winter Paralympics. We could invite athletes to teach children to skate, like I taught you. I can ask Linc to donate his time. A mentor-mentee program we can sponsor."

"So you like the idea?"

"I love the idea." I trace her lower lip with my thumb. "I love you."

She kisses my fingers and backs me into the desk. "Prove it."

My happiness lies in making Rose happy. My hands on her waist, I lift her onto the desk and step between her parted legs. I run my lips along her neck, pausing below her ear. "You want us to christen this desk too?"

"Yes." Her fingers tug at my zipper. Her tone is low and seductive, her fingers urgent. The desk creaks beneath her, an unwilling witness.

"Oh, fuck off," Callum's voice booms. "Can't you two keep your hands off each other for two seconds?"

I face my friend. "If you had a woman this amazing in your arms, would you?"

He shrugs. "Fair point."

"To be continued," she whispers in my ear. Rose untangles herself and pops off the desk. "Hi, Callum. Thanks for coming."

He hoists a magnum of champagne in the air. "I bought the cheapest stuff I could find. For old time's sake."

I snatch the wet-with-condensation bottle and wipe it off with my sleeve. The coldness of the glass bites into my palm.

"Hey, if you don't like it, I'm happy to smash the bottle against the side of my boat." Callum leans against the door-frame. "I hear that's tradition for sending off sailors on long journeys."

Mine and Rose's gazes lock. With mischief in her eyes, she raises her eyebrows. Her meaning is clear: you ask him. He's your friend.

I glance at my watch. "Before our partnership dissolves, I have one last favor to ask."

"I told you years ago that I don't swing that way."

Rose's nose crinkles. "What way?"

"Not that. Even with Rose's help, Second Chance is taking more of my time than I anticipated."

"My mother is enforcing the clause in the contract that someone from TRI be on-site at HH Group for six months to ensure a smooth transition." Rose's hand finds mine. "We're pretty sure this is a tactic to erode our relationship. To overwork Alek and try to separate us."

Callum shakes his head. "Waste of time. Will that woman never learn?"

I squeeze Rose's hand. Her thumb traces a slow design into the back of mine. We're in this together. "She's not currently an ally, but we're trying to at least not make her an enemy."

"I don't see how I can help. Your mother barely knows me." Callum pushes off the doorframe. "But I'm happy to explain the situation to her."

I take a deep breath. This is the ask that matters. I step closer. "Glad you said that." My voice is steadier than I feel. "Can you postpone your trip around the world for, say, six months?"

Callum freezes. "You can't be serious."

"Mom expressly mentioned that you'd be an asset to HH Group." Rose nods slowly, her eyes waiting for Callum's reaction.

I step forward. "I need you to protect our people. Make sure they get everything we negotiated for them."

Callum shakes his head. "I'm done with all that. There's a bunkbed in a sailboat with my name on it. The only negotiating I'll be doing is not walking the plank."

Rose places a hand over her heart. "Please, Callum. It's only six months. You won't have to deal with my mother alone." Her voice is gentle, and I know how well that voice of hers works, peeling off resistance layer by layer, at least where I'm concerned. "My sister Olivia is overseeing the transition."

Callum's head snaps up. "Olivia?"

"You remember her." I tip my head, watching him closely. He's trying to play it cool, but I see the flicker in his eye. "You might've talked at the Orlov Thanksgiving party? She also went to the Halloween fundraiser?"

A smile I know only too well creeps across Callum's face. He adjusts his tie. "Pumpkin."

"That's right." Rose laughs. "I forgot I made her wear that child's costume from the lost and found." She shifts her weight from one foot to another, crossing her arms loosely. "She's grown up a lot since those days. I'm sure you'll enjoy working with her."

Callum's smile wavers. "Did she agree to this? Me . . . working with her?"

Rose nods. "She wants what's best for HH Group. This transition is important to my sister. It's her chance to prove to Mom she's CEO material."

I grip his shoulder. "I know this is a lot to ask. I promise it'll be the last time you bail me out. Business-wise, at least." I glance at Rose. "Rose and I will make it up to you."

"You better." He pulls me into a one-armed hug that turns into a headlock, ruffling my hair like we're back in college again. "With the good champagne."

Read Callum and Olivia's second chance romance in Not A Second Chance.

  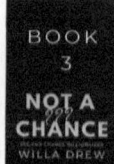 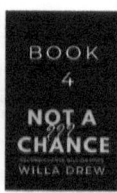 

Meet Leanne and Ezra's son Asher Menken and his best friend's younger sister Siobhan

in

Star Struck

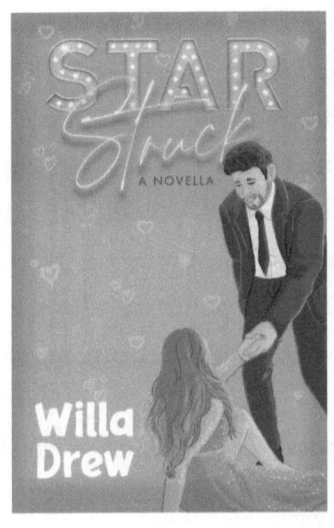

Tonight on *Extra*.

Maria Fernandez: Maria Fernandez here covering the prestigious Starlight Foundation Gala. On the red carpet with me is Asher Menken, star of romantic comedies like *Legally Hot* and the now-classic heartwarming historical tale *Tomorrow's Love*. Such a pleasure. It's been a couple of years since anyone on this side of the pond interviewed you. Where have you been?

Asher Menken: Thank you for the glowing introduction. Glad to be back in LA. I've enjoyed what the stages of Dublin and London have to offer, but I sure missed the California sunshine.

Maria Fernandez: We're glad to have you back. Hopefully, for good?

Asher Menken: For a while. My project—a collaboration with the winners of this year's Starlight competition—is the first movie my production company will take on. And I have my own reasons to stick around for the next nine months.

ONE

Siobhan

A cardboard tube with a shred of toilet paper mocks me. Of course, I end up in the bathroom stall that's missing the key element. My parents ran out of Irish luck when they had me: I'm the only member of the Casey clan born on US soil.

"Can't open the flippin' holder." My best friend isn't her usual happy-go-lucky self. She's nervous for a reason. Months of hard work, and the possibility of writing for a big Hollywood movie comes down to tonight.

"Don't break your new nails. Just shove a bunch under the divider."

The coveted wad of white toilet paper and Sarah's undamaged red nails appear beside the spike of my stiletto.

"Got it." My voice sounds strangled, because I'm holding the bottom of my floor-length sequined dress between my chin and my chest.

"Good. Now hurry. We don't want to miss the opening number," says Sarah. "I hope we'll be celebrating more than just your birthday tonight."

The best birthday present would be hearing, "And the Starlight award goes to Sarah Connor." Ever since I met her two years ago when she moved to LA, Sarah's been the one with a plan: become a screenwriter. May have hit a few bumps (okay, craters) on the road, but my girl is making her dreams come true.

The shapewear I have on at the insistence of Mrs. Marino, my boss who lent me this elaborate golden gown worth a year of my salary, doesn't want to go back up. How do people spend all night in these things?

"We were so sorry to hear about you and Leyla," the interviewer says on the TV in the lounge part of the restroom.

My ears perk up. I'm not sorry at all. I've been obsessing over my favorite romantic star's newfound freedom for weeks now.

"Well," Asher Menken's deep baritone loses its smoothness, "all I can say is—"

"Ladies and Gentlemen"—the TV switches from the pre-recorded interview to the real-time coverage of the awards ceremony—"welcome to the Fifth Annual Starlight Foundation Gala."

For feck's sake. The world is dying to know Asher's take on his ex. Okay, I'm dying to know. Even if I get a chance to see him, it's not like I could ask him myself.

"How much longer?" Sarah can't hide her impatience. "I don't want to miss anything."

"Just go." I wave my free hand at the closed door as if Sarah can see me. "I'll be in as soon as I can wrangle this tiny torture device back onto my crotch."

"You sure?"

"Aye, go already. Nick's waiting." Probably cursing me. Boyo is also nervous tonight, and we don't get along at the best of times. "Enjoy yourself. You've worked so hard for tonight."

A few clicks of her high heels plus the sound of the door closing, and I'm left alone with my tight beige nemesis.

I tuck the bottom of the dress into my décolleté. This is bollocks. I peel the undergarment off my thighs and balance on one, then the other silver strappy sandal as I struggle to free myself. Dress righted, I take my first deep breath of the night, ball up the offending material, toss it into the bin, give it the finger, and exit the stall.

A quick check of my stomach in the mirror shows it's as flat as it was with the awful contraption. I wash my hands and ensure my hair survived the battle of the bulge. The aquamarine dye I've been using this summer is starting to bore me. Might be time for a change.

The blue corner of the tattoo on the inside of my wrist is showing. I tug the long sleeves of the dress down, causing the neckline to plunge even more. Gotta make sure I cover up my body art tonight. While highly unlikely, Mum and Da might see pictures. They don't exactly know about this version of my artwork. My tastes run more towards black ink than gold sequins, but I do rock this dress. I blow myself a kiss in the mirror. Time to get this show on the road.

I reach for the door handle when the painted wood panel flies open and smashes into my shoulder. For a moment I teeter on my heels, sure I can save myself, but this battle I don't win. I land hard on the solid tiles of the bathroom floor.

"Bloody hell," I yelp.

The door slams shut, then opens again, and a tuxedo-clad figure enters the room. "Damn it, sorry, I didn't mean to . . . didn't know . . . are you hurt?" The crisp black silk of men's trousers crinkles as the offender crouches down and stretches his hand my way.

I blink. Then blink again. Wide pools the color of whiskey I've drooled over during movie nights with the girls peer at me.

"Are you okay?" An expression worthy of an Oscar nomination graces Asher Menken's face as he scans my body for broken bits.

I wiggle my toes, rub my shoulder, and swivel my head around. "All in one piece, no thanks to you." I've wanted to approach him since I first saw Ash on the red carpet a couple of feet ahead of us, but he was in the middle of an interview, probably the one I'd just been listening to. He and my big brother

Owen are still best friends, but over a decade has passed since the superstar and I have been in the same room together.

"What can I do?" There is no spark of recognition in his eyes despite the fact that other than the long hair, I'm a mini copy of my brother. I wait to see if anything clicks, but his focus is not on my face. Rather, he gawks at my naked leg, exposed in all its glory thanks to the thigh-high slit in this fancy dress. His gaze travels up my leg and I follow, until we get to where the lace of my aquamarine thong is visible, no longer shielded by the Spanx. He looks at my hair, then my thong, and swallows.

"I still like matching things," I say.

"Sorry?"

"My hair matches my thong. Like my hair bows used to match my clothes, remember?"

His eyes narrow, and he tilts his head. "I think you might've hit your head."

"I'm Siobhan." I lift the sleeve off my left wrist and show him the tiny star, my very first tattoo. I got the memento as soon as I moved here seven years ago: my design, based on the one I drew for Ash a lifetime ago. "Réiltín?"

Another sweep of his eyes takes in more of my face as he scans me up and down, or left to right, or however the horizontal plane is looked at. "Owen's little sister?" His eyebrow rises.

"Aye."

"Unbelievable." He reaches inside his jacket, pulls out his wallet, and takes out a piece of paper. Ash sits next to me on the icy floor as I tug at the dress in a too-late attempt to cover up. He gives the paper to me. "My good luck charm."

I stare. In my hand is a faded copy of what I now have on my wrist. The original little star I drew for him when I was nine.

"You . . . kept this?"

Asher casts his eyes to the floor, and my pulse takes off. I mean, I've seen the expression before, both on and off the screen, yet up close and personal like this he's . . . gorgeous. Yes, the teeth are perfect, the chin is chiseled, and the hair—oh, how I want to run my hands through his hair to test if those strands are as tuggable as they appear. But this is more than the good looks. He's lit up from within.

I hand the piece of paper from the past back to him and will my heart to slow.

"Owen did say you lived here." Ash tucks the drawing carefully back in his wallet and puts it away. "Of all places to run into you." He smiles, and there's the "I'm sorry" smile that got him out of a trip to the police when he bumped into a car in front of us. The lady who owned the Peugeot let him go with, "What's one more scratch on this old heap of metal?" She would've berated any of my brothers for doing the same thing.

"I promised my friends not to get starstruck, but I didn't think they meant literally." I smile back. "Howeyeh, Ash? Can I still call you that?"

He nods, giving me the once over again. "Can't call you Little Star anymore. You're no longer . . . little."

My turn to swallow. The way he said little sends a shiver through me that I can't blame on the chill of the tile floor. My name is a puzzle for most people in LA. At work I heard a million attempts at my name until I came up with "she-Vaughn." Sarah shortens it to just Sio, "she." Back in Ireland my family calls me Shiv, and Mum insists on Baby Girl. But Asher's nickname for me, Réiltín, which means Little Star, might be my favorite. "I don't mind." He can call me anything.

"Réiltín it is, then." He runs his hand through the thick light brown strands he inherited from his movie star mother and rests his fingers on the nape of his neck. "We should probably get off this floor." He jumps to his feet, wraps his fingers around my wrist, and lifts me up. I wince in pain.

"Did I hurt you?"

"The shoulder is a bit tender." I lower the neckline and see a red line across my skin. Ash's thumb traces the mark from the door. His touch doesn't make the pain go away, but I'm both nervous and more secure with his skin on mine. His presence has always had this effect on me. The thrill and the comfort at the same time.

The first time I met him, my nine-year-old self didn't know what to think about Ash. He wasn't a famous Hollywood star then, just the nineteen-year-old friend my brother brought home for Christmas break because Ash had no family in Ireland to spend the holiday with. A breath of fresh air all the way from California to light up our middle-of-nowhere in County Kerry.

I fix my dress. "We should get going. My friend Sarah must be wondering where I am."

"Sure you're okay?"

"I'm tougher than I seem."

"You look"—he pauses—"great in this dress. All grown-up." His eyes stray to my cleavage.

"Yup." I straighten and push my chest forward. "Got me big girl boobs and everything."

"I didn't mean to . . ." His "I'm sorry" smile is back. "This isn't what I—"

"Just having a laugh." I tap him on the arm, like we're old pals. "Great way to start my next quarter century."

"Today?"

"'Tis."

"Well, happy birthday to you." He purses his lips, and his eyes brighten. "We could have a drink after the gala? Celebrate? Catch up?"

"Bang on." I don't jump up and down like I used to when I got to spend time with him, but I flash him my "thank you for a great tip" smile. Asher Menken wants to have drinks with me. I ain't saying no.

"Great. But"—he rubs the wrinkles between his eyebrows—"a favor? Could you check if there is a guy in a red velvet tuxedo hanging around by any chance? If he is, I'll stay here a while longer."

"Aye." I peek out of the door and see empty hallways. "The coast is clear."

Reporter 1: Did you see Asher on the red carpet tonight? No Leyla by his side.

Reporter 2: My heart broke when I heard about the demise of #AshLa.

Reporter 1: But he did look fine. Like, rebound fine. Any bets who the next lucky girl will be?

Reporter 2: One-night stand with Asher Menken? Sign me up.

★ ★ ★

TWO

Siobhan Casey.

I can't believe Owen's baby sister scared my bathroom stalker off with foul language worthy of an R-rated movie. The creep thought he was clever hiding around the corner, ready to accost Siobhan and me on our way to the ceremony. Her vocabulary, among other things, has grown. In fact, there isn't much left of the little girl with a short bob, matching hair accessories, and hand-me-down outfits from her brothers. Although the eyes, those sometimes green, sometimes blue, sometimes gray eyes of hers, and Owen's, and their Ma's. I should've recognized those eyes.

When my publicist Jackson asked me to be part of tonight's ceremony, I almost said no. I hate these types of affairs. The fakeness. The shallowness. The constant vying for attention. I never dreamed my night would be like this.

I glance out into the sea of creativity, and the rush of youthful exuberance hits me like a tidal wave. My partnership with the Starlight Foundation was the right decision. This is the perfect project to kickstart my new production company. I already got the green light for two TV shows, and this movie, with the proper amount of press, will give me the cachet to do more.

Still, the best part is the opportunity to give back, do something worthwhile with the fame I've been lucky enough to achieve. And when the tall kid accepts his Best Director award, he's genuinely ecstatic. I can't help grinning like a fool along with him.

"That's Nick." Siobhan sits down after she finishes clapping her hands raw. An empty seat next to me had been an open invitation for the opportunists looking to pitch, but now I'm glad the organizers assumed I would bring a date. "He's been in LA less than six months, and look at him. I'm here seven years and keep slinging drinks."

"You want to be in the movie business?"

"God, no. Owen is the one with the acting bug in our family."

"Why LA then?" Owen refused to tell me the full story.

"Farthest place I could escape to with my American passport that met my criteria."

"Which were?"

"Far from Ireland, fun, sunny, and not an island." She winks at me. Good to see she hasn't lost her spunky attitude. "Had a string of jobs. Let's see, I was the Belgian waffle girl at Disneyland first. Girl's gotta start somewhere. Graduated to waitressing at a fifties themed diner. Gawd, that was horrible. They put that yellow American plastic they call cheese on everything. Who puts cheese on pie?"

Siobhan has the right to judge. Her family's cheese is the best I've ever tasted. Of course, I've had the privilege of stealing the stuff fresh from the cheese fridge when no one was looking. As a teenager I preferred to ask for forgiveness rather than permission. The bonus of performing in Dublin was that in three hours I could be at the Casey farm indulging in unlimited quantities of first-rate cheese. Well, and pretending I'm part of their large warm family. Owen is so lucky.

"Anyhow, now I work at a swanky resort bartending with my girl Sarah over there"—she swings her champagne glass in the direction of a group of young people, of which Sarah could be any one of three girls—"but the hours give me time to play artist."

"Well, lucky me. You saved me from being cornered by overeager fans and wannabe writers." And she saved me before. The first Christmas I spent at her family's farm, she saw me struggle to memorize my part for *The Little Prince*. I was ready to throw in the towel. Maybe the acting gene skipped a generation, maybe the tabloids were right and my good looks and family connections were the only reasons Trinity's theatre program accepted me.

Siobhan didn't let me give up. She ran lines with me, jumped up and down every time I got one right, and even drew me a picture of a little star, a réiltín, for good luck. The folded piece of paper with her design was in my pocket when I first went on stage and has been with me ever since, calming me when I'm nervous. And being back in the States has me super nervous tonight.

"He deserved the tongue-lashing. Shoving his script at you in the middle of the event is the worst way to get your attention."

"Hollywood is hard, I get it. But he was going to stuff the flash drive inside my jacket if you didn't interfere. I should've just shoved him off, but that'd end up in the papers with me as the unreasonable superstar, too stuck-up to talk to his fans." I take another sip from the flute the server keeps refilling. "The guy's face matched his red suit after you told him off. You're more effective than my bodyguards."

She laughs. Not the polite tut-tut of reporters reacting to my lame jokes or the light tinkle that warmed my heart when I managed to get Leyla to break character. No, this is a roaring, full-bodied, full-of-life laugh.

And I'm laughing along with her, feeling lighter than I've felt in months. No, years.

My real smile hasn't graced my face in forever. The world thinks Leyla and I broke up a few weeks ago. In reality, we've been apart for over a year. Our publicists timed the news for maximum impact, every step calculated to advance our careers. Well, her career. It's always been about her career. Every fight, a tug of war between her need to shoot for the stars and mine to settle down. In the end, our marriage came down to one thing: I can't wait to have kids, and she didn't want any.

"Gotta stand up for myself and those I care about," Siobhan says. "You know my older brothers; add waitressing in LA, and there's no better verbal self-defense school." She curls her arm and almost spills champagne onto herself. I catch the glass in time. "I know how to punch too, if it comes to it. Owen made sure to teach me. And I always keep my thumb out."

She puts her glass down and demonstrates the proper fist technique. "Brothers." Her eyes widen. "Oh." She holds out her hand. "Give me your phone. Let's send Owen a selfie. It'll freak him out."

I like nothing more than pulling pranks on my best friend. My phone in hand, Siobhan leans in, her shoulder brushing against mine, and I inhale a mixture of honey and something spicy. "Smile," she instructs.

Easily done.

She plucks my cell from my fingers, her thumbs fly over the screen, and in a second, she flashes our smiling faces at me. "Check out who I bumped into," is written underneath our picture.

"Bumped into, huh." I chuckle at her play on how we met in the bathroom. She sends the text.

Siobhan opens my jacket, the gesture she berated the guy in the red suit for. "Done."

My body shrunk away from the rando's touch, but with my grown-up réiltín, I savor the contact. She puts my phone in the inside pocket and adjusts my sky-blue tie. Her eyes narrow, and she runs her fingers against the dots on the smooth silk.

"This tie, doesn't it remind you of the *Infinity* exhibit Yayoi Kusama did with the mirrors at The Broad a few years ago?"

I nod. "Like being inside a kaleidoscope." I took Leyla on a private tour of the immersive art installation at The Broad Modern Art Museum. We spent the evening lost in the multi-reflective rooms.

"Exactly." She smooths my tie one more time. The touch of her hand on my chest does things to me it should not. "Wasn't it deadly? Blows you only got five minutes in each room."

She's deadly. Real and beautiful. And alluring.

Gone is the little girl who doodled on anything she could get her hands on. Before me sits this vivacious, gorgeous woman. Her green—or are they blue—eyes twinkle in the low light of the reception hall.

"Did you study art?"

"I take classes when I can, but nothing official. I love to explore—oils, watercolors, sculpture, loom, pottery, print—tried them all. I even thought about costume design. But I think skin is my favorite canvas." She looks down at the star on her wrist.

This woman is a bright star in the dark night that has been my life lately. I can't look away; I won't, not when there's so much to see.

Even her dress teases by covering up practically everything yet accentuating her body in a way no garment should be allowed to. But I've glimpsed the secrets the fabric hides. Thinking about her long leg and how I'd run my hand up the curves to . . . I feel a twitch I haven't felt in a long time.

What am I doing? How can I be thinking like this? What would Owen say if he saw me ogling his sister?

Hey, boyo, don't even think about touching her.

Which is exactly what I'm doing. Thinking. And that's where I'll be stopping.

"So, you've traveled the world?" Siobhan reaches for another glass from the server walking by and our hands brush.

There it is again, the little electric shock like when I touched her in the bathroom. What is she doing to me? Am I having any effect on her? It's so hard for me to tell these days, reality and fiction always blurring. Is a woman truly interested in me, or is she just caught up in my fame and fortune?

It was easy when I met Leyla. We were both unknowns at the time, just starting out in the business. When our movie hit number one at the box office everything changed overnight. I was used to my parents' fame and seeing my face on the cover of tabloids wasn't new, but with my own fame, the frenzy reached a whole different level. Leyla and I relied on each other, bonded in the fire of chaos.

Siobhan is different. She knows me and doesn't have the starstruck expression my fans get. Talking to her brings the instant comfort I associate with my visits to her family farm. She taps her glass to mine, and I enjoy another brush of our fingers.

Her skin is cool. No, comfort isn't the right word. Connection? There's something here. We're on our third glass and I should be feeling the haziness of the alcohol, but instead, everything is crystal clear. For the first time in a long time, I'm alert and aware.

Four delicate fingers brush over the back of my hand, as if she's painting me with invisible watercolors. Her pupils dilate, and I'm sure mine do too. A slender index finger wraps around my thumb and slides up, down, and up again. If I'm reading her right, my year of celibacy is ending tonight.

She touches a sensitive part at the base of my thumb. "Wanna get out of here?" Siobhan's eyes confirm her invitation.

"Yes" escapes my lips before I even think about consequences.

"Give me a minute."

As she walks away, I text my security detail to let them know I'm ready to leave and there's going to be a plus one. Hopefully, we can slip out the back door and not get noticed.

Across the room, Siobhan's talking to a short blonde in an even shorter silver dress. They hug, and my little star's walking back toward me. Her slender hips swing with the movement, glittering gold. My body reacts with more than a twitch this time.

"Where to, sir?" asks the limo driver.

"The hotel," says Siobhan.

"How'd you—"

"Know? Figured you'd be staying with your parents since you just got back. Their house is in Malibu, right? A tad too far for tonight."

She's too smart for me.

The hotel is only a short ride from the venue, and in no time we're in the underground garage. I hop out of the car hoping to open the door for Siobhan, but she's too quick for me too. Leyla would've waited, expecting a grand gesture from me in case there were any cameras around. Always a show with that woman.

This girl—woman—however, pinches my security guard's arm. "Oh, you're a tough one." The guard sticks out his chest and eyes Siobhan up and down. "Spend every day at the gym, do we?"

I feel a pang in my chest. Jealousy? I jut out my arm. "Shall we?" Siobhan slinks hers through and leans into me. My temperature rises with the contact of her warm body as we make our way to the private elevator.

The metal doors slide together and once again we're alone.

"What is it about elevators?" she asks, a hand running down my arm.

"What d'you mean?"

"They're just so damn sexy."

"You think?"

She reaches up and tugs on my tie, giving me a low, breathy, "Yes."

I'm done for. Reason, propriety, and resistance are out the window. My lips collide with hers, one hand circling her waist to pull her closer, the other finally getting to touch the soft skin of the long lean leg she's hooked over my hip. My palm travels up her thigh and cups her butt.

The sequins of her dress scratch against my thin shirt as if they are clawing to get at me. She's amazing, and so alive. Her taste, her scent, her heat invade me, send currents through my body, and light me up like no other. The twitch is now a throb.

I don't have enough hands. I need to touch more of her, but there's no way I'm letting go of this luscious ass. I tear my mouth from hers and explore her chin, her neck. I pause, pressing my lips against her pulsing artery, the thump matching my own racing heartbeat.

The soft ding of the elevator indicates we've hit my floor, but I don't want to leave our little cocoon. Siobhan has other ideas and starts backing out of the elevator, my tie still clutched in her hand. I'm happy to follow, as long as I get to keep kissing those amazing lips.

We move down the hall, and I reluctantly break the kiss. "Wait."

"What? Bored already?"

"Not in the slightest." More like alive for the first time. "My room is this way." I clutch her arm and haul her down the hallway in the opposite direction, searching for my hotel room key with my free hand. I jam the card into the reader, the light goes green, and we burst into my suite.

Before the door closes, her fingers are undoing my belt.

"Careful of the gown. It's not mine."

The first time I roll a condom on, she doesn't even take her dress off.

Read the rest of Asher and Siobhan's romance in Star Struck.

Out Now

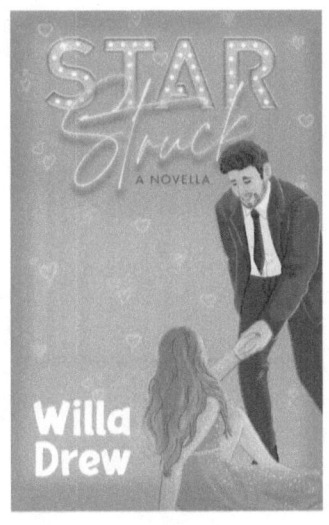

ACKNOWLEDGEMENTS

This Second Chance Billionaires series is a second chance for us as writers.

When we created Willa Drew in 2021, we had been writing together for about a year and had several years of writing series individually under our belts, but we were still what we call emerging writers. We knew a lot, but we also didn't know a lot more. And one of the things we weren't sure of was what we wanted to write about. The first series we created were not planned. They happened either because we decided to try writing together for the first time (Kisses, Lies, & Us), because our friends asked us to write for them (Star Struck), or because we were invited to write a serial story from scratch (WE Blend).

We tried writing in the Young Adult, New Adult, and Adult categories. We tried to write sweet, no spice stories and angsty, lightly peppered ones. We were experimenting, learning, and finding our voices. We discovered that we can be funny (especially DL), that we love writing about family drama (especially Gala), and that our male characters always are gooey inside, whether their exterior is rough or cheeky. They fall hard and pine and would do anything for the people they love.

At the end of 2024, we completed the two series we've been working on since the beginning of Willa Drew. We paused and took time to ponder what we'd do next. What is it that we want to write now that we know ourselves better? What do our readers love to read from us? The survey of our street team and our own observations yielded an interesting answer: the readers loved the sweet and gooey aspects of our books and the emotional rollercoasters we took them on, but they also wondered if we could add more . . . spice.

We took this advice and decided to try something new. In our individual stories as DL Croisette and Gala Russ, spice was definitely more prevalent on the page. So we combined our expertise in that area and created a new addition to our Willa Drew Universe: the five men of Second Chance Billionaires.

Although they started as roommates and teammates on their college hockey team, when they grow up, they each had a different life path. Playing around with a tight group of men who care about each other, offering support and advice, was an ultimate fantasy of what found family could look like and how friends play a huge role in our lives.

Here's a secret for you: DL and Gala each have a running list of their favorite things to write about, and we infused the Second Chance Billionaires series with them.

DL is a die-hard fan of hockey, and although you've seen some of that in the & Us series with Nick being a former hockey player, she gets to fully lean into her passion in the Second Chance Billionaires series, especially when you meet Linc. He's a professional hockey player who is chasing a Stanley Cup win one last time before he retires.

Gala loves using academia in her stories, and writing about the project Rose and Alek are working on in *Not a Fake Chance* was a special treat for her.

You'll see our shared love of music and travel represented as well. Each book has at least one character who has immigrant or international roots, another thing we love inserting into our books as a Canadian and a Russian American.

The second chance aspect allows us to showcase these characters in both their college days and their time as adults, combining our love for writing younger characters and the more impulsive decisions they make with showing how the older versions of them had matured and grown, and are making different choices.

The second chance aspect is also for us as writers to restart our career with a new angle and hopefully one you, the readers, would want more of. We poured our hearts, souls, and imaginations into these five guys finding love (yes, we have the entire series planned out already). We want you to get to know each one of them and their love interests as we write their journeys, each very different yet centered around their second chance at love.

To those readers who stuck with us from the very beginning, thank you for following along on this twisty journey. We are eternally grateful for your support, reviews, comments, and emails. Thank you for being our cheerleaders when we go through rough patches, as well as for celebrating with us when we're sharing the good news. You are such a vital part of this writing journey for us.

To those readers who are just discovering our Willa Drew coauthorship: Welcome! We are looking forward to hearing from you. The Willa Drew Universe is already a big space, so if you liked this book and are waiting for the next one in this series, make sure to go and check out what we've already created. You'll recognize some of the names from this book in our other series. We love creating fun cameos and easter eggs of existing characters throughout our universe of books.

Don't know where to start? We suggest you begin with the story that brought us together, the & Us series, followed by *Star Struck*, a novella, and the WE series. For more specific interconnections in these books, check out the reading order graphic on our website, willadrew.com.

If you ever want to get your hands on a signed copy of our books, you will find a link to our shop on our website as well.

If you are still reading, you get a special thank you from us. Use code JPGAPHRMEK on willadrew.com and get 15% off any product until August 31, 2025.

Being entrepreneurs as indie authors is another big thing we had to learn. Thank you for supporting our small business.

As always, there is an ever-growing list of people we'd like to thank who have been instrumental in making this book and this series happen.

Our families who accommodate our all-nighters, hold us through meltdowns, and always tell us we can do this writing career thing. Your support is the backbone of why we are still writing.

To our friends who were our beta readers, advisers, and back-patters. Thank you for reading the spicy scenes and giving us valuable advice on how some positions could be improved.

Thank you for giving us your honest feedback and not holding back. Thank you for volunteering your time and lending us your expertise. This enormous thank you is for Tanya, Kate, Leslie, Susan, Sal, and Finn.

To our street team for answering our many polls about what blurb, cover, and visuals will best represent our characters and make other readers fall in love with them.

To our editors, Jessica and Victoria, you are the best, and we are so lucky to have you. Thank you for making this book the best it can be, especially on such a short timeline.

To our ARC and Street teams. We are so delighted to welcome so many new faces. Your reviews help spread the word about this series and make such a difference. Thank you for being our hype people.

And thank you to you, our readers. Thank you for letting our characters live in your heads. Thank you for treating these imaginary people seriously. Thank you for worrying about them. Thank you for rejoicing with them. Thank you for falling in love with them. Without you, our author journey wouldn't be a success.

And as is our tradition, here's a thank you we wanted to write to each other.

Gala: Thank you for still being with me on this twistiest of the roller coasters called coauthorship. The previous year was tough. Thank you for still moving forward and lending me your creative mind even when you were barely able to get through the day. Our Venn diagram somehow works: the complementary things and the very different ones we bring to this writing table make us so much stronger. You are a partner I never realized I needed, and although I'll be cranky and tired and ready to give up as I go through my anxiety cycles, deep down I know I can stumble and fall and you'll be there to catch me, just like Alek caught Rose. Your kindness, strength, imagination, and love are just some of the many qualities that I admire. I hope this new experiment of ours brings us into a new era of writing, and I can't wait to put each of the many stories we have planned out into the world.

DL: I adore writing romance. I came to it rather late in life, so you might say it's my second chance. There's something about writing with you, Gala, that makes my blood hum. The words are different, the storylines are elevated, and the romance is richer and deeper. Having a partner to bounce ideas off of, to solve plot holes with, to laugh at the silly errors our editors point out, to be creative with, to suss out minute details like if American's put milk or cream in their coffee with, to argue with over how our characters should or would react, to lean on in the moments when I wasn't sure I would ever be able to write again, and to share this journey with is a unique experience not many authors, never mind people, get to partake in. I'm doubly lucky and grateful because you are the partner that chose to work with me. I never understand why you have this perception that you are difficult to work with. What we do is exhilarating and exhausting. It's creative and challenging. It's rewarding and bloody hard work. You are not perfect, Gala, and I love you for that. I love your deficiencies as well as your advantages. You are a delight. You are sunshine. You are brilliant and dedicated and passionate. You are still here. I'm thrilled we got to write this romance book together. And I'm ready and willing to write more romances until our creative well of ideas runs dry. Which might take a hundred years.

SERIES BY WILLA DREW

SECOND CHANCE BILLIONAIRES

The Second Chance Billionaires series follows five lifelong friends—a grumpy CEO, a charming playboy, a retiring hockey pro, a British aristocrat, and a sci-fi author—from college roommates to billionaire boardrooms as they each get one more shot at love.

Not a Fake Chance – ROSE & ALEK

Not a Second Chance – CALLUM & OLIVIA

Book 3 – LINC & ???

Book 4 – BLAKE & ???

Book 5 – SOREN & ???

  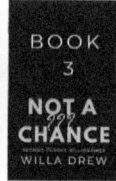 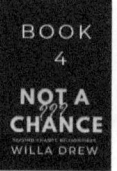 

AND US

Watch movies and real life collide with Sarah and Nick in a right person/wrong time, hidden identity, new adult romance. One year, five parts, six major holidays, many twists.

Kisses, Lies, & Us

Passions, Hopes, & Us

Distance, Love, & Us

or binge the complete series with bonus scenes in

Friendzoned By My Crush

FALLING FOR THE ROCKSTAR'S DAUGHTER

An upper young adult, friends-to-lovers, slow burn romance

featuring a reluctant collaboration between two musicians.

WE Blend

WE Breathe

WE Balance

ANDERS INVESTIGATIONS

Meet the men of Anders Investigations, a new contemporary romance series with a romantic suspense element.

Taming the Grumpy Bodyguard

Loving the Grumpy Bodyguard

FALLING FOR THE MOVIE STAR

If you like an age gap, brother's best friend romance featuring LA's red-carpet glamor, Irish charm, and a reunion written in the stars, Siobhan and Asher's story is for you.

Star Struck

Two authors. Two countries. One obsession with love stories.

Willa Drew's contemporary slow-burn romances are full of feels, playful banter, and high-stakes emotions. Their globe-trotting characters fight for love as they discover who they are and where they belong.

Willa, a proud Canadian and devoted Leafs hockey fan, and Drew, a Russian American with a lifelong love of languages, always search for the perfect words to capture heartbreak and connection.

Their books guarantee swoon-worthy kisses and happily ever afters.

Come hang out with them
@willadrewauthor
willadrew.com